CAFÉ PARADISE BOOK 2

MARILYN'S DAUGHTERS

Patricia Comb

2QT Limited (Publishing)

First Edition published 2015
2QT Limited (Publishing)
Settle, North Yorkshire BD24 9RH
www.2qt.co.uk

Cover design Hilary Pitt
Cover images supplied by Shutterstock.com

Author website www.patriciacomb.com

Printed in Great Britain by Lightning Source UK Ltd

A CIP catalogue record for this book is available
from the British Library
ISBN 978-1-910077-29-0

To Mother and Pop
With Love

Acknowledgements

I would like to thank Catherine Cousins and all the staff at 2QT for their help with this book, and Hilary Pitt for the lovely cover. My thanks to Karen Holmes for her help, friendship and support in editing this second book in the Café Paradise trilogy. Also, Nikita Vine-Scatchard for her culinary information; Pam Cropper for her wide-ranging general knowledge and advice, and Mary Wilhemy and Christine Anderson for their constant encouragement.

My thanks too, to Gerrie and Susan Douglas-Scott at ReadingLasses Bookshop/Café for allowing me free run of their RoomsAboveTheBooks to write in.

Grateful thanks also to Wattie McCutcheon for introducing me to the game of cricket; Brian Box for his amazing maps and patience in route-planning; Preston and Chester Harley Davidson Chapters for their advice on biking through Europe; Douglas Holliday, M.B.E. for directing me through the centre of Rome; Lorraine Thompson for her Italian translation, and Geraldine Simpson for her French translation. I hope the village of Upper Poppleton, York will forgive me for saddling them with a fictional cricket ground.

Lastly, my thanks and love as always to my funny, kind husband, Peter, who patiently shares his life with an ever-changing cast of characters.

PROLOGUE

Mayfield Road, York. September 2012

Barney Anderson swung the car into the drive and switched off the engine. He turned to look at his new wife and smiled. 'Home Mrs Anderson,' he said. 'The start of a whole new chapter in our lives.'

Jackie smiled back at him. 'After such a fantastic honeymoon it's going to be hard to open the book, never mind begin a chapter.'

'It's still going to be wonderful, you'll see. Wait there a minute,' he commanded. He got out of the car, opened the front door and came back. 'Now you can get out,' he said.

Jackie got out of the car and Barney swept her up into his arms. 'Hey, what's going on?' But she knew very well and locked her arms around his neck, laughing.

Barney grinned. 'I'm carrying you across the threshold. You're entering this house for the first time as a new bride. Must keep up the traditions.' He strode the short distance to the front door and carried her through to the sitting room.

'Enough, enough,' Jackie cried. 'You'll do yourself a mischief. Put me down.'

Barney paused for a moment before letting her down gently. 'You're as light as a feather, my darling. I could carry you all day and not notice.'

'Flattery will get ... ouch, what the hell...?'

Seeing the front door open, Samson, Marilyn's beloved cat, had come in to see what was going on. Spotting Jackie, he made

7

a beeline for her. He was very cross at having been left at home for two weeks and fed tinned cat food by Mrs Scott from next door. He vented his anger by sinking his claws into Jackie's leg and dragging them down hard.

'Bloody cat,' Jackie yelled. 'That's some welcome home.'

Barney bent down and scooped up Samson. He held him tight and looked him squarely in the eyes. 'Do that one more time Samson, and I think you might find yourself *in* a tin of cat meat. Get my meaning?'

Samson glared back at him and spat furiously.

Barney regarded him calmly. 'Listen, my friend.' He spoke softly now, into Samson's face. 'Times are changing and you will have to change with them. I will not have you do that to my lovely wife. Not now, not ever. Because if you do, you will never be welcome here again and, as I said, *cat meat*,' he hissed into Samson's ear. 'Now, I'm going to put you down and you will behave nicely.'

He put Samson gently back on the ground and tensed, waiting for him to strike. But something of what he said must have got through. The cat stalked disdainfully back to the front door, his tail high in the air, and disappeared down the drive.

'Well,' said Jackie admiringly, 'you must be on his wavelength. Do you think he's got the message?'

'I think we understand each other,' said Barney. 'One man to another and all that.'

'Oh, that's it. I've been the wrong sex all these years.'

Barney took her in his arms and kissed her. 'Definitely not, Mrs Anderson. Most definitely not.'

CHAPTER 1

Café Paradise, Castlegate, York. April 2013

'It's a royal command, Jackie. I can't say no to the Queen, can I?' Alastair Middleton, the Café Paradise chef, smiled disarmingly at his employer.

'Oh, she offered you the job personally, did she?' Jackie asked sceptically. 'Wrote to you on Buck House notepaper, "I command Alastair Middleton to be my very junior chef as from next week. You've a very taking way with lobster pâté, the American Ambassador will love it, so you must come immediately and never mind leaving your present employer in the lurch, your monarch needs you."'

Alastair had the grace to blush. 'It wasn't quite like that.'

'I'll bet it wasn't,' Jackie said grimly. 'How long have you been sitting on this?'

'Weeks and weeks.' He saw the look on Jackie's face and hurried on. 'I had to. You've no idea of the references they need, almost back to when I was in nappies. Now it's down to you. If you speak well of me, they'll take me like a shot.'

'As the saying goes, you've got me between a rock and a hard place, Alastair. If I give you a good reference, I lose you; if I don't, you'll stomp around here with a face to frighten off any customers or, worse still, poison us all.'

'I just want my chance,' he said mutinously. 'I've said I'm sorry it's such short notice, but if I hadn't been successful, you would never have been any the wiser. But as it is...'

'As it is, from next week I need a new chef.'

Alastair flushed and grasped Jackie's hand warmly. 'You won't regret this, Jackie.'

'Won't I? That depends on which end of the telescope you're looking through.'

*****

'When you two women have finished jabbering, I'll have a fat rascal and a pot of tea.' Walter Breckenridge sat down at a table near to the pine dresser that housed the crockery and cutlery used by the Café Paradise.

Kate Peterson flicked a tea towel at him affectionately. 'Don't even try, Walter. Just because you're the father of the boss. It doesn't cut the mustard, you know. You're the greasy-spoon cook to us and always will be.'

Walter grinned. 'Aye, those were the days, Kate. Sausage, egg and chips, fried bread and baked beans. Toast and marmalade and a pot of tea.' Walter closed his eyes dreamily. 'Or a bacon and egg bap with ketchup ... a few chips on the side...'

'Ellie's a good cook, Walter,' said Penny Montague, the other waitress. She came across and sat down opposite him. 'By the look of you, you get well fed at home.'

'Oh aye, Ellie's a grand cook, Penny, don't get me wrong. Only she's on a bit of a health kick at the moment. Muesli and bran for breakfast with skimmed milk. It looks like the stuff I used to give to the horses. She's cut down on the red meat and we have lots of oily fish. Fish!' Walter exclaimed bitterly. 'I've eaten that much lately, I'll soon have webbed feet and fins. I won't need to cycle anywhere, I'll get in the river and swim.'

'Is that what you're doing here then?' Penny asked. 'Breaking out?'

Walter looked sheepish. 'Aye. She's busy at home. She's that many goats and sheep now, I don't think she knows which way to turn for milking 'em. I'm not good with 'em. She says I'm too rough, I upset 'em and the milk dries up. So I offered to do the early morning fruit and veg run for Jackie and thought I might just get a cup of tea for my troubles.'

'And maybe get on the outside of half a dozen fat rascals at the same time.' Penny smiled at him. They had worked together at the café for many years. She knew how much he loved the Yorkshire staples like fat rascals and curd tarts. 'Coming up, Walter.' Penny rose and made her way to the counter.

Walter was happily munching when his daughter, Jackie, emerged red faced from the kitchen. 'Bugger and blast it all,' she exclaimed, making her way to Penny at the counter.

Penny pointed to Walter sitting at the nearby table and put her finger to her lips.

'Dad, what are you doing here?' said Jackie. 'I didn't expect to see you for another half hour, at least.'

'And how lovely it is to see you too, my beloved daughter,' replied Walter. 'Mind, I could do without the language.'

Jackie slumped down into the chair opposite. 'You'd swear if you'd just heard what I heard,' she said.

'And what have you just heard? Hang on, if it's that bad, we'd best have a cup of tea.' He rose and brought another cup to the table.

He sat down. Every time he looked at his daughter his heart swelled with pride. He could hardly believe she was his. Slim, with fair hair and violet eyes, she took after her mother, Marilyn, the love of Walter's life for forty years. Only when Jackie was in trouble last year was Walter able to reveal himself as her father. Now Jackie was married to the love of her life, she and Walter remained very close, in spite of a very feisty relationship.

He poured Jackie's tea and handed it to her. 'What's up, lass?'

'Alastair, the chef. He's just given a week's notice. A week! What am I going to do? I can't find a good chef in a week, they don't grow on trees.'

Walter took a deep breath. Here we go, he told himself, she's off on one at the drop of a hat. He tried a joke. 'Be nice if they did, then you could just pick one when you fancied a change.' Jackie scowled. Ooh, definitely a bad idea, Walter. She's not in the mood.

'Thanks, Dad, you're a real help.' She paused and then her face cleared as a smile spread slowly across her face. 'That's it!' She beamed sunnily at Walter.

'That's what?' said Walter warily.

'How you can help. Ellie's a brilliant cook. She could stand in here whilst I look for a new chef.' Jackie relaxed against the chair and sipped her tea.

'I could ask her.' Walter rubbed his head thoughtfully. 'She is a wonderful cook, but she can't do all those fancy dishes your Alastair does. You'd have to manage on Yorkshire fayre for a while.'

Jackie got up and kissed the top of his head. 'She'll be brilliant. I could advertise her as a feature for the spring. "New Yorkshire specialist chef comes to York café." Right, I must be off. I'll leave it with you, Dad. Bide your time and pick the right moment. Use your charm and, for once, don't frighten the horses.'

CHAPTER 2

Janet Bailey stood outside the gates of HM East Sutton Park Prison and shivered in the cold morning air. As she had no family, there was no one to meet her on her release. Over the last six months she had been on work experience at different companies in the area as part of her early release programme, and had got used to being outside the prison gates. But now, standing here on the pavement on her own, life felt very different.

She picked up her small bag and straightened up. The world was waiting. She must put the past behind her and make the most of these next years. She was thirty-nine and in her prime. That was what the governor had said in her exit interview. Janet couldn't remember much of what she'd waffled on about, but that bit had stuck. Yes, she was in her prime and after all her years in care and in prison, she was going to find out who she really was and where she came from.

After years with a dysfunctional adopted family she had been cast back into the care system, which she'd hated just as much. She'd left at sixteen and had survived on her own very well until the day her boyfriend had taken her into a jeweller's shop and used her as bait for a robbery, complete with firearms. She thought he was taking her for an engagement ring, instead of which she got six years because no one believed her story, not even her own solicitor.

And now, Janet Bailey was free. Only she wasn't Janet Bailey, that much she did know. Maybe she had a family somewhere. Did they even know about her? Her mother had given her up for adoption, that's all she knew. The time had come to find who she really was and she would do it on her own. No way was she going back to Social Services for help.

Janet set off resolutely up the road to the railway station. Her future started here.

CHAPTER 3

Penny was putting the finishing touches to a lasagne for supper when she heard a roaring noise outside. Looking out of the kitchen window, she saw a huge, gleaming motorbike parked on the drive and a tall, leather-clad figure standing beside it, leisurely drawing long gauntlets from his hands. She could not see who the visitor was as a black helmet covered his face.

Penny was puzzled. They had no friends with motorbikes. Quickly she wiped her hands and went out of the back door to see what this person wanted. 'Hello?' she said uncertainly to the black-clad giant who was polishing an already pristine chrome exhaust pipe. 'Can I help you?'

The figure turned towards her and took off his helmet. He shook his head and ran his fingers through his thick black hair.

'George!' Penny took a step back and looked at her husband in horror. 'George. Is that really you? What are you doing in that get-up and riding that ... that thing?'

George stroked the bike lovingly. 'It's not a "thing", Penny. It's a Harley.' He breathed the word reverently, like a man newly in love. 'A Harley Davidson. Isn't she beautiful?'

Penny felt a little dizzy. Please, God, please, if there's any good in You at all, please don't let George tell me this is his new hobby. I can't bear it. Trying out cross-dressing last year was bad enough and now you want me to live with leathers and engine oil? No, please, give me a break.

'It's my new hobby,' George announced proudly. 'I've given up fancy clothes for good now. I said I would and I've gone for biking instead. It's a real man's machine. All that power and thrust between my legs, make a man of me again. I'll soon drive any lingering thoughts you might have about that Enrique Gonzalez fella right out of your head. Forget all that zumba dancing nonsense, I'll show you *lurve.*'

He twirled about in front of Penny, showing off his new outfit.'Don't you fancy a dark, handsome man in leather, Penny?'

Before she could answer 'absolutely not and I couldn't think of anything worse, except being locked up with George Formby and his ukulele when someone has thrown away the key,' George swept her off her feet and planted her on the back of the Harley.

'Oh yeah, a real biker babe! We're really going places this summer, Penny. We can ride anywhere we like. Where do you fancy?' George's face was alight with his latest enthusiasm. He stood tall and proud, his dark figure sharply outlined against the whitewashed walls of the house.

She was fifty-three, George fifty-five. Middle-aged bikers? What if he went in for piercings, tattoos or grew his hair into a spindly pony tail? And worse, expected her to go in for piercings and tattoos as well. Penny shuddered. Whenever she saw a pretty girl with a stud in her nose or tongue, she felt queasy. Imagine chewing on a nice piece of steak or engaging in a bit of passionate kissing with that thing in the way.

'Well?' George asked impatiently. 'Where would you like to go?'

'Helmsley?' she ventured. It wasn't too far away and she didn't know anyone there.

'Helmsley,' roared George. 'When I said go somewhere, Penny, I really meant go somewhere. As in London, Paris, Spain, that kind of somewhere.'

With some difficulty, Penny swung herself off the bike and tottered towards the kitchen door. 'You've just brought it home, George, give me a chance to get used to the idea. Half an hour ago all I had to think about was whether I had enough lettuce to make a salad to go with the lasagne and now you want me to think about biking and Spain. It's a bit of a leap, even for me. Give me time to take it in.'

'You'll love it,' George called after her enthusiastically and returned to polishing the exhaust pipe.

Inside the house, Penny leaned against the back door and looked upwards. 'I'll say this for You, God, You've got a sense of humour. You don't let up, do You? Last year it was frocks and now it's bikes. What next? Scuba diving? Sailing? Lion taming? A woman can only take so much, you know.'

She pictured herself in leathers, clinging on for dear life as they made their way through France, George steering them unsteadily through the narrow village streets.

It wasn't what she had imagined their lives would be after the boys left home, but then she hadn't imagined George cross-dressing either. If she ever thought about it, she had vague ideas of sedate cruising, sunbathing by a pool in a pink bikini by day and dressing up to the nines at night, she in a beautiful frock and George in a suit. At the end of a superb meal, he would lead her onto the floor to dance the night away to the big bands they always had on these ships. A cruise with all those hot, starry nights might have re-kindled the romance between them – instead of which she now had to contemplate black leathers, chafed thighs and eating dust.

Outside, George leaned back against his new bike and let his imagination run riot. He pictured himself and Penny riding romantically through narrow French village streets, staying in *pensions* and sampling the local *vin rouge* or a delicate rosé, before making their way down through Spain, swimming in the warm Mediterranean seas, sharing a paella supper under the stars before ... before... Sweating profusely at these pleasurable images, George forced himself from his reverie and returned to buffing his bike.

CHAPTER 4

Kate sank down gratefully into a comfy armchair in the new staffroom at Café Paradise. It was the end of a busy Saturday and a cup of tea with Penny before making her way home was very welcome.

'I'm glad that's the end of our day,' she said as Penny flopped down in the chair opposite.

'Mm,' agreed Penny. 'I don't know where Jackie gets the energy to run the Café Paradise restaurant at the weekends. If I did have the energy though, I'd be happy to stay on at the moment,' she continued glumly.

Kate looked at her questioningly. 'I thought you were a bit quiet today. Come on, out with it. What's up? George hasn't gone back to his naughty ways has he?' she asked teasingly.

Penny sighed. 'I don't know which is worse, that or this.'

'Throw in a bit of the other and we've got a full house,' said Kate. 'What is "*this*", then?'

'Motorbikes,' Penny said flatly and then corrected herself. 'Well, *a* motorbike. He's only gone and bought one.'

'Whoah,' breathed Kate admiringly. 'What kind of bike?'

'Harley,' said Penny.

Kate spluttered over a mouthful of tea, the drops splattering down her apron. 'A Harley! As in Harley Davidson! You're kidding. We are talking a real, full-size Harley here, he hasn't just bought a toy? You know, little boys, brm, brm and all that.'

Penny looked at Kate in exasperation. 'Does George look like a man who plays with toy cars or bikes?'

'He didn't look like a man who would get into cross-dressing and look what happened. Anything is possible with George.' She paused and the penny dropped. 'He's bought a Harley Davidson? A big one?'

'Huge, black, shiny and lethal.'

'Has he had a bike before?' Kate enquired.

'If he did it was probably a penny farthing.' Penny was quiet for a few moments and then continued. 'He says he had one for years *and* got his licence, but I find that hard to believe after watching him wobble around yesterday. You've never seen anything like it, Kate. Typical George, never does things by halves. He's got all the gear, black leathers, black helmet, he looks like Boon, only not as good.'

'Boon?'

'Oh, you're too young to remember. Michael Elphick played a private detective called Boon and he dressed in black and rode a motorbike.'

Kate thought about being tactful, but decided against it. Cutting to the chase always worked best with Penny. 'At least he's not prancing about in frocks any more. He's got himself a manly hobby and you wouldn't be embarrassed to be seen out with him. Not like last year when you had the disastrous outing to Thirsk, with George dressed in a girlie outfit.'

Penny agreed. 'But that's part of the trouble. George can't just go off and do his own thing, he always wants to drag me into it with him.'

'I think they call it marriage, Penny,' Kate said drily. 'Your boys are all grown up. Of course George wants to share his interests and time with you now. Sounds fairly natural to me.'

'He wants us to go on a trip.' Penny was glummer still. 'Imagine, me on the back of a bike wearing all the kit.'

'Sexyyy,' drawled Kate. 'You've got a fabulous figure, he'll be drooling.'

'Why couldn't he do something normal, like ... like ... oh, I don't know, take up bowls, or gardening, or...' Penny's brow creased in concentration, 'stamp collecting. That's it. It's clean, it's quiet and I wouldn't have to get involved.'

'And it would bore the pants off George, as well you know. He's action man or woman, depending upon his mood. Sitting quietly with his stamps, he ain't. Embrace it and thank your lucky stars he's still got some get up and go. Who knows, it could be a whole new adventure for you both. I wish we could do it.' Kate was wistful.

'How are things with Stan and the bakery?' asked Penny.

Kate got up from the armchair and trailed over to the sink to wash her mug. 'Couldn't be worse really. The bakery's gone bust. It's in the hands of administrators and Stan will soon be made redundant. That's put an end to our savings programme for now and an end to our new home and baby plans.'

Penny leapt up from her chair. 'I'm so sorry Kate.' She flung her arms around her. 'Here's me going on about George and you've got real problems. What is Stan going to do?'

Kate pushed her long red-gold hair off her face and frowned consideringly. 'Well, I have been wondering about applying for a bursary for him from the Historical Trust. We've found a permanent site within the city walls where we can build a replica settlement of early Ebacorum. I need to be there full time to supervise it when it gets underway. Stan has an extensive knowledge of Roman soldiers and battles and if he could widen his field to take in Roman domestic life, he would be invaluable to our education programme. I know there's a vacancy on a training programme at the International College in Rome and it may be possible for him to get the place.'

Penny crossed her fingers on both hands and held them up to Kate. 'Good luck, Kate, and don't worry too much. I'm sure things will sort themselves out.'

Kate smiled. 'Yeah, that goes for all of us.'

CHAPTER 5

'Mummy?' The slightly panicky voice at the other end of the phone did not bode well for Barney's mother, Grace Anderson.

'Genevieve? Where are you? Your train came in an hour ago and I'm still waiting for you.'

'Now don't be cross, Mummy. I'm at...'

Grace waited patiently whilst a muffled conversation was conducted at the other end of the line.

'He says I'm at Newark. Hang on. What? Oh, Newark Northgate.'

Newark! How in God's name...? Genevieve was thirty years old but she could still thwart their carefully laid plans. Grace took a deep breath and drew on all her years of experience with her daughter. Getting cross would get them nowhere. Only patient questioning would unravel this latest twist in Genevieve's eventful life.

'Is there a gentleman there helping you, darling?' she asked carefully. Visions of her beautiful but brainless daughter trustingly following an unknown stranger into a who-knew-what scenario flitted across her mind.

'Sort of, Mummy,' Genevieve replied. 'He says this is Newark. I thought it was York. I am coming to York, aren't I?' she asked, a note of doubt creeping into her voice. 'I'm sure Daddy said York when he put me on the train at King's Cross.'

Grace fought down the irritation Genevieve always invoked in her. How did she come to have such an airhead for a daughter? They had managed to teach her to read, at least that extremely expensive private school with extra tuition had.

So all Genevieve had to do was sit on a train until it drew into York station and read at least four signs that clearly said York and then get off the blessed train. She even knew she should be coming to York, so how was she in Newark?

'You are coming to York, darling,' Grace said calmly. 'Now tell me slowly, why are you in Newark and who is the gentleman with you? Can you do that for me?'

'Well…'

In the silence that followed, Grace could almost see her beautiful daughter wrinkling her short, freckled nose and the little furrow creasing her smooth white forehead as she tried hard to remember the latest events in her muddled life.

'Take your time darling,' Grace crooned gently.

'I know,' Genevieve said brightly. 'It was very hot on the train and I fell asleep and then the train must have jerked a bit and I fell against this nice man. He said the driver put the brakes on suddenly and that's why I… Anyway, I saw the end of this sign and I saw the R and the K and I just knew it was my stop, Mummy. Really, I just knew it. You would have been so proud of me. I got up and the nice man helped me off with my bags and I waited there on the platform, just like you told me to do. I didn't move. I remembered you said to get off the train and you would collect me. So I did, but you didn't come. I waited for ages and then I asked this man in a uniform what time it was and he said it was six o'clock and I'm sure you said you would be there by five and then this man said it was Newark.'

'Was that the man in the uniform, Genevieve?' Grace had been here before. Genevieve attracted men and trouble.

'Yes Mummy. Could he have a word with you?'

Two hours later, having driven down the A1, clogged with Saturday evening traffic, Grace collected her daughter from the stationmaster's office, where she and all her baggage was being carefully guarded. The look of relief on the stationmaster's face when she appeared told Grace all she needed to know. An hour with Genevieve was enough for most mortals.

******

Barney was appalled. 'Have Genevieve here? In my office? Mother! Have you completely lost your marbles?'

Grace regarded her son dispassionately. He was extremely handsome. Tall, blond and blue-eyed. He had it all: a new wife he adored and a new business in the centre of York city, working in partnership with his old friend Jake. They had served together at the Citizens Advice Bureau and had recently set up a solicitors' practice. Yes, Barney was very fortunate and now it was time, if Grace had any say in the matter, that he took his share of family responsibilities, in the form of minding his sister, Genevieve.

'I would remind you, Barnabas,' she began.

Barney groaned. He knew he was losing. When his mother called him Barnabas, she was like the Rock of Gibraltar and about as immovable.

'I would remind you, Barnabas,' Grace continued 'you have been very fortunate to have been born with a good brain which your father and I have spent a lot of time and money nurturing to ensure you can lead a happy and fulfilled life.'

'For which, as you know, I am grateful.' He knew he was swimming against the outgoing tide, but a bit of timely grovelling would not go amiss if it would prevent Genevieve being foisted upon him.

'Don't give me grateful, Barnabas.' Grace was in no mood to be sidetracked. 'The fact is, my dear boy, it's your turn to look after your little sister. Juliet has had her for six months, quite heroic of her in my opinion, especially as Genevieve nearly managed to electrocute the dog, burn the house down and lose their new baby in the middle of Bellingham. Juliet's done her bit for the cause and so has your father. He's lucky he's any members of his Chambers left, let alone staff to run them, since he let Genevieve loose in the office. He's going to be a high court judge soon and he won't do that with Genevieve in tow. No, there's nothing for it, you'll have to take your turn.'

Barney sagged back against the richly upholstered armchair in his mother's drawing room. Genevieve! A five-foot-ten lamppost, all legs, long red hair and freckles. His staff were fairly new and were just beginning to work well together. Barney wondered if they would be strong enough to work with his little sister.

'Couldn't you leave it for a while?' he pleaded. 'If she's driven Dad's staff up the wall, what's she going to do to mine? Have a heart, Mother.'

Grace rose and Barney knew that he had lost the battle. 'Brotherly love, Barnabas. To whom much is given...'

Barney trailed miserably in his mother's wake. 'Yeah, I know: much is expected.'

'Quite.' Grace smiled at her son and embraced him fondly. 'Just do your best with her. You'll hardly know you've got her.'

Well, that would be a first. Genevieve was not a loud, noisy girl, quite the opposite really, but somehow... Barney could never work it out. Things just happened when Genevieve was around and before you knew it, chaos ensued. He felt far from sanguine at the prospect of having his sister in the office. Jake had only met her once, at Barney's wedding to Jackie last year. Barney winced inwardly as he remembered Jake leading Genevieve onto the dance floor at the reception. She had tied him up in knots as she tried to avoid treading on his toes and talking to him at the same time. Jake had the look of a man sorely tried as he returned shakily to his seat. Barney did not look forward to breaking this latest news to Jake tomorrow, when work resumed after the weekend.

CHAPTER 6

Ellie Breckenridge was having a very busy morning. Her nanny goats were milking well and she was making cheeses in the new dairy Walter had created for her in one of his disused barns. Walter had gone out very early to the fruit and vegetable wholesalers, armed with a long list from Jackie. Even though he had volunteered for the trip, he grumbled about it. Jackie had a husband now, plenty of staff and a fancy chef who should be going and choosing his own fruit and veg, not sending a clapped-out old bloke like him out at the crack of dawn in a bloody great big van...

Ellie smiled to herself as she recalled Walter's monologue the previous evening as he prepared for his early morning excursion. She knew he adored his daughter and son-in-law and was quietly pleased to be involved with Café Paradise, even though Jackie had taken over the running of it.

'Cooee, anyone at home?' A light female voice echoed around the farmyard.

Ellie grabbed a towel to wipe her hands as she went to the dairy door.

'Hello?' came the voice again, a little more uncertain this time.

'Jane! What a nice surprise.' Ellie regarded her old friend Jane Bradley with pleasure. Before Ellie had married Walter the previous year, she had lived in Dunnington, a pretty village on the outskirts of York. Jane and her husband, Michael, farmed nearby and Ellie had spent a lot of time with them.

'Ellie! Thank God you're at home. You're my only hope.'

Ellie looked at her friend with concern. Jane looked flustered and upset, quite unlike her usual calm self. Ellie put her arm about her and led her towards the farmhouse. 'Come inside and you can tell me all about it over a cup of tea. And I've freshly made scones and your favourite raspberry jam. Now, if they don't help I don't know what will.'

Ten minutes later, at the end of Jane's story, Ellie sipped her tea and reflected quietly on what she had just heard.

'Mike's never done this before?' she said.

'Never had to.' Jane was calmer now that she had unburdened herself to her old friend. 'I think the economic situation made him want to do it. We're struggling to make ends meet and it would be another mouth to feed, and with it being the runt of the litter, it'll be a slow grower, so extra feed with no guarantee at the end that we'd be able to get anything for it. He was going to drown it.' Jane's eyes filled with tears. 'He's never done anything like that before, not to a healthy animal, and I couldn't bear it Ellie, not for me and not for him. It just can't happen, so I thought of you, scooped the poor thing up and here I am.'

'I could do with a dog,' Ellie said slowly. 'Walter's away seeing to his own sheep a lot and then working in his fruit and veg gardens. A dog would be company and we could train a Border collie for my sheep and goats. It could be just the thing.'

Five minutes later Ellie was in possession of a black-and-white puppy. Although it was eleven weeks old, it was tiny, the size of a newborn. Ellie fell in love straight away.

'Does he have a name yet?' she asked her friend.

'No, best not to on a farm. Once you do that they become your friends and then it's too hard to let them go. If you'll take him, you can call him whatever you like.'

Ellie gazed down at the little furry bundle snuffling on her lap. 'Elvis,' she said dreamily. 'I fell in love with Elvis when I was young and I think I've just fallen in love with this little fellow too. Elvis it is.'

'Elvis,' Jane said doubtfully. 'Ellie, are you sure you'd be happy shouting "come-bye Elvis" at the top of your voice?'

'Ecstatic,' replied Ellie, a broad smile spreading across her face.

******

'Elvis!' Walter was inclined to feel his wife's forehead and tell her she needed to lie down in a darkened room. 'Bloody Elvis! What kind of a name is that for a sheepdog? Not that you can call that *thing* a sheepdog. Nor it never will be neither. Look at it!' Walter said in disgust.

He took the puppy from Ellie's arms and held it up for inspection. 'Aye, it's a runt alright. What do you think you're going to do with it?' Walter brought the puppy down to eye level and it tried to lick his nose. 'Elvis!' he snorted again.

Alarmed at the tone of his voice, the puppy promptly peed down Walter's shirt. 'Oh God, that's all I need. Here, have him back.' Walter dumped Elvis back in Ellie's lap.

'I'm going to train him to round up my sheep and goats for milking,' Ellie said tranquilly.

'You don't need a dog, you've got me,' he said.

Ellie's lips twitched in amusement. 'You can't round up my sheep for me and herd my goats, now can you?'

'Shouldn't need to if you do it right,' said Walter. 'Time you had 'em trained to come to a feed bucket. That way you don't need a dog, especially not that one. He's a runt, he'll never amount to anything, no matter how much you try to train him. Another mouth to feed – and you can bet he'll eat for England as he's a runt. Never got near enough to his mum to get his share. Them ones are greedy for ever after.'

As if on cue, the puppy reached up and licked Ellie's face, whilst squeaking and wagging his stubby tail enthusiastically. Ellie rose, hugging him to her. 'Elvis stays,' she stated quietly, 'and now I'm going to get his lunch.'

'*His* lunch! What about *my* lunch?'

Ellie shot a look at him as she passed.

'Well, our lunch then?' Walter asked feebly. 'I was up at

three this morning. I bet he wasn't.' He watched enviously as Ellie scrambled eggs and cut bread for Elvis's lunch.

'You got breakfast; he didn't because he had a hot date with a farm pond, as I told you. And what's more,' Ellie rounded on Walter, uncharacteristically fierce, 'another word about this poor little puppy and he won't be the only one with no food and a hot date with a farm pond today. OK?'

Walter took a step back. Ellie was a force to be reckoned with when roused. Tigers protecting their young could take lessons from her. 'OK. But we will be getting lunch today, won't we?' His stomach was rolling. Walter hoped it wasn't going to be carrot juice and salad again.

'When I've seen to Elvis.' As if she had read his thoughts, Ellie added, 'Go and find me some carrots and salad and I'll call you when lunch is ready.'

Grumbling to himself, Walter headed outside to the cold store. He loved his wife and in the nine months they had been married, Walter had never known such tenderness and care in his life. But, by the heck, he thought, she's bloody daft about her animals. If she could tuck her sheep and goats up in bed at night I think she would, and now we're saddled with this little runt. She'll never make owt of him. Walter sighed as he gathered up carrots as instructed. Women. They always knew best, didn't they? And what did he know? He was only a man who'd just been demoted in the pecking order by the looks of it. He foresaw trouble ahead with little Elvis. He might be a cute little puppy now but wait until he grew into a great galumphing dog. Walter shook his head and went to find the lettuce.

CHAPTER 7

The April days were lengthening, bringing visitors and locals out to dine in the city. The following Monday evening, Barney was helping Jackie re-stock the café after a hectic day's trading. It was obvious they were going to need more staff for the summer season and, thinking of the conversation with his mother, Barney broached the subject.

'Maybe a couple more waitresses,' he suggested.

Jackie considered this idea. 'Mm, you're right. If we're going to be this busy all season, we'll certainly need more help.'

'It so happens, Genevieve's home just now, she could lend a hand,' her husband said airily.

'Genevieve! Barney, have you lost the plot entirely?'

'What?' Barney tried to maintain his offhand manner.

'You know very well *what* and I know very well *what*, so don't *what* me, Barney Anderson. You are not fobbing your little sister off on me. What's going on, anyhow? What's she doing home? Has London got too hot for her?'

Barney raised his eyes heavenwards. 'Honestly, Jackie, you always think the worst where my sister is concerned.'

'With good reason,' Jackie shot back. 'I haven't forgotten her treading on my dress at our wedding, dropping my bouquet and then locking herself out of the house so we had to rescue her, on our wedding night! Not to mention her recent sojourn at Juliet's in Bellingham.'

Barney groaned. 'Has Jules grassed her up already?'

'Big time, so you can forget any ideas you may have harboured about Genevieve coming here.' Jackie's furrowed

29

brow suddenly cleared. 'Oh I see,' she breathed. 'No wonder you've worked your butt off tonight. Softening me up, Mr Smoothie?'

Jackie put her arms around Barney and kissed him tenderly on the lips. Maybe, just maybe... Barney was hopeful. He held her tightly and caressed her.

Slowly, Jackie withdrew. 'Not a chance,' she whispered sweetly.

'Jackie, please.' Barney was desperate. If she wouldn't take Genevieve, he would have to.

Jackie picked up her coat and walked to the door. She opened it, turned the sign to closed and stepped outside. She gestured up the street, to the main squares of the city. 'There's all of York out there for Genevieve to be let loose on, Barney. Petergate – High and Low, Stonegate, Coppergate and all the other Gates hereabouts. You wouldn't want to cramp her style, now would you?' She grinned and began punching in the numbers for the burglar alarm code.

If only he *could* cramp her style. Genevieve anywhere was a loose cannon and most definitely the last person he needed on his new team. He gritted his teeth and followed his wife out. She would be a tough nut to crack but he wasn't giving up yet. This was only an opening skirmish.

CHAPTER 8

Two days had gone by since Alastair had given in his notice to Jackie, and Walter still hadn't been able to get Ellie to sit down and relax long enough so he could talk to her about the situation at the café.

On the Tuesday evening he devised a plan. He came into the kitchen at their Claygate farm with a dozen freshly cleaned eggs, a bunch of daffodils from the garden and a bottle of wine. He placed his offerings carefully on the table and smiled at Ellie.

'It's not my birthday,' she said, eyeing the flowers and wine suspiciously.

'Doesn't have to be.' Walter tried for laconic. 'Thought we'd celebrate the new pup. Light the fire in the sitting room and relax a bit.'

Ellie wasn't convinced. 'You don't even like him. You've only called him "runt" so far.'

'Well,' Walter shifted uncomfortably. 'Not easy, Elvis, is it? If you'd called him Shep, or Rex, something decent, maybe I'd get my tongue round it a bit better. But I'll try, for you.'

Ellie was won round and after supper they settled by the fire. Walter poured them another glass of wine and allowed Elvis to crawl onto his lap. Ellie smiled her approval. 'There, I knew you'd love him once you'd given him a chance. Isn't he just gorgeous?'

Walter looked down at the pup and sighed inwardly. Gorgeous was not the first word that sprang to mind. Elvis had a big head perched on a small body, one raggy ear flopped over and the other stayed upright, as if permanently to attention. His large paws made his legs look like sticks.

'It's to be hoped he never grows into them paws or he'll be bloody enormous,' Walter observed. 'That's if we can ever make anything of him.'

Elvis cocked his head and stared brightly up at Walter, his long pink tongue lolling out of the side of his mouth. He barked. It came out as more of a high-pitched squeak. He almost fell off Walter's lap in surprise as he looked round to see where the noise had come from.

Walter steadied him. 'Less of that, young fella,' he said firmly. 'Speak when you're spoken to.' He stroked him gently and Elvis responded by jumping up and licking his face enthusiastically. 'Aye, aye, alright lad.'

Feeling he'd done his bit by the pup, he passed him back to Ellie and took a large gulp of wine to fortify his nerves. This next bit might be tricky. He smiled his most winning smile. Ellie smiled fondly back at him, stroking Elvis as he snuggled down on her lap.

'You couldn't run to the chocolates as well, then?' she said.

'Chocolates?' Walter sat up in alarm. Had she been expecting chocolates? It wasn't really her birthday, was it? No, surely he hadn't got that wrong? 'Erm, I hadn't thought of buying chocolates, Ellie. Thought we were eating healthily just now.' Bloody chocolates, what's she on about?

'I've had the washed eggs, daffs and wine. Thought you might have run to chocolates too. You're obviously currying favour in advance and I think I'm worth it, whatever it is.'

Walter looked at his wife in surprise. 'Currying favour?'

'You didn't think I was taken in by all that eyewash about celebrating Elvis, did you, Walter? I'm not that daft. So what is this all about?'

Walter shuffled in his seat, avoiding her gaze. 'Well, you're sort of right,' he said slowly.

'No sort of about it. Come on, out with it. I'm wined and dined and mellow and I might even say yes to whatever is going on in that head of yours.'

Encouraged by her tone, Walter took the plunge. 'Jackie needs a cook at the café for a while. That Alastair's given a week's notice. He's off to work at Buckingham Palace, taking that daft Melissa with him, and Jackie can't get a good chef just like that. She asked if you could step into the breach and I said I was sure you would. Help out like.' Walter looked at Ellie hopefully.

Ellie eyed him levelly and continued stroking Elvis. 'I'm sure I won't, Walter,' she said calmly.

'But...' Walter began.

Ellie held her hand up. 'Listen for a minute, lad. I've got my goats and sheep to milk, then cheeses to make. I've booked my stall at Newgate Market, don't forget, and now there's Elvis to look after and train. If you can see space in the day to go and cook at Café Paradise, I can't.'

'I could do the milking for you,' Walter offered.

'We've been here before, Walter. You're too rough and you upset them, then their milk dries up. I'm not having that again. No. I've got a better idea. I'll stay at home with the animals and you can go to the café.'

Walter stared at her. 'Me!'

'Yes you, my dear. From what I hear, you used to turn out the best sausage and bacon baps in the whole of York. It won't take you long to get back in the swing of things.' Ellie grinned happily at him and placed Elvis back on the floor. 'Well, now we've sorted that out, I must get on. Elvis needs his supper and a little walk before bedtime.' She made for the door. Walter had not moved. He was staring straight ahead. 'Walter?' she called back to him.

'Me? Back at the café, with Jackie? I can't do that. I only do fry-ups – I can't do all that fancy food she offers now. Please, Ellie, have a heart. We can't see Jackie left in the lurch like this.'

'We're not, Walter.' Ellie smiled her sweetest smile at him. 'I am looking after my animals and my cheeses and you are looking after the cooking at the café. You'll be able to see to the vegetable garden when you come home. There we are, all angles covered. Now come along, Elvis is waiting and we need to check on the stock before bed.'

How did he end up playing third fiddle behind sheep, goats and a runt named Elvis? And now volunteered for a stint at the café? Walter got up from his chair. Life was even more of a mystery to him than ever.

CHAPTER 9

Even before the jury had pronounced her guilty, Janet Bailey could not remember feeling this sense of apprehension. Her mouth was dry and her chest so tight she could hardly breathe. Even though she was innocent of the charges of robbing a jeweller's shop, there had been some sense of relief when the trial was over. Things were at an end.

But now? She desperately wanted to know who she really was but what if she didn't like what she found out? Supposing her mother had been a prostitute and she was a by-product? What if ... what if? Janet shivered in the April sunshine and squared her shoulders. Come on, she told herself, it can't be any worse than your imaginings. Go in and find out, the lady's waiting for you.

******

Two hours later, Janet was drinking scalding coffee with hands that were still shaking after her interview at the adoption agency. Mrs Lawson had been sympathetic, understanding and very helpful with offers of counselling and referrals to other agencies. Janet politely took the details but knew she would not follow them up. She just needed to know who she was.

And now she did. She was born to a woman called Marilyn Langley who, according to the birth certificate, had named her child Annabel. Janet stared unseeingly down the long room of the café and pondered the name. Annabel. She mouthed it silently. Mm, it felt good, quite sophisticated. She liked it. Better than a plain old Janet; worthy, dependable Janet . Perhaps this Marilyn, her mother, had been sophisticated. There was no way of knowing now. Marilyn had died at her home in York not so very long ago, Mrs Lawson informed her. The only clue Janet had to Marilyn's personality was a garnet necklace and earrings she had left behind for her child when she reached sixteen. Janet had received them when she left the children's home. A strange legacy, especially as there was no letter or information about herself or who had fathered her child, not even a photograph of them together. It looked like Marilyn Langley would remain a sophisticated mystery.

Janet grimaced to herself. She hadn't been wanted as Annabel, or as Janet in her adopted family. The placement hadn't lasted for long but she was stuck with being known as Janet ever after. Drinking the cooling coffee, she pondered this point. She didn't have to be Janet now, she could be Annabel again. Her mother had at least given her a name. She nodded to herself; from now on she would be Annabel, Annabel Langley, the person on the birth certificate.

Clutching her bag containing the precious certificate, Annabel made her way out of the coffee shop and on to the street. She had a whole new life to make. Perhaps she would visit York and see where her mother came from and where she was born. She smiled to herself. She was a Yorkshire lass; there was nothing wrong with that.

CHAPTER 10

A tower of red bread trays appeared at the back door of the Café Paradise and moved towards the storeroom.

'Is that you behind there Stan?' asked Kate.

'None other than me, light of my life, my beloved, beautiful angel-wife.'

Kate sighed and raised her eyebrows queryingly. 'Cut the cackle. What have you forgotten, oh very, very late in your deliveries, husband of mine?'

'I have twenty packs of bagels, enough baguettes to feed the whole of France, fifteen large linseed and pumpkin loaves, but no fish, hundreds of wholemeal and a wagon load of teacakes, fruit cakes, sponge cakes, cheesecakes, tarts, pies. Bloody hell, doesn't that Alastair cook anything himself? You've got half of Henderson's Bakery here.'

'He's busy with his nouvelle cuisine. When you've been summoned to cook for the Queen, your mind's not on curd tarts and fat rascals. It's all mousseline, scallops and quenelles these days.'

Kate went to help her husband unpack the bread trays. Stan swept her up in his arms and embraced her. 'I am not in the least interested in Alastair and his quenelles, whatever they are, but I *am* interested in a certain weekend waitress and project leader of the Historical Trust, aka Mrs Peterson.'

Kate wriggled out of his arms. 'Out with it. What haven't we got – and you can tell Her Majesty's chef yourself. He'll likely throw a tantrum if he's got to set to and start baking now. That's all so beneath him.'

'None of the fancy stuff, no gateaux, chocolate or coffee cakes, lemon drizzle...'

'He'll have a nervous breakdown. What's happened?' Kate wasn't sure she really wanted to know.

Stan picked up his bread trays and headed for the door. 'I'll bring in the rest of the stuff and then break the glad tidings to him. It's looking like when it's gone, it's gone. No more cakes, bread only and that's for one more week and then it's shutdown. We'll all be out on our ear and down to the Job Centre.'

Stan departed and Kate stared sadly at the open door. Her lovely, hardworking husband. His pride was hurt, especially as their plans for buying their new home and starting a family were now on hold. He only had a week of employment left. She had to do something to give them their future back. She would email Sofia at the International College in Rome tonight. Stan must get a place on that course.

******

Jake stared at his friend in disbelief. 'Genevieve? Here? Have you got a touch of sun, Barney? We can't let her loose in the office, she'll cause havoc.' Jake ran his hands through his short brown hair, leaving it standing up in spikes.

Barney's heart sank. If he couldn't rely on Jake's support, this wasn't going to work. 'Please Jake, just for a week or two. I've had the three-line whip from Mother and Jackie won't have her in the café. What else can I do with her?'

'Does it have to be here? We've only just got the office up and running. Throwing Genevieve into the mix could be disaster.'

'I won't let her loose in the office, I promise Jake. I'll keep her under my eye all the time. You'll hardly know she's there. Honestly.' Barney was ready to go down on his knees, lick Jake's boots, anything, just to get his agreement on this one. He looked pleadingly at his friend.

Jake looked steadily back at him and sighed. 'I know I'm

going to regret this, but, OK. Just a week or two mind. I still have vivid memories of Genevieve at your wedding. I know what she's capable of, so keep her close Barney or I may not be responsible for my actions.'

Barney heaved a sigh of relief. A breathing space at least. It would give him time to work on Jackie. Genevieve would be an asset to the Café Paradise, wouldn't she?

CHAPTER 11

Penny Montague stared at the figure looking back at her in the mirror and had difficulty in recognising herself encased in tight leather trousers and heavy jacket. She paced to and fro before the mirror, torn between amazement at how good she looked in the get-up and embarrassment at a woman of her age strutting about trying to be a biker babe. She was surprised at how the soft leather encased her legs. She stroked it experimentally. It was surprisingly warm to the touch. Quite sexy. Yes, she definitely liked the leather look. If only she could just wear the stuff and not go on that wretched bike. Maybe she could talk George out of it.

A long whistle interrupted her thoughts. George leaned in the doorway, smiling wolfishly at her. 'Phoah. Penny Montague! I knew you'd look good in leathers, but not this good. Wait 'til the Helmsley boys get a look at you! Come on you biker babe, let's go.'

'Are you sure about this, George?' Penny made a last-ditch attempt to talk him out of it. 'I mean us, in our fifties, biking? Aren't we a bit old? And maybe you need a bit more practice?'

'Old? Don't be ridiculous Penny. We're in our prime and I've had all the practice I need. I'll be competing in the TT races next year at this rate. So come on, sexy, Harley awaits.'

Penny picked up the new motorcycle helmet from the bed and jammed it on her head. At least with that on, no one would recognise her.

Fifteen minutes later, all Penny's misgivings were confirmed. They wobbled their way precariously on the A64 out of York and along the winding roads that led to Helmsley. George was enthralled with the new experience and insisted on shouting out with delight every time he changed gear, extolling the virtues of the smoothness of the engine, the precision engineering that went into the making of a Harley and how special a machine it was. He spent so much time with his head turned back towards Penny that every bend came as a new surprise to him and he only managed to keep the bike upright at the last moment.

Over the roar of the engine, Penny screamed at George to 'shut up and face forwards'. She wasn't the least bit interested in the performance of the bike, only in getting to Helmsley alive, in preference to being scraped off this awful road. She shut her eyes and fastened her arms even more tightly around George's waist.

George took her screams as shrieks of delight. 'Better than the fairground rides any day,' he shouted and swung deeply into the next bend, the Harley angled at thirty degrees, almost grazing his knees on the road.

Approaching the outskirts of Helmsley, George slowed his speed and coasted into the market square, where dozens of other motorbikes were already parked up. With a flourish, George parked alongside them and switched the engine off. He took in the scene with delight. Biker's paradise. The conversations he could have – optimum performance, the best engine oils, polishes, servicing. Oh, the fun was going to be endless. Penny would love it.

'You're going to love it, Penny,' he echoed his own thoughts to his wife. No reply came. George looked round. Penny was still holding on to his waist, her eyes tight shut. 'We're here, Penny love,' he said. 'What have you got your eyes shut for? You love Helmsley.'

There was no response. George removed Penny's arms and managed to shuffle awkwardly off the bike. He turned and looked at her. She neither moved nor spoke. He removed the motorcycle helmet from her head and saw the fixed, terrified expression on her face. Perhaps she hadn't enjoyed the ride quite as much as him after all.

George shook her gently. 'Penny love, we're here,' he repeated. 'Shall we go and have a nice cup of tea? I expect that's just what you need.' George brightened up. Yes, that was it. It was still early spring; maybe it had been a bit cold, in spite of the leathers. 'Tea.' He spoke loudly, directly into her ear.

This roused Penny. She stared at him blankly.

'Tea.' George mimed drinking a cup of tea. 'Let's go and have a cup of tea. You're in Helmsley, Penny. We can get a cup of tea.'

Realisation dawned and the look of stark terror slowly left Penny's face. 'Tea,' she said. 'Tea. Lovely. Let's go and get some tea.' As she made to get off the bike, she cried out in pain and sat back down again. 'My back, George, my back. I've hurt my back. I can't get off. Help me please.'

George tried but Penny cried out loudly as he attempted to lift her off the seat. A burly man idling by his bike nearby strolled over and offered to help.

'Maybe one of us each side and we lift her clean off will do it,' he suggested.

And so Penny was lifted clear of the bike and deposited safely on the ground. To her horror she could not straighten up, seemingly locked into her passenger position.

An interested crowd of bikers was gathering round them. Offers of help and advice flowed. 'Can we give you a hand, love?' 'You wants to lie down, lass,' and 'Expect the cold's got into your bones. You need a rub down with some Deep Heat, that's what you want,' proffered a woman of Penny's vintage. 'I was like that, my first time. It gets better.'

Flushed with embarrassment, Penny thanked the onlookers and clutched on tightly to George. 'Let's get that tea, shall we?' She began to totter towards The Black Swan Hotel, an old stone building facing onto the market square.

The fine spring day had brought the visitors to Helmsley and the well-appointed visitors' lounge was already full with people taking morning coffee, fresh scones and scrumptious-looking cakes.

George guided Penny to a comfortable sofa and lowered her down gently. Penny sat well back into the deep sofa and felt the pain in her back ease considerably. George sat beside her, smiling at the prospect of tea and scones. He looked about with interest and smiled at the two elderly ladies seated opposite. The ladies smiled slightly and acknowledged George with a tilt of their heads, then carried on with their conversation.

The waitress brought tea and scones and set the tray before Penny. Penny looked at it. 'I'm stuck, George, I can't move. You'll have to be mother and butter my scone for me. I can't do a thing.'

Unused to these manoeuvres, George set to, splashing tea about and sawing away at the scones. He handed Penny her plate of broken bits of scone and pools of jam. 'There you are, love. Sorry it's not in one piece but it all goes down the same way, doesn't it?'

Penny's pained glance at her plate was wasted as George happily picked up a teaspoon and began shovelling jammy lumps of scone into his mouth.

The two matrons opposite broke off their conversation and stared covertly at Penny and George. They shook their heads and whispered earnestly together. 'Fancy leaving it all to her husband,' one hissed to the other.

'I know. The young folk these days. Just won't do anything, will they? Expect to be waited on hand and foot. And you can see he's not up to it. What a mess he's made.' They shook their heads again and took up their china teacups, little fingers crooked.

Penny caught the flow of their disapproval and her cheeks burned. She shuffled lower in her seat and passed her empty plate to George. 'Could you pass my tea please, George, as I am unable to get it myself?' She glared defiantly at the two ladies opposite but their conversation had moved on and they were busy shredding the reputation of the waitress, who was quietly replenishing coffee and teapots.

'The old cats!' Penny burst out as they made their way out of The Black Swan Hotel.

'Cats?' George looked back into the hotel foyer. 'I never saw them. Shouldn't have cats in a place like this. Not in the daytime at any rate. Not everyone likes cats. Night-time maybe, if you need a good mouser. Some do a grand job.'

'Not cats, George,' Penny cried, exasperated. 'Those old women opposite us, they were like a pair of old cats.'

'Didn't look a bit like cats to me.' George looked hard at Penny. 'You alright love. Seeing cats and all that...'

'Oh, God.' Penny ground her teeth and held on tightly to George. 'I am not seeing cats; I just want to go home. I've had enough for one day. Let's go and find the Harley and ride home. *Very gently please.*'

George looked down at Penny and patted her hand. 'I rode here gently,' he said. 'Anyway, we haven't looked round the shops yet. We've plenty of time. Don't you want to look in your favourite dress shops?'

Penny ground her teeth. 'No. I might see someone I know.'

'That would be nice,' George said happily. 'I can tell them all about the Harley.'

'Oh Harley, Harley!' Penny said crossly. 'I don't want to meet anyone, not dressed like this. Just take me home.'

George looked down at his wife and shook his head, mystified. Women were funny creatures. Penny looked gorgeous, wouldn't she want to show off to her friends?

'Home, George,' Penny said firmly.

They arrived at the bike and George fished out the keys from his pocket. Selecting the ignition key, he tried to insert it into its slot on the control panel. The key would not fit. George grunted to himself and wiggled the key in again. He had no luck. He stepped back, puzzled, scratching his head.

'George!' Penny squeaked. He looked across at her and saw a familiar look of fright on her face.

'It's alright, Penny, it's just a bit stiff, that's all. We'll get home, don't you worry.'

'No, George, it's not that.' Penny pointed to something behind George. 'It's ... it's behind you. Him...'

George spun round on his heel, almost into the chest of the large man standing immediately behind him. The man did not move or speak. George's gaze slowly travelled up from the chest, took in the powerful shoulders and bull-like neck and on to the massive head, topped with a mane of shaggy grey hair flowing around a thick grey beard. George's first thought was that this was Hagrid on an away day from Hogwarts. He was enormous.

George stepped back. 'Nice day,' he offered.

'It is,' agreed the man. 'Are you trying to steal my bike?' He took a step towards George, who backed off again. 'Because if you are...'

'Your bike! No, no. Not at all, Hagrid, I mean... Sorry, we haven't been introduced. I'm George Montague and this is my wife Penny. This is *my* bike. My new Harley. Well, I know it's not new new, but it's new to me and this is our first outing on it. We've been having tea at The Black Swan and now we're going home.' George knew he was gabbling, but the guy was huge. Any misunderstandings and he could be flattened by a wave of one of those huge paws.

'Hagrid, eh?' The man's lips twitched and a smile played about his mouth. 'I've been called some names by the boys, but this is a new one. I've not heard it before at any rate.'

'B-b-b-boys?' George looked around at the gathering of bikers in the square. A moment ago they had seemed a friendly bunch but with Hagrid looming over him, the atmosphere seemed to change.

Hagrid took the ignition key from George's hand. George began to protest but the man stopped him and put his finger to his lips. Keeping his gaze fixed unwaveringly on George, he reached into the pocket of his leather jacket and slowly extracted an ignition key. He leaned across and fitted it into the slot on the bike. It slid in easily.

'So you see, Mr Montague – may I call you George? This is

my bike. Although, if you were trying to steal it, it isn't actually my bike. It belongs to one of the parents. He loans it to me sometimes when I get an afternoon off. Such a kind man. He knows how much I love biking.'

Hagrid stroked the bike lovingly. 'We take a vow of poverty, though. Keeping a Harley wouldn't sit too well with that, would it?'

George stared at the bike and then up at Hagrid. 'A parent's bike?' he managed.

'Yes.' The man held out his hand. 'Father Jerome, Ampleforth Abbey, on a day off.' He smiled down at George. 'I'm sorry, I shouldn't have said "steal". I didn't think for a moment that you were trying to take it. You've just come to the wrong bike, I can see that.'

George nodded wordlessly. He looked across to Penny. She was speechless too. Father Jerome, six foot seven of him if he was an inch, long hair, beard and biker's leathers. A monk!

Father Jerome pointed to a Harley parked a short distance away. 'Is that yours?' he asked. 'It's almost identical to this one. No wonder you made a mistake. Peace be with you, George. I must be off.' He grinned down at George and swung his leg over the Harley. In a moment it roared into life and the biker monk rode off, smiling and waving to the groups left behind, his grey hair flowing behind him, glinting in the spring sunshine.

Luckily there was still plenty of help to hand. Penny's back was so bad, she had to be lifted back onto the seat. Soon they were underway again, Penny as vocal in her requests for riding home slowly as George had been for fast riding on the way out.

The morning sunshine had faded, to be replaced by a grey and mizzly afternoon. All too soon the mizzle gave way to a downpour. George enjoyed throwing up the spray as he splashed his way home, like a small boy jumping into puddles. Penny did not enjoy the journey at all. Leaning forward to hold on to George exposed a gap in her leather collar for the rain to drip steadily down her neck and soak her through. The heavy raindrops hammered on her helmet, bringing on a migraine.

Switching the Harley off in their driveway, George jumped off the bike, ready to help Penny down. 'What a great ride,' he enthused. 'Rain, hail or shine, bring it on. It's the best way to travel.'

'Best way...' Penny hobbled up the drive and to the back door. She stepped inside and slammed it forcefully behind her. George stared after her. Women, there was no pleasing them.

CHAPTER 12

It was early Monday morning and Barney was nervously pacing about his office, wondering how he was going to explain away the new member who was joining the staff.

Their new assistant, Joanna Starling, a leggy blonde Australian, was sorting the post at her desk. 'Say Barney, will you stop jumping around like that? You're worse than a kangaroo gone walkabout.'

Barney paused for a moment, opened his mouth, closed it again and continued pacing.

'Spit it out, boss. Has old Ma Jones been fiddling the tea money, or Sarah put the wrong letter in the wrong envelopes and sent them out to clients, or are you going to dispense with my invaluable services already, on the grounds that I'm the most useless Aussie girl you've ever had the misfortune to meet?'

'If only that were it,' Barney answered, wearing out a little more of the pale-green carpet.

Joanna laughed. 'So I'm not the most useless!'

'No. No, I didn't mean that. You're not useless at all, far from it.'

'Well, for God's and Australia's sake, sit your ass on your chair and tell me what's up. Come on, bite on the bullet, boss.' Joanna pulled out Barney's new leather chair and motioned to him to sit on it. He obeyed and sat down gingerly, like a naughty schoolboy caught in the headmaster's study.

'It's my sister,' he began.

'Lot of 'em about,' Joanna commented.

'Mm, not like mine', said Barney. He picked up a pencil and

began chewing on it.

Joanna took it gently from him. 'Didn't you get breakfast this morning?'

'What? Oh, yes, a mango something-or-other smoothie. Jackie's trying it out for the café.'

'Your sister?' Joanna prompted.

'Ah,' Barney paused. 'Genevieve.'

'Genevieve, beautiful name.' Joanna waited. She was trying to acquire the art of playing the waiting game as the English did but was finding it hard.

'Beautiful name and a beautiful girl,' Barney agreed. 'She's, er, she happens to be joining our little team today.' He saw Joanna's eyebrows rise and hastily continued. 'Just for a short while, I hope. It's just that, well, she's been working in my father's Chambers in London and they sort of found they were a bit overstaffed and as Genevieve was last in, so to speak...'

'First out, eh? Yeah, I get the picture, boss. So she's handed on to us? We're pretty much full strength right now, Barney. I don't know what I can do with her. Can she type, do shorthand, spreadsheets, that kind of thing? Maybe I could teach her.'

'Genevieve? Good God, no!' Barney was appalled at the thought of Joanna attempting any of these things with Genevieve. 'I thought perhaps a little filing,' he said. 'The thing is, my sister, well, she's not exactly the brightest button in the box and...'

'What's she doing here then?' Joanna asked bluntly, all thoughts of English tact temporarily forgotten.

Barney gave in. 'Because my mother insists on it. We have to take turns you see, minding Genevieve.' He looked glumly at his young assistant. 'And now it's my turn. She's not dangerous or anything,' he went on. 'Quite the opposite in fact. She's very serene and has a lovely air of calm about her. It's just... Oh, I don't know, things always seem to happen when Genevieve's around.'

'She sounds like she could be fun,' said Joanna brightly. 'Don't worry. As it happens, there's a backlog of filing I can keep her busy with. I'll keep an eye on her. I'm sure she won't be any trouble.'

On past experience, Barney was not so sanguine.

******

Monday morning was a new start for Genevieve. She presented herself, scrubbed and soberly dressed, at Barney's office promptly at 9.00am. Barney was already busy at his desk when Joanna Starling showed Genevieve in.

'Hello, big brother,' Genevieve greeted him merrily. 'Mummy said you were looking forward to having me here with you. I know a lot already. I was in Daddy's office in London for quite a while. I think I was getting good at it, this law stuff, you know. They said I was almost a law unto myself. Quite a compliment,' she ended complacently.

'They said that, did they?' Barney pulled up a chair for his sister. She sat down and looked at him across the desk, her luminous green eyes staring innocently back at him.

'Genevieve,' Barney began.

'Yes, Barney dear.' Genevieve flicked her red hair back and studied her nail polish attentively.

'Genevieve!' Barney spoke sharply to get his sister's attention.

'No need to shout, Barney. I'm right here.' She smiled sweetly at him. 'And I'm not deaf you know.'

Oh God. The old familiar irritation with his bird-brained sister rose up again in Barney. How did she always manage to wrong-foot him? He took a deep breath and went on in a more moderate tone. 'Genevieve. We are a very new team here, still knitting together. You are the newest member, here on a trial basis, and I don't want you to do anything that will upset the applecart. Do you understand me?'

Genevieve stared back at him for a moment, her fine eyebrows raised. 'Mummy did show me how to knit when I was little, Barney, but I never quite got the hang of it. All that casting on and off and needles everywhere.' She hesitated. 'I can't do knitting…' she trailed off and went back to examining her nails.

Barney felt like a drowning man. Very slowly, he said, 'Just do as Joanna tells you and *nothing else*. Do you understand, Genevieve? *Absolutely nothing else.*'

Barney wrung his hands as he said this. Genevieve reached out and patted them comfortingly. 'Of course, Barney, nothing else.' She rose to go. At the door she turned back. 'You shouldn't worry so, Barney. It's not good for you. Daddy's just the same. I really don't know why. There's nothing to worry about.'

Barney stared at the door as Genevieve closed it. When Genevieve said that, he knew it was time to worry. He only hoped he would still have a team left by the end of the week.

*****

Joanna passed a thick sheaf of papers across the desk to Genevieve. 'This is the general office correspondence; the stationery orders, utility bills, insurance, council tax and so on. We're filing them alphabetically at the moment, just to see how it goes. We may change it later. So have a go with that lot.'

Genevieve looked down at the papers. 'Alphabetical,' she said hesitantly, a furrow appearing on her brow.

'Yeah, you know, Gen. Alphabetical order. A, B, C, that kind of stuff.'

Genevieve's brow cleared. 'Oh yes,' she said. 'I know my alphabet. D, E,' she continued and then stopped. 'Well, I'm sure it will come back to me,' she said brightly.

'Tell you what, Gen,' Joanna had an idea. 'What's your favourite thing? Eating out, clothes, fashion, pop stars, anything like that?'

'Fashion and clothes,' Genevieve said dreamily, 'all the designers.'

'Why don't you see how many names you can get into the alphabet and that would help you remember the letters for the filing.'

Linking fashion and filing appealed to Genevieve. Relieved that she didn't have to stand over her, Joanna left Genevieve to the task.

After Joanna had departed, Genevieve doubtfully eyed the large sheaf of papers sitting on the desk and picked the first one from the pile. Council tax, she read. That was easy. C for Chanel. It came between B for Balenciaga and D for Dior. She set off happily for the filing cabinet and placed the paper in the correct drawer. Unfortunately her knowledge of designer names from the world of fashion did not extend to every letter of the alphabet and soon she was stumped. Where did 'I' for insurance come in the scheme of things, or 'R' for road tax? Genevieve gave up and pushed those papers into the nearest drawer.

Some time later, a distracted Joanna entered Barney's office. 'Pretty thick, your sister, right?' she suggested.

Barney prevaricated. 'Well, I wouldn't say that exactly,' he replied.

'Hey, I would, mate.' Joanna perched on the edge of his desk, shook her head and looked sadly at Barney. 'She gives hope to a short plank.'

CHAPTER 13

'Did you tell Stan to try and make it snappy today, Kate?' Jackie was looking anxiously out of the café window. 'With Walter starting this morning, I need all the cakes and pies I can lay my hands on.'

'Yes, I did.' Kate joined Jackie at the window. 'He knows we need the bakery order early. He promised we'd be his first call. I hope everything's alright.'

As they watched, Stan's bakery van turned into the rear yard of the café. Mightily relieved, Kate rushed to the back door to let him in. Stan quickly unloaded several bread trays and brought them into the storeroom. There was no cheery smile and bear hug for his adored wife this morning. 'That's it, Mrs P,' he said, slapping the trays down on the counter, 'the very last of the very last orders from the bakery today. They're ceasing trading and I'm out of a job when I've completed this run.'

Stan leaned back against the cupboards, his head slumped onto his chest. 'It's a hard world out there.' The unusual sombre note in his voice alarmed Kate. Stan was always so happy-go-lucky and upbeat. 'All our dreams, hopes of our new home and a family...' He straightened up and looked Kate square in the eyes. 'We'll not be beat, oh lovely Katie mine. I may have to sell my body on the streets, for which I know there will be huge demand, but we will not starve.'

The tight knot dissolved in Kate's chest. This was more like the old Stan. The bakery closure had come sooner than they had expected, pulled the rug from under them, but at least he was coming out fighting. She had emailed Sofia at the International College in Rome. Stan might be able to get a place on the course just starting. Perhaps he could join it next week. She reached up and kissed her husband slowly and lingeringly on the lips. 'We will not starve indeed, Mr P. I have great plans, just you wait and see.'

Stan pulled Kate into a tight embrace. 'Plans, mm? Now just what could they be? I know you and your ideas and they usually mean trouble.'

Kate put Stan away from her. 'Not this time my darling. Just be patient and all will be revealed. Now go and finish your deliveries and I'll see you later. I might even have some good news for you.' Kate hustled a resisting Stan out of the door, ignoring all his protests at being kept in the dark. 'Later, later,' she said mysteriously and shut the door behind him.

******

Walter Breckenridge parked his bike in the rear yard of Café Paradise and squelched inside. He walked through the storeroom and into the main café. 'Bloody motorists! They've no consideration for us poor cyclists. Look at me, I'm soaked through!' Walter stood in the centre of the room, pointing at his wet, muddy trousers. Water splashed onto his muddy boots and dripped onto the floor around him.

'Get out, Dad,' Jackie screeched at him.

Walter looked indignantly at his daughter. 'Now there's a fine welcome, I'm sure. You ask me to come and help you out and here I am, and then you tell me to get out. Make your mind up.'

'Even a pea-brained mouse would have the sense not to walk all the way through here in muddy clothes, Dad. Go to the changing room – I've left your chef's whites ready for you.' She shook her head at him. 'Don't worry your pretty little head about it, Dad. I'll fetch the mop and bucket and clean up the mess. Just another little thing to throw into the mix of a mad

Monday. Alastair's gone, the bakery's closed as from today and I'll have to find a new supplier pronto. Fantastic. Welcome to my day.'

Walter turned to go. 'I could have been flattened by a juggernaut or caught triple pneumonia for all you care. Never mind, long as I get my chef's whites on, that's all that matters.'

'Correct.'

Seeing there was no sympathy to be had, Walter trailed away to change his clothes. He was pleased to find the old tumble drier was still in the cloakroom and pushed his wet clothes in. He set the dial to hot for thirty minutes and went off to get to grips with the new kitchen.

Walter looked around his new domain. It would be like the old days when he reigned in the kitchen: fry-ups, baps and chips with everything. His mouth watered at the prospect. Ellie was miles away in Claygate with that daft Elvis, she'd never know if the occasional sausage buttie crossed his lips.

Penny Montague popped her head around the door. 'I've to carry out your induction training for all the kitchen equipment and apparatus. Are you ready to start, Walter?'

'Induction training?' Walter shook his head incredulously. 'I think I know how to turn a gas switch on and stick a pan on the stove, lass.'

'I know that, Walter, but it's health and safety these days. As a new employee, you have to be induced, or is it inducted?' Penny looked at him doubtfully.

'I'm not having a baby, just lighting the gas and I promise I won't blow meself up.'

'Rules are rules, Walter,' Penny said firmly and went to the microwave. 'Now, look at this. This is a new oven and microwave combined. It's got a digital timer, ten different heat settings that can be used alternately for the same dish. It can defrost, make bread and cakes, do roasts, grill anything you want...'

'Sing, dance and serve your supper whilst it's on with it.' Walter eyed the machine dubiously. 'Awful lot of buttons, Penny. By the time you've worked out which is which, isn't it as quick just to whack something in a pan or a real oven?'

'And don't forget it's kilograms now, Walter. It doesn't know pounds and ounces, so don't try that on it.'

'Kilograms! Them bloody new-fangled European things.' He wasn't having any truck with them. 'I'm a Yorkshireman, our Penny. "Walter", remember, not some jumped-up French Johnny. We're not in the euro.'

'It's nothing to do with...'

'What is that awful smell?' Jackie burst into the kitchen, wrinkling her nose in disgust. 'The whole place pongs of goat. What have you brought with you, Dad, and where is it? You've only been here five minutes and there's trouble already.'

'That's right, blame me,' Walter said indignantly. 'I left my bike outside and I walked in the door. Am I likely to drag a goat along with me all the way from Claygate?' Walter bowed. '"Come along Esmerelda, leave off chewing all that lovely grass, come and have a day at Café Paradise. Sit amongst the chips and coffee cups all day."' He glared at Jackie.

Penny wrinkled her nose. 'There is something amiss, Walter.'

Kate put her head around the door. 'For God's sake, open the doors and get rid of that pong. We'll never get any customers today, smelling like we've a herd of Mongolian goats in the back.'

'I'll find it if it kills me.' Jackie stormed to the door. 'And if I find it's you at the bottom of this, Dad, I might well kill you too.'

'Don't know what she's on about, I can't smell anything,' Walter said, staring at the closed door.

'Can't smell...?' Penny cried.

Before she could say any more, Jackie was back, holding a bundle of clothes out in front of her. 'I don't suppose you know anything about these, do you?' Her voice had a dangerous edge to it.

'Well, you knew I was soaked. I put me clothes in the drier. You wouldn't want me to cycle home in wet clothes, would you?' Walter appealed.

The room was silent for a moment. He looked round for support. Kate had followed Jackie in and was frowning. Penny was too and Jackie looked thunderous.

'You could cycle home in your long johns with a rose between your teeth for all I care right now, Dad, but never, ever use that drier for your clothes again. It's only for the café laundry.'

'But I'm part of the café...' Walter caught Jackie's eye and subsided.

Jackie thrust the clothes at Walter. 'Put them outside,' she ordered.

'They'll get wet,' Walter protested.

'Out,' shouted Jackie. 'And leave the doors open.'

'I'll get cold.'

'The freezer's colder. Would you like to try it?' She stalked out, banging the door behind her.

'Typical,' Walter said with feeling. 'She never changes. Goes off on one at the drop of a hat.'

CHAPTER 14

The April morning sunshine bathed the wide, leafy squares and reached into the narrow, cobbled Shambles, lending a golden glow to the ancient, overhanging timber-framed houses. The shops in the centre of York were slowly coming to life and in Castlegate, the Café Paradise was opening up for the day's trade. As usual, Penny Montague had made a tray of coffee and carried it through to the new staffroom at the rear of the café, where Jackie and Penny joined her.

Jackie looked towards the kitchen. 'Is Dad busy already?'

'Not in yet,' said Kate. 'Hope he's alright, the traffic's heavy this morning.'

'That old bike! Why does he insist on using it? He's got a perfectly good van and we have the works' van for the fruit and veg run, but oh no, he must wobble all the way from Claygate on a clapped-out old penny farthing lookalike that was probably around in the Boer War.'

'Not that you ever exaggerate, Jackie,' Kate said drily. 'Calm down. He'll be here soon enough.'

Penny passed the coffee around. 'I've got some news,' she said tentatively.

Jackie looked up from her coffee. She knew it. They were just getting the café running again after Alastair's departure and now here was something else. In the short time she had been running the café, 'news' wasn't always welcome. 'Good or bad?' she asked warily.

'I don't know,' said Penny. 'It depends. George thinks it's good, I don't, but you might. But, there again, you might not. I mean, I don't think it's going to be very comfortable. All that dust and the elements...' Penny trailed off and looked around expectantly. 'What do you think?'

'We don't know what to think, because we don't know what we're thinking about,' said Kate.

Penny looked at her in surprise. 'You always know what you're thinking about, Kate. You're so ... together, somehow.'

'I know what *I* think about, Penny, but I don't know what *you* think about.' She paused and waited for Penny to continue, but nothing came. 'You haven't told us what your news is yet.'

'I did,' Penny insisted. 'You weren't listening. George wants us to go on a road trip. To Spain or Italy, on the bike. I said, didn't I? I'm not sure about it. But we've been to Helmsley and I've got over it now. George is very keen. He wants to take at least six weeks, make a real trip of it. Soon.' Penny stopped uncertainly.

Jackie put down her coffee cup carefully. The beginning of a hectic season in the centre of York. The tourists, the visitors, thirsty shoppers, looking for refreshments, day and night. How would she cope without one of the most experienced members of staff? Penny might be a bit ditzy but she was hardworking and loyal. And such a friend.

Kate and Penny sipped their coffee. The silence lengthened. Jackie's thoughts turned to her mother, Marilyn. What would she have done in this situation? Not let her go, of course. She had worked Penny far too hard for years, salting away the tips that were meant for her and only grudgingly giving her time off. Jackie made her decision. Penny deserved this trip. She would have to let her go and with her blessing.

'It sounds fantastic,' Jackie said, smiling across the table to Penny. 'The trip of a lifetime. Good old George. Now that *is* different from being Georgina. Biker boy and biker babe! As soon as you like, Penny. We'll manage, won't we Kate?'

Kate nodded enthusiastically. She loved Penny dearly and they were close friends, but if Penny was gone for the summer, Kate might pick up much-needed extra hours at the café. She had her own news to impart. Now was the time.

'I've got some news too, Jackie,' she announced brightly.

Jackie slid down in the chair until her chin was level with the table top. 'Not you too. Don't tell me. You and Stan are going to study Roman remains in darkest Uzbekistan for the next five years, or excavate the new site around the Minster and I'm going to lose you too.'

Kate chuckled at this idea. 'I wish. Nothing so grand, I assure you, and I'm not going anywhere. Stan is. I'm keeping my job at the Historical Trust three days a week and next year, with a bit of luck, we'll be establishing a permanent site to create a small replica of a Roman town. We could employ Stan as information officer and events co-ordinator if we can widen his overall knowledge of Ancient Roman life. So ... I've managed to get him on a training course at the International College in Rome and he can start next week. So,' she smiled at Jackie and patted Penny's hand, 'I'm home alone and up for extra hours to help fund his trip. Penny can go with our blessing and hopefully have a wonderful time.'

Slowly, Jackie recovered her sitting position and smiled. 'Bloody marvellous! God doesn't entirely hate me, after all.' She thought for a moment. 'I know you're very hardworking, Kate, but even you can't do two people's work, plus days at the Historical Trust. We'll need some extra help. I'll put a card in the window.'

'What about Genevieve?' Penny suggested tentatively. 'Didn't you say she was home and looking for work? Perhaps she could take on some hours here.'

'Are you out of your...?' Jackie began and then stopped as the possibilities of this new scenario played out in her mind. 'Mmm. Maybe.' Genevieve had only been at Barney's office for four days and Jackie knew it was hard going. Yes. Jackie got up decisively and hugged Penny. 'What a great idea. What wouldn't Barney do to get rid of her? And what an amazing wife I would be if I nobly offered to have her here. Thank you, Penny. Go and enjoy Europe with George. Kate and I will manage and keep Genevieve employed but away from the customers, if we can, and my darling husband will worship the ground I walk on for evermore!'

Jackie skipped out of the staffroom and met Walter entering by the back door. She embraced him. 'Morning, Daddy dear. How lovely to see you. What a beautiful day it is. God is in His heaven and all's right with the world.' She disappeared into the café.

Walter gaped after her. He would never understand women if he lived to be a hundred. He was very late and had expected dark looks from his daughter. Instead, she'd kissed him. Women were queer creatures.

*****

Café Paradise was closed. The treasured cleaner, Mrs Featherstone, had done her work and departed and the city was settling down for the night. For the tenth time Jackie peered out into the dark April evening, wondering what was keeping Barney. He should have been here an hour ago and wasn't answering her calls or texts. Uneasily, she trailed back to her office and tried to get to grips with the mountain of paperwork on her desk.

It was gone midnight before Barney finally appeared. His blond hair stood on end, his lovely suit was rumpled and somewhere along the way he had lost his tie. Tonight, the usually buoyant and sunny Barney looked tired and defeated.

Jackie had been going to greet him with 'I hope she was worth it,' but the remark died on her lips. 'What...?'

Barney shook his head. 'Genevieve. Let's go home. I'm knackered.'

They were silent on the way home. Jackie's mind was racing. Four days in and Genevieve had reduced her lovely husband to this defeated wreck. In the darkness, Jackie tilted her chin determinedly. She wasn't Marilyn's daughter for nothing. If she'd had any reservations about accommodating Genevieve at the café before, now they had fled. She would keep Genevieve out of everyone's way and for once in that young lady's life, she would make her do some proper work. But … everything came at a price and she was determined to extract top whack from Barney for this.

******

'Barnabas, she's only been with you four days. She can't possibly have wreaked such havoc in that time. You're getting just like your father, prone to exaggeration. No. I'm not listening to any more. Get a grip, my son. It's Genevieve you're dealing with and you're learning the hard way like the rest of us. Get on with it.'

The telephone clicked as Barney's mother ended their brief conversation. Jackie turned her head away to hide her smile. God bless her lovely mother-in-law. Jackie could already see herself being pampered at the fabulous spa at Bishopthorpe Hall, sampling the fine cuisine in the restaurant and then sipping the best champagne in their suite before falling into the biggest mega-king-sized bed with a deliriously happy Barney, newly freed from the shackles of his eccentric sister.

Barney knew he was exhausted and his brain was fuddled. The problem of Genevieve would have to wait until the morning. He rose from his chair. 'That's it then. Mother has kiboshed any idea of moving Genevieve on. Only I don't know how long Anderson and Cranton, Solicitors and Commissioners for Oaths, can survive her.' He moved to the door, looking back at Jackie stacking the cups in the dishwasher. 'I don't suppose you would…? No. Why would you? Asking for trouble isn't it? Who'd take on Genevieve? Madness.'

'What happened today?' Jackie asked.

'Which bit of Genevieve havoc would you like? She couldn't do the filing, so she dumped all the papers in a drawer. I ended up doing it all myself yesterday, or Joanna would have slung her hook. Making the office tea and coffee shouldn't be a dangerous task, unless you ask Gen to do it and then she fuses all the lights and we lose the programmes on the computers. Finally, Jake thought it would be a good idea just to get her out of the office, so he sent her to fill up his car with petrol at the supermarket. Mistake big time, believe me. She got the new coffee supplies in the supermarket and went off to get the petrol at their pumps. She managed that fine, went in to pay and found she didn't have her card. So far, not too bad. The petrol shop phoned the food shop and sure enough, Gen had left her card in the till machine. All she had to do was go and retrieve it and go back and pay for the petrol.'

'I take it that didn't happen?'

Barney drew a deep breath and let it out slowly. 'No. She drove back to the supermarket, parked up in the car park and went in and got the card. This is where only Genevieve could get it wrong. She *says* the supermarket had different entrances and she must have come out a different entrance from going in. She couldn't find the car and got in a real flap. She had to really search round for it and was so relieved when she eventually did find it, she forgot all about paying for the petrol and just drove back to the office. She'd given her name as Genevieve Anderson to the petrol station. The car reg was in Jake's name but he's moved house and so it's a different address with DVLA. By the time the police caught up with us, it was teatime. Jake and Gen had gone home. I tried to explain the situation but they weren't taking my word for it and there was an unpaid petrol bill. Jake, Genevieve and I ended up at York Police Station. He's going to get fined for not notifying DVLA of his new address, we're lucky we're not going to be struck off the Law Society Register for behaviour likely to bring the profession into disrepute and Genevieve, as usual, bedazzled them all until they were almost begging us to take her home. As you see, just another day in paradise.'

Barney went out. Jackie heard his footsteps slowly going up the stairs. Now was the moment. She followed him into their bedroom and slipped her arms around him. 'I think I just might,' she whispered softly.

Barney tried to connect this statement to any of their earlier conversations, but couldn't make anything of it. 'You might what?'

'I *might* take Genevieve on at the café.' Jackie smiled up at him and stroked his back.

Barney knew he was tired, but not yet at the hallucinating stage. Jackie hadn't just said 'take Genevieve on' had she? 'Did you say...?'

She drew him down onto the bed and lay beside him. 'Poor Barney. Genevieve is too much for you. She's only been there four days and look at you. I love you far too much to stand by and do nothing. So I am willing to take her off your hands and find her something to do at the café.'

Barney sat bolt upright, astounded at this unexpected news. 'Take Genevieve?'

'Providing a little R and R is thrown in to alleviate the stress of it, now and again,' Jackie drawled.

'Anything! Anything at all! You name it, we'll do it. Home makeover, gold-plated taps, a new iron, anything,' Barney promised recklessly.

A new iron! This was 2013 York and he was thinking new irons. How wrong could a man be? 'R and R as in Bishopthorpe Hall, best suite for us and regular spa days for me. Stress, remember, darling. Genevieve around my neck seven days a week. I'll need to escape sometimes.'

Bishopthorpe Hall! Suites! Spas! Barney groaned. He knew when he was beaten. Jackie had more of Marilyn in her than she knew. She drove a hard bargain. He had no choice and she knew it.

'Bishopthorpe Hall it is,' he agreed.

'Yesss.' Jackie kissed him hard on the lips. 'I love you, Barney Anderson.'

A week of Genevieve and would she still love him, he wondered.

CHAPTER 15

In the two weeks since Annabel Langley had discovered her real identity, she had set about creating a new life and image for herself. Whilst in prison, she had squirrelled away every pound that she could and on her release was able to update herself and her wardrobe.

Now, in late April, smartly dressed and with her long brown hair newly washed and cut, she stood outside the offices of the *York News*, ready to discover more about her mother, Marilyn Langley. Annabel had watched the programmes where people traced their families and knew newspaper obituaries were a good starting point. She felt a mixture of excitement and apprehension. There would be no going back from here. Even though she disliked it, she knew her own history intimately and was ready to leave it all behind her: the dreadful adoption, the abrupt thrust back into the children's home, then out on the streets to fend for herself at sixteen. Annabel shuddered in the cool spring breeze. Come on, she told herself, whatever you learn about your real background can't be any worse than what you've come from. Stop dawdling. Your real roots are here in this beautiful city, maybe even some family.

Yes. Maybe even some family. Until now, Annabel had not acknowledged that finding her family was part of this pilgrimage. She hesitated halfway up the steps to the newspaper's offices. Family. Family? Even if she had family, ten to one they knew nothing about her. She was thirty-nine and no one had ever come looking for her. She'd been cast out and Marilyn had got on with her life. Annabel remembered her adoptive mother, in one of her many rages, screaming at her one day, 'You're a little bitch just like your mother, and she's no better than she should be. She tried to be posh but she's not – and you take after her.'

Annabel continued slowly up the steps. Out in this new, unfamiliar world, she desperately needed to anchor herself to something. Whatever she found out today, at least she would know a little more about her mother and what sort of life she had led.

Annabel wasn't sure what she had expected to find, but instead of a two-line obituary notice, there was a large black-and-white photograph of Marilyn underneath the headline, 'Death of Well-Known York Businesswoman and Benefactor.' Annabel stared at the headline, a hard knot of disappointment in her stomach. She could never meet Marilyn now. She looked at the grainy photograph, trying to connect with her mother. Marilyn was slim, fair haired and dressed in a smart suit. Was there something about her eyes? Annabel read and re-read the obituary, charting her mother's business life, support of local organisations and more importantly, mention of her daughter, Jacqueline.

An archive assistant passed by. Seeing Annabel staring silently into space, she paused. 'Everything OK, Miss Langley? Did you find what you were looking for?'

Annabel jumped, startled out of her reverie. 'Yes, I did, thanks. Look, can I take a copy of this? I think she might be part of my extended family.' Best not reveal her true relationship to Marilyn in here. If her mother was so well known in the city, the existence of Annabel herself would be news and she didn't want to make those kind of waves.

Half an hour later, sitting in Harkers Bar in St Helen's Square, Annabel read through the obituary again and again and tried to see something of herself in the photograph. Marilyn looked fair, fine-boned and petite, whereas she, Annabel, although slender, was tall with brown hair and brown eyes. Maybe it was just as well there was no resemblance between them. She could blend into the crowd and no one would be any the wiser.

She tried to absorb the details of her mother's busy life. She had obviously got married three years after she'd given birth to Annabel. A Barry Dalrymple-Jones, estate agent. So that's where the name came from. Jacqueline was born seven months later. Interesting. Very premature, or had Marilyn got herself into trouble again but got out of it more neatly second time around?

So, she actually had a sister. Half-sister probably, but still a real blood relation, alive and maybe still living in York. Did this Jacqueline know about her? Somehow, Annabel felt she would not. Reading Marilyn's obituary, her life and times in York seemed to really start when she married Mr Dalrymple-Jones and opened a café in Castlegate. Café Paradise. Annabel let this information roll around her head. Barry, Marilyn and Jacqueline. A happy family unit. According to the obituary, Marilyn was a loving and doting mother, an astute businesswoman who ran a very successful business, and a pillar of the York Trades Council who encouraged and mentored emerging entrepreneurs in the city. All round wonder woman by the sound of it, Annabel reflected wryly.

Café Paradise. She was intrigued. Lovely name. Would it still be there on Castlegate? Annabel urgently needed to know, to experience something tangible of her mother. Walk the streets *she* had walked, be in the place *she* had spent so much of her life, feel something of the life *she* had led here. She jumped up from her seat, ready for immediate action and then abruptly sat down again. Six years of prison life had instilled the need to proceed cautiously, think through the consequences of her actions.

To hell with all that now, Annabel announced to herself. I'm here and Café Paradise can't be far away. Go girl, you're Marilyn's daughter too. Mother obviously had drive and initiative. Take your lead from her. It's time you stopped apologising for your life and started being Annabel Langley, intelligent, creative and go-getting.

******

The spring was well advanced and the trees were in full leaf. The city centre was bustling with Saturday shoppers and the first wave of visitors to the majestic Minster and quaint cobbled streets and alleys of York. Weary tourists sat on benches in the squares, grateful to rest under the shade of the newly green trees.

It was Saturday morning and Café Paradise was already full. Penny and Kate were busy ferrying food from Walter's kitchen, whilst Jackie manned the counter for coffee and cakes. Outside, Annabel stood on the pavement and stared. Café Paradise. This was where so much of her mother's life had been spent. She wasn't sure what she'd expected, but not this elegant and very fashionable-looking place. There were large plate-glass windows either side of a green door which stood open, revealing the busy café within.

Controlling her excitement, Annabel stepped inside. Her eyes widened in surprise. It was beautiful, large and airy with tables well spaced so that customers and staff could easily move around. It was decorated in restful, neutral colours, with splashes of colour from the few pictures on the walls. This was not any old café; it spoke of good food and wine, in anyone's language.

The woman manning the coffee counter looked up as Annabel approached and smiled a friendly greeting. 'Good morning. Would you like a table?'

Annabel nodded, unable to speak. The lady was about her own age, fair-haired with large violet eyes. Could this be...?

Jackie pointed to a table for two near the coffee counter. 'Would that be alright for you?'

Annabel nodded again and sat down. She picked up the menu and pretended to study it. Maybe she should have more than a cup of coffee, order a meal perhaps. But would she be able to eat it? Her chest felt tight and there was a lump in her throat. Her eyes were hot and prickly with tears. She felt flustered by the unexpected mix of emotions now that she was finally in the heart of her mother's world.

Kate appeared at her side, smiling and ready to take her order. Annabel managed to croak out, 'Could you give me a few minutes? I'm just a bit...' She couldn't finish the sentence. Kate was all concern and quietly brought her some water and a glass and, seeing that Annabel was alright, left her to recover.

Annabel drank the water thirstily and took deep breaths to calm herself down. Slowly she adjusted to her new surroundings and looked at the menu. What would slip down easily and yet prolong her visit? She decided on soup, followed by egg mayonnaise. Not the most exciting meal in the world but manageable in the circumstances.

Kate returned to take her order. She was polite and friendly but asked no questions about Annabel's earlier distress. Annabel's mood improved. If that was indeed Jacqueline at the counter, and she did seem in some indefinable way to be in charge, then Annabel could relax. There was no resemblance between them. Jackie was medium height, fair, with a heart-shaped face and violet eyes. Jackie wasn't looking for a sister right here in her café today and even if she had been, she would never think it was this tall, angular woman with brown hair and eyes.

Annabel sat back in her chair and looked around. The café was obviously a popular meeting place. People coming in and out greeted each other and the staff as old friends. Annabel approved. Nothing seemed too much trouble for the waitresses and the food and service flowed effortlessly.

When it came, the tomato and basil soup was delicious. Annabel ate it slowly, trying to listen to snatches of conversation flying around her. After a while, she discovered the waitresses were Penny and Kate and there would be a new one called Genevieve starting on Monday.

Annabel ate her sandwich slowly, her eyes fixed on the lady at the counter. She watched her serve tea and coffee at high speed, dispense scones, cakes and gateaux on white china plates for those staying in and putting up coffee and food-to-go for those on the hoof.

And then it happened: Jackie looked up from her work and smiled across at Annabel as she steamed milk for a large latte. A memory stirred in Annabel; a loving smile, just like that. Marilyn? Don't be ridiculous, she told herself. Marilyn left you at a few weeks old, you have no memories of her at all. Don't go imagining things. In spite of this common-sense reasoning, Annabel was sure that this was Jacqueline, her own flesh and blood, so near for the first time.

Kate, the waitress who had served Annabel, rushed up to the coffee counter. 'Are there any cheese scones left, Jackie? It's Mrs Parry's treat on a Saturday.'

Annabel's heart thumped. Jackie. It was her. Jacqueline! No, Jackie, she corrected herself. Jackie. She had been right. And that smile. It was like coming home.

Suddenly, it was all too much. Too many discoveries in one day. She needed to get away, to think, walk round, anything, just not be here with her sister a stone's throw away.

She went quickly to the counter. Jackie looked up and smiled her bright smile. 'Did you enjoy your lunch?' she enquired.

Annabel swallowed hard. 'Thank you. Yes. Very much. I ... I'd like to come again ... soon.' She proffered a ten-pound note to Jackie, who quickly rang it into the till and gave Annabel her change.

'We'd be delighted to see you back,' Jackie said. 'We love to make new friends at Café Paradise. We're quite a little family here.' She held out her hand. 'I'm Jackie Anderson by the way. This used to be my mother's café and I took it over after she died last year. She was Marilyn Dalrymple-Jones, quite a well-known character in York.'

Annabel was almost ready to faint away. Here was all the confirmation that she needed and here was Jackie looking at her expectantly. 'I'm Annabel. Annabel La ... Lewis-Langley,' she improvised. It was too soon for the Langley connection. She needed time to properly assess the situation. Slowly, she reached across the counter and joined her hand to Jackie's outstretched one. For the first time, she touched her sister.

CHAPTER 16

Elvis had been at Claygate for three weeks. With Ellie's loving care and good food, he had grown from a weak runt into a sleek, gawky puppy, full of energy and mischief. He had a very sunny nature and charmed everyone who came to the farm as he licked and nuzzled them enthusiastically. He still hadn't quite got the hang of house-training and was apt to pee when excited, which was unfortunate as he got excited over most things.

For the second time on Sunday morning, Walter had changed his trousers. Whenever Elvis saw him, he jumped up and peed down Walter's leg.

'How come it's always on me?' Walter grumbled to Ellie. 'He never does it to you.'

'He gets excited when he sees you,' Ellie said, smiling fondly down at the dog.

'Humph,' snorted Walter. 'I get excited when I see you, but I don't go peeing everywhere.'

'Maybe you should, then I might know.' Ellie moved about the kitchen in her tranquil way, mixing up yet another special dish for Elvis.

Walter knew his place in the house and farm pecking order, but behave like the runt to get his wife's attention? That was too much. He stooped down and picked Elvis up by the scruff of the neck, his face close to the pup's. 'The gloves are off, young fella. If you want to stay at Claygate, you've got to learn your manners and I'm the one who's going to teach you, starting now.'

Elvis licked Walter's nose affectionately and peed down his chest. Walter tapped his nose gently. 'Stop it,' he commanded, 'you're too big for all that now.'

Ellie protested, 'Don't smack him, Walter, you'll make him worse.'

Walter made for the door, carrying Elvis. 'He's getting spoilt, Ellie. It's a pity I'm having to be at the café at the moment or I'd have had him licked into shape by now. But time's going on and if we're ever going to make anything of him, he's going to get some training every day. You're too soft and we'll end up with a big daft mutt. We might anyway. He doesn't seem to catch on too quick, but I'm going to give it a try. And you'll have to keep to the rules when I'm gone.' He eyed Ellie sternly. 'No spoiling him.'

Walter went out, carrying Elvis with him. Ellie's lips twitched into a smile. She knew Elvis wasn't the keenest brain in the doggie world, but he had the natural wit of the Border collie. She wondered who would come off worst in these training sessions. Maybe not Elvis.

Out in the yard, Walter put the pup down and fixed him with a hard stare. 'Right lad, you've had enough time in the house with Ellie and eating like a bloody carthorse. Women! She's too soft and you've got her trained. She looks into them big brown eyes of yours and that's it. You can have anything you want.'

Elvis flattened his ears at Walter's tone and looked up at him expectantly.

'You're a working dog, not a poncey house pet. It's time you were out in the real world, starting to learn your trade.'

Elvis peed on the grass.

'I've told you, stop that.'

Elvis peed again.

Walter looked at him wonderingly. 'Where d'you keep it all, lad? Right. First things first. We're going to visit the hens and you're going to have to get used to squawks and feathers.'

Walter found a length of baler twine in the yard and

attached it to Elvis's collar. 'We're going to watch 'em for a bit and then mebbe have a bit of a walk amongst 'em. And *you*,' he said sternly, 'will have to keep by me and walk gently too. Got it?'

Elvis made no response, eyeing Walter warily.

They set off across the yard towards the small paddock where the hens spent their days, scratching in the grass for their favourite seeds and insects. A sturdy little house nestled behind a dry-stone wall, where the hens could lay their eggs and roost on the perches at night.

Elvis gambolled in front of Walter and was brought up sharply as he reached the end of the baler-twine lead. He had never been restrained before and took exception to this. He yapped and spun round and round, trying to break free, to no avail. Walter kept a firm hold of him and continued walking slowly forward, bringing the pup behind him. Elvis yapped and struggled all the way. Walter ignored him. Elvis must learn.

By the time they arrived at the paddock, Elvis had given in and was walking beside Walter. They stopped at the gate and the hens came running up, squawking expectantly. A visitor could mean barley or mash. The hens crowded at the gate, pecking at Elvis. He yapped and backed off, alarmed by the noise and the fluttering wings.

'Don't be such a girl,' Walter chided him. 'It's only a daft hen. They've even less brains than you have.'

Finding there was no food on offer, the hens soon wandered away and began scratching at the grass again. When they were at a safe distance, Walter opened the gate and took Elvis into the paddock. The pup peed and sat down just inside the gateway. Walter tried pulling gently at the baler-twine lead, but Elvis wasn't having any of it. He dug his paws hard into the ground and sat back on his haunches. Walter was surprised at the strength of his resistance. 'It's only a bloody hen, for God's sake. Just think of 'em as your dinner; eggs or chicken when their coats are off. It's win-win for you.'

Elvis wouldn't budge and the moment a curious hen came

to investigate, he set up a shrill yapping and headed for the gate. Maybe hens weren't his thing, Walter mused. He thought about his sheep but they had just lambed and the last thing they needed right now was a wayward Border collie pup.

Walter was determined he would not go home to Ellie without making progress. His reputation was at stake. What about the goats? They were a recent addition to the farm and were a feisty bunch. Elvis wouldn't frighten *them* off in a hurry.

Once out of the hens' paddock, Elvis recovered his confidence. As they walked over the fields to where Ellie kept her goats, he bounced along shaking his head, trying to get free of the lead again. Several times Walter stumbled as Elvis darted between his feet, but he persevered and led the reluctant dog on. The fields were still puddled after the winter rains. Walter, in his wellingtons, strode through them but Elvis strongly objected to this. At every small pool he halted and then tip-toed carefully around the edge. Walter was disgusted.

But he did not give up hope. Puddles were one thing, Ellie's goats were another. At least they looked a bit like sheep. Elvis could practice on them. Walter wasn't a natural optimist but he wanted to have at least one small success with Elvis's training before they headed home for lunch, some sign that Elvis wasn't the complete mutt that he suspected.

But Elvis was. 'Just as I said from the start,' Walter said later, taking a break from his roast beef and waving his knife in the air. 'Great wussy thing. You should have seen him, Ellie. Yon goat of yours just walked towards him and he was off, hiding behind me and yapping away. Big soft lump.'

Elvis had returned to the farmhouse, eaten an enormous lunch and now lay asleep in his basket by the stove. Every so often he squeaked as he relived his morning's escapades in his dreams.

'You're trying too much, too soon, that's what it is.' Ellie defended her beloved puppy.

'How long do we have to wait, Ellie?' demanded Walter. 'In a very short time he's going to be the Incredible Hulk and about as much use around here as that toothless old ram in the field out there.'

'Exactly,' said Ellie. 'So you're just as bad.'

'Me? I'm not a useless runt of a dog, costing a fortune and eating my head off.'

'You've kept that old ram, what good is he?' Ellie persisted.

'He's earned his keep,' said Walter. 'He did his job, year in, year out. Which is more than that mutt of yours will ever do. Monty's earned his retirement.'

'Elvis will in time. Just give him a chance. He was the runt, a late developer. We'll make something of him yet.' Ellie smiled affectionately at the sleeping Elvis. 'He'll be a champ. You'll see.'

Walter choked on his roast beef. Did women always believe what they wanted to believe, in spite of everything? Elvis, a champ? Walter felt the need of a pint of strong ale at the pub. Who'd have thought it? Driven to drink by a mutt.

CHAPTER 17

Across the city, Sunday was proving a very trying day for Kate Peterson as she attempted to organise Stan for his study trip to Rome.

'What do you mean you haven't got enough pants?' she asked as Stan rifled through the clothes she had laid out on the bed.

'Just that,' Stan replied. 'I can't go tomorrow. I need proper clothes. Pants, socks.' He picked out a pair at random from the heap. 'Look at these. I can't take these through customs. Suppose I had to open my suitcase and they saw my kit? Imagine the smirks from those Italian guys. No, I can't go.'

'I'll head off right now and get you several pairs of tighty-whiteys, if that'll make you get on the plane, Stan,' Kate said distractedly. He 'had no euros'. Kate produced them. His 'passport was out of date'. How could it be? They only honeymooned last year and he'd renewed it then. OK, he 'needed immunisations for this trip'. For Rome? Kate didn't think so.

What was wrong with Stan? He had been devastated when the bakery closed and he'd been made redundant and then over the moon when Kate got him a place at the International College in Rome. Yet today, on the eve of the trip, he was trying everything he could to get out of going.

Stan sat down on the bed, his head in his hands. 'I can't go,' he said, his deep voice muffled.

Kate's heart sank. Now what? She hadn't envisaged anything like this happening. Stan had to go. There was no Plan B, only the Job Centre and there wasn't much on offer there. She sat beside him on the bed, took his hands away from his face and kissed him. 'Come on, big man. Out with it. What's the deal?'

Stan stared out of the window. 'You're so beautiful,' he said softly.

Kate was taken aback. This was not the discussion she'd expected to have. 'Well, thank you, my darling,' she said evenly. 'Now, can we cut to the chase and you tell me why you can't go to Rome tomorrow?'

Stan turned to look at her, drinking in her long corn-coloured hair, deep-green eyes and porcelain skin. 'You're so very beautiful,' he repeated. 'When you walk down the street, every man's head turns to watch you. I've seen them, watched them watching you. I've seen their desire. I would be over a thousand miles away, mouldering in Rome. How can I keep you mine? Keep all the men in York away from you? The minute I'm gone, you'll be surrounded by them.'

'Sounds like a bunch of tom cats round an old tabby,' said Kate tartly. 'No.' She held up her hand as Stan was about to protest. 'Listen to me, Stan Peterson. Of course I want you out of the way in Rome. After all, we've only been married a few months and I'm tired of you already and need pastures new. So ... the minute your back's turned I'm signing up with the best executive escort agency in York and I'm going to earn "shed loads of money darling", to quote the lovely Melissa. I can have my fun and you'll be none the wiser. How does that sound?'

Stan groaned and buried his head in his hands again.

'That's settled then,' Kate said brightly. 'I'll go and buy those tighty-whitey's, shall I?'

CHAPTER 18

Walter cycled into the rear yard of the café and braked sharply. Jackie's white van was carelessly parked in the centre, making it difficult for Walter to squeeze past. The world was full of inconsiderate daughters, rubbish drivers, useless sheepdogs... He removed his waterproofs at the back door and made for the staff changing room.

'This is our kitchen, Genevieve.'

Walter recognised Kate's voice. Genevieve? Genevieve! No. It couldn't be. What the hell was she doing here? He put his head round the door. Genevieve, dressed in a brightly flowered dress, stood looking about her.

'Morning, Kate,' Walter said warily, eyeing Genevieve. 'Another Monday at Café Paradise. Hello ... Genevieve. Are you visiting?' he asked hopefully.

Genevieve came forward, smiling her wide, friendly smile and holding her hand out. 'Mr Breckenridge, you remember me.'

'Aye, who could forget you, Genevieve?' Walter said with feeling. 'Jackie and Barney's wedding, wasn't it? Something to do with champagne and locking yourself out, as I remember. Didn't you tread on her train and drop the bouquet, all that kind of stuff?' It was all coming back. Genevieve was lovely to look at but there didn't seem to be much between her ears.

'You're very kind.' Genevieve continued to pump his hand and beam at him.

Walter looked helplessly at Kate. She cleared her throat. 'Well now, Genevieve. We mustn't delay Walter. He needs to get changed and we need to start your induction training.' Kate looked at the wall above Walter's head.

'Induction trai...' Had he just walked into someone else's nightmare? He stared at Genevieve. 'Are you...?' He looked at Kate. 'Is she...?'

'Well, yes,' Kate said evenly. 'Penny's starting her holidays today, preparing for her trip abroad with George. Luckily for us, Genevieve was available to step in at short notice and help us out.'

Help us out! God help us all if we need Genevieve to help, Walter thought. She could hardly help herself, what use would she be at Café Paradise? Hang on a minute. She was in his kitchen. If Jackie thought for one moment he was having Genevieve trotting in and out, she could have several more thinks. Never in her wildest dreams was that going to happen.

He backed out of the kitchen and, still clutching his waterproofs, marched into the café. Jackie was at the coffee counter, carefully placing decorated cupcakes on a stand. 'Morning, Dad,' she said cheerily. 'Had a good weekend?'

'No, I didn't,' Walter replied shortly. 'Ellie's that busy with her goats and sheep and now with that bloody daft Elvis, I hardly get a look in. Anyway...'

Jackie eyed him sympathetically. 'Always the bridesmaid, never the bride. Elvis will grow up,' she added brightly.

'Never mind bloody Elvis.' Walter glared at his daughter. 'And speaking of bridesmaids, what's she doing in my kitchen?'

'You've met our new waitress.' Jackie frowned, considering the placement of the last cupcake.

'Have you lost it altogether, lass?' he spluttered. 'She's a walking disaster area and you're going to let her loose here?'

'Not straight away.' Jackie stood back to admire her handiwork and placed the cake stand in the display cabinet. 'We thought we could put her in charge of the dishwasher and teach her to set and clear the tables, initially. That way, she'll be very useful and get used to learning the café routine, without doing anything that requires a brain. She won't be in your way,

I promise you.' Jackie kissed Walter's cheek affectionately and reached for a new cake stand. 'You'll hardly notice she's here.'

As he changed into his chef's whites in the cloakroom, Walter contemplated his day. A brainless redhead in his kitchen getting under his feet all day and then home to training a brainless sheepdog who was scared of sheep, water and his own shadow. Thank you, God, and welcome to Monday. You know how to make a man happy.

******

'It can be a bit of a jigsaw puzzle fitting everything in sometimes,' said Kate, finding a space for the last few serving spoons. 'The top tray's alright, you just stack cups and glasses on it and then take it out when they're washed to carry through to the café, and stack them up at the coffee counter again. You need to pack the bottom tray fairly tightly to get as many plates in as possible and fill up the cutlery containers. We can get through a lot of plates and cutlery on a busy lunchtime.' Kate looked up to see if Genevieve was following this new information.

Genevieve laughed uncertainly. 'Ha, jigsaw puzzles. I remember those at school. All those little pieces. I never could quite ... they always seemed, I don't know. I mean, the pictures on the box looked so lovely. I always wanted to complete one. The straight bits weren't too bad, but all the other pieces... My sister, Juliet, was very good at them. Crosswords too. How did she ever make all the connections...?' Genevieve trailed off vaguely.

'The dishwashers.' Patiently, Kate bought Genevieve's attention back to the task in hand. 'Next time they need filling, do you think you could manage it?'

'Mm. Yes, I'm sure I could. Plates, spoons, saucers. It's all a jigsaw.' Genevieve smiled at Kate.

Feeling less than confident, Kate returned to the café and her waitressing duties. She would be away three days a week at the Historical Trust. She fervently hoped Genevieve would soon get the hang of things and not be any trouble to the agency temp who would be standing in.

The morning rush was soon underway and Jackie and Kate were kept busy supplying coffee, breakfasts and snacks to hungry customers. Periodically, Genevieve emerged from the kitchen proudly bearing trays of clean cups and mugs, fresh from the dishwashers.

Jackie smiled encouragingly at her. 'Well done, Gen. You're doing a great job. Couldn't do without you today.' She was pleasantly surprised at how well the morning was going. Maybe Barney had exaggerated things. Typical man, making a fuss for nothing. Still, if things went on like this, she would soon be able to enjoy a spa day at Bishopthorpe Hall. Jackie grinned happily to herself. Genevieve was a lamb.

Life in the kitchen was not so serene. Walter had now got used to most of the new-fangled equipment, but still had to stop and think when it came to programming the combination microwave and oven. It slowed his progress and as he rushed to complete orders, the kitchen worktops soon became littered with used pans and utensils. Where was that girl with the clean ones? Walter wondered as he hurtled from stove to refridgerator.

'Genevieve,' he called in the general direction of the washing-up area. 'Bring the clean pans and spoons, please. I've none left and Kate's still piling up the orders. We'll be into lunches soon. I need clean pots. Hurry up, lass.'

Genevieve appeared in the doorway carrying a fresh tray of clean cups. 'I'll just take these in to Jackie and then I'll be right with you. It's the jigsaw, you know. It's not easy. It looks easy, but it isn't. And it's not as if there are any straight bits to worry about.' She disappeared.

Walter looked after her, mystified. Jigsaws? He thought she was meant to be loading dishwashers. He left his work and went to investigate. The room off the kitchen contained two dishwashers, deep stainless-steel sinks and draining boards for washing large items. Usually this area was clear as the staff loaded and unloaded the dishwasher through the day.

Something had gone radically wrong. Dirty plates, cutlery and pans were stacked high on every available surface. What had the lass been doing? Filing her highly-polished nails in the corner? Certainly not attending to her job in here.

Genevieve came into the room, loaded up with a tray of dirty cups. She slid them deftly into the first dishwasher and set it going. Walter goggled. The thing was half-empty. What was she thinking about?

'You can't do that, lass,' Walter chided her.

'Jackie needs the cups. Everyone wants tea and she's running low,' Genevieve said serenely.

'What about this lot?' Walter gestured to the worktops overflowing with dirty plates and pans.

'Well, it's the jigsaw thing, isn't it?' Genevieve looked about her helplessly. 'I told you. Fitting it all in. I tried, I really did. I think the plates should go one way and knives and forks somewhere else, but I'm not too sure about them, and then there's all those horrid pans of yours. I mean, where do they go? It's all a bit of a puzzle.'

Without doing anything that requires a brain, Jackie had said. Wait until she saw this lot, Walter thought grimly. She'd been right about one thing though. You certainly didn't notice Genevieve was there, 'cos she didn't do anything.

Walter washed out a pan and stalked back to his kitchen. 'Go and tell Jackie she was right. I wouldn't even know you were here.' He slammed the door.

Genevieve smiled and shook her head. Mr Breckenridge was quite funny sometimes.

CHAPTER 19

After that first visit to Café Paradise, Annabel decided to stay on in York. She had some savings and wanted to give herself time to adjust to her new life. What better place to find her feet? After some careful searching she found a room on the outskirts of the city and settled in. It was the first week in May and the weather was glorious. Armed with a guidebook and an armful of brochures from the tourist information centre, Annabel explored, visiting the Minster, walking the Roman walls that surrounded the city and discovering the ancient, cobbled Shambles.

Café Paradise drew her like a magnet. Every day she sat at her table to the side of Jackie's coffee counter. She was a familiar face now and was warmly welcomed by the staff. She lingered over lunch, watching and listening to Jackie greeting and serving the endless line of customers as they queued for their coffee and sandwiches to take out into the spring sunshine.

After a week of watching, Annabel felt even more confused and mixed-up. She longed to reveal herself to Jackie, but now that she was here it was impossible to see how to do it. She couldn't just walk up and say, 'Hello, I'm your big sister. Did you know about me?' After all, it was more than likely that Jackie did not. Marilyn had married and had another child and that was it. She'd never tried to find Annabel again; Annabel was her past. Jackie probably adored her mother; the news of an illegitimate half-sister might be a horrible shock to her.

Every time Annabel left Café Paradise, she felt frustrated and sad. She had found the place where her mother had spent so much of her life, but knew little more about her. She had found her sister, but had not even had a proper conversation with her. She was no better off than she had been in prison. She was still alone, with nothing.

Walking up Stonegate, Annabel stopped abruptly. Yes, that was it. Annabel walked slowly on, along Lendal and into the Museum Gardens. She sat down on a bench and watched the tourists posing for photographs with the grey squirrels that abounded in the gardens. Everybody had somebody. Unable to bear it, she got up and walked away, feeling lonelier than ever.

******

Annabel had spent the morning visiting the Yorkshire Museum and was drawn, as if on strings, back to Café Paradise for lunch.

'Hi Annabel.' Jackie was in her usual place at the coffee counter as Annabel made her way to her table. 'How are you today?' She smiled warmly.

Jackie's large violet eyes held such warmth and welcome. Annabel was aware of the sharp contrast in the thoughts tumbling round in her head. She stumbled over her reply. 'I'm, I'm OK, thank you.'

'Are you enjoying your holiday?' Jackie moved at speed, cutting an enormous wedge of chocolate cake and putting the lid on a take-out coffee, all at the same time, or so it seemed to Annabel.

'I've loved it.' Annabel wanted to prolong the conversation. She hesitated, trying to think of something to say. 'Although it can't go on forever. The trouble is, I've fallen in love with the city.' She tried for a light tone. 'Perhaps I could find a job and a flat.' Where had that come from? She made it sound like she was staying put. Was she?

'What's your field?' Jackie asked. 'If I heard of anything...' She turned away briefly to give a waiting customer his change.

Annabel thought quickly. 'Administration. I'm a very good PA. Good computer skills and shorthand, a good organiser.'

This was no lie. She'd had a successful career before prison and had excelled in her pre-release work placements. They would give her good references, without disclosing the circumstances of her employment.

Jackie eyed her thoughtfully. 'I wonder ... look, give me five minutes. I might be able to help you.'

Annabel took her place at the usual table and picked up the menu. Her hands were shaking. Yes, she would stay in York. It felt like home already and there might be an opportunity to get to know Jackie a bit more. She was almost sick with excitement.

When the rush had died down, Jackie left Louise, the new waitress, to mind the counter and went to her office. She returned a short while later and slid into the seat opposite Annabel.

'This could be your lucky day and mine,' she began, smiling across the table.

Annabel smiled tentatively back and waited.

'My husband, Barney, has recently started a solicitor's practice with his friend in Little Stonegate. I don't know if you've spotted my sister-in-law, Genevieve, floating about here?'

Annabel nodded.

'Yeah, well she was at Barney's offices for a while. She was supposed to do the filing and sort the bills out, all that kind of stuff. Actually, she's useless and everything's in a right old muddle now. They've been very lucky and have tons of work on and a great legal secretary to help out on that side of things, but the actual running of the offices has gone to pot. I hardly see Barney these days. He spends his evenings trying to catch up on invoices and VAT, and comes home exhausted. It's not the best scenario. We've only been married for eight months and I'm spending my evenings on my own again.'

Annabel nodded sympathetically.

'Which is where you come in, that's if you're interested. Now that they're shot of Genevieve, they can take on an administrator. Seems to me, you're heaven sent, Annabel. If you pop round this afternoon about three o'clock, with a bit of luck, you'll have a job by half past and then I'll get my husband back.'

Annabel could hardly believe it. A job in Barney's office and a chance not only to stay in touch with Jackie but maybe learn more about her. And, just as importantly, to learn about Marilyn. She smiled at Jackie. 'Wow, you're amazing. Thank you.'

'Thank you, Annabel. As I said, you're heaven sent.'

Would she say that if she really knew? Annabel wondered as she made her way out of the café. Only time would tell.

CHAPTER 20

'There you are.' George Montague stood back to admire his handiwork. He had fixed black panniers to a frame and placed them over the back wheel of the Harley. 'Ah, this is the life. Travelling light, we can go where we please, no baggage to worry about.'

Penny eyed the panniers with dismay. 'Is that it?'

'Is that what?'

'Our bags?'

'Yep. That's it. Fantastic. There's plenty of room for your stuff – you'll get everything you need in there: toothbrush, swimsuit, camera...'

'Yes, George. I don't suppose we need clean knickers, socks, shirts, anything like that, do we?' Penny's tone was sarcastic.

'Well, take a change if you must,' George said reluctantly. 'We don't want to be loaded down. We're bikers, free spirits. Real bikers don't worry about clean socks.'

'Well I do, and take clean socks I will – and a lot more besides. My hair drier, for instance.'

'Hair drier!' George was appalled. 'I said free spirits, Penny. We take life as it comes for the next few weeks. Leave all that stuff behind.'

'It's me and my hair drier or nothing,' Penny said firmly. 'That's final.'

'Bah,' said George.

*****

It was a long and dusty ride to Hull. The day was bright and sunny and Penny was hot inside her new leathers. Beads of perspiration gathered on her forehead and ran down her face, misting up the inside of her helmet. It took a few miles for her to get into the rhythm of swaying with the bike as George followed the gentle contours of the road, but after half an hour Penny felt more comfortable. Unfortunately for her, they hit a series of roundabouts on the A1033 that led to the ferry. George let rip, slewing the bike around the bends at terrifying angles and deaf to Penny's entreaties to slow down. She shut her eyes and hung on grimly, hoping that driving on the right in Europe would slow him down.

At Hull, Penny was amazed by the size of the ferry. She lost count of the decks they drove through before they were finally waved into their parking bay. As they removed their helmets, George sniffed the air appreciatively. 'Ah, that's better. Fresh air again.'

Penny thought the air was foul. A strong smell of diesel and old engine oil hung in the massive hall. George was inclined to linger, wanting to take in the sight of the lorries with their long trailers piling onto the loading bay. Penny shivered. 'Let's go and find our cabin.'

They unhooked their bags from the Harley and made their way up the steps, into the heart of the ship. It was like a floating hotel with stairs up and down; to dining rooms, bars, quiet lounge rooms and shops. The cabins were located at the rear of the ship. They seemed to walk miles down endless corridors, turning left and right and left again into yet another corridor, identical to the one they had just left. Eventually they found their cabin, the last in an anonymous line of doors.

Penny was dismayed to find bunk beds. She eyed the ladder up to the top bunk. 'I'm not going up there,' she announced firmly. 'You could fall out if the ship rolls.'

'Don't be daft, 'course you wouldn't. I'll go up there if you like, anything for a quiet life.'

A quiet life! They would be roaring noisily through Europe

for weeks on end. Sometimes Penny wondered what went on in her husband's head.

George was keen to explore. 'Come on, Penny. Let's have a good look around the ship. It's like a floating town out there. I bet it's a fantastic view from the top deck.'

The thought of standing at such a height, watching the open sea rush by made Penny shudder. 'You won't get me up there. I think I'll stay safely indoors, thank you.'

'Alright,' George said unwillingly. 'But we've come away for adventure, Penny, not to be old stick in the muds. Come on, there's lots to see.'

After the hot and dusty ride, Penny needed to freshen up. She decided on a shower and change of clothes first. 'You go on ahead,' she said to George. 'We could meet in the dining room for dinner, when I've tidied myself up.'

Eager to be off, George agreed and left Penny to it. An hour later, Penny emerged feeling more like her old self in light summer clothes and careful make-up. She knew she looked good for fifty-three and sashayed confidently up the corridor.

Her sense of direction was not good and it took her a long time to find her way out of the maze of passageways and up onto the main deck. The ship was moving smoothly along, the throbbing of the engines providing a low background hum. The Friday evening crossing was fully booked; anxious mothers held tightly on to children, couples strolled hand in hand and others sat alone, staring out to sea.

Penny found the main dining room and looked for George, but he was not there. She was hungry and hoped George would hurry up. Half an hour later and George had still not appeared. She decided to eat. Maybe then George would arrive.

The food was surprisingly good. Penny enjoyed her meal and kept an eye out for George between mouthfuls. She sat on for some time after she had finished, but the dining room was hot and crowded and as George didn't appear she decided to seek cooler air.

It was still early evening. Penny decided to explore the ship and look for her husband. Where could he have got to? George loved his food and would never miss a meal. Perhaps he had gone for a drink, got into conversation and lost track of the time. There were several bars and lounges on board and as dusk was falling, passengers turned from watching the sea and went in search of new entertainment.

Penny looked for George. She tried every bar, lounge, coffee shop, brasserie and diner, finishing up at the main entertainment lounge, where a live band played for the enthusiastic dancers on the floor. Penny was worn out from walking up and down endless flights of stairs. She perched on a stool at the bar to rest her aching feet.

'Yes Madam?' enquired the barman. 'What can I get you?'

'Oh. Oh,' Penny was taken aback. She hadn't been thinking about ordering, but now she was here, why not? She could spend the whole night looking for George and never find him. 'A gin and tonic, please,' she said and settled herself properly on the stool.

As she took in the scene, she was startled to see a group of young men dressed in grass skirts, with garlands of flowers around their necks and in their hair. They sang along with the band, waving their drinks in the air and clapping enthusiastically. At the end of the performance, they crowded round the bar, grinning merrily at Penny.

'Oh, ho,' said one. 'What have we here? A pretty lady.'

'Now, lads,' said the barman. 'Leave the lady alone. Behave yourselves or you'll be out.'

'Of course we'll behave ourselves,' said the young man. 'We're only having a bit of fun.' He held his hand out to Penny. 'James Ritchie at your service,' he said, slurring his words slightly. 'Stag do this weekend. Mine. Last fling before the padlock goes on. Don't know where I'm going, that lot won't tell me.' He jerked his head towards his friends. They grinned knowingly at Penny.

'That would be telling, Jamie boy,' said one. 'Time for another round. Sir.' He summoned the barman and indicated

Penny's glass. 'One for this beautiful lady, too.'

'You're just like my boys,' she smiled. 'They're about your age and just as daft.'

The young man toasted her with his beer glass. 'I may be daft but you don't look anything like my mother.'

The band struck up again and soon the floor was crowded with dancers. The boys piled onto the floor, their grass skirts swaying in time to the music. At first, Penny watched them, too shy to join in, but as the music got louder and the beat faster, she couldn't resist. James put his garland around her neck as she danced around the floor. He drew closer to her. 'In New Zealand they touch their noses and foreheads together when they meet. They call it a hongi. Well, we've just met...'

'And you won't be meeting any more,' George roared, dragging Penny away from James and holding up his fists.

'George. No,' Penny shrieked and got between them. 'We were only dancing. He's on his stag weekend with all his friends. Where have you been? I looked everywhere for you.'

'Stag weekend?' George ground his teeth. 'We all know what stags get up to. Well, not with my wife, sunshine.'

The floor around them had cleared and a burly member of staff was at their side. George and Penny were hustled out very quickly, George still shouting, 'Just keep away, that's all, or I'll have you. I wasn't the York county champion for nothing, you know.'

All the way back to their cabin, George seethed. 'I leave you for half an hour and what do I find? You, jumping about a dance floor with a bunch of half-naked lads young enough to be your sons. It's disgusting.'

Penny smiled to herself. It wasn't. It had been grand. If this was what a trip to Europe was about, she was all for it. 'Never mind me, where did you get to George?' she finally got a word in.

'Nowhere special,' he said. 'Just mooching.' Penny looked up at him. That tone of voice meant he had been somewhere and it wasn't just 'mooching'.

'You've been to the casino, haven't you?' she said accusingly. 'Now, don't lie.' She slumped against their cabin door. He had promised he wouldn't go near it. 'How much?' she asked.'

'Just a pound, or two,' George admitted.

Penny slid further down the door. 'How much?' she repeated.

'Two hundred pounds,' said George.

Penny closed her eyes and moaned. They might just as well stay on the boat and go home. He'd just lost a chunk of their holiday money.

George squatted down beside her and took her hand. 'I won it Penny. I won,' he repeated as her eyes remained closed.

'You won,' Penny said tonelessly and then it registered. 'You won? Two hundred pounds!' She flung her arms around him. 'You promised me not to play, promised faithfully and you did and now you've won and ... and...'

George gave up. He pulled Penny, still gabbling, to her feet and guided her into the cabin. When she was ready for bed, George said, 'Seeing as I've won all this money and no doubt you'll be spending it on this trip, how about you take the top bunk?'

'You promised me you wouldn't go to the casino in the first place, George, then you throw punches around on the dance floor and now you expect me to risk sleeping up there.' Penny stretched out on the lower bunk. 'Not a chance,' and put her light out.

*****

The night crossing was calm and Penny slept well. Not so, George. The bunk was too small, he had been hungry all night, the ship rocked, and he could hear the people next door snoring...

Penny was glad when they left Zebrugge and were on their way down through Belgium, heading towards Lille. The morning was grey and overcast. Driving on the right side of the road forced George to keep his speed down, although Penny still held on tightly and shut her eyes as he wobbled up to junctions, uncertain of which way to go. Once they were clear of Bruges the road was straightforward to Lille, just over the French border. It was only an hour away and George wanted to keep going, but Penny had read about the cafés and art galleries in the town and was keen to stay overnight and see the sights.

'Ah, we're doing all that stuff in Paris,' said George. 'I'm not being dragged around art galleries today *and* tomorrow. We'll go to a café for lunch and you can look at the wildlife, then we're off to Paris.'

They lunched in a little café in Lille. George studied the map as he ate.

'I think I've got our route sorted in my mind,' he said, folding the map and putting it back in his jacket. 'It seems easy enough to get to this *pension* place I've booked, just down a side street on the outskirts.'

'On the outskirts? I thought we were staying in a nice hotel in the centre of Paris. I thought you were treating me.'

'Do you know how much a hotel in the centre of Paris costs? A fortune, that's how much. This *pension* place is fine. I saw the rooms on the website and they look great. We can go into Paris on the bike.'

'Can't we take the bus?' Penny asked hopefully.

'Bus!' George was scornful. 'And miss the fun of riding round Paris on a Harley? Not likely. It'll be fantastic, weaving in and out of the traffic, ducking and diving. You'll love it. Hurry up and finish your coffee. It's time we were off.'

Three hours later they arrived at the *pension*. It was at the end of a dreary street of houses built of flaking limestone, with ancient shutters at the windows keeping out the little spring sunshine that penetrated the narrow street.

Any hopes Penny had entertained of a memorable stay in Paris vanished as she looked around their room. It was tiny and only just accommodated a double bed and dressing table, with the tiniest en-suite she had ever seen. How George would fit in the shower, she didn't know.

'Well, this is grand,' George enthused, dumping their bags on the bed. 'Just the job for a couple of nights. We'll have a great time, you'll see. I've got a surprise for you.'

Penny thought longingly of a proper hotel suite with a deep bath, TV and mini-bar. This cupboard wasn't her idea of 'just the job'. She wondered what other accommodation George had been booking for them online. Could it be much worse than this? She hoped not. And the surprise? On past experience, George's surprises were things to be wary of.

******

Riding through the centre of Paris was every bit the nightmare that Penny suspected it would be. It was early evening but the traffic was still heavy. George whooped with delight as he roared around the Arc de Triomphe, sounding his horn and waving to everyone as if he were making a victory lap at the TT races. There were several close shaves with vans and cars that made Penny squeal and shut her eyes as she endured what she was sure would be her final moments on this earth.

When George finally came to a halt and switched off the engine, Penny opened her eyes and to her surprise found they were at the Eiffel Tower. She gaped speechlessly up at the tower, brilliantly lit against the evening sky.

George removed his helmet and gestured towards it. 'Madame,' he announced in his best French accent, 'your table awaits. You dine tonight at Le 58 Tour Restaurant. Your clever 'usband Georges has fixed it all up for you. Champagne awaits and the best cuisine France can provide.'

Dinner, at the Eiffel Tower? One minute they're in a cheap dive of a B&B and the next in the most exciting restaurant in Paris. Life with George might be exasperating but it was never dull.

They went up in the lift and stepped out into a very modern, chic brasserie. Dark wooden tables lined the room, with floor to ceiling plate-glass windows, allowing panoramic views of

Paris. A smartly dressed waitress conducted them to a table by a window overlooking the city. Penny looked out eagerly. 'There's Notre Dame Cathedral.' After a few moments, she looked away. 'I'd better not look too much. We're so high up, it's a bit scary.'

George thrust a menu at her. 'Look at this instead. I hope you can find something you like on it. All *nouvelle cuisine* from what I can see. I fancy steak and chips, I wonder if they can do me some. Don't suppose I'll get ketchup with it though.' He contemplated the menu gloomily.

The large menu rather flummoxed Penny too. She was thrilled to be here, actually in the Eiffel Tower restaurant – well one of them – but although she didn't like to admit it, nouvelle cuisine wasn't for her either. She didn't like her food messed about with, all those coloured sauces and bits of meat dotted about the plate with that jus stuff scattered about. Maybe they *should* see if they could get steak and chips here.

The waitress came with the champagne on ice that was included with their meal. 'Ask about the steak, Penny,' George urged her.

'Why can't you?' Penny wanted to know.

'You've got the lingo better than me. Go on.'

Penny smiled shyly at the woman hovering over her and managed to get out *'Avez vous bifteck et frites sur votre menu, sil vous plaît?'*

The waitress's eyebrows rose to her hairline and the pen poised over her pad stopped in mid-air. *'Bifteck et frites?'* A slight twitch at the corner of her mouth betrayed her astonishment, but she soon controlled it. *'Oui, madame. Pour monsieur aussi?'* she said faintly.

'Oui,' Penny said happily. Closing the vast menu, she handed it back to the waitress.

'I knew you could do it, Penny,' George said enthusiastically and poured the champagne. They clinked glasses in a toast and relaxed back in their seats, looking about them. The interior was very simple; the dark wood of the small, square tables contrasting with the crisp white napkins. Glasses and cutlery sparkled in the subdued light, the backdrop to the myriad, twinkling lights of night-time Paris spread out below.

Penny looked out of the window again. She could see for miles across the city. Paris was lit up by millions of lights, lighting the way for the never-ending flow of cars on the roads far below them. They were so far down, they looked like toys.

'I bet you don't mind that B&B now, do you?' said George, grinning broadly at her. 'It's not many that can say they've had dinner at the Eiffel Tower. Took some arranging, I can tell you. I had help from Frenchy Joe at The Green Man. I couldn't have done it otherwise.'

Penny couldn't take her eyes off the cars below. They mesmerised her and she began to feel a bit dizzy. She continued to look even though it made her queasy. George's voice rolled on in the background, mingling with the other diners. Eventually, Penny could stand no more. She got up abruptly from the table. 'It's no good, I can't do it, George,' she said, holding her hand to her mouth.

'Do what? No one's asking you to do anything. Sit down, folk are looking.'

'I can't. I can't stay here. It's too high up. It's making me feel funny. I feel quite sick.'

Penny rushed from the room in search of the Ladies and didn't immediately return. George stirred uneasily in his seat. Another two or three minutes passed and then the waitress arrived with their steaks. She looked questioningly at Penny's seat. '*Madame?*' she queried.

George mimed Penny being sick. The waitress hesitated, holding aloft their dishes piled with crisp, golden chips. George's mouth watered. He held up two fingers. '*Deux* minutes,' he suggested.

The waitress nodded. '*Oui monsieur, ou il sera gâté.*'

George had no idea what she meant, but waved her away confidently. 'Yeah, whatever. She won't be long.'

The waitress wheeled about and returned to the kitchen.

George sat back in his chair and looked out of the window. The lights outside were dazzling, constantly changing, re-configuring in a silent dance below him. He enjoyed watching the lines of traffic snaking around the streets and the flashing neon lights randomly lighting a building here, a square there.

After some time of watching the lights, George grew restless and peered anxiously round the restaurant, hoping Penny would materialise from the shadows. Ten minutes later he sighed with relief as Penny walked towards their table.

George got up to usher her back to her seat. 'Feeling better, love?'

Penny sat down, smiling at him. 'Much better, thank you. I'll be fine now as long as I don't look out of the window.' She kept her gaze fixed on George and then turned to take in the detail of the restaurant.

George shook his head. Right up in the heart of the Eiffel Tower and she turns her back on the view. He wouldn't be telling Frenchy Joe at The Green Man about that. Never mind, he could murder that steak and chips now. He poured them some more champagne and they drank a toast.

'To France and many happy memories,' said Penny.

'To France,' George agreed. He spotted their waitress passing by with plates of food for other guests and gave her the thumbs up. Seeing Penny back in her seat and smiling happily, she nodded.

'*Deux minutes, monsieur. Madame est bien? Bon. Bifteck et frites.*' She tripped lightly off to the kitchen, giggling.

A few minutes later she returned and set their dinner down before them with a flourish. '*Monsieur, madame, bifteck et frites.*' She stood back triumphantly.

George gazed down in horror at his plate. 'No, no. This won't do. It isn't cooked. It's raw. We can't eat this.' He looked up at the waitress. She stared back, uncomprehending.

'Tell her, Penny,' George pleaded with Penny.

The waitress looked at Penny enquiringly.

'*Le bifteck,*' she began.

'*Oui?*'

'*C'est* raw.'

'Raw?' The waitress looked blank.

'Raw, woman. Raw. Not cooked. Inedible. Tell her, Penny,' George repeated.

'Oh George, I don't know the French for raw.' She thought a moment. 'I know.' Penny pointed to the steak on her plate. '*C'est rouge.*'

The waitress rolled her eyes. '*Oui, madame. Bifteck est rouge.*'

'Hang on a minute,' said George. 'Frenchy Joe had a phrase. *Bien cuit.* That's it.' He turned to the waitress. 'Steak *bien cuit, s'il vous plaît.*'

'*Mais non, monsieur. Vous êtes en France. Le steak est cuit de ce façon. Nous ne commeçons pas à l'assassiner comme chez vous. C'est une insulte à la viande. Notre chef ne le fera pas. Bon appetit.*' The veiled contempt in her parting remark was not lost on Penny.

'I think that was take it or leave it, George.'

George gazed sadly down at the large and very red steak on his plate. 'It looks like he's just sawn it off the cow and put it on our plates. I don't think it ever saw the frying pan. I can't eat that. Not even for you, Penny.'

Penny looked at her own steak and agreed. Blood oozing from the meat ran onto the chips. It didn't look appetising.

'I know it isn't what you wanted, Penny,' George said. 'But I think I've had an idea. How about we get a doggie bag for these and cook them up for breakfast at our B&B?'

The waitress was passing by. George stopped her. 'Can you do us a doggie bag?' he asked.

The waitress looked at him blankly.

George racked his brains for his schoolboy French. '*Le sac,*' he tried. '*Un sac de chien.*'

The waitress looked horrified. '*Un chien!* No, no, *monsieur. C'est une vache de première qualité. Pas de chien dans notre restaurant.*' She bore the food away, anger and contempt in every bone of her rigid back.

Two minutes later the manager appeared at the table. 'You

are causing problem, *monsieur*,' he began.

Someone who spoke English. George was mightily relieved. 'I don't mean to, Moosewer. We ordered our meal and then my wife was feeling poorly, too much looking down, all that traffic and she's at a funny time of life, if you know what I mean, so she didn't want her dinner and I thought, seeing as we'd paid for it, how about a doggie bag?'

'Exactly, *monsieur*. This doggie bag, we put the dog in it for you?'

George beamed. 'Now you've got it!'

The manager bristled. 'Oh no, *monsieur*, you have got it. Your ticket out of here, as you say. Right now. There are no dogs in my restaurant. You will leave, now.'

Ten minutes later they were standing disconsolately on the pavement outside, looking up at the brilliantly lit Tower.

'Tell you what, Penny,' George suggested. 'I'll walk you along the Seine and buy you a burger. How about that?'

'You really know how to treat a girl,' Penny said flatly. 'I bet there's not many girls get an offer like that.'

'I know,' George said as they set off. 'You were lucky when you met me.'

'Keep telling me George. Keep telling me.'

CHAPTER 21

Coming out of the airport, Stan was bathed in the warm Rome sunshine. He found a taxi and gave the address, Via Bartolemeo, to the driver. It was a short drive and Villa San Paolo was the middle of a terrace of large houses that looked as if they had been there for centuries. When the taxi had driven off, Stan paused apprehensively on the doorstep. Kate had said that her friend Sofia spoke good English. He hoped so; his Italian was limited to *si* and *no*. He rang the doorbell and heard light footsteps approaching, whilst at the same time, a loud and animated argument seemed to be in progress.

'È ora che tu ti sposi,' cried Maria.

'Voglio un uomo vero nella mia vita non un bambino!'

'Per te qualsiasi uomo puo andare bene!'

'Oh, *Dia*,' shouted an enraged Sofia and flung open the door.

Standing on the doorstep, a little alarmed at this greeting, Stan tried to smile and get out his much-practised greeting. *'Buon giorno, La signorina,'* he began.

'Stanlee.' Sofia drew the door closed behind her. 'The husband of Kate, no?' She smiled and kissed him warmly on both cheeks.

Flustered at this unexpected welcome, Stan flushed and managed to stammer out, 'Yes, yes, Kate's my wife. You know her, of course.'

'*Si*, she spent some time at the university here, when she was studying. I was studying too. We make the friends.'

Sofia looked Stan up and down admiringly. 'Come,' she

commanded. 'You will meet my mother and then I will take you to your room, show you your bed, help you to be comfortable. You, who are far from home.' She smiled knowingly at him.

Sofia Anastasio was built on generous lines. She was nearly as tall as Stan, olive skinned, with deep-set brown eyes beneath fine brows. Her raven-black hair was piled high on her head. She led the way into the house, her movements fluid and sinuous. Stan followed in her wake, feeling like a boy on his first day at school.

Signora Maria Anastasio was the opposite of her daughter in every way. She was small and dumpy, with a round face and black button eyes. Her skin had the dry, papery quality of the elderly and she was dressed in the traditional widow's black. She smiled shyly at Stan and welcomed him in halting English. 'Hope you enjoy stay here. You ask Sofia,' she gestured to her daughter, 'you need anythings.'

Stan shook her hand warmly. He liked this little Italian lady, with her old-fashioned dress and scraped-back hair. She reminded him of his grandmother back in Yorkshire.

'I'll show him to his room,' Sofia threw over her shoulder to her mother as she headed for the door.

'Stanlee,' Maria enquired, 'have you wife in England?'

'I have, Maria,' Stan replied. 'Her name is Kate. She is very beautiful and wise.'

Maria's face fell. 'Piittee, I need good husband for Sofia. You would be nice one.'

Were all Italians this frank on first meeting? Stan wondered. He picked up his bags and followed Sofia to the door.

As they made their way up the stairs to the rooms on the first floor, Stan asked shyly, 'Are you looking for a husband, Sofia? Or is that just what your mother wants?'

'Oh, may the blessed Jesus help us all! No I'm definitely not. That is just my mother's way. She wants more *nipotini*, grandchildren.' Sofia shrugged. 'I love my work at the International College, Stanlee.' She turned to face him. 'I love men too,' she smiled. 'But to be married, keep house, cook, no.

Not for me, Stanlee. My sister has four children. Mother will have to be content.'

She showed him into a large and pleasant room. It had a bed against one wall and a desk and chair under the window overlooking the street below. 'There is a bathroom just opposite,' said Sofia, 'but is for you only. We have bathroom upstairs.'

Stan put his bags on the bed and looked round appreciatively. 'It's a lovely room, thank you. I think I'll unpack and freshen up a bit and maybe have a stroll around, get to know the lie of the land.'

'If you need any help...' Sofia drifted to the bed and caressed the coverlet, smiling at him.

'No thank you,' Stan said hastily. 'I can manage quite well.'

Sofia looked a little disappointed but left him to it. At the door she said, 'Term begins in the morning. I give you a lift this first time. We start early to avoid the heat, so be awake early, Stanlee. Would you like me to wake you?' she asked hopefully.

'No thank you,' Stan said firmly. 'I have a good alarm clock.'

Stan spent a pleasant couple of hours with his street map, walking around Rome. He could hardly believe he was here. He soaked up the atmosphere, listening to many different languages as he stood at the Trevi Fountain and wishing Kate was with him. But it could not be and it wasn't for ever. He resolved to do his best in the short time he had here.

Back at Villa San Paolo, he ate a delicious supper with *signora* Maria. Sofia was out at a college function. At least, that's what Stan thought Maria was trying to say. Tired after his journey and afternoon's ramblings, Stan went early to bed. Awake in the early hours, he heard light footsteps pass his door and pause. Stan held his breath. It could only be Sofia. After a few moments, he heard the footsteps move away. Stan breathed a sigh of relief. Maybe he needed to lock his door at night.

*****

Sofia should have been a rally driver, Stan thought. He held tightly on to his seat as she swerved around the narrow Roman streets. Her little Fiat 500 convertible was short on interior springs. Stan was glad the top was down as he bounced up and down all the way to the International College.

She brought energy and zest to everything she did. She drove at speed into the college car park, jammed on the brakes and was out of the car in a flash, striding towards the entrance before Stan had time to collect himself.

'Come on, Stanlee,' she grinned back at him, swinging her big leather bag over her shoulder. 'You had a good sleep last night, didn't you?'

Stan made no comment and hurried to catch her up.

The International College for Roman Studies was a large building in the heart of the city. Sofia led Stan through a maze of corridors with high windows. On every ledge there were busts of Roman emperors and gods. Stan would have liked to linger at several of them but Sofia strode on and eventually flung open the door to a small room with windows looking out over a piazza, lined on all sides with shops and cafés. Tables and chairs filled the square and already they were filled with visitors, sitting under the striped umbrellas.

Stan chose a seat away from the windows, fearing his attention would wander to the colourful scenes below. After a brief welcome, Sofia launched into her lecture on Roman gods and goddesses. She was a good speaker and the class was kept busy making notes. There was a mid-morning break and Sofia led the way to her favourite coffee shop out on the Piazza Navona.

The group took over a table and the waiter quickly brought out small cups of espresso. Talk of the gods continued. A student asked Sofia if she had a favourite amongst the ancient gods.

Sofia sipped her coffee thoughtfully. 'I do. I think the goddess Venus is my favourite.' She looked across the table at Stan and smiled at him, as if they shared a naughty secret. 'Venus, the goddess of beauty, sex, fertility and prosperity.' She breathed the words slowly, emphasising 'sex', keeping her eyes fixed on Stan. 'We Romans,' she continued, 'for us, the gods and goddesses are still very much a part of our lives and culture. They pre-date Christianity and are in our blood, our bodies, our very being. So,' she paused and looked around, 'I am a follower of Venus. She guides the choices in my life.' Sofia paused and ran her tongue around her lips, eyeing Stan speculatively. 'And she sends me new lovers. What more can I ask of her?'

I just hope she hasn't asked for an English one, thought Stan, taking a deep draught of the bitter black coffee.

CHAPTER 22

In the staffroom at Café Paradise, Kate thoughtfully circled the advert in the *York Herald*. *Model required for Evening Life Classes at York College of Art. Start immediately.* The pay was exceptionally good. It would have to be, she thought wryly. Taking all your clothes off, even if you were discreetly posed, was a big deal. But Stan was away in Rome for the term and the money would go a long way to building up the deposit for the new house they wanted. He need never know.

Kate got up and took her mug over to the sink to wash. Jackie came in and put her tray down on the table. 'I've left Louise on the coffee counter for ten minutes,' she said and flopped down into a chair. 'I've had nothing to eat since six this morning and I'm beginning to feel a bit light-headed.' She bit hungrily into her sandwich and sat back contentedly.

She saw the newspaper on the table and immediately spotted the advert Kate had ringed. 'Life class modelling! Who's this for?' She glanced up and saw Kate colouring up. 'You're not serious, Kate? Why on earth would you do that?'

'Why would anybody do it, Jackie?' There was a note of steely defiance in Kate's voice. 'Look at the money they're offering to take your clothes off and sit still. I could save every penny of that and we'd finally have the down payment on that house we want. By the time Stan gets back, we'd be ready to go.'

Jackie took another bite of her sandwich and considered. 'How are you going to explain this sudden wealth to Stan?'

'Extra shifts here,' Kate said promptly. 'You'll be opening the bistro in the evenings again when you get the new chef.

106

Well, I've done a lot of evenings.'

'Have you now? Well you'd better do a few, Kate, and then I'll be telling some of the truth.' Jackie looked again at the advertisement and sighed. 'I wish I could afford to pay you that kind of money. If Stan ever found out...'

'He won't,' Kate said shortly. 'Not if we don't tell him.' She picked up the paper from the table and made for the door. 'It'll be fine, Jackie, you'll see. Anyway, I might not be what they're looking for. They might have dozens of more suitable applicants.'

When she had gone, Jackie contemplated her mug of coffee. None as beautiful as you, Kate Peterson. They'll snap you up.

*****

That evening, Kate made her way to the College of Art. It was a graceful, three-storeyed building of red brick, blending in with the neighbouring buildings. Kate's heart beat a little faster than usual as she followed the directions to Studio Four, as instructed.

She walked up a flight of worn stone stairs and on to a landing that opened out to a wide bay, with several doors off it. One was marked Studio Four. She looked through the glass panels, but could not see anyone about. She knocked and waited and when this drew no response, she opened the door and went in.

Studio Four was a long, bright room, with large windows all down one side. Paintings of every description were hanging on the walls and unfinished canvasses were stacked everywhere: on the floor, on easels and on the tables that lined the far side of the room.

A man with his back to Kate was bending over one of these tables, examining a painting. 'Mr Rawlings?' Kate called out.

The figure spun round and saw Kate. For a few moments he stood perfectly still, studying her. Kate flushed uncomfortably under his gaze. This was no good. If she got the job, she would have to get used to people staring at her. That was what she was there for.

The man hurried towards her, hands outstretched in welcome. He was tall and thin, with suspiciously black hair. He wore a suit that was too large, the trousers held up by braces. A knitted, multi-coloured scarf wound round his neck and flowed down, almost to his knees. 'Miss Johnson? Come in, come in.' He took her hands and smiled down at her.

'Remarkable,' he commented. 'Quite remarkable. I never expected such beauty, such ...' he studied her, 'such purity.'

Kate had no idea what to say to this and stood, feeling foolish, as he continued to hold her hands. 'Mr Rawlings,' she began.

'Frederick, please.' As if she had broken the spell, Frederick pulled her arm through his and led her further into the studio. 'Come and sit down, Miss Johnson. Kate, isn't it?'

Kate nodded. She was using her maiden name and had, with a sense of anguish, removed her wedding ring before entering the building.

'May I call you Kate?' Frederick drew her to a chaise longue in the centre of the room, where a group of easels were set up. Sitting on the sofa, Frederick gazed at her intently. 'Perfect, Kate. I never thought I would ever be so fortunate to have a model such as you.' He breathed the words slowly, reverently, as he absently stroked her hands. 'You are a wonderful person, Kate,' he announced when he'd finished studying her.

'I'm not so sure about...'

'Yes,' he commanded. 'Yes. You have the most perfect face and body. My students will love to draw and paint you. But it is not that, lovely Kate. Not that at all.' Frederick leaned towards her, close enough for Kate to catch the waft of garlic on his breath. 'True beauty comes from within.' He nodded solemnly at his own pronouncement. 'Through your eyes, Kate. You gaze out at this bleak, troubled world with the eyes of an unsullied child, unknowing of the foul deeds men do to each other. I see goodness in your eyes, pure, undefiled goodness. I will paint you, my students will paint you. Such inspiration!'

'Does that mean I've got the job then?' asked Kate.

'Tomorrow. 7.00pm. We will drape you,' Frederick said dramatically. 'The Goddess Aphrodite, goddess of love and beauty.' He jumped up from the sofa, took a pencil from his pocket and began sketching at the nearest easel. Kate sat still and waited. After a few minutes, Frederick flung the pencil from him. 'Oh, you'll be a challenge, Kate.' He smiled in delight. 'Your essence eludes me tonight.' He threw his head back and laughed, stretching his arms out wide. 'There is always tomorrow, oh goddess. Always tomorrow.'

His breathing slowed as he focused intently on her. 'See you tomorrow, beautiful Kate, oh purest of goddesses.'

Stepping out into the evening twilight, Kate felt apprehensive about the following evening. All this talk of purity and goodness gave her the creeps. Just sit still when they ask you and think of the pay cheque, she told herself sternly. They're studying you objectively, that's all. Even so, she was more daunted than she'd expected.

CHAPTER 23

Annabel Lewis-Langley could hardly believe it was only three short weeks since she had come to work for Barney and Jake. She had slotted in as if she had been working there for months. Joanna Starling was kept very busy as their legal secretary and everyone was very relieved when Annabel stepped in to unravel the administrative nightmare that Genevieve had left behind.

How her life had changed in the short time since her release from prison. She had a job and now rented a tiny flat at Clifton Moor and, best of all, she had found her half-sister.

Annabel mused on all these changes as she moved about her flat. This was her first real home in years. She had her own front door key to prove it. She still felt a sense of wonder every time she shut the door behind her. She had very little in the way of furnishings: a bed, the basics for the bathroom and kitchen, and a deckchair in the tiny lounge, but she knew she would soon make it cosy. She'd enjoyed using the computers in prison and learned a lot about furniture and design.

And she had a job. Barney and Jake were great to work for. They trusted her. The firm was so new it didn't have any established administrative systems and Annabel was free to devise her own. One day she hoped to develop a career as an interior designer but for now she was happy to have a decent job.

A job that enabled her to see something of Jackie. Annabel still went to Café Paradise two or three times a week for lunch. Jackie always greeted her in a friendly manner as Annabel

made her way through to her usual table near to the coffee counter. Frustratingly, Annabel never got any further than this. She knew Jackie and Barney lived in Marilyn's old home, a large detached house near the river at Acaster Malbis, but she was no nearer learning any more about Jackie or her mother, or how Walter Breckenridge had fitted into the picture in the past. Annabel had gone to look at Marilyn's house one day. She'd stood on the pavement opposite, an ache in her heart. She would love to take a look inside, get some sense of this woman who had left her behind but kept Jackie.

Well, maybe tonight she would learn a little bit more. Jake Cranton, Barney's partner, was holding a fortieth birthday party at The Golden Lion Hotel and had invited friends, family and colleagues. 'Including you, Annabel Lewis-Langley,' he had smiled at her as he dropped the invitation on her desk.

Annabel was delighted and bought a new dress for the occasion. It was dark red with a tight waist and full skirt that showed off her slender figure. She carefully applied her make-up and brushed her hair until it gleamed. Surveying herself in the mirror, she felt something was missing. She went to the box by the bed and took out the garnet necklace and earrings Marilyn had left her. They looked perfect with the dress.

By the time Annabel arrived, the party was in full swing. Jake was still a single man about town and Annabel was soon introduced to a group of his friends who were of her own age.

She spotted Jackie and Barney at the far side of the room, sitting at a table with Walter and his wife. What a handsome couple they made: both so fair, Barney with his blue eyes and Jackie's so deep violet. Did she get them from Marilyn? Annabel had brown eyes. She must take after her father. So many questions but none she dared ask. After all, Jackie didn't need a sister in her life and might not welcome such a surprise. Annabel pushed these thoughts away. Jackie waved to her and Annabel waved back. It looked promising. Maybe she would get an opportunity for a proper conversation later. It might be a long time before another chance presented itself.

A tall, serious-looking man joined the group and Annabel was introduced. 'David Hall,' said her new friend, Sarah. 'Meet Annabel Lewis-Langley. She works with Jake and Barney, for her sins.'

Annabel shook hands with David and liked what she saw. She judged him to be about six foot two, in his early forties. He had wiry brown hair and brown eyes and a wide, smiling mouth.

'Jake's kept you a secret,' said David, admiration for Annabel evident in his eyes.

'I've only been there for three weeks,' she replied. 'I recently moved into the area from the south and I was very lucky to land a job almost straight away. Barney and Jake are lovely to work for.'

David Hall laughed. 'Well, you must have got them tamed. I've heard many a tale about those two.'

'And I don't tell tales out of school,' Annabel replied, smiling back at David.

He nodded his approval. 'Good girl. That's what I like to hear. Loyalty.' He paused. 'I wonder, would you like to dance?'

Annabel nodded, feeling suddenly shy. They joined the throng on the dance floor and the band struck up a slow waltz. Annabel hadn't danced with a man for years and hoped David couldn't feel the fast beat of her heart as he held her close.

When the dance was over, Jake announced the buffet supper and invited everyone to come along and enjoy it. David looked down at Annabel. 'Would you join me for supper?' Annabel agreed, hoping a glass of wine and some food would calm her nerves.

As they stood in the queue, they talked quietly together. Annabel learned that David was a very old friend of Jake's and he worked as a quantity surveyor in private practice in the city. He was unmarried and lived on his own in Copmanthorpe village. He continued to look at Annabel with undisguised admiration. Annabel flushed under his gaze. Unused to such attention, she felt a mixture of emotions. It was balm to her

lonely spirit to bask in David's admiration, but panic shot through her as he gently questioned her about herself. She had prepared a background to fill in the missing years in prison, a story about working in London and the south-west, but it was hard to deliver it and meet his eyes.

'So what brought you to Yorkshire?' David asked.

'I needed a change and I believe my ancestors came from around here,' she said.

'Oh, really.' David looked interested.

'Yes, well.' Annabel was alarmed. She'd said too much. She didn't want any connections being made. 'It was only vague hearsay but once I was here, I fell in love with the city and thought I'd like to stay. Make it my home,' she added.

David Hall looked delighted at this news and they continued their way in to supper.

Sitting at the table with Jackie and Barney, Walter was trying to identify some of the guests. He watched David and Annabel make their way to the buffet, their heads close together in conversation. Ellie followed his gaze. 'Who's that lovely girl?' she asked.

'Annabel, they call her. Don't know her surname. She's just started working for Barney and Jake, getting them out of the mess Genevieve made, by all accounts.'

'Annabel. What a lovely name.' Ellie leaned across the table and questioned Barney. 'Your new lady, what's her name?'

'Annabel Lewis-Langley,' said Barney. 'Jackie found her for me. She's a treasure.'

'Lewis-Langley,' mused Walter. 'Does that ring a bell somewhere?'

'Bells ring with you all the time, Dad,' said Jackie. 'It never means anything. Except you've got bells in your head.'

David and Annabel passed near to the table carrying their plates of food and wine. Barney waved them over.

'David. Annabel. Come and join us. There's plenty of room on our table. You can spread out here. Don't want to be cramped there with the hoi-polloi.'

David glanced questioningly at Annabel and she nodded. He was a little disappointed – he'd hoped to keep her to himself over supper – but Annabel looked eager and Barney was already clearing a space for them.

Jackie patted the seat beside her. 'This is lovely, Annabel. No noisy café, no customers to see to. We can have a proper chat for a change.' She smiled. 'I've been looking forward to meeting you properly. Life at the café is always so mad, there's just never any time.'

Annabel sipped her wine, trying to steady her nerves. 'I've been looking forward to getting to know you too,' she said. 'Everything's happened so quickly, getting the job and then finding my flat. It's been a busy time.' She laughed nervously. Now that her opportunity was here, how on earth was she going to grasp it? There were too many people: Walter, Ellie, David, Barney. Just sitting right beside Jackie was almost too much.

She took another sip of wine and, as she looked up, she saw Walter staring at her. She blushed under his gaze, looked away and tried to give all her attention to Jackie who was asking if she was settling in to her new flat.

'It's a slow process,' Annabel admitted. 'It will take time to make it my own but I'm very happy there.' She would love to ask Jackie to drop round, but how to explain one dilapidated deckchair for lounge furniture? 'I'd love you to come and see it when I've re-decorated,' she said. 'Give me a few weeks.'

'Great,' said Jackie, 'and you must come and visit us at Acaster Malbis, when you can manage it. Mind you, the season's in full swing and the evening bistro will be open again soon. I think I've found a new chef, so you may only find me at home on a Sunday.'

'I'm sure we'll manage to...'

Walter leaned across the table, interrupting them. 'Are they garnets?' he demanded.

Taken aback, Annabel fingered the heavy necklace. 'Er, yes.'

Walter stared hard at her. 'Bit old-fashioned for these days. Where did you get them from?'

'Walter!' Jackie and Ellie chimed together.

'Don't be so personal, Dad,' Jackie said, embarrassed at Walter's sharp tone.

'It's alright.' Annabel lifted her chin and met Walter's eyes. 'They were a gift from my family, long ago.'

'Family, eh?' Walter continued staring at Annabel. She felt as if he saw right through to her soul. 'Where do you come from then, lass?'

'Now Walter,' chided Ellie. 'Leave the young lady alone. She needs her supper, not listening to you with your twenty questions.' Ellie smiled encouragingly at Annabel. 'Don't mind him, love. He gets a bee in his bonnet...'

'And bats in his belfry,' added Jackie, smiling at Annabel. 'He likes to turn people inside out. I know how off-putting it is.' She turned to Walter and frowned at him. 'So if you'd like to get your supper, Dad, we'll get on with ours in peace, thank you.'

Ellie took the hint and hustled Walter off to the supper queue. When they were at a safe distance, she asked, 'What was all that about?'

'That jewellery. I'd know it anywhere and it's not hers.'

'How do you make that out, Walter?'

'Because I gave it to Marilyn over forty years ago. Saw it and the matching earrings in a jeweller's shop that used to be just off Kirkgate Market and I put a deposit on it. It took me two years of saving but I got it in the end and bought it for her.'

'So what? There could have been dozens of them.'

'No.' Walter was adamant. 'Hand-made, a one-off set. They had a certificate in the fancy case. So what's our Annabel doing with them? That's what I want to know.'

'I don't want to upset you, Walter, but perhaps Marilyn sold them,' ventured Ellie.

'Not her,' asserted Walter. 'To have and to hold, that should have been her motto. She never let nowt go, didn't Marilyn. No, there's a mystery here and I'm going to get to the bottom of it. Annabel Lewis-Langley? Where's she come from and what's she doing here? I'll find out, Ellie.'

'Maybe you will, Walter,' Ellie soothed, 'and maybe you won't. Maybe the jeweller wasn't straight with you. Tonight's a party, remember. We're here to enjoy ourselves, not solve riddles. Come on, let's get some supper before it's all gone. Forget about jewellery for now.'

'For now,' Walter growled, 'but I know what I know and I know I'm right.'

Ellie sighed and handed him a plate. 'Eat now and forever hold your peace.'

******

The early morning June sunshine streamed in through the bedroom windows. It was time to get up. Samson wanted his breakfast. He jumped lithely onto the bed and sat watching the sleeping Jackie and Barney for a few moments. He crept further up the bed and sat on Jackie's stomach, purring loudly. Jackie was fast asleep and did not respond. Samson moved up and tried patting her face gently with his paw. That usually did the trick. 'Get off, Barney, it's too early,' she muttered drowsily.

Samson moved over to Barney. He trod his paws on Barney's chest. That often worked. But Barney was in a deep sleep. Samson was hungry and was not giving up on his mission. It took a lot of swipes with his paws to bring Barney to wakefulness.

Feeling the gentle tapping on his nose, Barney rolled over, gathering Jackie into his arms. 'Playing games, are we?' he murmured. 'I'm game if you are.'

Samson dug his claws hard into Barney's back, making him yell out in pain.

'Samson! Bloody cat! Where the hell did you come from?'

Samson retreated to the end of the bed and regarded them inscrutably, meowing plaintively and kneading the quilt.

Jackie groaned and rubbed her eyes sleepily. 'What time is it?'

'Six o'clock,' groaned Barney, rubbing his back.

'He wants his breakfast,' said Jackie. 'I've been feeding him early lately, before doing the fruit and veg run for the café. He doesn't know it's Sunday, so he's come to see what's happened to us.'

'Since when did you stick up for Samson?' asked Barney, scowling at the cat.

'Absolutely never,' Jackie shuddered. 'He's a fiend incarnate but he's our fiend and if we want any peace today, one of us has to feed him. Now.' Jackie snuggled further down the bed and smiled invitingly up at Barney. 'But it is Sunday, only six o'clock. You can come back to bed and, who knows...'

Barney flung back the covers with alacrity. 'Come on, Samson, I'll give you a feast fit for a king. Just promise to stay away for at least three hours and leave us in peace.'

'Three hours!' Jackie burst out laughing. 'I thought we'd already had the Marathon.'

Barney grinned as he followed Samson to the door. 'Not here in York, we haven't, Mrs Anderson.'

******

That same Sunday morning, Ellie Breckenridge was getting ready for the farmers' market in York city centre. 'Those two trays there, Walter,' she directed. 'Oh, and there's two more still in the dairy. If you can put those in the van whilst you're out there, please.'

Walter picked up the trays of goat's and sheep's cheese and went to the door. 'But it's Sunday, Ellie,' he grumbled. 'You never go to the market on a Sunday.'

'Too good an opportunity to miss,' said Ellie, loading jars of jams and fruit curds onto a new tray. 'Every producer worth his or her salt will be there today. It's a big affair and I'm not missing out on it. Claygate Produce and Preserves could do really well there today. It's going to be a regular monthly affair; if we're lucky, people will come looking for us in the future.'

'Every month?' Walter contemplated this prospect mournfully. 'But Sunday's roast beef and Yorkshire pudding, Ellie, the highlight of the week. What are we going to do for lunch today if you're at this market affair?'

'Elvis's lunch is on the side there. Minced beef, biscuits and gravy. Give it to him about twelve o'clock.'

'What about me?' asked Walter.

'There's a cheese sandwich ready in the fridge. Help yourself.'

A cheese ... and he gets... Walter shook his head and went out. It was the pecking order; he knew it well enough and he was the last chick to get a leg on the perch these days.

When he had loaded everything up as Ellie had asked, he came back into the house and picked up the Sunday paper.

'It's a lovely morning, Walter,' said Ellie briskly. 'Why don't you take Elvis out and go and put the netting up over the new fruit canes? I got the poles last week. It shouldn't take you too long and we really need to keep the birds off everything now.'

No roast beef, no newspaper. It wasn't the Sunday Walter had been anticipating. Stuck at home with Elvis and a load of fruit canes to net. Thank you God. Thanks a lot. Try not to do me too many favours, will you?

Ellie smiled and kissed him goodbye. 'Think what you've got to look forward to. I might throw you a dry crust when I get back. It is Sunday after all.'

Walter wandered about the house disconsolately after she had gone. He tried sitting with the paper but Elvis was full of energy and bounded about the room with his toys, throwing and catching them, pouncing on them with fierce growls. When he got bored with this, he made a start on Walter's slippers, quietly nibbling the toes until his sharp little teeth connected with Walter's flesh.

Walter gave up. Whatever happened to 'they married and lived happily ever after'? He stared down at Elvis, now busy demolishing a furry elephant. 'S'pose it's me and thee then, lad,' he said glumly. 'Come on, let's go and get the netting and poles.

118

You need a walk and I need something to do.' He went outside, with Elvis running madly round him. 'She's gone off without me for the day,' he mused to the little dog. 'Not so long ago, we'd all have gone. Had a bit of fun while we were about it. But now? Have I turned back into a frog, do you think?'

Walter had made a large vegetable garden many years ago, when he came to Claygate. When Ellie joined him as his wife, they had spent a lot of time in the autumn planting fruit bushes and raspberry canes. Standing in the June sunshine, Walter realised Ellie was right. He needed to erect a stout fruit cage around this plot or the birds would get the lot.

He decided to make a job of it and discarded the thin poles Ellie had purchased. He had plenty of wood in his workshop and was soon engrossed in sorting out suitable timbers and carrying them down to the fruit garden. Elvis got plenty of exercise running to and fro with him but after several journeys he grew tired and flopped down under the shade of a gooseberry bush. Walter didn't think he would come to much harm, so left him to sleep whilst he made a last trip to his workshop.

Time slipped quickly by as Walter gathered together his tools. He loaded them into a barrow and set off for the fruit garden. He made his way slowly down the sharply sloping field, concentrating on avoiding protruding rocks and large tussocks of grass. As he drew near to the flatter ground where they had made the fruit garden, he heard Elvis wailing loudly.

Bloody Elvis. What's up now? Walter wondered. Couldn't leave that darned dog for five minutes... Scared of sheep, scared of goats, doesn't like hens. He's probably seen his own shadow and got scared. I told Ellie he'd be useless and now, here we are saddled with him, the great lump. *And* he gets best mince and gravy.

Leaving his barrow, Walter went to investigate. He had left a large roll of garden netting beside the timbers he had collected for the framework. Elvis must have only had a short nap, woken up and found the netting irresistible. He'd had huge fun dragging it away from the timbers and unravelling it all,

119

and in the process got caught up in it and rolled over and over in his panic to escape. When he saw Walter approaching, Elvis wailed loudly and struggled to get out of the netting, getting even more tangled up in it.

Whichever way Walter pulled, Elvis seemed to become more tightly bound up. He struggled and howled plaintively. Walter knew there was nothing for it. There was only one way Elvis would be extracted from that lot. He pulled his knife from his pocket and began to cut away at the netting. It was slow work and Elvis would not keep still. Walter was frightened of cutting him; it wouldn't be Elvis in the doghouse if he did that.

Eventually he cut away enough of the netting to slide Elvis out. The little dog bounded into his arms, trembling and licking Walter's face. Walter held him away and looked him in the eye. 'Now, I'm not going to shout at you, Elvis,' he said carefully, 'but that was a very naughty thing to do. That was brand new netting and now we have none, so the job can't get finished. Do not do anything like that again.'

Walter had been very careful to use soft tones, only too aware what would happen if he shouted at Elvis. But it made no difference. Elvis snuggled into Walter and peed thankfully down his shirt.

With Elvis now safely tied up and dozing in the sunshine, Walter worked on until lunchtime, hammering in posts for the new fruit cage. Feeling hungry and thirsty, he untied Elvis and they made their way back up to the farmhouse. It was later than Walter realised and he hastily made preparations for his and Elvis's lunch. As he was mixing the rich brown gravy into the mince and biscuits as Ellie had instructed, Walter's stomach rolled. It looked and smelled so delicious. Lucky old Elvis and all he had to look forward to was a cheese sandwich. Or did he?

Walter looked down at Elvis drooling at his feet and yapping impatiently. 'Time you had a change of flavours, young Elvis,' Walter said and dived into the fridge for his cheese sandwich. Quickly he sliced it into small squares and put it down on the floor for the little dog. Taking a spoon from the drawer, Walter turned the meat and gravy out into a clean bowl, took it to the kitchen table and started eating. In a few minutes it was gone. Walter smacked his lips in satisfaction and looked pityingly at Elvis. 'Yes, it was grand, lad,' he told him. 'You would have loved it. But see here, young fella, I earned it. I did all the work this morning and what did you do? Get caught up in a load of netting that was nowt to do with you in the first place. Let that be a lesson to you. If you work, you eat. If not, well, there you are. It's a cheese sandwich.'

There was a knock at the door. 'Anyone home?' Jackie called out.

Walter got up hastily, took his dish over to the sink and ran water into it. 'In here, love, come on in.'

Jackie walked into the kitchen, followed by Barney. She kissed her father warmly. 'Hi Dad. Home alone?'

'Not entirely,' Walter said drily. 'I've got Elvis looking after me.'

'Where's Ellie?' asked Barney.

Walter told them about the new farmers' market and Ellie's determination to make the most of it.

'Wow, she's really got her teeth into this smallholding lark, hasn't she?' whistled Barney admiringly.

'Aye, too much,' grumbled Walter. 'She left me a cheese sandwich for my lunch. Imagine that, and Sunday too.'

'It's only once a month,' soothed Jackie. 'Come over to us. We might spare you an old bone or two. That's if Elvis doesn't get there first.' She picked Elvis up and held him close. He licked her face and snuggled in.

'Careful,' warned Walter. 'He's a reputation to maintain has that one.'

'What's that then?' asked Barney.

'No bladder control.'

Jackie hastily put Elvis back on the floor and took a seat at the kitchen table. Walter went to put the kettle on.

'It was a good night last night,' he said.

'Yeah, Jake really went to town for his fortieth,' agreed

Barney. 'It got a bit rowdy with a few of his mates later, I gather. I hope he's settled down a bit by the time he reaches fifty. I can't stand the pace.'

Jackie ruffled his blond hair. 'Forty-one and knackered. What have I taken on?'

'Speaking of taking on,' Walter seized his opportunity, 'that new lass of yours, that Annabel. Do you know much about her?'

Barney shrugged. 'Not a lot really. She came with good references from her previous employers, which was what I really needed to know about. I can't go prying into her personal life. Haven't had much opportunity up to now, anyway, we've been too busy. Why do you ask, Walter?'

Walter kept his back to them and busied himself getting out the china cups and saucers Ellie liked to use. He didn't want to cause any alarm and he didn't have anything tangible yet, other than those garnets. If Barney didn't have any information, he would have to do some digging himself.

He brought the tea to the table. 'I'm just being nosey Barney, that's all,' he said at last. 'New face on the scene. You know me, I like to know the far end of the donkey's tail. She seems an OK lass,' he ventured.

'She's great,' Barney enthused. 'Super efficient and hardworking and is getting us all organised. She's a gift from heaven.'

'Gift from me, more like,' Jackie laughed. 'I found her for you. But you're right, she's a lovely girl. There's something about her. I don't know what it is. She reminds me of someone but I can't put my finger on it.'

Walter opened his mouth and quickly closed it again. That was it. She was like someone, someone they knew – or had known. But he couldn't put his finger on it either. Before he had time to ponder further, Jackie jumped in with her latest news. 'I've found a new chef, Dad, at last.'

'Well, thank God for that,' said Walter. 'Does that mean I can have a lie-in tomorrow morning?'

'No,' Jackie said sweetly. 'It means you get up early, get on that old boneshaker of yours and head down to Café Paradise as usual.'

'But if you've got a new chef...' Walter protested.

'Henri will need time to find his way around the kitchen and construct the new menus for the evening bistro. He's a fine chef but I don't want to just throw him in at the deep end. I want to keep him long term, ease him in gently for now.'

'Henri?' Walter asked suspiciously.

Jackie was tranquil. 'Yes, Henri. French for Henry. He's from south-west France and very, very French.'

An anguished cry died in Walter's throat. He looked appealingly at Barney. Barney shook his head. 'Not my fight, Walter. I stick to what I know.'

'A Frenchy!'

'Oh, come on, Dad. This is 2013 and you know very well I want Café Paradise to have a more international flavour. That's what the evening bistro is all about.'

'So where do I come into all this?' he demanded. 'Because if you think I'm spending my life playing second fiddle to Moosieur Henry and carving up frogs' legs and snails' heads, or whatever...'

'I just want you to stay on for the next couple of weeks, that's all,' Jackie said mildly, fixing him with her violet eyes. 'Just be an assistant and show him the ropes until he finds his feet. Then, when he's up and running, you can retire again.'

'Aye, I've heard that one before an' all,' said Walter morosely. 'We all know these Frenchies. Throw a tantrum if the béchamel doesn't turn out right and hurl pans about. Then they stalk out and won't come back unless you triple their wages. I bet I'll be back frying sausages in Café Paradise before you can say knife. Why couldn't you choose a good Yorkshireman, that's what I want to know?'

Jackie finished her tea and got up. She kissed the top of Walter's head and smiled at him. 'Always the dinosaur, Dad. Wait 'til you meet Henri, you'll love him.'

'Take her away, Barney,' groaned Walter. 'My Sunday was

bad enough and now I have to get my head around Henri for the morning.'

Barney patted Walter consolingly on the shoulder. 'It won't be nearly as bad as you think, Walter,' he said and shepherded Jackie to the door.

'That's all you know, lad,' Walter said to himself as they departed. 'Trouble is, it usually is – and a damned sight worse as well.'

CHAPTER 24

After Jake's party, Annabel became friends with Sarah Woods and some of the group that had been at The Golden Lion Hotel that night. She went out with David Hall a few times and really liked him, but found him a bit overwhelming. David seemed to have instantly made up his mind about her and wanted to monopolise her company and Annabel was not sure she was ready for a serious relationship yet.

In the lovely summer evenings after work, she was happy to explore the city and surrounding areas, sometimes with David and often with Sarah. Sarah was a nurse at the city's teaching hospital on Wigginton Road. She specialised in the care of the elderly and was always interesting to listen to as she talked of the varied lives her patients had led and her compassion for them in their infirmity shone through.

Annabel was growing in confidence now that she had a steady job and a small group of friends, but the habits of prison life were not easy to shake off. She was always wary when meeting new people and careful in everything she said. She had constructed a background for herself but tried not to get into conversations about the past, preferring to talk of the present and future hopes and plans.

In the course of her conversations with Sarah, she had confided her dream of one day having her own interior design business. On one of their evening rambles around the city, Sarah brought along the *York Herald* and showed Annabel an advertisement. The York Trades Council was holding an evening for prospective new members. Anyone interested in starting their own business, or looking for grants towards starting up, was welcome to come along and meet existing members for support, advice and information about doing business in York.

'What do you think about that?' Sarah asked eagerly.

'I think it sounds a great organisation but why are you showing it to me?'

'Because you'd like to start your own business, that's why. Looks like a golden opportunity,' said her friend.

Annabel wasn't sure. Yes, she wanted to have her own business one day but she was a long way from being in a position to do that yet.

Seeing her hesitate, Sarah tried again. 'You've nothing to lose and everything to gain. You could make useful contacts, maybe find out about training courses for the self-employed, that kind of thing.' She consulted the advert again. 'Yes, see, even if you're only thinking about starting your own business, you're welcome. So why not give it a go?'

'Alright,' Annabel agreed. 'I'll go. I've got the dream, a shoe-box of a flat, no capital and no backer, but hey, empires were built on vision.'

'Nothing ventured,' Sarah said confidently.

Briefly, Annabel thought of Marilyn. Her mother had come from nothing and made her way in this city. Maybe she could too.

******

The White Hart Hotel was a handsome, four-storeyed building nestling in a quiet square in the shadow of York Minster. On a warm Friday evening in late June, Annabel made her way up the steps of the smart hotel and into the plush foyer. A notice board directed her up the stairs to the Green Room and, as she made her way, she could hear music and voices. She felt nervous: how would she get on in a room full of strangers? She smiled to herself. It couldn't be any worse than moving prisons and having to get to know a whole new set of women very quickly and she'd done that a few times. She threw her head back and fixed a bright smile on her face, drawing her thin shawl around her shoulders.

Tom Young, President of the Trades Council, was at the door to greet her. Annabel had spoken briefly to his secretary to book a ticket for the evening. She gave her name and looked up at the most handsome man she had ever seen. For a moment, she was bereft of speech. A dinner suit set off his lean, muscular frame to perfection. Melting brown eyes glowed in a tanned face. This man belonged on a Hollywood film set.

Tom shook her hand and held on to it with both of his. He smiled warmly. 'Miss Lewis-Langley, you are very welcome.'

'Annabel, please,' she managed to say.

'Annabel,' Tom purred. 'A beautiful name. I'm surprised our paths haven't crossed before. Are you in business in the city?'

'Not yet,' Annabel replied, mesmerised. 'I haven't been in York very long. I thought I would come along tonight, see what the organisation was about and explore the possibilities for a new business in York.' She tried to sound relaxed and confident, as if she did this every day.

'Well, as President of the Trades Council, I'm your man,' said Tom. He stopped a passing waiter and presented Annabel with a glass of champagne. 'I can be with you in about ten minutes and we can continue our conversation. If you'd like to go in, look at the stalls and maybe talk to some of our existing members, I'll join you shortly.'

Annabel moved into the crowded Green Room, tingling with anticipation. It was a large function room, with ornate plasterwork covering the ceiling. Huge chandeliers cast circular patterns on the plush green carpet. Annabel sipped the champagne and drifted past the stalls set out around the room. They represented trades and services of every description: the Whyte Knight Fund, Finance Yorkshire, Connect Yorkshire, Yorkshire Association of Business Angels. There seemed to be a lot of organisations that could offer financial help and training for new businesses. Annabel felt more optimistic. Maybe her dreams would become reality.

Tom Young pushed his way through the chattering crowds, bringing fresh champagne. He drew Annabel to a small sofa and they sat down, clinking glasses in a toast. 'To the beautiful Miss Lewis-Langley,' Tom said solemnly, 'and to the Trades Council, which is fortunate enough to enjoy her company tonight.'

Annabel laughed. She took refuge in the champagne, furious with herself for blushing like a schoolgirl. Tom relaxed into the sofa and looked at her with interest. 'So,' he began, 'tell me about yourself, Annabel. What brought you to our city?'

Annabel had decided to play down the ancestry theme in her decision to come to York. Luckily, she did not look at all like Jackie, but she did not want to risk anyone making a connection between them. Sudden revelations might prove too shocking for Jackie to handle and that was the last thing Annabel wanted. Instead, she opted for the notion of family holidays in the area when she was a child.

'We loved exploring the area and the Yorkshire Dales and I knew that I wanted to return one day. Now seems an ideal time,' she said. 'I've no family ties, I can go where I want and what better place than beautiful York?'

'There is no better place,' agreed Tom. 'Tell me, are you working here or just exploring the area?'

'I have a job with Anderson and Cranton, Solicitors,' said Annabel. 'I've only been there a short while, working as an administrator. They're lovely people and I'm enjoying it, but I don't want to do it forever.'

An expression Annabel found hard to read crossed Tom's face. There was a pause and then he said smoothly, 'Anderson and Cranton, eh? The new boys off Stonegate. Yes, I know them slightly. So, you work there. Interesting.'

Annabel wasn't sure it was interesting, but if Tom Young wanted to think so, that was fine by her.

Suddenly he leaned closer to her, a smile playing around his mouth. 'How about dinner soon, Annabel? I know a lovely restaurant down by the river. We could dine on the balcony and watch the boats go by in the evening sunshine. Is that tempting enough? Please say yes. I'd love to get to know you and talk about your business ideas. Not all evening, of course. Can't have all work and no play. There's time for a little fun, too.' He ran his hand along the back of the sofa and slowly stroked the fabric.

Mr Hollywood dreamboat was actually asking her for a date! Gripping her champagne glass tightly, Annabel tried to keep a lid on her excitement. 'That sounds lovely, Tom,' she said coolly. 'I'll look forward to it.'

Annabel left The White Hart some time later, with armfuls of leaflets for every organisation involved in business start-ups in York. She had a lot to think about, not least a date with Tom Young.

CHAPTER 25

Kate had been modelling for the life class at the College of Art for a month. To her relief, she was not required to pose entirely without clothes. On the first evening, she felt sick with dread as she mounted the stone steps to Studio Four. She'd brought a robe with her, as Frederick Rawlings had suggested, and slipped into it behind the screen discreetly placed near to the chaise longue where she was to pose.

When she was ready, she stood for a few moments, forcing herself to breathe deeply to calm herself down. All she had to do was step round the screen, drop her robe and drape herself tastefully on the chaise longue. But all the deep breathing in the world would not still her racing heart and Kate could not delay any longer. Jerkily, she took the few steps and almost fell onto the sofa, looking anywhere but at Frederick as he bustled about arranging the canvasses for the students.

The moment Kate appeared, he stopped and stared at her.

Oh God, I bet I won't do, Kate thought dismally. He's going to tell me to get dressed and push off, I just know it. I'm not curvy enough.

'Oh, no,' Frederick breathed softly. 'This will never do.' His chin sank slowly to his chest as he regarded Kate.

Kate reached for her robe, embarrassed. This was a huge mistake. Why ever had she come here?

'I was right,' Frederick pronounced. 'You are perfect in every detail, oh Goddess Aphrodite. You are pure and unsullied maidenhood. You cannot be exposed to the lascivious eyes of men. I was right. You must be draped!' He rushed off to the far side of the studio and returned with a length of purple satin. 'You must always wear this, Aphrodite. I will make you garlands, bring you sweet wine, rich grapes...'

As the words tumbled out, he wrapped Kate in the purple cloth, fashioning a Grecian-style gown. He stood back to admire his work. 'Beautiful Aphrodite,' he murmured to himself. 'Quite beautiful. So perfect.' He gestured to the chaise longue and Kate reclined on to it. Frederick was ecstatic. 'The canvas ... I must...'

Kate was so relieved to be clothed, even if it was as Goddess Aphrodite, she was able to keep her pose as the students came in. Frederick continued to apply paint feverishly to the canvas and waved the students away as they tried to view his work. One by one, they set up their easels and started work. Some students opted for drawing, some worked in oils.

Kate was surprised at how quiet they were. They all wore the same intense expression as Frederick, the only difference being that Frederick continually muttered to himself as he painted, looking up frequently and pausing with wonder on his face, before bending again to his labours.

Over the course of the following three weeks Frederick dressed Kate in all colours but always in Grecian dress; sometimes she wore garlands in her hair, sometimes she held a lamp, sometimes an urn. Kate felt foolish and uncomfortable, but it seemed Frederick could never paint her enough times. The students were growing restless. They had signed up for life classes but Frederick would not allow Kate to step out of the Greek goddess role he had assigned to her.

Kate found his silent adoration very spooky. He was very possessive. Eventually he employed another more experienced model for the students, an older, buxom lady named Michelle. The students were happy again and Frederick returned to his obsessive painting of Kate. He did not allow her to go to the coffee bar with the students during the evening break time, insisting she remain in pose for him. Kate was not sure how long she could continue with these classes. Being with Frederick was getting claustrophobic.

CHAPTER 26

Walter Breckenridge left the Claygate smallholding early on Monday morning. He was used to cycling the few miles into the city centre and timed his journey to avoid the rush hour. York in June is a busy place with residents going to work and visitors up early, keen to make the most of their stay.

Unusually, he was in a sunny mood. After three weeks of the strict diet, Ellie was satisfied with Walter's improved physique and had eased up on her draconian regime. He'd had poached eggs and grilled bacon this morning and, joy of joys, some toast and marmalade. Even Elvis had behaved like a half-sensible dog and managed not to pee on the floor at the sight of him.

Walter needed all his wits as he made his way into the city. Cars were parked in an unbroken line almost to Bootham Bar. He cycled slowly, enjoying the morning sunshine. Suddenly an enormous Alsatian dog lunged at him from the open window of one of the parked cars, baring its strong white teeth and barking fiercely. Walter fell off his bike in fright and narrowly escaped being run down by the car behind him. Shakily, he picked up his bike and wheeled it onto the pavement. The handlebars and one of the pedals were bent. 'Bloody dogs, bloody cars,' he shouted and shook his fist in the direction of the dog, who was still watching him and growling.

Walter turned away and wheeled his bike through the Museum Gardens and on to Café Paradise on Castlegate.

Inside, Jackie was showing around her new chef, Henri Beaupariant. Henri's olive skin and merry brown eyes glowed against his traditional chef's whites and the pleated white chef's toque which confined his mass of curly brown hair.

Henri was delighted with the modern café and new kitchen. He was exclaiming over the spacious preparation areas and separate room for the deep sinks and dishwashers when Walter made his way in from the back door.

'And how am I going to get home tonight with my bike in that state?' he said to no one in particular. 'Bloody Alsatians. They shouldn't be allowed to stick their heads out of car windows. Look what happens.'

'Dad,' Jackie said pointedly. 'I'm showing Henri round the café and kitchen. Shall I introduce you?'

Walter looked up from studying his broken pedal. 'Oh. Henri, is it?' He offered an oily hand to the Frenchman. Henri backed off.

Jackie scowled. 'Dad!'

'What?' Walter looked at her, puzzled.

She nodded to his hands. 'What have you been doing?'

'Getting knocked off my bike, mangling my handlebars and pedal, that's all. A marauding Alsatian,' he added in explanation. 'Anyway, let's not worry about that. Daresay I've got nine lives, like that cat of yours.' Walter rubbed his dirty hand down his trousers and offered it again to Henri. 'How do Henry, pleased to meet you. I'm Walter, your sidekick, for now.'

Henri shook Walter's hand, looking bemused. 'Sidekick? We play a game?'

Walter rolled his eyes. 'Here we go.' He looked accusingly at Jackie. 'You never said he couldn't speak the lingo. I suppose I'm going to have to explain everything to him.'

'Don't start, Dad. His English is very good. You can't expect him to know colloquial words.'

'Colloq...' Walter rubbed his nose, transferring some of the oil to his face. 'Is that fancy for local?'

'Yes. Now go and get cleaned up and changed and maybe we can get some work done around here today.'

Walter trailed off to the staff cloakroom, still talking to himself. 'She should have stuck to a Yorkshireman. I bet that

Brian Turner off the telly could have found her any amount of good lads. And the size of his hat. Wonder what he's got under there?'

******

From the off, Jackie knew it was going to be a difficult day. Walter was in one of his querulous moods and disposed to argue with his own shadow. He didn't like the idea of carrot batons or julienne; what was wrong with plain old slicing? A carrot was a carrot, wasn't it?

Kate was down in the dumps; she hardly ever heard from Stan in Rome and imagined him in the arms of every *signorina* he met.

Worst of all, Genevieve was driving her round the bend. Whenever there was a lull and she could escape from the kitchen, she hung around the café, watching Louise and Kate as they went about their duties. 'I could do that,' she asserted to Jackie. 'I've watched them for weeks now and I know how it's done. I just need a chance. Pleeease, Jackie,' she wheedled. 'Let me try. I won't mess it up, I promise. It's so easy.'

Jackie looked at Genevieve. Easy it was not. Kate and Louise made their work *look* easy, but that only came with practice. And the idea of allowing Genevieve to practise on her customers filled her with horror.

'And it's such a ducky apron,' enthused Genevieve. 'So smart. I'd love to wear one and whizz about the tables.'

'If it's the apron you want...'

'No.' Genevieve looked serious. 'It's the *responsibility*. Taking the order correctly and making sure the right meal gets to the right person. It's a proper job. I've never had a proper job,' she said wistfully. 'I have tried. I was at Daddy's office for three months, but...' Genevieve looked puzzled. 'I never quite got the hang of it there.'

'Well, there you are then,' Jackie said firmly. 'You only had to make the coffee and do the filing.'

'This is different,' Genevieve insisted. 'Look, I've been practising.' She produced a small notebook from her pocket and showed it to Jackie. 'When Kate or Louise take an order, I've been copying them and writing it all down. And getting it right.' Genevieve was lit with enthusiasm. 'I just need to practise the other bit now.'

'The other bit?' Jackie felt Genevieve was cutting the ground from under her feet.

'Bringing it from the kitchen and giving it to the customer! I know, you could pretend to be a customer and I could serve you.'

What planet was this girl on? Carefully, Jackie said, 'I don't know whether you've noticed, Genevieve, but I have a café full of customers and more waiting to be served. I don't have time to play waitresses.'

'But I'll never have a proper job if no one will let me do anything.'

'Genevieve, you've been given proper jobs in the past and you haven't exactly got a wonderful track record of success, have you? I want to keep my customers.'

'Pleeease, Jackie, just one chance,' Genevieve pleaded.

The longing in Genevieve's green eyes touched Jackie. Maybe this was something Genevieve *could* do. 'Tell you what, Gen. Go and tidy yourself up, tie your hair back and get a uniform on and then try shadowing Kate.'

'Oh, great!' Genevieve hugged Jackie. 'Thank you.'

'*Don't do anything,*' she warned. 'Just shadow her and watch what she does. And don't get in the way.'

'I will, I mean I won't.' Genevieve was already rushing to the staffroom.

'What have I done?' Jackie asked herself. A bag of monkeys let loose in the café might do less damage. Only time would tell.

*****

Genevieve looked very striking in the waitress's uniform. The black dress hugged her slender figure and contrasted with her long red hair, which she'd fastened back in a stylish ponytail threaded with a black ribbon. Her green eyes sparkled as she followed at Kate's heels, her smile very reminiscent of Barney's. Jackie's heart softened. Genevieve might be brainless but there was no harm in her. Perhaps, finally, she might find a job she was good at and make a success of it. Jackie hoped so. And success with Genevieve equalled mega-brownie points with Barney.

Imagining herself wallowing in the heated baths of Bishopthorpe Hall Spa, followed by a gentle massage, Jackie did not notice David Hall. He waved in her face to attract her attention. She jumped sharply back to reality.

'I don't know where you were, but I wish I'd been there with you,' he said. 'You have the biggest smile on your face.'

'Bishopthorpe Hall Spa,' she replied. 'Enjoying the hot baths and a massage.'

David wrinkled his nose. 'Girlie stuff. Give me a flowing trout river and a rod any day. Now that's *my* idea of happiness. Except this time of year, when it's cricket.'

Jackie laughed. 'Each to his own. How's things, David? Have you seen much of Annabel?'

David looked downcast. 'Not as much as I would like. She's keeping me at a distance. I'm not sure that she wants to get involved, so I think I'm solo again. Anyway, I know one thing. I'm starving hungry and I need coffee and lunch, so what better place to come to.'

Now here was an opportunity. David was a friend, maybe he wouldn't mind Genevieve practising on him. He was a real customer and maybe she would get it right.

'Yeah, that's fine,' David agreed. 'What could be nicer than to be served by the beautiful Genevieve? I'm glad I came.' He made his way to a table and Jackie called her sister-in-law over.

'Here's your chance,' she told her. 'You know David, don't you?'

'Not really,' Genevieve said doubtfully, looking at him.

'He's a friend of Barney's. Not that that matters. But as he's a friend, I thought it would be a good idea for you to practise on him. Now concentrate, Gen. Go and take his order then deliver it to Henri in the kitchen. OK?'

'Oh, a real customer and I'm a real waitress!' Genevieve looked as if she'd just won the lottery.

'Just concentrate, Genevieve,' Jackie repeated. 'Take his order and take it slowly. That way, you've a chance of getting it right.'

Notepad in hand, Genevieve made her way to David's table. 'Hi David,' she said. 'And what can we get you today?' She had been listening carefully to Kate.

David smiled. The usually bubbly Genevieve looked so serious. 'I think I would like the cassoulet and a cafetiere for one, please.'

Genevieve's pen hung over her notepad. Her fine, white brow wrinkled. 'Cassoulet,' she echoed David doubtfully. 'Is that on the menu?'

David showed her and Genevieve copied it down. 'What is it?' she whispered.

'French casserole,' he said succinctly.

'Oh.' Genevieve considered this and added, 'There's a new chef. Henri. Do you think...?'

David nodded. 'Bound to be. Hope it comes with lots of crusty bread. I'm starving.'

'Why can't he just call it casserole?'

'Because he's French.'

'Is that cafetiere thing...?'

'Yes, it's a pot of coffee.'

Genevieve looked a lot happier. 'There's a lot more to waitressing than you think,' she said, writing busily on her pad. A thought struck her and she looked anxiously at David. 'It's not all going to be in French, is it? I'll never do it if it is. I couldn't learn it at school, no matter how hard Mamzelle tried with me. I'll never manage a French menu.' She looked so crestfallen, David felt sorry for her.

He put his hand out to comfort her. 'It's all right, Genevieve. There's only one or two dishes in French, the rest are all English. Listen, why don't you go and give your order to Henri and bring us both a cup of coffee and we can have a little talk about all this.'

'That caff ... caff...'

'Tell you what, you order lunch and I'll get the coffee.'

Genevieve trotted off to the kitchen and, after clearing it with Jackie, David brought the coffee back to the table. Soon Genevieve was back and sitting opposite David, looking more cheery.

'I like Henri,' she said. 'He didn't get cross, even though he couldn't read my spelling of that cassoulet thing. He wrote it down for me and said I was his *petite choux*. Wonder what he meant?'

David laughed at Genevieve's puzzlement. 'You are his little cabbage.'

'I don't look like a cabbage. Do I? Why does he think I look like a cabbage?'

'You don't, not a bit.' In fact, now he came to think about it, Genevieve was beautiful with her green eyes and powdering of freckles. 'It's just a French term of endearment. Like we would say "my lovely", or "my dear".' David stirred sugar into his coffee. 'About this waitressing, Genevieve.'

'You didn't tell Jackie I got it wrong, did you? Oh David, say you didn't. She won't let me try again if you did. You're my sort of...'

'Guinea pig?' David supplied.

'I didn't mean you look like a guinea pig?'

Feeling they were getting away from the point, David pressed on. 'As I am your guinea pig, I'd just like to give you a piece of advice to help you in this new venture of yours.'

Genevieve gazed at him anxiously. David was reminded of a devoted spaniel he once owned.

'Do your homework. In the morning, go over the menu

with Henri and if there are French dishes, which there are bound to be, don't be afraid to ask him about them. Ten to one, some of your customers will want to know too and you could explain to them. Same with Jackie's coffee counter. Check what coffees and cakes she has on the go.' He nodded solemnly at her. 'Knowledge is power, Genevieve. When you know, you can do.'

She mouthed his words slowly to herself. 'Knowledge is power ... ask Henri, ask Jackie...'

'And last of all,' David said boldly, 'how about coming out with me on Sunday? There's a cricket match over at Upper Poppleton. I'll bring a picnic and some wine, we can sit out in the sunshine and watch the match. How does that sound?'

Genevieve beamed at him. She didn't know the first thing about cricket, but a picnic and wine sounded good. She nodded. 'Yes, please. Although you might have to explain a bit about cricket. I've never been to a match before.'

'It will be a pleasure,' said David.

CHAPTER 27

That afternoon, Annabel made her way to Café Paradise for a late lunch. She had been busy in the office and lost track of the time. It was nearly three o'clock before she stepped out of Little Stonegate.

Her mouth watered when she saw cassoulet on the menu and she placed her order with Kate. She was lucky, there was just enough left for her.

Walter pricked his ears up when he heard Annabel was in the café. This might be a good opportunity to renew their acquaintance and learn more about her. He made sure Henri could manage on his own for half an hour and cautiously looked out on the café. He was in luck: Louise was at the coffee counter, which meant Jackie was in her office or, with more luck, out altogether.

Annabel was flicking through the pages of a magazine and looked up in surprise as Walter sat down opposite. She smiled uncertainly at him.

'It's Annabel, isn't it?' Walter began. Annabel nodded. 'Aye, I thought it was. I'm Walter, Jackie's Dad. We met at Jake's party, do you remember?'

'Yeah, I think so.' A wariness came into Annabel's eyes.

Walter tried for affable. 'You're quite a regular here now, aren't you lass? Nearly part of the furniture, even though you haven't been here long.'

'It's a lovely café and very welcoming.'

'Aye, we're all very friendly. Quite a little family, all in all.' Walter looked directly at her. 'Have you any family, Annabel?'

he asked.

Annabel flushed under his steady gaze. 'No. My parents are dead, I believe, and I was an only child. And as I'm not married, I can please myself.'

'You believe your parents are dead? Don't you know?' Walter's tone was sharp and Annabel bridled.

'I was adopted at birth, Walter. It didn't work out and so I grew up in a children's home.' She shrugged. 'It was alright.'

'Where were you born, lass?' Walter asked.

'You ask a lot of questions, Walter?'

'I'm just interested lass. You're friendly with my daughter and work for my son-in-law. You spend a lot of time in here. As I say, you're almost family.' He regarded her steadily, watching for her reaction.

There was none. Annabel was used to keeping her emotions hidden under a blank expression. 'That's a very nice thought, Walter,' she said.

'Have you ever looked for your family?' he asked. There, he'd struck a chord with that one. Briefly, there was pain in Annabel's eyes. She looked away and when she turned back to him, she had herself under control.

'I tried, but I was too late. My mother died some time ago and my father ... I dont know.' She shrugged her shoulders. 'I'm over it now, getting on with my life.'

'Settling in York,' Walter said reflectively. 'Long term?'

'I hope so,' Annabel said evenly. 'Is that alright with you?'

'It's alright with me, lass. It's you that has to make a life for yourself. But there's just one thing I can't work out. Those garnets you had on at Jake's party. You said they were your family's. But if you didn't know your mother, nor your father, how come you've got them now?'

'You want to know a lot, don't you?' A faint flush stained Annabel's cheeks. Walter knew he was on to something. She was rattled. He waited. 'When my mother placed me for adoption, she left the jewellery with the adoption agency to give to my adoptive parents. They were passed to the children's home, to be given to me when I left at sixteen. There,' Annabel finished. 'I don't know why you're so interested, but I'd like you to keep that information to yourself, please. It's the only bit of my mother I have and...'

'She sounds a good woman,' Walter reflected. 'She cared about you. What was her...?'

Kate arrived with the cassoulet and was putting it down in front of Annabel as Jackie walked back into the café. She frowned when she saw Walter sitting with Annabel. 'I hope you haven't left Henri on his own, Dad. It's only his first day.'

'He's fine,' Walter said breezily. 'I think he was glad to get me out of his way for a while. I've just been getting to know your friend here a bit better.'

Looking at Annabel's flushed face, Jackie wondered what Walter had been saying to her. 'I think you should leave her to enjoy her lunch in peace,' she said firmly and nodded towards the kitchen. 'I'm sure Henri will need you by now.'

Reluctantly, Walter took the hint and got up. He'd been so near to asking her mother's name. If he could have had another five minutes… If he tried again, she would be on her guard, probably have a ready-made tale to give him. But Walter knew it wouldn't be the truth.

CHAPTER 28

Tom Young slipped a twenty-pound note to the waiter at the Riverside Restaurant. The young man nodded. The best table overlooking the river had been booked and they were not to be disturbed. He led Tom to the table placed in a sheltered spot with a view of the river below. Cabin cruisers and tourist boats passed slowly beneath them, swans bobbing gracefully up and down in their wake. 'Perfect,' Tom said in satisfaction. 'I'm sure my guest will be here soon.'

He was right. A few minutes later, Annabel was conducted across the room, looking striking in a sleeveless cream dress that showed off her summer-tanned skin. Tom rose to greet her, kissing her lightly on the cheek. 'Stunning, my dear,' he murmured, helping her to her seat.

Annabel flushed with pleasure. Since leaving the prison, she had tried hard to update her style and wardrobe. David Hall's admiration, and now Tom's, increased her self-confidence and made all the effort and expense worthwhile.

The waiter brought champagne and expertly poured two glasses before melting discreetly away.

Tom raised his glass in a toast. 'To a beautiful lady.' He set his glass down carefully. 'I hope you don't mind,' he continued. 'I took the liberty of ordering in advance from their special menu, entitled The Romance of Midsummer Night.' He smiled warmly at Annabel. 'It seemed appropriate.'

Life did not get much better, Annabel thought. The perfect setting, the perfect man. Her heart turned over as his brown eyes met hers.

It was a very romantic dinner. A light soup, tagliatelle, followed by a triumph of a dessert: chocolate hearts with raspberries and cream, with fine wines accompanying every course. Tom was an interesting companion. He said little about himself, talking instead about the different characters involved with the Trades Council.

As the meal progressed, he questioned Annabel gently about her work at Anderson and Cranton and her hopes for her own business. He was interested in her ideas for opening an interior design gallery and promised to put her in touch with people he knew who might help her realise her dream.

Afterwards, when Annabel looked back on that evening, she was amazed at how much of herself she had revealed. She, who was always so careful to guard her tongue, talked freely of her childhood, the failed adoption and life in the children's home in London. She was not sure whether it was the champagne and wine, or Tom's skilful questioning, or her infatuation with him that had led her to such personal disclosures.

Late that night he saw her home in a taxi and walked her to her door, kissing her gently on the mouth. She returned his kisses and invited him in for a nightcap. He glanced at the waiting taxi and shook his head regretfully. She was too distracting and he had to be up early the next morning for a shooting party some distance away. He promised to see her again soon and, kissing her goodnight, took his leave.

Floating on air, Annabel let herself into her flat. Midsummer night had been the best night of her life.

*****

Early on Saturday morning, Tom Young telephoned Matt Carstairs, a private detective who owed him a big favour. 'Her name is Annabel Lewis-Langley,' he said and gave the background details he had winkled out of Annabel the previous evening. 'There's a mystery there and I want you to find out about it. She told me a lot about herself but it doesn't all ring true. Do some digging, Matt, and get back to me as soon as. OK?'

When the details were settled between them, Tom rang off. He gazed unseeingly at the phone for a long while, a grim smile playing about his lips.

CHAPTER 29

David Hall got up in good time on Sunday morning and packed a picnic basket with the food he had purchased from Marks & Spencer the day before. He added plates, glasses and napkins and was soon ready to go. He was looking forward to the day ahead. The weather was perfect for cricket: bright-blue sky dotted with fluffy clouds scudding along in the light breeze. They should be able to sit out comfortably without frazzling in the sun.

He drove to Mrs Anderson's home in Pocklington and collected Genevieve promptly at 11.00am, as arranged.

Grace opened the door and invited him in. 'Genevieve won't be long, David,' she said. 'She lost her shoe and is turning her room upside down looking for it. Some strappy sandal thing. She's so thrilled to be going out, she wants to look her best. I'm glad to catch you before you go,' she went on. 'This may sound a bit odd, but do keep an eye on her. Genevieve has a tendency to ... wander off. She's easily mislaid and this often leads to...'

David was going to ask Grace, 'leads to what?' when Genevieve appeared at the top of the stairs. She floated down, a vision in a green silk dress, carrying a straw hat. Her hair was loose around her shoulders. She looked as if she had stepped straight out of a Rossetti painting. David looked up at her in awe.

She was breathless. 'It was on top of the wardrobe,' she announced. 'How ever do you suppose it got up there?'

Nothing surprised Grace about her daughter. 'Never mind that now. David's waiting for you.' She handed Genevieve a wrap and sun umbrella and hustled her out of the door. 'Look after her, David,' she called as they made their way to the car.

It was only half an hour to Upper Poppleton cricket ground. Genevieve chattered all the way about how she was getting on waitressing at the café, learning Henri's new dishes and about Jackie's different coffees.

'You've no idea how many different combinations there are,' she said. 'I was listening yesterday and a customer asked for a double shot skinny with sprinkles, a full mocha with extra and a regular chai. They all turned out to be coffees with different things added. There's such a lot to remember but I'd love to have a try.'

David chuckled. 'I don't think Jackie would let you loose on the coffee counter yet, Genevieve. One thing at a time. You need to learn waitressing first.'

At the cricket ground, David began unloading the food from the boot. 'Let's find a shady spot and settle ourselves for the afternoon,' he suggested.

'I'll find us the best spot,' Genevieve said excitedly and grabbed the rugs. She headed off in the direction of the field, her long legs quickly covering the ground. By the time David had found extra cushions and loaded himself up with the chairs and their picnic, Genevieve was nowhere to be seen.

He toured the whole field, becoming increasingly hot. Arriving back almost to where he started he spotted the rugs in a neat pile under a tree, but Genevieve was nowhere to be seen. David looked around anxiously. Grace had instructed him to look after her. They hadn't been here five minutes and he'd already lost her. Where could she be?

The field was filling up rapidly. Families were staking their claim to small patches of grass and laying out rugs and food around the perimeter. David scanned the faces. Genevieve was not among them.

Leaving the chairs and rugs, David moved off and began walking around the pitch, stopping to ask everyone he could if they had seen a tall, red-headed lady in a green dress. No one had. He made a full circuit, there was no sighting of Genevieve. Perspiring heavily now, his heart thumping in his chest, David saw one last place to try: the hut where the teams were served tea at the halfway point in the match.

He ran towards the door, pushing past a group of women chatting in the doorway. Ignoring them, he rushed into the body of the hall and stared round, frantically searching for any sign of Genevieve.

And there she was. Standing at the buffet, happily eating cake and chatting with the lady in charge.. David rushed over. 'Genevieve, here you are! I've been looking everywhere for you.'

Genevieve smiled her dazzling smile and offered him a piece of cake. 'Well, I haven't been anywhere, only here. Try this, it's delicious. It's Mrs Martin's great-grandmother's. Jackie would love it at the café. I'm going to take her the recipe.'

David was so relieved to have found her, he took the cake meekly and vowed to stick to her like glue for the rest of the afternoon. No wonder Grace had warned him.

When Genevieve had finished discussing the finer points of the fruit cake with Mrs Martin, they walked back to the field and made themselves comfortable under a tree, a safe distance from the pitch. Genevieve was fun to be with, finding pleasure in everything. She did justice to the picnic; sandwiches and cake rapidly disappeared, washed down with chilled wine. David enjoyed watching her sparkling eyes and happy smile as she relaxed in her deckchair, taking in the scene around her.

'The match will be starting soon,' he said.

Genevieve turned to him. 'Barney used to make me bowl for him when we were small, but he never really explained what it was all about,' she said seriously. 'I've often wondered. It looks complicated.'

'It's straightforward enough.' David leaned forward in his chair and used their empty plates as markers. 'This is the pitch. Two teams of eleven men play against each other. Two batsmen come out and stand here and here,' he indicated both sets of wickets. 'The eleven men from the opposing team come out, ten of them go to fielding positions and one bowler goes to bowl to the batsman.'

'Well, that's not fair,' said Genevieve indignantly. 'Eleven men against two – one really.'

'It's the game,' David said. 'The pitch is large and the batsman can hit the ball anywhere he likes. It's up to the fielders to catch it before it bounces, or chase it down and throw it at the wicket and run the batsman out. It's a game of skill,' he went on. 'There are all styles of bowlers, fast, slow, medium-pace, spinners. Now, spinners. They can make the ball spin in the air, bowl googlies, yorkers, or drop it right at the batsman's feet so he can't see it.'

'Well what's the point of that?' Genevieve asked. 'How ever would he hit it?'

'That's the whole idea. Get him out, LBW.'

'It's a funny game. You send one man out to bat against eleven, then you bowl so he can't bat and then tell him he's out.'

'There's a lot more to it,' David said and placed their glasses and cutlery in fielding positions around the imaginary wickets. 'The wicket keeper stands behind the batsman to catch the ball if it comes his way and then, spread out a bit behind him are the slips. The silly mid-on and silly mid-off fielders are just above the batsmen, and further down are long off and long on, fine leg, square leg and then the boundary fielders have to spread themselves about, because as I said, that ball can go anywhere and a good batsman can get them all on the run.'

Genevieve laughed as David rolled out the fielding positions. 'Silly mid-on and mid-off? Who ever made up names like that?' she asked.

'Who knows?' David answered. 'It's an old game, the origins of these positions are long forgotten. Then there's gully and slips...'

'Don't say any more,' Genevieve begged. 'I'll never remember it all.'

There was a ripple of applause as the players came onto the pitch and the captain deployed them to their positions. The batsmen took their places at the creases and soon the game began.

The first bowler was a spinner. Each time he bowled, he took a long run before releasing the ball. Each time it bounced up and away from the batsman, who lunged awkwardly for it, chipping it carefully away but not enough to be able to make any runs. After four such deliveries, Genevieve was bouncing up and down in her chair. 'He's not very good, is he?' she said in a loud voice. 'He's not aiming it straight. He's supposed to bowl to the batsman, not send it all over the place like that.'

People around them overheard and tittered. David shushed Genevieve. 'No, Gen. Keep your voice down, you've got it all wrong. He's doing his job.'

'I bowled better to Barney than that when I was little,' Genevieve said, not keeping her voice down. 'If the bowler didn't run up so fast, he might aim better.'

'Just watch the match Gen, and I'll try and explain a bit more at the next changeover.'

But Genevieve could not just watch. She tried to put her new-found knowledge to use, commenting indiscriminately on fielders, bowlers and batsmen, until the umpire gave the batsman out to LBW. She thought it was quite unfair, the ball was nowhere in line with the wicket. The umpire needed glasses, probably magnifying glasses, and she would buy him a pair.

David was red with embarrassment. This was not the happy Genevieve he knew. Was it the wine? He tried to calm her down, aware that they were attracting attention. 'Gen, it's village cricket, not premier league. We don't diss the umpires like they do at a football match.'

'Perhaps we should, then they'd make better decisions.'

'It was a correct decision, Gen. By the rules he was LBW.' David was beginning to wish he'd never brought her to the match. 'Now, settle down and keep quiet.'

The match continued, new batsmen and bowlers taking their turn in the field. David tried to explain more of the bowling and fielding tactics to Genevieve, but he could see he was not holding her attention. Her eyes were fixed on the match. The bowler let fly a particularly fast ball and the batsman went for it, hitting it with all his might, sending it soaring through the air towards the boundary. The crowd cheered. The ball was dropping in their direction. Genevieve, carried away in the moment, jumped to her feet and caught the ball.

A roar of disbelief went up from the crowd as Genevieve, in one fluid move, threw the ball at the wicket and neatly toppled the bails before the batsman reached his crease. 'Yippee, I did it,' she shouted, jumping up and down.

'You've done it alright.' David was aghast. The batsman was looking murderously at her and the umpire was striding purposefully over to them.

'Time to go, I think,' he said and began hastily to throw their plates and glasses into the hamper.

'Oh, we can't go,' Genevieve exclaimed. 'I'm just getting the hang of it.'

'You might not live to see your second cricket match if we don't.' David grabbed Genevieve by the arm and hauled her away. 'We're just leaving,' he called over his shoulder as the umpire advanced.

'Not a minute too soon, lad,' the umpire called after them. 'And don't ever bring her again.'

'What did I do?' Genevieve wailed as he bundled her into the car. 'I only gave them their ball back.'

CHAPTER 30

For the hundredth time, Kate checked her phone and saw that there was no missed call or message from Stan. It had been three days and no word from him. She decided to ring him in Italy when she got home that night. Something must be wrong for him not to be in touch.

Two days previously, on a baking hot afternoon in the centre of Rome, a snatch thief had taken Stan's mobile phone from his back pocket and run off down an alley before Stan realised what had happened. He did not have any spare cash to buy a new one and was reluctant to ask Sofia if he could use the house phone. To be in any way indebted to her would be inviting trouble. She made no secret of what she would like to do with Stan, given the opportunity. So, he had written to Kate and hoped the Italian post was efficient. He knew she would be worried at his silence.

Now it was Wednesday and class was finished for the day. Stan had bought himself a small scooter to get around on. He felt a bit silly sometimes, as most of the other riders were men at least twenty years younger than him, but it got him about and – most importantly – he was not dependent on Sofia for lifts.

The afternoon was very hot as Stan rode away from the college. He decided to go back to his room and put in some intensive studying before the evening meal. He made his way up the Via San Sebastiano and turned into Via dei Pellegrini. Halfway down, the little Vespa engine coughed and sputtered jerkily, finally dying away at the end of the road.

Cursing all things Italian, Stan got off the bike. This was all he needed. He was sure he had enough petrol in the tank the day before. He sighed. Maybe the battery wasn't charging properly. It looked old and had probably come to the end of its life. Luckily there was a garage not far away. Stan decided to take the battery off and see if he could get a replacement straight away. There would still be time to get home and do some work.

He had some tools in his saddlebag and set to work unscrewing the nuts that held the battery in place. He was concentrating on his work and didn't hear the *poliziotti* walking up behind him. The first thing he knew was the screwdriver being whipped out of his hands.

'Hey, what's going on?' Stan exclaimed.

He spun round to find two large policemen rapidly checking over his Vespa and then turning their attention to him, dusting him down for any weapons about his person.

'The scooter's mine, I'm fixing it,' said Stan. 'The battery. Caput.' He made the thumbs down sign, hoping they would get his drift. He couldn't believe what happened next.

'Che cosa stai facendo, amico? Stai cercando di rubare una batteria, eh? Sei in arresto. Vieni con noi alla stazione di polizia.' They stared at him fixedly and then huge grins spread across their faces as they pointed at his face. *'Eh! Eh!'* they exclaimed and nodded in complete agreement with each other.

Stan could only stare at them. What was so interesting? He was not prepared for what happened next.

The two policemen hustled him away. He tried to explain himself, but his inadequate Italian was no match for this situation. They bundled him into their police car and drove at high speed through the streets of Rome to the main police station. All the way the two men kept turning around and pointing at Stan, exclaiming excitedly in rapid Italian. He had no idea what was taking their interest. He gave up on the Italian, loudly insisting, 'No Italiano. English, English.' That made them laugh all the more.

Once at the station, the officers set about fingerprinting him. Stan resisted vigorously but was no match for the burly men, especially when one thrust a fist into his face. His wallet and cards were examined and laughed over and then he was marched down a corridor and thrown into a cold, dank cell.

Long after they had left him there, he banged on the bars of his cell, but no one came. He gave up and sat down on the bed to review his situation. He had been removing the battery from his own scooter and then arrested. Why? And on sight, no questions asked. Just carted off, although he had done nothing wrong. Here he was in an Italian jail; no one knew where he was and the police took no notice of his protests that he was English. Where were his papers? How long could they keep him here? The questions chased round and round in Stan's head.

Eventually one of the young *poliziotti* who had arrested him came to his cell. 'What your name?' he asked.

Stan jumped up from the hard bed and clutched eagerly at the bars of the cell door. 'Stanley Peterson,' he replied. 'You've made some mistake. Are you going to release me now?'

The *poliziotto* ignored him. 'You live in Via Bartolemeo. Who you live with?'

'Sofia Anastasio and her mother, *signora* Maria.' Stan's heart lifted. 'Can you contact them? Get them down here to identify me?'

The *poliziotto* unlocked the cell door and motioned to Stan to step out. 'Come you, with me,' he said, and pushed him up the corridor.

Stan was relieved to see Sofia at the main station office, leaning nonchalantly at the counter, her head thrown back, magnificent dark eyes flashing as she shared a joke with the police officers.

'Sofia,' Stan gabbled with relief. 'For God's sake, tell them you know me. For some reason they arrested me and won't believe who I am. I've been in a filthy cell for hours.'

'Calm down, Stanlee,' Sofia soothed. 'It was a little

misunderstanding. All is well now.' She turned back to the *poliziotto* at the counter and a rapid exchange in Italian took place. Stan's papers were handed over.

The policeman was all smiles now. 'A leetle misunderstanding, *signore*. So sorry.'

'A little...' Stan was incredulous.

'We go.' Sofia commanded. 'No more trouble with la *polizia*, ah?' She swept out of the station with Stan in her wake.

Outside, Stan breathed the warm evening air with relief. 'What about my scooter? They took it away.'

Sofia stared at him in disbelief. 'They were going to lock you up and throw away the key. They think you the spy they are looking for. I miss two classes for you and come across the city to rescue you and all you can say is your scooter. Bah!' Sofia tossed her head angrily and marched away to her car. Stan followed anxiously. 'Get in,' she ordered.

Stan slid into the passenger seat and started apologising for the trouble he had caused her.

'You cause plenty,' she agreed. As quickly as it came, her anger melted away. She turned to face him and smiled broadly. 'You big in my debt now, Stanlee.' Sofia eyed him speculatively. 'You're going to have to work very hard to make this up to me. I get you out of big trouble with *la polizia*. So.' She let in the handbrake and joined the stream of traffic on the Via Concorde. 'A little dinner at Gino's tomorrow maybe. A little wine, a little...' She smiled to herself. 'Mmm, a little more wine and then, who knows, Stanlee? You can show me how grateful you really are.'

Stan's heart sank. He was certainly grateful to Sofia for getting him out of the police station and he didn't mind standing her dinner, even though he couldn't afford it. How would he explain all that expense to Kate? He might have to ask her to transfer some more money to his account and he still needed a battery for his scooter and a new phone. He hadn't spoken to Kate for days. Whatever would she be thinking?

*****

The next evening, when Kate got home from the café, she telephoned Sofia's number in Italy. To her frustration, old Maria answered. Kate asked for Stan.

'Stanlee?' Maria hesitated, searching for her few English words. 'He out. In Rome. With Sofia. Dinner.'

Kate slowly replaced the telephone in its cradle. So, Stan was out on the town with Sofia, was he? Having a cosy dinner for two, no doubt. No wonder he didn't want to return her calls.

Angrily, she got ready for her evening modelling class. If Frederick wanted to paint her in the nude, he could go right ahead. What did she care? Stan obviously didn't. A few weeks in the most romantic city in the world and he forgot all about her. Sofia was incredibly beautiful and Stan loved beautiful women...

CHAPTER 31

Any romantic notions Penny had entertained about her motorbike trip through Europe being largely cultural were rapidly left behind in Paris. George grumbled all the way up the queue for the Louvre and pronounced the Mona Lisa 'a plain old duck'. He didn't like churches, he had enough of them at home he said, after they had visited the Basilique du Sacré Coeur and Notre Dame cathedral. By the time they had done the Versailles Palace and the Palais Garnier, where Penny was hoping to purchase tickets for the opera, George had had his fill of culture and flatly refused to attend a performance of anything – and certainly not opera. 'Caterwauling women and men in tights,' he said dismissively. Instead they ate burgers at MacDonald's on the Champs-Elysées and went back to their *pension* early, so George could clean and polish his beloved Harley ready for the next leg of their journey.

Penny had always wanted to visit the town of Bolzano in Italy, where Ōtzi man was exhibited at the Museum of Archaeology. George looked at her as if she had finally taken leave of all her senses. 'You want to visit an old corpse?'

Penny sighed. This was going to be a tough one. George couldn't see the purpose of studying ancient civilisations; they were dead and gone. Science and technology were far more relevant. Best concentrate on them.

'He's not just a corpse,' Penny protested. 'He's over five thousand years old and there's a huge amount to be learned from him and from the artefacts that were buried in the snow with him.'

'He's a dead bloke in a glass case and anyone who wants to visit that is a bit weird, if you ask me.' George gave the bike a final wipe and stood back to admire his handiwork.

'That's rich coming from a man who liked to dress up in women's clothes.'

'No, it's not, I was just embracing the feminine side of my personality, not repressing it. Think how it might have come out in other ways. I might have rampaged the streets murdering women out of jealousy and frustration. As it is, my dressing up didn't hurt anyone. It fed my inner woman. Freud had a lot to say about that, you know.'

Penny gaped at him. Since when had George read Sigmund Freud? And if he had, the effect never showed. George always did exactly as he liked. She'd never known him repress anything.

Penny was not to be sidetracked. She'd endured heat, dust, driving rain and even a hailstorm in Brussels. She was not going to be denied Õtzi man. 'Bolzano or bust,' she said firmly.

'What do you mean? Whose bust?' George twisted the cloth in his hands.

'No one's bust,' said Penny. 'I mean, no Bolzano, no more road trip for me. I'll get on the next plane home. Take it or leave it.' Even as she said the words, Penny was amazed at her own daring. There were a few moments of silence as George contemplated this idea. Penny held her breath. George could be very stubborn when he didn't get his own way.

'Alright,' George said at last. 'Bolzano it is.' He stowed away his cloth and went into the *pension* to find his maps. Penny watched him go, hugging herself with excitement.

Up in their room, George smiled broadly as he studied the map. It would be three days hard biking and over the mountains to get to Bolzano. Penny would hate it. With a bit of luck, it would put her off archaeology for life.

CHAPTER 32

Jackie stood back. The dining table looked elegant, with her mother's best linen cloth on the table and the crystal wine glasses twinkling in the evening sunshine. Barney's favourite supper was simmering gently in the oven. All she had to do now was attend to her make-up, slip into a slinky dress and be ready to greet him with champagne and kisses, before bringing him up to date with the news.

The summer sunshine faded into gentle twilight and still Barney did not appear or answer his phone. His office phone was switched to the night answering service and his mobile went straight to voicemail. Working late again. Jackie was angry and disappointed that her carefully planned evening had been ruined and he didn't even let her know. She turned the oven off on a dried-out casserole and trailed away to bed.

Samson was already there, curled up on Barney's side. Jackie got in beside him. 'Maybe I should have married you, Samson,' she said, stroking his glossy black coat. 'I see more of you than my husband. What is he up to?'

Later that night, Barney crept into their room and slipped quietly into bed.

'She must have something I don't,' Jackie said.

Barney chuckled. 'Not a chance. I've been with a smart-arse fat man with too much money, who thinks he can buy up MPs to see things his way. But beggars can't be choosers. I just wish the police wouldn't decide to start interviewing at six o'clock. Sorry darling. I would have let you know, but it was all a bit relentless.' He lay back on the pillows and in a moment was asleep, exhausted by the long day.

Not even a goodnight kiss, Jackie thought bitterly. I go to all that trouble and I get passed up for a fat businessman. Is this how it's going to be? Angrily, she turned her back on him, staring into the darkness. She'd spent a lot of evenings on her own lately.

CHAPTER 33

The day had started well for Walter Breckenridge. Elvis had gone the whole night and not peed everywhere and, when praised by Walter, managed not to pee in delight. Ellie, thrilled at this progress, eased up on the hamster-food regime and rewarded both of them with eggs and bacon. As Walter cycled into York, the sunshine bathing the city in a golden glow enhanced his mood of contentment.

It was too early for shoppers and tourists and the Museum Gardens were deserted. Cycling was prohibited but as he was a little later than usual, Walter decided to press on. He could do without Henri throwing a French wobbly and waving those lethal-looking knives of his about if his carrots julienne weren't ready on time.

Walter wasn't the only traffic in the Gardens. Ahead of him, a lorry piled with scaffolding was backing into the ruins of St Mary's Abbey. The driver had made too wide a turn and, instead of gaining the firm traction of the path, was slipping on the wet, grassy bank. The engine noise rose shrilly as he slammed the gears into first and jumped hard on the accelerator. The back end slewed and the lorry jack-knifed down the bank, its load of scaffolding smashing through the sides onto the path below.

Walter, still musing on the vagaries of the French, looked up and saw the scaffolding coming towards him. For a moment, paralysed with shock, time stopped. Then, as if in slow motion, he saw a chunk of scaffolding whirling directly into his path. Seeing its trajectory galvanised Walter into action. He raced away from it, hitting a large decorative pot and vaulting over the handlebars into a formal rose bed.

Walter parked his battered bike in the yard at the rear of Café Paradise and limped into the kitchen. It was only 8.30a.m. but the gloss of the new day had already dissipated for everyone. He was going to launch into his near-death experience in the Museum Gardens and exhibit his wounds from the rose bed, but no one was interested.

Henri Beaupariant was infuriated at Walter's tardy appearance and expressed his feelings in voluble French. Walter understood none of it but got his drift. He wandered out into the café in search of sympathy from Kate and Jackie.

Kate was busy stocking up the dresser with crockery and cutlery for the morning rush. She had always been his ally and Walter was ready to receive her sympathy and first-aid ministrations. He launched into the account of his brush with death and bared his scratched and bleeding arms. 'I'm lucky to be here, a few more seconds and I'd be...'

Kate, not pausing to look at him, continued to stack the cups on the shelves.

'I'd have been a goner.' Walter waited for the drama of the situation to sink in.

'Mm. Well you're here now,' Kate replied, still not looking at him. 'Best give those scratches a wash and get your kit on quick. Henri's been shouting for you for some time. We've all got problems, Walter, and we've all got work to do...' She tailed off absently.

Puzzled by her unusual response, Walter tried Jackie at her usual place at the coffee counter. 'You nearly lost your old Dad this morning,' he began.

Jackie looked up and scowled. 'Hah! Another bloke with another tale. You're all the same, a story for every occasion. Don't tell me, this time a piece of scaffolding miraculously happened to fly through the air at you, as it does in the middle of a park, and you fell off your bike again and it really wasn't your fault. Da dee da dee da. Swallow that one, Jackie. Well, no, Dad, I don't. Stop wasting my time. Just get your kit on and get into that kitchen before Henri blows a gasket.'

Walter limped off to the changing room. 'And stop bloody limping,' Jackie shouted after him. 'No one buys that story, or any other story you men try to palm us off with.'

'Hear, hear,' Kate added her voice to Jackie's.

Women. Walter would never understand them. As he changed into his chef's whites, he wondered what had upset the Café Paradise applecart today. One thing was for sure, those two were in no mood to tell him and it would be no good asking Henri or Genevieve. He was too French and she was too daft. All the same, Walter mused uneasily, Jackie had been so happy since she married Barney and suddenly ... she had the look of the unhappy Jackie of old.

Walter didn't like that, or Kate being so brusque with him. Men trouble? Walter hoped not. Jackie used to be like this around Barney when she first met him and thought he was an unemployed dosser, and Stan used to infuriate Kate with his persistent requests for a date, even though he had the reputation as Stan the Man with a girl in every store. But now Barney was established with Jake in a flourishing solicitor's practice and happily married and so was Stan, even though he was temporarily away in Rome. He couldn't do much harm from there, could he?

It's all that Elvis's fault, Walter mused bitterly. I should have known it was too good to last. A beautiful morning, a halfway sensible dog for once and a great breakfast. All too good.

CHAPTER 34

It was late Monday evening when Matt Carstairs, of Carstairs and Green, Private Detective Agency, slipped unobtrusively into Tom Young's offices in Swinegate. When he left half an hour later, he was seven hundred pounds better off.

Tom Young decided to treat himself to a celebratory cigar. A broad smile spread across his face as he relaxed in his chair. The news was even better than he had expected.

******

Annabel was busy decorating the sitting room in her flat when Tom Young telephoned. Ever since their dinner at the riverside restaurant, she'd been on tenterhooks, waiting for him to call and now he was on the other end of the line and she was like a tongue-tied schoolgirl. She stared at the telephone as if it were about to bite her.

'Are you still there?' Tom asked into the silence.

'Yes. Yes, of course. Hello, Tom. How lovely to hear from you.' Did that sound too gushing? She needed to be cool, not too eager.

Tom Young leaned back in the leather chair in his office and put his feet up on the desk. 'Sorry I've been a while getting back to you. You know how it is, business, business, always business.'

Annabel waited. She hoped another invitation was going to be forthcoming.

'Anyway, you don't want to hear all that,' Tom continued. 'I was wondering, can you spare me half an hour tomorrow evening? Something's come up which I need to discuss with you. Can you make Sancho's in Low Petergate, say seven o'clock?'

Sancho's was the new wine bar. Annabel had passed by a few times and it was always crowded with young professionals, unwinding after the working day.

'I'd love to,' Annabel agreed, disappointed there wasn't another romantic dinner in the offing.

'Great. See you there.' Tom's tone was brisk as he said goodbye.

Annabel picked up her paintbrush and carried on with the sitting-room wall. She was puzzled by Tom's invitation. It seemed to be social, but his brisk tone and 'something I need to discuss' gave it a businesslike flavour. She tried to swallow her disappointment. She had really fallen for him and thought he felt the same about her.

She shrugged her shoulders. Better not get too excited. Maybe he only had her business idea in mind.

******

Annabel made her way through the throng of people crowding into Sancho's that evening. Young people talked and laughed as they happily downed their favourite cocktails or Sancho's top-quality house wine.

Tom Young had secured a private, screened-off booth for them. He was waiting for her, his jacket thrown carelessly on the bench, sparkling white shirt unbuttoned and tie loosened to reveal his tanned throat. He lounged lazily back in his seat sipping chilled white wine. He was even more handsome than Annabel remembered. She paused a moment to collect herself.

Tom spotted her and rose to greet her with a chaste kiss on the cheek. He gestured to the seat opposite. Annabel took her place, concealing her disappointment. It was going to be a business meeting. But maybe afterwards...? She smiled expectantly as he poured her a glass of wine from the bottle chilling in an ice bucket. They clinked glasses.

She looked at him. 'Is this a toast?' she asked quizzically.

Tom sat back against the bench, considering for a moment. 'Let's say, to a fruitful partnership.'

Partnership? Annabel took a sip of her wine and wondered what kind of partnership he had in mind. Business? Romantic? Both? Her heart was ready to burst. He wanted to take things forward, she knew it. She looked across the table. How lucky she was to have this handsome and charming man smiling at her. This was their moment.

Abruptly, Tom leaned across the table and looked her in the eye. 'A situation has arisen, my dear, which I believe we should take advantage of.'

Annabel smiled back at him, every nerve tingling in her body.

'We share an interest in certain parties of this city.'

Parties? What did he mean?

'You are very interested in Jackie Anderson, nee Dalrymple-Jones, daughter of the late Marilyn. Which is natural, as she is your half-sister.'

Annabel leaned back, putting as much distance between herself and Tom as she could. Alarm bells were screaming in her head but years of masking her feelings in prison stood her in good stead. Carefully she put her glass down on the table and looked steadily back at Tom. 'Am I?'

'Oh yes. You were in East Sutton Park Prison for six years, released a few months ago, and came to York to track down your half-sister. *And,* if I'm not mistaken, your share of a substantial inheritance in the form of a large residential property at Acaster Malbis and a thriving business in the centre of York City. How's that for starters?'

'How did you come by this mis-information about me?' she asked.

'Not *mis*-information, Annabel. Hard facts.' Tom's voice had lost its silken tones. 'In my line of business people tell me things. Things you would not want your new set of friends to know. It wouldn't help you to set up a business in the city. Who would do business with you, an ex-con? That nice David Hall?'

Annabel flushed.

Tom pressed home the point. 'Yes, he may be running around with that airhead, Genevieve Anderson, but his heart's not in it.'

'And you would know.' Annabel kept her voice even.

'I make it my business to know. Everything about everyone. Knowledge is power.'

Annabel winced. That phrase had resonated around the prison walls, where blackmail was rife.

Tom let his words hang in the air. For a few moments all was quiet in their private space, in contrast to the chatter around them.

Annabel made herself look at him. Oh yes, he was handsome and charming. She had fallen heavily for it all, fool that she was. Why had she not seen through him, never noticed that dead look in his eyes before? She had been stupid and let down her guard. Missed the signs she'd known so well in prison – and now it was too late. Her new life, her new world, was about to come crashing down.

'And what do you intend to do with this knowledge?' She kept her gaze on him, knowing she needed to meet cool with cool.

'Do? My dear, I won't do anything.' He smiled fondly at her. The cat playing with the mouse. Annabel was not convinced.

'I don't want to do anything,' he repeated. He leaned towards her and took her hand. 'I want you to do something for me.'

East Sutton Park Prison all over again. This man was on the wrong side of the gates.

'You see, your sister's not the "all sweetness and light" character she makes herself out to be. Neither is that husband of hers, come to that. Between them they worked an insurance fraud that swindled me out of fifty thousand pounds commission. *She* took out new insurance for that café of hers and immediately made a claim for asbestos removal and *he* came round threatening to sue me if I didn't honour the claim. My unblemished record with the company was ruined, all due to them. I can't prove she knew about the asbestos and take *them* to court. But they owe me and I don't forget.'

His words whirled about in Annabel's head. She knew they were lies.

'And now they owe you too,'Tom continued. 'They're living in your mother's house and reaping the rewards of her years of building up that thriving business. It was handed to them on a plate and half of that plate is yours.'Tom's mouth was set in a grim line. His cold eyes made Annabel shiver.

'But I don't want it.' Annabel pulled her hand away, forcing herself not to shrink away from him. 'I'm happy with my life and I've got a good future here. Well, I did have, unless you intend to destroy it.'

'No, my lovely Annabel, I do not. You shall have your life here, just do me a little favour and your secret is safe. You may not want your share of the pot, but I do. I want some kind of redress, to upset their smug little applecart and let them feel even a quarter of the pain I felt when they did the dirty on me.'

'What do you want me to do?' Annabel asked dully.

'Send Barney a text, you know the kind of thing a girlfriend would send. Sexy. How good he was last night, can't wait to see him again. When's he coming round? That kind of stuff. That's all I want you to do. Jackie's bound to find it. She's the type who'll check his mobile messages. Plain girl married to good-looking bloke, she must feel insecure. Give her something to think about. Now that's not much to ask, is it?'

Annabel was filled with outrage and disgust. He was asking her to put the skids under her sister's marriage. 'No, no, absolutely no.'

'Oh, I think so. You have too much to lose if you don't,' purred Tom.

'I'll disappear. You can't do anything then.'

'I'd find you soon enough, Annabel. I have contacts everywhere and, of course, I wouldn't hesitate to relate your history to your oh-so-dear sister. With some embellishments. She'd never want to see you then, would she?'

He had set his trap so well and she had walked blindly into it. Wining and dining her, getting her to talk, quizzing her about her home, her family. Again, she cursed herself for her stupidity. Her new family would be lost to her forever if she did not do what this man said. He expected results, or else.

She gathered her bag and got up from her seat. 'Leave it with me,' she said abruptly and made to leave.

Tom rose. 'Don't leave it too long, dear girl. I'll hear from you soon, or...' He kissed her cheek.

Annabel drew back sharply and stepped out of the booth, pushing her way through the laughing crowds.

CHAPTER 35

Realising he'd worked late at his office for too many evenings, Barney made sure he got home early every night for the next week and life returned to normal in the Anderson house. Jackie's niggling worries disappeared as Barney was attentive and loving. She decided to have a re-run of the previous week's special dinner and arranged time off from the café. This time, she made sure Barney knew she was cooking his favourite meal.

'Wow, I must be in the good books! I'll make sure I'm home in good time, with a bottle of the best.' He went off jauntily to work.

Things were running smoothly at the café. Henri was settling in nicely and Genevieve managed to create only a few daily disasters. It was odd how quickly they had got used to her and accommodated her erratic ways. In some respects her presence was quite enjoyable and kept them on their toes as they tried to anticipate the next catastrophe. Walter grumbled about her, but Walter grumbled about everything.

Confident that they could manage without her, Jackie enjoyed a rare afternoon at home, tidying the garden and preparing for an evening with her beloved Barney. As she worked she meditated on all the changes in her life since her mother had died. She'd thought then that she was quite alone in the world and now here she was with a doting, if sometimes curmudgeonly, father and a wonderful husband. However had she imagined Barney was a lazy, good-for-nothing layabout? But then Barney had never tried to disabuse her of this impression. She suspected he'd quite enjoyed her confusion. Now all that was in the past. The future looked good for them all.

Barney came home early, carrying an expensive bottle of red wine. 'Only the best for the best,' he said, kissing Jackie soundly before going to change his clothes.

Jackie poured herself a glass of red grape juice and poured the wine for Barney. She smiled to herself. She didn't want him to guess too quickly. Maybe, after dinner, when they were relaxing in the garden...

Dinner was everything she wanted it to be. Just the two of them in their own world, the evening sunshine streaming in through the dining-room windows. Barney was smiling and happy, gazing at her with such love, Jackie felt her heart would burst.

A loud buzzing interrupted them. Barney's mobile phone lit up on the sideboard, intruding on the peace of the evening. 'Blast that thing,' Barney said. 'Let's leave it, darling. Nothing's going to spoil tonight. Let's take our drinks outside and enjoy the evening.'

He picked up the bottle and glasses and went outside to the garden. Jackie hesitated. If someone was texting at this time of night, could it be important? She picked up the phone and opened the text.

'Missing u tonite my darling. My bed is cold and lonely without u. When r u coming to me again? Amy xxx'

Jackie put the phone down on the table with shaking hands. Was this the explanation for all those late nights at the 'office'? Her lovely Barney, straying already? It had all been so wonderful. Too wonderful. She should have known she would have to share him. He was so good-looking and charming, women almost threw themselves at him.

Her chin went up. She was Marilyn's daughter and she had made a success of Café Paradise in her own right. He might be about to break her heart but she could manage on her own if she had to. One thing was for sure, in the light of this text, her news would have to wait. Right now, she needed to summon every ounce of dignity she could muster.

She stood very still, breathed deeply for a few moments and then marched out to the garden. Barney was dozing in a deckchair, the evening rays of sun dappling his blond hair. Jackie flung the phone on to his lap.

'You should have opened that text,' she said tersely. 'She's missing you.' She stalked back into the house and went up the stairs. She was in the process of collecting her night things when Barney appeared, white faced, in the doorway.

'This has got to be a joke,' he said. 'I don't know anyone called Amy. I've never been near another woman.'

Jackie straightened up from retrieving clothes from a drawer. 'She knows your number, she knows you're not available tonight. It seems she knows a great deal. Working late at the office, Barney? Working late on her, by the look of it.'

Barney strode across the room and took her in his arms. Jackie struggled but he held her tightly. 'Look at me, Jackie,' he insisted. 'I've never lied to you and I'm not doing so now. I've no idea who sent this text. The number is barred. I've never looked at another woman since I met you. I love you, love you to distraction. You're always in my thoughts. All I want is to spend the rest of my life with *you*.'

Jackie stood still in his arms. She didn't know what to think. His words had tumbled out so easily. Were they true?

'Someone's out to make trouble between us,' Barney went on.

'Why would anyone do that?'

'In my line of work, I'm not everyone's buddy, am I? I can think of quite a few people who would like to see Jake and I fail. They'd dance on our business graves.'

'Only this isn't business, is it?' Jackie twisted out of his arms and picked up her clothes. 'It's our personal lives and that was a very personal message.'

She walked towards the door. Barney rushed to bar her way. 'I have never been unfaithful to you, Jackie,' he said steadily, 'and I never will be. Don't walk out on me. We'll find out who's done this and when we do ... God help them.'

Jackie looked up at him. His clear blue eyes were fixed unwaveringly on her. She so wanted to believe him. She must believe him; as he said, he'd never lied to her. Maybe this was all a hoax. She turned and threw her clothes down on the bed.

'If there's an explanation, I'll be waiting to hear it,' she said flatly. 'In the meantime, let's just go to bed.'

CHAPTER 36

There was a subdued atmosphere at the offices of Anderson and Cranton the next morning. Even the breezy Joanna Starling noticed it. Usually when she took the morning post in to Barney he greeted her with a smile and a joke, but not this morning. She entered his office to find him with his head in his hands, studying his blotter intently.

'Have you found it?' she asked.

Barney looked up and Joanna was shocked to see the difference in him since the day before. His face was haggard, his eyes bloodshot with lack of sleep.

'Hey, boss. You OK?'

'No,' Barney replied shortly. He had spent most of the night pacing the floor, wondering who could be trying to cause him so much anguish. He decided his office staff needed to know what was going on; four heads might be better than one.

Joanna sat down opposite Barney. 'What's up?' she asked.

Barney reached for his phone and showed her the text. Joanna whistled long and loud. 'Is this for real?' She looked closely at him. 'It's not true is it?'

'No, of course it's not true! When have I got the time, never mind the inclination, to slope off to some mythical mistress? I've only been married five minutes. Why would I want to do that?'

'Keep your wool on,' Joanna said. 'I had to ask. So who's doing the dirty on you?'

'I wish I knew. That's why I'm showing it to you, then you're in the picture. Jake knows and I can't bear to go through

174

the whole rigmarole again. Tell Annabel about it for me and then get your thinking caps on. Someone's up to no good and if I want to keep my marriage, I need to find out who it is.'

'No worries, boss,' said Joanna, getting to her feet. 'We're on to it.'

Which is more than I am, Barney thought gloomily as she went out.

Joanna made straight for Annabel and explained the situation to her. Annabel hadn't worked at the offices for very long but was already very much part of the team and Joanna was pleased to see her genuine concern.

'Yeah,' Joanna threw over her shoulder as she left the office. 'You can bet it's some right bastard looking to cause trouble for Barney. The sooner we find out who it is, the better.'

When she'd gone, Annabel continued sitting at her desk, white faced and tense. After the meeting with Tom Young, she had struggled, looking for a way out of the situation. She couldn't see one. She knew Tom would keep his word, find her wherever she went and ruin whatever new life she carved for herself. At least she might be able to stay here and build on what she had already started, maybe in time, get close to Jackie.

Getting impatient at her silence, Tom Young had phoned again, giving her a last chance before he told everyone the truth about her. So, the previous evening she had sent Barney a message, hating herself, hating the deed. But it was done now, she couldn't take it back. She might have saved her own skin but at what cost to her lovely sister and to Barney? They had trusted her and had given her a job here, her chance for a clean start away from East Sutton Park Prison. And why, oh why, had she cold-shouldered lovely David Hall? She should have stayed away from Tom Young and never told him anything about herself.

Yes, she had saved her skin, but could she live with the consequences? By the sounds of it her text had interrupted a lovely evening. Barney and Jackie were finally getting everything off the ground and then ... she'd ruined it for them.

How could she continue to work here, taking their friendship, their kindness? The thought was unbearable.

CHAPTER 37

Nothing George could do to her again could ever be as bad as the experiences of the last three days. Penny had clung on to George for mile after relentless mile as the Harley roared across hot and dusty France. Blurry memories of endless motorway ribboning out in front of them. Then a cheap hotel in Metz with the world's most uncomfortable bed, in a stiflingly hot room where the window did not open. George slept like a baby; Penny thought she would die.

The erratic water pressure in the hotel meant the shower stopped just as it reached lukewarm. George didn't know what she was making a fuss about. 'You're going to get dusty again anyway, so why bother?'

He was right, of course. The next day's biking was worse. Another baking day, passing lorries and cars, the air full of exhaust fumes and grit. They made their way to Strasbourg and over the Rhine to Munich. Another dodgy hotel down a side street. George had a gift for nosing them out.

By now, Penny was gritting her teeth and enduring. Only the thought of getting to Bolzano and the Ötzi man kept her from jumping off the bike and heading for the nearest airport and home.

Had she known about the Brenner Pass she might have stayed in Innsbruck and thrown in the towel. First, they had to negotiate the toll booth on the outskirts of Innsbruck. George read the headings, rode confidently up to a window and produced his credit card.

'*Nein, nein,*' said the woman at the booth.

'What do you mean, *nein, nein*. It's a credit card, woman, Visa. It's international. Take the money and let's get on.'

The attendant pointed across the lanes of traffic to the last booth. 'Cards, cards,' she intoned.

'Bloody hell,' grumbled George. 'Why can't they be multi-functional, like at home?'

By now, a queue of traffic had built up behind them. The booth was not wide enough for George to turn the bike around. He motioned to Penny to get off and he gingerly manoeuvred it past the stream of waiting cars. She trailed in his wake, hot and embarrassed as the queuing drivers hooted impatiently.

Once through the toll, George settled them back on the bike with a cheery, 'It's a grand ride ahead, all the way up into the mountains and then all the way down.'

Penny groaned. The Brenner Pass. Thirty miles of motorway and another toll booth. It was no use telling George to slow down, he only knew where the throttle was. All the same, she tried. 'Don't go too fast, will you, George.'

'Fast? I never go fast. Sit back and enjoy the scenery. You have some great ideas Penny. Who'd have thought going to see some old bones could be so much fun? We're having the ride of a lifetime. Hold tight, Bolzano here we come.'

George sped on, whistling tunelessly. The ride of a lifetime. Penny, clinging on tightly at the back, hoped they had nine lives. Eight must have been used up already.

*****

Having endured a lightning descent down the Italian side of the Brenner Pass, Penny tottered off the bike at Bolzano and insisted on choosing a decent hotel for their stay.

'Need a fancy hotel after that? You do exaggerate, Penny.' George was plaintive. 'I've always said so. We had a nice, gentle ride. The view was fantastic: the mountains, sheep, goats, everything. I could have gone a lot faster, but I showed consideration for you and meandered around those bends and you still say it was a nightmare. It was no such thing.'

'I've had better nightmares in my own bed at home, so don't tell me what class of nightmare I've had, George Montague. That was one of the worst and don't think you're going to fob me off with some backstreet B&B tonight.'

Bolzano was a pretty town of ancient winding streets and cobbled medieval alleyways. Stone arcades housed fruit and flower stalls and fashionable shops, with outdoor cafés and restaurants on every street. Penny and George found a hotel in the town centre that offered all the facilities Penny had been dreaming of for days. She soaked in a deep tub, the water fragranced with luxurious oils, rested on a king-size bed made up with fine linen and ate the best dinner that the hotel could offer.

'Steady on!' George protested as Penny requested more warm rolls and another cappuccino with her breakfast the next morning. 'It's costing an arm and a leg already. All this lot's extra.'

'I know.' Penny smiled sweetly at George across the table. 'You're getting off very lightly, George. After all I've put up with these last few days, you're lucky I'm not renting a top-floor suite with indoor pool.' The dangerous sparkle in Penny's eyes quashed any more comments George might have come up with.

The flower-decked streets of Bolzano sparkled in the late June sunshine. Pampered and refreshed, Penny ran ahead of George to the South Tyrol Museum of Archaeology. George, in his beloved biker boots, strolled more slowly. When he entered the museum Penny had already purchased their tickets.

'How much?' Incredulous at the alarming sum Penny had shelled out without batting an eyelid, George sat down on the nearest chair to get over the shock. Fancy hotels were one thing but exorbitant entrance fees to see a load of bones and a bow and arrow that any self-respecting schoolboy could make were quite another. If he'd known Penny was so keen on archaeology, she could have done some digging at home for free. York was full of Roman and Viking bones. Too late now though. When he got up, she was already away to the Ötzi Iceman viewing room.

George followed and found Penny glued to the small viewing window that opened on to the Ötzi man. 'Let's have a look at this bloke then,' he said.

Penny moved aside and George peered in. A small skeleton, the skin like wrinkled brown parchment dried and shrunken to the bones, lay partly on its side inside a temperature-controlled glass case. George stared at it for a long time. Penny waited patiently, pleased that George was so impressed.

Eventually George drew back and shook his head in wonderment. 'We've travelled hundreds of miles, forked out three nights bed and breakfast and two nights in a fancy hotel here in Bolzano – and all for this. I need my head examining, lass. I sometimes thought you were a bit off the wall, now I know it for sure.'

'Oh!' Penny exclaimed in disgust. 'Just because you've no sense of history. We're not all straight out of the swamps. Go and have a look at the exhibits. He was found with his hunting equipment almost intact. Surely you're interested in that.'

Penny pointed out the exhibition area for Ötzi man and returned to the viewing window. George drifted off disconsolately. He hoped they could get off for Rome early tomorrow. He was looking forward to seeing Stan again. Now there was a man who understood about bikes and the freedom of the road. George couldn't wait to show off the Harley to him. What a blast they'd have.

They were the first visitors of the day to the museum and, having the space to himself, George imagined himself on the Harley with Stan on the back. He kicked the bike into gear and revved it up, weaving at speed in and out of the stands displaying the life-size replica of Ötzi and his tools. Then his heavy boots caught in one of the posts holding up the rope that cordoned off the display area and George came crashing down, crushing the Ötzi model beneath him.

Immediately a loud siren went off. Penny looked up from

the viewing window and saw George prostrate among the wreckage of bones and tattered clothing. She moved towards her husband but was overtaken by the museum's security staff, who lifted George to his feet and dragged him out of the room.

Penny screamed in protest and ran after them, clutching vainly at George's T-shirt. The guards dumped him unceremoniously at the entrance, where the museum director joined them.

George scrambled to his feet. 'I'll pay for the repairs,' he offered. Hopefully that would be enough to stop them pressing charges for criminal damage.

The director shook his head and replied in perfect English, 'No, no, Sir. It happens all the time. People cannot resist touching the exhibits and then ... bumph.'

'Bumph?' echoed George.

'Yes. Bumph. Over they go. We're putting everything behind glass next month, but in the meantime ...' he shrugged, 'we'll do something. I'm sorry, but we cannot allow you back in the museum, or your good lady.'

'But I haven't done anything,' Penny protested.

The director shrugged. 'No, but,' he gestured to George, 'your husband obviously needs a little supervision.' He turned and looked hard at George. 'Perhaps you would like to look at our gift shop on your way out,' he suggested. 'A little recompense...'

George spluttered indignantly at 'supervision'. Penny dug him hard in the ribs.

'The gift shop? Oh, the gift shop. Yes, we'll have a trawl through, bound to find a memento of our visit, short though it was.'

The director conducted them to the shop entrance, bowed and left them.

'Why couldn't you behave yourself, just for once, George?' Penny was furious. 'All you had to do was walk quietly around a museum and look at a few exhibits, yet somehow, you managed to wreck the place.'

'I didn't do it on purpose.' George was aggrieved.

'That wouldn't surprise me,' Penny snapped.

'Come on, love.' George drew her into the gift shop. 'There's bound to be something in here you'd like to remember your visit by. You get whatever you want. There, what more can I say?'

Penny briefly glanced up and stalked past him into the shop. Unfortunately for George, it was an Aladdin's cave, with merchandise to please every age and taste. Penny cheered up as she walked round, exclaiming and picking up Ötzi memorabilia: tea towels, mugs, stationery of all kinds, history books about the area, Ötzi brooches, and all manner of small treasures. She piled the basket up with small but very expensive gifts for all their family.

George followed her, swallowing his groans as her basket filled up. 'Steady on, Penny, where are we going to put all this stuff?'

'Not my problem, George,' Penny said serenely.

The final reckoning at the till almost made his heart stop. How could anyone spend so much money in such a short time? Penny's expression dared him to utter a sound.

Still in shock and weighed down with merchandise, George tottered out of the gift shop. He moaned softly to himself. 'I need a drink.'

'Good idea,' Penny said brightly. 'There's a coffee shop right here. Let's get a cappuccino and a cake. Shopping always makes me hungry.'

'Well don't shop then, love,' George said gloomily. 'Bad for your waistline.'

'Are you suggesting I'm fat?' Penny demanded.

'No, I never meant...' George wasn't going down that road. He was in enough trouble for one day.

He led the way into the coffee shop and offloaded the bags by a table near the window. 'Enjoy the view, Penny love, and I'll fetch the coffee and cakes.'

Large glass windows gave a good view of the busy streets outside and Penny settled happily to watch the crowds of shoppers and tourists drifting around the ancient square outside.

George managed the coffee and cakes very well. The well-trained staff would have understood his request for cappuccino and cakes without the elaborate pantomime he gave them to obtain the particular cakes he fancied. Nonetheless, they enjoyed his performance.

Smiling happily, George made his way to the table, looking forward to sinking his teeth into the large cream pastry he had chosen. He made to set the tray down and stumbled over his own feet. As he tried to regain his balance, he lost control of the tray, and coffee and cakes slid off and into Penny's lap.

She screamed and leapt from her chair as the scalding liquid soaked through her trousers and onto her legs. Coffee and cake squelched beneath her feet. She too lost her balance and fell to the floor, landing in a tangle with George.

'Penny!' George reached out to help her to her feet. 'Are you alright? I'm so sorry. I don't know what happened.'

He helped Penny to her feet. Coffee stained the front of her crisp white trousers and splodges of cream adorned her hair.

'What happened?' Penny ground her teeth. 'You happened, that's what happened, George. I might have known. Why ever did I think you might manage to carry a tray without something happening to it? My best trousers. No, don't.' She batted George away as he attempted to remove the cream from her hair.

'I could fetch us another cup,' George offered.

'So you can have another go at throwing it over me? I don't think so, George.' Penny gathered her bags and scowled across the table at her husband. 'I'm going back to the hotel to change and after that I'm going to buy the most expensive pair of Italian trousers I can find and after *that*, the best pair of Italian shoes and maybe by then, *maybe*, I'll feel like speaking to you again.'

Penny marched out of the coffee shop, damp and dishevelled but with her head held high. George stared after her mournfully. Penny had said 'expensive'. He was going to need more than a cappuccino to face the results of her next shopping spree.

Whoever would have thought a guy who'd been dead for five thousand years could cause so much bother. George shook his head. History. It never did anyone any good so far as he could see. The sooner they got back on the bike the better.

CHAPTER 38

Life was not going well for Stan in Rome. Sofia was more of a menace than ever. She played her 'get Stanlee out of jail' card at every opportunity. She slunk around him like a hungry cat, lightly stroking his hair, letting her hands slip down his neck and his back.

'You would still be in that preeson but for me, darling,' she told him. 'Now you are in my debt. You must show me just how grateful you really are.'

Stan felt besieged. Kate, at home in York, continued to give him the frosty treatment. His letter had never reached her and how unlucky was he that when she'd telephoned the house, she'd been told that he was out on the town with Sofia. He knew it sounded bad. If only Kate had let him explain properly. When he said Sofia had got him out of jail, Kate had snorted derisively and said, 'Yeah and I'm the next Pope.' Then the line went dead. Now her phone went straight to voicemail.

Stan could not hide his unhappiness and Sofia took advantage of it. She had no sympathy for 'the leetle Kate at home'.

'She is there and you are here, Stanlee. 'Ow you say, you're up for grabs. More fool her for letting you out of her sight.' Sofia gyrated sensuously around him. 'I am here, Stanlee,' she smiled invitingly at him.

'And I'm not.' Stan dived for the door and was away on his Vespa, Sofia's laughter ringing in his ears.

Unfortunately, the next day Sofia's car was due at the garage for servicing. She knew it would not be ready by the afternoon. 'I could come home with you, Stanlee.' She smiled mischievously at him. 'I will have to hold on, oh so tight, my arms around you. Like this.' She slid her arms around his waist and rubbed herself against him.

'Maybe not quite that tight, Sofia,' Stan suggested. 'I do need room to manoeuvre.'

She smiled wickedly at him, her eyes dancing. 'I like the sound of that Stanlee. You can manoeuvre as much as you like with me.'

Waiting for Sofia at the garage the next morning, Stan felt a wave of homesickness. He longed to see his beautiful Kate and explain things properly to her, tell her how much he missed her and his own city. Explain about Sofia the sex siren and her mother throwing them together, his stolen mobile phone, being mistaken for a spy... He needed to speak to Kate so much, and resolved to buy a new phone that day, however short of cash it might leave him.

All these thoughts jostled in his head. He did not see Sofia come from the garage until she was on the pillion behind him, nuzzling softly into his ear.

'Stanlee, darling. You are so good. Mmm.' She inhaled the scent of his aftershave. 'Delicious. I could eat you.'

Startled by her fervour, Stan quickly started up the Vespa and weaved his way in to join the chaotic lines of traffic beeping and honking their way about the city.

Sofia was a bad passenger. Unable to sit quietly on the pillion seat, she wriggled about, pointing out ancient sights one minute and the next holding him so tightly he could hardly breathe. She saw a male acquaintance near the Trevi Fountain and waved wildly at him, laughing and throwing kisses. It was too much for the little scooter. The back end slewed round into the side of a small van.

Sofia screamed but fortunately kept tight hold of Stan. Gently freeing her hands from his waist, he jumped off the bike to see if she was alright. She seemed to be unharmed, other than holding her neck, and was giving the van driver a voluble telling off in Italian. He screamed back at her in turn. Stan didn't understand a word, but the gestures were familiar. He thought Sofia was getting the better of the argument.

Five minutes later, after a lot of shouting and hand waving, the driver jumped into his van and drove away.

Sofia turned triumphantly to Stan. *'Stronzo! Guidava come un pazzo e poi incolpiva noi! Che idiota!'*

'Eh?' said Stan

'He drives like an idiot and then blames us! How dare he? He was looking at a pretty girl, I saw him. Don't worry, Stanlee. He threatened to get the *polizia*. I told him, "No, I will get the *polizia*. You were not looking where you were going. You look at a pretty girl." *Ah! Polizia!* He didn't want them, Stanlee. I could tell.'

In spite of her spirited attack on the hapless van driver, Sofia looked shaken and was still holding her neck.

'Are you hurt?' Stan asked anxiously.

'My neck, I think. A leetle whiplash.'

'Had we better get you to the hospital to check it out?'

'No, I don't think it's that bad, but I may have strained the muscles in my neck. I need to get an ice-pack on it straight away. How is your bike, Stanlee?'

Stan righted the scooter and checked it over. It looked undamaged except for a small dent in the rear mudguard. 'It's OK,' he said cheerfully. 'Could have been a lot worse.'

He helped Sofia onto the seat and said sternly, 'Now, sit still this time. No wobbling about on the back. Don't speak, don't wave, just hold on tight and I may have a chance of getting you home safely.'

Sofia pouted up at him. 'You are so ungracious, Stanlee. I rescue you from jail, then you nearly kill me on this oh-so dangerous scooter of yours that I never wanted to come on. I save you from that angry van driver with no thought for myself and my injuries – and that is all you can say.' A tear escaped from her eye and rolled slowly down her cheek. 'I did not think you could be so ungallant, Stanlee, when you are so much in my debt.'

Stan raised his eyes heavenwards. Women. Why did they always turn on the taps and make a man feel so helpless? What could he do against that? 'I know, I know,' he muttered.

Sofia slid her arms around his waist once more and whispered softly in his ear, 'I will lie down on my bed when we get home. Perhaps you could bring the ice-packs to me, look after me a leetle, eh? I will need lots of ice for the next three days at least.' She sighed dramatically. 'What a good thing you are here, Stanlee. I could not manage without you.'

'You've got your mother,' he said shortly, starting up the engine.

'Didn't I tell you? She is going to visit her sister in Madrid for a week. She will be gone when we get home. The taxi was due at nine. It's just you and me, Stanlee.' Sofia held him tightly. 'You, me and the ice-packs and after that ... with luck, the warm baths for the tender muscles. I will be relying on you, Stanlee.'

Stan rode slowly back to the house. He'd thought that things couldn't get any worse but they just had. Cold-shouldered by Kate and marooned with an Italian sex-siren. Years ago, he'd have gone for it, hook, line and sinker, but now?

Sofia made the most of having Stan to herself. Although she had caused the accident, she had got them out of a difficult situation and made sure Stan danced attendance on her in return. Over the next three days she called for regular ice-packs for her injured neck. When the swelling went down, she demanded warm baths followed by hot towels to be draped around her neck. Stan was run ragged between looking after Sofia, bringing her meals on a tray and completing his college work, which continued as another lecturer took over Sofia's duties.

Stan needed all his imagination to keep out of Sofia's clutches. He was happy to run her bath, but not to help her into it, ignoring her pouts of disappointment when he declined. Her hands were everywhere. When he brought her warm towels, she could never just take them from him. Somehow, magically, she managed to stroke his arms and try to pull him onto the bed.

On the plus side, Kate had finally taken one of his calls and accepted his explanation of recent events, although she was less happy about him being alone with Sofia for a week.

'I think I'll speak to her, maybe a gentle hands-off hint wouldn't go amiss,' Kate suggested.

'No, don't do that,' Stan said hurriedly. 'I'm managing it, honestly, and it's only for a few more days. Her mother will be home soon.'

If only Stan had agreed, Sofia might not have tried again and put Stan right back where he started. She had been up all day and in the evening she cooked supper and produced a fine bottle of wine.

After a hectic week, Stan was glad to relax and unwind a little. As he sipped his wine, feeling full after the meal, Sofia joined him on the sofa and snuggled up to him. He didn't immediately push her away. She slowly stroked his chest and, sleepily, Stan enjoyed the sensation. Sofia slid her hand caressingly down his thighs.

His new phone rang, piercing the quiet of the room and bringing Stan back to his senses. He sat up and fished in his pockets. He flicked the phone open. It was Kate.

'H-h-hello, darling,' he began, struggling to get off the sofa. Sofia held him down.

'Stan? Are you there? Are you alright?' Kate could hear strange snuffling noises.

Stan tried to remove Sofia's hands from his thighs. 'Get off,' he whispered.

Sofia's laugh could be heard back in York. 'Who's there, Stan? Have you got someone with you? Are you with Sofia again? I knew it. I knew you weren't telling me the truth.'

'Kate, darling, it's not what you...'

Whatever Kate did or did not think, he did not find out. She cut off the call.

Sofia tried to drape herself over Stan again, but he leapt up, shoving his phone back in his pocket. 'Thanks, Sofia,' he said bitterly. 'That's all I need. Just as I get Kate talking to me again, you have to ruin it all.'

Sofia ignored his remarks and patted the sofa invitingly. 'Come, Stanlee. We were just getting to know each other,' she purred.

'I think we know each other quite well enough, thank you, Sofia. I'll say goodnight and go to my room. Maybe I can get Kate to speak to me when she's cooled down a bit.'

Stan tried several times to contact Kate, but her phone went to voicemail. If she picked up his messages, she did not answer them. How long would he have to wait this time before she got in touch again? Well, maybe he wouldn't wait at all.

CHAPTER 39

At Acaster Malbis, Jackie was up early, getting ready for the fruit and veg run for the café. She had not slept well and looking at herself in the mirror, thought she had aged ten years. She put on make-up to cover the bags under her eyes and applied a bright lipstick to cheer herself up. Feeling a little better, she tiptoed down the stairs and into the kitchen, only to find Barney already there, waiting for her with a cup of tea.

'Oh.' She stopped short in the doorway. 'I'm just off.'

'I've made you some tea. Have a drink before you go.'

'No thanks,' Jackie said shortly. 'I'm late as it is.'

She picked up her car keys and headed for the door. 'Bye.'

Through the kitchen window, Barney watched her jump into the van and drive off. She looked a million dollars in smart clothes and full make-up. She was only going to the veg market and the café. Wasn't she? Was she? Since that awful text he knew nothing of his wife's doings. She'd shut him out completely.

In a moment he was in his car and driving down the road after her. Interestingly, instead of turning right at the end of the road, she turned off in the opposite direction, making for the ring road around the city. Wherever she was heading, it wasn't the veg market.

Barney stayed a few cars behind Jackie, trying to guess where her final destination might be. He didn't have long to find out. She turned in at the gates to Bishopthorpe Hall and drove around the back. Barney followed suit and parked at the front of the Hall, jumping out and running lightly to the gable end of the building. All the way, following Jackie, Barney's mind had been in a whirl. She had never shown any sign of lying to him, no hint of deception had ever crossed his mind. Quite what he had expected to find out, he wasn't sure. But it hadn't been this.

Jackie was held in a tight embrace, kissing a man unknown to Barney, at the back door of the Hall. Barney was frozen in horror as he watched his wife, hand in hand with the man, turn and go inside the building.

What did it all mean? Had this been going on for some time or was Jackie taking some weird revenge on him for the unknown Amy? Barney waited as long as he could for them to come out, but Jackie did not appear. Feeling sick and dazed, he made his way back to his car and slowly drove to the office. His world had gone mad.

*****

It was a miserable, wet morning in York, which chimed with the mood of the staff at

Café Paradise. Except for Genevieve who was, irritatingly, more buoyant than ever.

'I'm going fishing, Walter,' she said brightly when he asked what she was so cheerful about.

'Fishing! There's enough water about here, lass. Just step outside with a bit of line, you're bound to catch something.'

Genevieve was not to be discouraged. 'Proper fishing, Walter. David's taking me. We're going on the river tomorrow. Bet I come back with loads of salmon and mackerel, lobster, crabs...'

Walter looked at her and shook his head wonderingly. Was there anything between her ears? 'For starters it's the wrong time of year for salmon and you don't catch crab or lobsters with a fishing line...'

Genevieve made a face. 'What are we going to catch then?'

'Who's we?' Walter asked

'I told you, David Hall. He took me to that cricket match at Upper Poppleton, do you remember?'

'Ha, who could forget? He's never asked you out again after that? He must be a glutton for punishment.' In Walter's opinion, anyone who went within five miles of Genevieve was certifiable.

'It wasn't my fault the ball came right at me. Anyway, what *are* we going to fish for, if it's not salmon?'

'Muddy old brown river trout by the sound of it. He'll have worms and maggots for bait, I don't doubt,' said Walter with relish.

Genevieve squealed. 'That's awful. I'm not touching any of those.'

Walter went back to his chopping board in disgust. Women were such girls when it came to anything slimy or wriggly, or leggy come to that. Show them a slug or snail and they ran a mile and if they found a spider in the café, you'd have thought it was a dinosaur, the way they went on.

******

'Flaming July,' Kate commented, looking gloomily out as the shoppers splashed their way through the rain-sodden streets. She turned over the OPEN sign.

'What's up, Kate?' asked Jackie. 'Are things going on alright at the Historical Trust?'

Kate sighed and moved back to folding napkins on the dresser. 'Yes, they're going fine. It's not that.' She hesitated.

'Go on,' Jackie encouraged. 'We're on our own. You can tell me.'

'It's Stan. He doesn't call or text me for days on end and when I rang him last night, he must have been up really close and personal with Sofia. He was breathing heavily when he answered the phone and she was right next to him. I could hear her. Ten o'clock! What were they doing together at that time of night? It looks like when her mother's away...'

'What is it with men?' Jackie shook her head. 'Why can't they be satisfied with what they've got? They're all the same.'

Kate smiled wanly. 'Not all of them. Barney's besotted with you.'

Jackie snorted fiercely and slashed a fruit cake into portions for the display case. 'So besotted he gets texts from a woman called Amy, saying she's missing him in her bed and when is he coming to her again? That's besotted for you, Kate.'

For a few moments Kate stood still, shocked by what Jackie had just said. Her sea-green eyes widened in disbelief. 'Not Barney...?'

'The very same,' Jackie said angrily. 'He'd gone out to the garden after dinner and I heard a text come into his inbox and checked it for him. I wasn't checking up on him. I thought it might be something from Ellie or Grace. They often text ... but this female, number barred, was wondering when he was going round, kiss, kiss, kiss.'

'He denies it, of course?' Kate asked.

'Of course,' Jackie said flatly. 'He's spent a lot of nights "working late at the office", though.'

'We've hardly been married five minutes,' Kate said miserably, reaching for her handkerchief.

'Don't count on us making it to ten.' Jackie wiped away the tears sliding down her cheeks

Genevieve bounced into the café. 'Walter says I'm to tell you he may have to slit Henri's throat if he goes on about fricassée, dauphinois or, or ... bloody rillettes any more. Oh, and guess what? David's taking me fishing tomorrow. Walter says he'll have worms and maggots. He won't, will he?' She looked anxiously from Jackie to Kate. They were starting to cry. Maybe they didn't like the sound of maggots either.

CHAPTER 40

There was no point in continuing to model for the life classes. The rosy future Kate had been saving for disappeared when she heard Sofia's husky laugh. The Italian woman must have been glued to him last night. Looking back over the weeks Stan had been in Rome, Kate could see how he had gradually withdrawn from her; fewer phone calls, not even bothering to text for days on end.

She would tell Frederick tonight as soon as she got to the College of Art. He had other models on his books that he could call on at short notice. Once she had made the decision, Kate realised how relieved she was to give up the work. It was well paid and it had been very interesting to see the work the students produced. But she would be very glad to get away from Frederick Rawlings. There was something creepy about him. His interest in her was unhealthy, almost obsessive. She knew the students had other life models to paint but they were getting fed-up with painting her every week in the Grecian get-up Frederick insisted she wore.

As soon as she arrived at the class, she told Frederick of her decision.

'But why?' He looked at Kate in disbelief.

'My plans are changing. When my husband comes back from Rome, I'm not sure there will be a future for us together.'

Frederick stared at Kate. 'Your husband! You said you were *Miss* Johnson. My perfect, untouched Kate. All these weeks you've let me dress you as Aphrodite, beautiful and pure, and all the time you were lying to me.'

'I wasn't lying,' Kate protested. 'You never asked and anyway, women keep their own names these days.'

There was no virginal goddess that night. Frederick threw a silk wrap at her and told his students to 'make what you can out of that', before stomping off to his office.

The atmosphere in Studio Four was very subdued. Hot and embarrassed, Kate adopted a pose on the chair and the students worked quietly for the next two hours, with a short break for Kate to stretch her limbs.

Frederick Rawlings was nowhere to be seen when it was time for her to leave. Kate would have liked to say goodbye but maybe Frederick was still too cross to talk to her. She said her farewells to the students, promised to come and see their end of term exhibition and stepped out into the balmy July night.

She was glad of the walk; every muscle in her body ached from holding a pose. It was only nine thirty and the streets were still thronged with tourists, hot and tired from packing every moment with the history and fine buildings York had to offer. Kate weaved her way through the crowds, envious of the happy diners filling every restaurant she passed. A tall, thin figure loped along with the crowds, keeping Kate in his sights as she made her way home.

Walking up Blossom Street, Kate left the crowds behind. She could hear her footsteps tapping on the flagged pavement and every now and again thought she caught others footsteps, but when she turned around to look, there was no one there.

She hurried on uneasily, glad to be within sight of her home, telling herself not to be an idiot. There was no one behind her. Reaching Park Street, she ran up the steps and tried to fit the key in the lock, ashamed to find her hands were shaking. After a few moments she managed to turn the lock and swung the door open, almost falling into the hall as her legs gave way beneath her.

Picking herself up, she turned to close the door – and found her way barred by Frederick Rawlings. He had leapt up the steps and shut Kate's door behind him.

She gasped with fear. 'Frederick! What are you doing here?

Please, get out of my house.'

Frederick grabbed her firmly and pushed her towards the open living-room door. 'Deceiver! Whore!' he hissed. 'Leading me on, letting me worship you as an unspoilt virgin, untouched by this world! And all the time you were sharing your favours, your bed, with men. Well, what's good enough for them...'

Frederick clasped Kate in a tight embrace and forced his lips down on hers, all the while pushing her back towards the sofa. Kate tried to fight him off but, in spite of his thin frame, Frederick was too strong for her.

Locked in a tight embrace, neither of them noticed another figure enter the room. Frederick felt himself being wrenched away from Kate, spun round and punched hard on the nose, before being dragged back down the hallway and thrown out of the door into the street.

Stan dusted his hands and scowled at Frederick. 'There'll be plenty more of that if you show your face here again, mister. I don't know who you are, but stay away from my wife or you'll get a lot more than a bloody nose.'

He slammed the door and marched back into the sitting room. Kate sat up, trembling and re-arranging her blouse. 'I've come all this way to explain about Sofia, how you've got it all wrong and I've never been near her, and what do I find? My lovely wife entangled with some bloke on my own sofa. No wonder you don't answer my texts or calls. Too busy with Daddy Long-legs.'

'It's not...' Kate protested, hot tears springing to her eyes.

Stan was grim. 'It is! I saw you. I'm off!'

'No,' Kate screamed.

Stan was already at the door, bag in hand. 'I might as well finish what I started in Rome. York's not the only place to study Roman history. I can go anywhere now. I suppose that's something to thank you for.'

Kate heard the door slam. The silence of the night wrapped itself around her. She flung herself on the sofa, heaving sobs tearing out her heart.

CHAPTER 41

Annabel. David Hall guiltily tried to banish her image from his mind as he drove to collect Genevieve on a bright Sunday morning. *When are you going to accept it? She's not for you. Even worse, she's been out with Tom Young.* Smooth charmer, David thought bitterly. *He can take his pick of the girls, why couldn't he leave me Annabel?* They had been getting on so well and then suddenly ... she seemed to have isolated herself from everyone. It was very odd. His heart stirred at the thought of her deep brown eyes and soft wavy hair. A longing for her swept over him.

He must stop this. It wasn't fair to Genevieve. In spite of their bumpy track record so far, a cricket match and a very muddy fishing trip, he was looking forward to spending the day with her. She was beautiful to look at, but it wasn't just that. David admired how she tried so hard at everything. She would never be a *Mastermind* champion but she was making a go of her work at the café, in spite of the occasional disaster.

He turned into the Anderson's driveway and pipped his horn. Genevieve was always choc-full of good intentions but her timescale seemed to be quite different from everyone else's.

Just to prove him wrong, Genevieve stepped out of the front door, breathtaking in a pale-blue dress with matching sandals. Her glossy red hair swung loose, framing her face. David's heart lifted. Genevieve was fun to be with. They would have a lovely day in Knaresborough.

The A59 was busy but there were no hold-ups along the way. David's work had kept him very busy over the last couple of weeks and he was out of touch with news about his friends and the café. Genevieve chattered on the journey, making David laugh as she imitated Walter and Henri in one of their many spats in the kitchen.

'No, no, no, not like zat, you stupeed Englishman. 'Ow can you present a cucumber like zat? Eef you were serving an elephant perhaps...'

David laughed as Genevieve mimicked first Henri, then Walter's thunderous face.

'"It's a bloody cucumber, Henry. A vegetable," says Walter. "You slice it, not make bloody flowers out of it. They want to eat it, not stick it in a vase." They'd had a lot of run-ins that day.' Genevieve smiled at the memory. 'Jackie had to go in and quieten the pair of them. She could hear the racket in the café.'

'Two cooks and all those knives. I hope you keep well out of the way, Genevieve,' David commented.

Genevieve laughed. 'No, it's fine.' She paused. 'I think they actually enjoy it. You know, all those arguments. They're very alike in a lot of ways. They both think they're right and want their own way, so they fight and they love it. You can see it. They thrive on it.'

I take it all back, David said to himself. Genevieve may be scatty and accident-prone, but she could be perceptive too.

'How's it going for you at the café?' he asked.

'I thought it was going well.' Genevieve's brow wrinkled as she thought about the situation.

'So...?'

'But these days I can't seem to do anything right. Everyone's in a bad mood. Not Walter and Henri. Like I said, they like their fights. No, it's the girls in the café, Jackie and Kate. They're not like they used to be. Sort of miserable and snappy, especially at me, whether I've done something wrong or not. They look unhappy and don't chat any more. Something must have happened but nobody will tell me.'

'Do you think you can stick at it?'

Genevieve looked determined. 'Yes. I'm learning all the

time and not making nearly so many mistakes. I know Henri's dishes and can say most of them to the customers, salmon and herby potato coulibiacs, crêpes, pineau pâté, and sometimes I get to take the orders. Mummy wants me to stay there, but maybe I could get a real job in another café. Only, I'd need a reference...'

'I'm sure they'd give you one but maybe you should wait a bit, get a bit more experience before you spread your wings. Don't want to be like Icarus.'

'Who's he?'

'Clever dick, thought he could fly to the sun. Got his wings burned and fell to earth.'

'Not a waitress then?'

'No.'

The pretty market town of Knaresborough banished all thoughts of work. They visited Mother Shipton's Cave and made a wish in the Petrifying Well.

'I wished for everyone to be happy again,' Genevieve smiled up at David as they walked through the park. 'What did you wish for?'

David started guiltily. 'We're not supposed to tell our wishes or they won't come true. It's a secret between you and Old Mother Shipton.' He'd wished to see Annabel again. How disloyal was that? Aware of how unfair that was to Genevieve, he took her hand and started walking briskly towards the town.

'Come on, let's have some lunch and then we can do the castle and museum and walk by the river this afternoon.' He grinned at her. 'Any trouble and you'll be clapped up in the dungeons and I'll go home without you.'

Genevieve's green eyes widened. 'Dungeons! I hate dungeons. So scary. Imagine being shut up in one for years on end.'

'In chains, half-starved and left in the dark.'

Genevieve shivered.

'We're having a lovely day,' David said cheerily. 'OK. No dungeons, I promise.'

After a pub lunch in the cobbled market square, they walked through the narrow streets to look at the remains of the old medieval castle and stroll in the grounds. Genevieve gazed at the view spread out below her, the huddle of houses cascading down the banks towards the River Nidd that sparkled in the sunshine as it wove its way between the green fields.

After a long time, she sighed. 'I would love to paint this scene,' she said.

David was surprised. 'Do you paint?' he asked.

'Yes. Well I try. Mummy said maybe I should go to art classes, but I don't know.'

'Why not?' he asked. 'Nothing to lose by it.' He was curious now. How long had she been painting? Was she any good? 'What type of painting?'

'Watercolours mostly,' Genevieve replied. 'I don't think they're very good but I enjoy trying. I'm not very good at anything really.'

She sounded so dismal that David put his arm around her and hugged her. 'Don't say that, Genevieve. It's not true. You're always cheerful and you make people happy. Not many people have that gift, you know.'

Genevieve stared at him as if he had just landed from Mars. 'People are generally cross with me. I never quite ... get it right somehow.' She stared out at the patchwork of fields beyond the river. 'Look at the café. The more I try, the worse it gets. I must be doing something wrong.'

'Come on,' David said firmly, leading her away from the castle. 'I'm sure it's not your fault. The girls must have troubles of their own that you don't know about. You're in the firing line, that's all. Let's go and have a walk by the river and an ice-cream. I'd like to hear more about your painting, too.'

They made their way down the hill and along Waterside. Finally, they sat down on the riverbank with ice-creams and watched people row up and down the river in gaily painted boats, hired from the nearby landing stage.

'That looks fun,' Genevieve said wistfully. 'I don't suppose...'

'No,' said David firmly. 'Our recent track record is not the best.'

'That's not fair,' Genevieve retorted. 'I bet everyone gets in a tangle with their fishing line the first time.'

'And winds it around a tree and then me and then you. Everywhere but around a fish.'

'There's nothing to get tangled in there,' Genevieve pointed out. 'I promise to sit perfectly still. Come on, don't be a stick in the mud. It looks gorgeous out there.' She smiled up at him so warmly, David could not resist.

True to her word, Genevieve stepped daintily into the wooden boat and sat down on the bench seat. David jumped in nimbly after her, took a firm grip of the oars and, with a few swift strokes, they were soon out on the open river.

With Genevieve sitting quietly in the boat, David relaxed and began to enjoy himself. He told her how he used to be a keen rower at university. 'Maybe I should take it up again,' he said. 'It gets you out in the fresh air and it's fun.'

'I love being the passenger,' Genevieve said happily. 'Daddy and Barney had a boat when I was little but they would never take me out in it. I don't know why.'

David tried to hide his smile. Small Genevieve and a boat. What a recipe for disaster. No wonder they left her at home. 'Well, you're out in a boat today and you can tell them it was perfectly alright. Maybe they'll change their minds if they get another one.'

It was a perfect afternoon to be on the river. The breeze kept them cool as they skimmed the surface of the water. Genevieve enjoyed the motion as the boat bobbed up and down in the cross-currents and backwash from the other craft.

All too soon it was time to turn around and head back to the landing stage. David felt a sense of triumph. For once, they'd had a day out and nothing had gone amiss. Mother Shipton's Cave, the castle dungeons and even a river trip. He smiled at Genevieve. She was fun and not always accident-prone, as everyone thought. They'd just proved it.

Fate must have read his thoughts. He was bringing the boat in towards the landing stage when Genevieve, without any warning, stood up and reached out for the banking. She lost her balance and panicked, swaying to and fro in an effort to stay upright, rocking the boat dangerously.

'Sit down,' David shouted.

'I can't.' Genevieve made things worse as she reached out for the safety of the bank again. The boat swung over like an empty hammock and they were both cast out into the waters of the Nidd. David surfaced first, gasping at the coldness of the river. He looked about for Genevieve, but she was nowhere to be seen.

Terror gripped him. Genevieve! Oh my God. Lovely, beautiful Genevieve. Was she still under the water? Drowning? No, she couldn't be.

'Help,' he shouted, waving his arms. Staff from Blenkhorns Boat Hire were already in the water. A muscular young man bobbed up beside David and gripped him firmly, towing him to the riverbank.

'Genevieve,' David gasped, trying to turn back to the river.

'They'll get her,' the young man replied. 'Let's just get you out, Sir.'

The image of Genevieve being brought to safety stayed with David for the rest of his life. She was like the John William Waterhouse painting of the Lady of Shallot, her blue dress floating in the water and her long red hair spread out behind her.

'I'm a good swimmer,' she told him earnestly afterwards. 'Only my feet got tangled up in my dress and I couldn't kick free of it. Lucky for me those boys came to get me.'

David shuddered. Lucky indeed. Never, never, never again would he let Genevieve anywhere near water. He sighed as they drove soggily home to York. The list was growing. No cricket balls, no fishing tackle, no water. He wondered about a simple country walk and a drink at a pub. Could she walk from A to B and manage half a bitter without mishap? He was beginning to think that, with Genevieve, the possibilities were endless.

CHAPTER 42

Jackie Anderson reached for the packet of Kattibix and poured some into Samson's bowl. He sat quietly on the floor, looking at her inscrutably, his long black tail curled around him.

'That's it, cat,' she told him. 'Salmon's off, chicken's off. If you get a lump of tired old mackerel chucked your way, you'll be very lucky. I'm not cooking for you ungrateful blokes any more.'

Samson made no move towards the Kattibix. What had gone wrong? Kattibix hadn't featured in his life for a long time now. He was used to better things. He meowed plaintively.

'Take it, or leave it,' Jackie snapped. 'It's more than your master's going to get.'

Barney came into the kitchen as she was saying this. The atmosphere between them had been very frosty since the night of the mysterious text message. Jackie slept in the spare bedroom and was out to the café early in the morning, not returning home until late in the evening. She often expressed surprise at finding him at home.

Tonight she said caustically, 'Not with your darling Amy? Missing you,' she reminded him, quoting the text. 'You'd better get round there and get her to cook your dinner, because I'm not.' With that, she made to go off to bed, but Barney stood in the doorway, barring her path.

'Bishopthorpe Hall.' he said.

'Your delightful sister, Genevieve, remember?' said Jackie. 'We had a deal. Don't tell me you're going to renege on that too?'

'I haven't reneged on anything,' Barney said quietly. 'I tell you again, I don't know anything about this Amy and I have never been unfaithful to you. But I do wonder about you, Jackie. There was no fruit and veg market, was there? I saw you at Bishopthorpe Hall, in a very fond embrace with a man and it wasn't me.'

Jackie flushed angrily. 'Spying on me now! Just because you are unfaithful, you think everyone is. Didn't you recognise him? The guy was at our wedding, or have you so easily forgotten that little event?' She pushed past him to go to bed. 'It's not me that's being unfaithful. When you can tear yourself away from your precious Amy, have a go at working it out. I'm sure as hell not going to tell you.'

Barney didn't try to stop her. She'd said quite clearly she wasn't being unfaithful. So what was Bishopthorpe Hall all about? If he'd seen anyone else in that kind of clinch and then they'd disappeared for a long time, he would be fairly certain what they were up to. But Jackie didn't lie... What a pass they were in. He didn't really believe her and she didn't believe him.

Barney had canvassed all his family, his friends and any contacts he could think of to try and find the mysterious Amy. No one numbered the lady among their acquaintances. He'd tried conveying all this to Jackie but she wasn't listening. He was miserable. He adored his wife and had no idea how he was going to put things right between them. As he pondered the situation he became aware of Samson looking up at him hopefully. Barney was always good for a titbit.

'Nothing today, old boy,' Barney told him. 'It's Kattibix or catch your own dinner. Looks like I'm going to have to catch my own too.'

They regarded each other sadly. Samson cast a contemptuous look at his bowl and padded out of the door.

Barney looked after him and made a decision. 'You're right, Samson. I have to look elsewhere for a solution. I wonder what Walter would have to say? I think I'll go and find out. But first, I have something to do...'

CHAPTER 43

It was late evening when Tom Young telephoned Annabel. When she heard his voice she had to stop herself from hitting the 'off' button. She had done what he asked and hated herself for it – and Tom Young even more. Now he was invading her life again.

'You did well, Annabel.' She could hear the pleasure in his voice. 'So well, in fact, that I want you to do just one more little thing for me.'

'No.' Annabel jumped up to ward him off as if he were physically in the room.

'No? Well maybe you would like me to tell Jackie who's been texting her husband?' Tom's sigh hung in the airwaves between them.

'You said it would only be the once and here you are again. I was a fool to think you would keep your word. You'll come back again and again. I don't know why you hate Jackie and Barney so much, but I like them and I'm not going to do anything else that will hurt them.' Annabel was trembling with anger, but she kept her voice steady.

'Newly out of prison, false references, dirty tricks and not only on Barney and Jackie. Mud sticks, my dear Annabel. I only have to hint at other activities you might have been involved in, bring forward my own witnesses, and you'll never be welcome in York again, least of all in the bosom of your loving family. Think about it.' Tom's tone changed, becoming brisk. 'All you have to do is collect a package from my office in the morning and leave the contents at the café.'

'What contents?'

'You'll know what to do when you see them,' Tom said tranquilly and rang off.

CHAPTER 44

'The Shroud of Turin! Are you mad, woman?' George looked at Penny across the breakfast table. 'First it was a load of old bones in a glass case and now it's an old cloth that isn't even what it's supposed to be. It was proved a fake years ago.'

'There has been lots of new research on the cloth, showing that it could be from the period of Christ's death. And they have no idea how the image was made. It's not painted or burned on, no one knows how it was done. So it could be real and I thought, as we're nearby, we could call in and see it.'

George spluttered into his coffee. Nearby. Call in. She made it sound like they were going for a drink with the neighbours. 'It isn't *nearby* as you seem to think. It's in the opposite direction, hundreds of miles away. We're on our way to Rome, remember.'

'I thought this was a holiday and we could...'

George held his hand up. 'Just listen a minute. How about a couple of days in Venice?' Penny stared at him. 'We could go sightseeing by day and then out in a gondola in the evenings. Just think of it, you and me, under the stars. I can't get more romantic than that, my love. Better than an old bit of cloth, surely?'

Venice! Never in her wildest dreams had Penny thought George would take her to Venice. She ran around the table and hugged him.

'Alright, alright. Don't be making an exhibition of yourself. Sit down a minute.'

Penny sat down, glowing with delight. At last, something other than bike oil and polish. George was showing an interest in history and culture.

'I've been studying the route. It's straightforward enough, but we can't take the bike all the way into Venice, seeing as how it's all water. We have to stop at a place called Mestre and get a bus or train into Venice. We can find a hotel for a couple of nights.'

All the gods of Italy must have been smiling on them as they made their way to Mestre. It was hot and dusty, but Penny didn't care. They were going to Venice.

Mestre came as a surprise. It was a modern, bustling town and George loved it straight away. Signposts pointed the way to the industrial zone. George could not resist and instead of going directly to the centre, he turned off and made a tour of the industrial estates and suburban blocks of flats. 'Great place,' he shouted over his shoulder to Penny. 'Glad we came. All got good windows. Don't suppose they need conservatories though, weather's too good. I wouldn't do much business here.'

Penny shook her head. Beautiful Italy and all he could think about was conservatories. Didn't he get enough of them in his work at home in York?

In the town centre they found a Best Western Hotel and booked in. Penny would have preferred an authentic Italian experience in a family-run B&B, but after Bolzano George insisted on a chain hotel, that way he knew what to expect. Penny gave in. After hours on the road, she was ready to sink into a warm scented bath.

They wandered around Mestre in the late afternoon and, to George's disgust, came upon the Centro Le Barche shopping mall. Penny, deprived of any shopping for weeks, looked set to spend a long time going into every store. George hadn't come to Italy to look in a load of dress shops. He decided to head off on the bike to the industrial estates again. He wouldn't mind taking a look at their window and conservatory businesses. He might learn a thing or two.

Both of them were very satisfied with their evening in Mestre and, after dinner in a small café and a night's rest, they were ready to take on Venice the next morning. Penny had cast off her biker leathers and was smartly dressed in tailored trousers and pumps. George complained when she chivvied him into good trousers, shirt and a light gilet. 'We're going sightseeing, not meeting King Juan Carlos.' But Penny was having none of it and a spick and span George stepped out from their hotel.

They caught the bus from the main square and travelled over the lagoon bridge to the Piazzale Roma in Venice. George had done some research on the internet and guided Penny to the ACTV offices to purchase tickets for the water buses that ferried the visitors around the canals and islands of Venice.

'I'd like two tickets for the *vaporetto*, please.' George spoke slowly, in his best English, so that the man in the ticket office would understand him.

'You stay a few days?'

'Two.'

'You want big ticket for *vaporetto* then. That's fifty-six euros, my friend.'

'How much?' George had heard this was the cheap way to travel. Fifty-six euros! Still, it would get Penny around Venice and if he got to ride in a gondola later, like James Bond did in *Moonraker*... He looked down at Penny. 'Oh, I suppose you're worth it.'

They made good use of the *vaporetto* during the morning, getting on and off to see the Rialto Bridge, then on to San Polo to the famous food market. After this, George had seen enough of shops for one day and suggested they buy some lunch in the market and picnic on the banks of the Grand Canal.

'I haven't come to Venice to make my own picnic,' Penny said indignantly. 'I'm looking forward to lunch in a little café. Come on.' She made a beeline for the *vaporetto* stop and, reluctantly, George followed.

Wandering around the side streets off St Mark's Square, Penny found a pretty café with tubs of flowers and plants outside and a tantalising menu. There were tables on the terrace overlooking the Grand Canal. Penny was delighted and sat at a table before George could protest.

Sitting opposite her was a group of gondoliers, recognisable by their blue-and-white-striped jerseys. Penny's eyes widened as she took them all in. Every one of them was drop-dead gorgeous.

'What are you staring at?' George asked.

Penny controlled her features. 'Oh, nothing. Just ... taking in the Venetian ambience.' Really, the boatmen were staggeringly good-looking. She picked up the menu and tried to study it. 'What shall we have, George?'

'Oh, I don't know, Penny. You pick something you think I'd like. Spaghetti, tagliatelle, linguine, it's all the same to me. It's all dressed-up pasta with tomato sauce and maybe a bit of a meatball thrown in and that Parmesan cheese on top that they charge you an arm and a leg for. Tastes funny anyway. Give me a good bit of Wensleydale any day.'

'Perhaps we should have gone to MacDonald's,' Penny said caustically.

George brightened. 'Now that's a good idea. Do you know, I could murder a burger and fries.'

Penny buried her face in the menu. Over her dead body. She decided on a Venetian speciality, *baccalà mantecato*, a mousse made from dried cod, served on grilled polenta and a carafe of house wine, hoping this would soften his mood.

The waiter came to take the order. Penny looked up. My goodness, were they all out of central casting for MGM? He was as impossibly handsome as the gondoliers. She gave their order in halting Italian but the waiter spoke perfect English. 'I spend time at my uncle's restaurant in London,' he told her. 'Is good for me and for my customers. Now you relax, *signora*, enjoy this beautiful day and I bring you *un aperitivo*, compliments of the 'ouse.' He smiled down at her. 'For a beautiful lady. Then you 'ave a little wine and ... polenta.' He winked at her 'No hurry, eh?'

Penny watched him leave with their order, admiring his tall, lithe figure and swaying hips. She thought of Enrique, her zumba dance partner. He had the same Latin good looks. Her imagination dwelt happily for a few moments on Enrique's sexy zumba technique.

'Water's mucky, isn't it? And it pongs.'

Penny was jerked back to the present. 'What? Oh George! We're in one of the most romantic places in the world and all you can think about is MacDonald's and the state of the water.'

'There's a good one back in Mestre.' George was enthusiastic. 'We could get the bike out tonight, have a ride round and top it off with burger and chips. Sounds good to me.' He smiled hopefully at Penny.

'So does fine dining under the stars in St Mark's Square, which is what we'll do later – after some more sightseeing.'

George recognised the finality in Penny's tone and sat back disconsolately. At least he had the gondola ride to look forward to. If it was good enough for James Bond...

The waiter arrived with their *antipasto;* mushrooms stuffed with goat's cheese with a herb breadcrumb topping and a carafe of light rosé wine, which he poured with a flourish. *'Buon appetito.'* He bowed and departed.

'Come again?'

'It's the Italian version of "enjoy", I think.'

The food was delicious. George tucked in happily. Penny relaxed, sipping her wine and looking about her. Her gaze lingered on the gondoliers sitting at the table behind George. They were all so gorgeous. Lucky Venetian women to have such hunks to go home to, to... Penny blushed at her own thoughts and blushed even more when the gondoliers raised their glasses in a toast to her. She realised she must have been staring too hard at them.

George glanced up from his food. 'What's up, lass? You're a bit pink.'

Penny picked up her glass and buried her face in it. 'The change, I expect,' she said after a few gulps of wine. 'The hot flushes take me by surprise sometimes.'

George grunted and went back to his mushrooms. Penny

tried a surreptitious glance at the gondoliers but they were ready for her. They mimed kisses and one showed how he would hold her in his arms.

She had not touched her food. 'Eat up, love,' said George.

Penny looked at the mushrooms. Just at that moment, she couldn't possibly... 'You eat them, George. I think I'll leave room for my main course.'

George didn't argue and started on Penny's plate. Behind him, the gondoliers got into their stride, playing violins and miming passionate songs to her. Penny loved it, stifling her giggles behind her wine glass. George, oblivious to the pantomime behind him, chomped his way through the mushrooms before putting his cutlery down with a sigh.

'Venice is turning out alright after all,' he observed.

A giggle escaped Penny. 'It is, isn't it?'

Soon after this the gondoliers, with much air kissing, left for their afternoon's work and Penny and George spent a leisurely hour enjoying their *baccalà* and watching the world go by on the Grand Canal. Eventually they summoned up the energy for more sightseeing. They decided on the Murano Glass Factory and took a *vaporetto* to the island where the glassworks were located.

Stepping off the water bus, Penny slipped her arm through George's. He looked at her in surprise. 'That's nice. Is Venice working its magic on you, love?'

'Not exactly, George. Letting you loose in a glassworks is a bit like letting the bull into the china shop. I'm keeping tight hold of you all the way round. We had enough trouble in Bolzano. Imagine what you could do in here?' Penny shuddered. 'No, don't. It doesn't bear thinking about. I'm not letting go of you until we're safely out of here.'

'You worry over nothing, Penny. I'll tell you something: if you didn't have anything to worry about, you'd worry.'

'The day I don't have anything to worry about will be the day I finally tie you to a chair and leave you there, where you can't get into mischief or do any damage to anything.'

'Charming. I work with glass all the time, Penny. If anyone knows about it, I do. I know to treat it with care.'

'All the same,' Penny said firmly, 'I'm staying very close to you.'

Penny's strategy worked and they managed to spend a happy afternoon at the glassworks, following a tour guide as he led them around the vast factory, explaining the glass-blowing processes to them. Every blower had his own speciality. George lingered to watch one artisan create a set of very large elephants, predominantly coloured blue and tinged with red and green. George adored them and would have taken them home if he could. Penny thought they were spectacularly hideous and for the only time on their trip, was glad they were on a motorbike and didn't have space for them.

The afternoon passed all too quickly and in no time they were watching the last glass-blower of the day. Penny was tired and now that all danger was past, relaxed her hold on George.

The man was making a glass lamp stand and George was fascinated by the way he stretched out the red-hot glass. He sidled around the table to stand behind the man and set up his camera to get the whole of the scene in shot. He leaned back a bit too far and his gilet wafted near the flames, instantly catching fire.

A woman screamed and pointed at George. Everyone turned to look as George, now aware that he was on fire, yelled out in alarm and tried to struggle out of his gilet. The glass-blower dropped his work, which smashed into a thousand pieces on the table and grabbed his fire extinguisher, spraying George liberally with icy foam and exclaiming at the situation in rapid Italian.

The foam worked immediately but drenched George from head to foot. He stood gasping like a newly landed fish in the middle of the puddled floor as Penny alternately cried, berated him and lamented over his ruined camera.

'I leave go for two minutes and look what's happened. I just can't take you anywhere, can I? Have you got a death wish, that you must set yourself on fire and ruin a good camera into the bargain? And you'll probably have to pay for his ruined work...'

On and on she went. George switched off. She was right. It had been a lovely afternoon and he had no idea how the accident had happened. But sometimes ... oh, how she did go on. There wasn't much harm done and he could soon buy a cheap change of clothes. Couldn't she just be glad he wasn't burnt to a cinder?

Obviously not. All the way back in the *vaporetto*, Penny relived the situation, letting her imagination roam over every conceivable permutation of events – George with severe burns, airlifted to hospital, months of skin grafts and would their insurance cover it or, worse, George burnt to a crisp on the floor, having to be flown home for burial.

This was too much for George. He swung round and eyeballed Penny, enunciating very clearly, 'I am perfectly alright Penny. Stop all that nonsense now. It was an unfortunate accident, I grant you, and I am a little damp and have no shirt, but I will buy one very shortly. We can have a drink and decide what to do with our evening. Everything back to normal.'

Normal. Penny wasn't sure she wanted 'normal'. George's 'normal' wasn't anyone else's 'normal'. She'd forgotten what 'normal' was. She sat back in the boat and sighed. Café Paradise and dear old York seemed a lifetime away.

CHAPTER 45

For the second time in a week Barney turned his car into the grounds of Bishopthorpe Hall and switched off the engine. Without giving himself time to think, he got out of the car and strode into the hallway of the hotel. The man he had seen with Jackie was leaning on the reception desk, going through a sheaf of papers.

At Barney's approach the man turned and smiled. 'Good morning, Sir. Can I help you?' A moment's hesitation and then, 'It's Barney isn't it? Mr Anderson?' he finished uncertainly.

Barney walked right up to Martin Woodside and stared closely into his face. Martin stepped back a pace.

'I don't know your name or what you do here, but here's a message for you and I want you to hear it loud and clear. I saw you with my wife the other day and I didn't like what I saw. My wife is *my wife*, got it? Stay away, or you'll be very sorry.'

'It's not...'

Barney wheeled about and made for the door. He waved the man away. 'I don't want to hear it. Just leave my wife alone.'

Martin Woodside gazed after him, open-mouthed. 'It really isn't...'

Barney was gone, roaring away down the drive and back to the city.

******

Annabel waited nervously in the reception area of Tom Young's offices in Swinegate. She looked around. It didn't look like business premises, having more the air of a private residence with its luxurious carpets and sofas, and discreet lighting enhancing the oil paintings hanging on the walls. Financed how? By hard work and good business practice? Annabel frowned. More likely to be funded by Tom's shady dealings. From what she could see, he seemed to have a finger in most dodgy pies in this city.

The office door opened and Tom appeared. 'Annabel,' he exclaimed with pleasure. 'So good to see you, do come in.' He ushered her into his office and drew a chair up to his opulent desk. He sat down at the other side and spent a few seconds openly admiring her. 'Looking more beautiful than ever.'

She could have said the same about him, only now she realised how skin-deep his good looks were. 'You have something for me,' she said, keeping her voice neutral.

'Ah, down to business. Very well.' Tom reached into his desk drawer and pulled out a box. He looked at it for a few moments, smiled and then passed it over to Annabel.

'And what do I do with this?' she asked.

Tom leant back in his chair and stretched languidly. 'I always feel that the Café Paradise lacks a little something, a certain *je ne sais quoi*, shall we say. I think the contents of the box might liven things up a little, discreetly distributed about the place. I can safely leave it to your inventiveness and dexterity to leave your, ah … little calling card at the premises.'

Annabel made to open the box. Tom's long, elegant fingers closed over hers. 'Not in here, my dear. Take them away and look at them, then implement our little plan soon.' He made to stroke her face and Annabel drew back sharply. 'Soon Annabel,' he said briskly. 'I look forward to hearing from you, as they say.'

Annabel placed the box in her bag, fighting down the impulse to slap Tom's handsome, smiling face. She got up and headed for the door.

'As I said, Annabel,' Tom repeated. 'Soon.'

When she got back to the office, Annabel went into the Ladies and opened up the box. It was full of mouse droppings.

In her immediate revulsion, she almost dropped the box and its contents on the floor. How could he? She didn't know what she had expected, but it wasn't this. How low could Tom Young stoop?

Annabel saw it all. Not content with trying to wreck Jackie and Barney's marriage, he wanted to wreck her sister's business too. If Environmental Health were called in, they could close her down until the place was deep-cleaned. By then, the café's reputation could be ruined. Why did he hate Jackie and Barney so much? She didn't believe his story about the asbestos but had no way of finding out without arousing suspicion.

All through the long, hot afternoon, the box lay in Annabel's bag in her office. She tiptoed around it, as if a ticking bomb had come to rest by her desk. As the hours went by, Annabel's resolve grew. There was no way she was going to spread those mouse droppings around the café, whatever the cost in the long term to herself. She had come to admire Barney for the compassion and care he showed to his clients and had seen how hard Jackie worked to create a friendly and welcoming café with the best food York could offer. She was not going to be instrumental in destroying all that.

She needed to warn Jackie and Barney about Tom Young, but how could she do that and not reveal the awful truth about herself and what she had already done to them?

CHAPTER 46

After their visit to the Murano Glassworks, George suggested a ride in a gondola and then back to the safety of Mestre for burgers and chips before anything else could befall them. Penny agreed. George attracted trouble. But they'd come all this way, it would be a shame to leave Venice without having coffee or a drink at the famous Caffè Florian in St Mark's Square.

She had read up in the guide books about this café and was determined to try it. It was the oldest in Italy and one of the best, famed for its orchestra and possibly its prices, if the reviews on TripAdvisor were to be believed. But George didn't know that.

They walked around the square until they came to the café, and Penny flopped down at one of the pavement tables. The orchestra was playing light, romantic music. Penny relaxed and closed her eyes, swaying along to the gentle rhythms.

'Bit tame, isn't it?' George mused. 'They could do with something a bit more zippy. More of a beat to it. Wonder if they know any Led Zeppelin or Eric Clapton.'

'It's elegant, sophisticated Venice, George.' Penny opened her eyes and glared at him. 'It's supposed to put you in the mood for romance, not make you behave like a banshee at a pop concert.'

'Since when did I...?'

A waiter in immaculate uniform appeared at the table. They ordered a carafe of wine and cake. After he'd gone, George returned to the conversation. 'I've never been a banshee.

If anyone was...'

'Shut up George, please.' Penny closed her eyes and let a Strauss waltz wash over her. She imagined herself wearing a floating pink dress, held gently in the arms of a handsome Venetian gondolier as they danced as one around the square.

'I remember when we went to Glastonbury before the lads were born,' George continued. 'It rained non-stop and all our kit was ruined. We had some rough old cider with us and we got drunk. Do you remember?' George paused and began to smile. 'You fell over into the mud and you were the one shrieking like a banshee. I started to laugh, so you pulled me down as well. Aye, shrieking like a...'

Penny kicked him under the table.

'What was that for?' he asked, confused.

'We're at the most famous café in Venice, George, I don't think I want reminding of Glastonbury.'

The waiter arrived and set down the wine and cake, along with small dishes of crisps and nuts. George poured the wine and passed a glass to Penny. She took a sip and resumed the imaginary waltzing with her gondolier. The orchestra moved on to Vivaldi. 'That's got a bit more life in it,' George said happily, emptying his wine glass. 'You know what? This wine isn't half bad either. I think we'll have another one.'

Penny wasn't listening. Lost in the music, she didn't notice George drain the carafe and order the next. He polished off the cake and all the crisps and nuts, and was well down the second carafe when the orchestra took a break. Penny opened her eyes. By now, George was smiling broadly and still swaying to the strains of the last piece of the Summer Concerto in G Major.

'George?'

'Romantic Venice, Penny. You were right.' George hummed loudly and carried on swaying.

'Sit still, George. You're making me feel dizzy.'

'Dizzy! That's it. Dizzy with delight at Venice. The sun, the water, the sights and most of all,' George focused hazily on Penny, 'the delight of my beautiful wife.' He sloshed the last of the wine into his glass and picked it up. 'Here's to ... here's to ... here's to ... wine.' He downed it in one and looked sadly at the empty carafe. ''Nother one?' he suggested.

'No.' Penny signalled to the waiter for the bill. 'Time to head back to Mestre. MacDonald's, remember?'

'MacDonald's.' George nodded solemnly. 'First. In Venice. Gotta ride in a gondola,' he said carefully. 'Take my wife in a gondola. S'romantic.'

Penny didn't think it would be very romantic with a tipsy George, who might fall asleep and snore. 'Give me your wallet,' she said.

'Why?'

'Because I have to pay the waiter. Can't leave without paying, can we?' she said patiently.

'Mm.' George obediently handed over his wallet and watched as Penny extracted an alarming number of twenty-euro notes and handed them over to the waiter.

'No, no, no. Can't do that.' George made to grab the notes. 'Far too many. Only had a giraffe. That could buy the whole zoo.'

Deftly, the waiter whipped the notes away. 'Good evening, *signore*. We hope you have enjoyed your visit to the Caffè Florian.' He wheeled away before George could react.

Penny guided George away, intending to board the *vaporetto* back to the bus station and on to Mestre, but George was having none of it. 'Gondola,' he said stubbornly. 'I am taking my wife on a gondola.'

'Your wife wants to go home,' said Penny.

'No. My wife wants to go on a gondola. And go on a gondola she will.'

It was no use arguing with George in this mood and it would be nice to experience the real thing. They found a waiting gondola and were helped into their seats by a good-looking youth and were soon floating gently down the Grand Canal.

The gondolier sang softly in a dreamy Italian baritone as he steered, smiling all the while at Penny. She hummed along with him.

George, who had been slouched back against the cushions, suddenly sat up. 'James Bond,' he said.

Penny frowned at him. She didn't want this lovely ride to be spoiled.

'Bang,' he said, shooting an imaginary gun at the gondolier. 'James Bond wouldn't stand for it, neither will I. *Moonraker*. No, that's wrong. It was a bloke in a coffin, throwing knives at Roger Moore.'

George sat up properly, throwing an imaginary knife at the gondolier. 'Right in your heart. You're dead. Now you fall overboard.' George rocked the gondola. 'Go on, fall out. You're dead. Won't be smiling at my wife like that again.'

He turned an imaginary steering wheel. 'Brm, brm, brm. James Bond. Car chase up the canal. Gondola turns into a hovercraft and he drives it right through St Mark's Square. Brm, brm, brm, brm, brm.'

George swayed around the imaginary bends and the gondola rocked along with him. The gondolier, alarmed and furious at his passenger's behaviour, poled to the nearest gondola station.

'*Cosa fate! Siete ubriaco! Rischiate di capovolgere la gondola! Scendete subito e andatevene via, via da Venezia!*'

Penny did not understand a word, but there was no mistaking his meaning. She dragged George out of the gondola and made her apologies to the young man. 'I'm so sorry. He must have had too much sun,' she said. 'And wine. He's not usually like this. I'd better get him back to Mestre before he does anything else.'

CHAPTER 47

Stan Peterson sat alone at a table in the Piazza Navona in Rome. Moodily, he drained his glass and seeing the waiter nearby, gestured to his empty glass. 'Vino, vino, encora,' he commanded.

'Si signore.' The waiter scurried away to collect a fresh bottle.

Stan watched the ebb and flow of people strolling idly in the evening sunshine. Happy couples, walking hand in hand, some twined together so tightly they seemed as one.

The waiter delivered the wine. Stan poured himself a glass and drank it down. He slumped in his chair, chin resting on his chest. In his pocket was an unopened letter from Kate that he'd received that morning. His first instinct had been to tear it up and hurl it in the bin, but he hesitated and stuffed it in his pocket before heading off to the International College. Now it was evening and, instead of going home to Via Bartolemeo to study, he was drowning his sorrows at the Bar Solesto.

Two glasses of wine later, he took out Kate's letter and looked at it. What bad news would it contain? He had not read any of her texts or answered her calls since he'd caught her in the arms of a man in their own home, two weeks ago. Had she realised she'd made a mistake in marrying him in the first place and sent him here to Rome to give herself space to think? She obviously hadn't wasted any time in finding another man when his back was turned. This letter might be intimations of divorce.

Stan could bear it no longer. He pulled the letter out of his pocket and tore it open. Fortifying himself with another glass of wine, he started to read.

Darling Stan,

It is two weeks now since you marched into our house and out again. The scene you witnessed was not what it seemed and I want you to give me a chance to explain it to you. You won't answer my calls or texts, so this letter is my only way of getting through to you. Please don't tear it up at this point. Give me a chance and read it through to the end.

Whilst you were away in Rome, I took up an evening modelling post at the College Of Art. I didn't tell you because I wasn't sure you would like the idea. The pay was fantastic and I was able to save it all towards the deposit on our new home. That's why I did it. Unfortunately, I went under my maiden name to keep the work separate from the Historical Trust, and Frederick Rawlings, the head of department, somehow seems to have developed a real 'thing' about me as the ideal of an unsullied virgin.

I knew nothing of this. When he found out I was married, he turned nasty and I decided to leave. I didn't know it, but he followed me home and got into our house and attacked me. I think he was intent on raping me. Believe me, Stan, I was terrified. I was trying to fight him off when you walked in on us. Yes, I was in his embrace, but please believe me, not willingly. It was wonderful when you knocked him down and threw him out. If only you had stayed to hear the truth of the situation.

Please believe me, my darling Stan. You are the centre of my life and I will always love you. Please, please, ring me or text me and tell me you understand. We have a wonderful future waiting here for us in York.

You are due home soon and I will be waiting here for you, loving you always.

Kate xxx

Stan put the letter down on the table with shaking hands. A nutcase had followed his wife home and attacked her and he had immediately got hold of the wrong end of the stick and blamed his lovely Kate. What an ass he had been. He should have known better. Kate loved him and had always been faithful. She was working so hard for their new home. Stan was overwhelmed with guilt and remorse. He didn't deserve a girl like her.

Over the next hour, Stan drained the bottle of wine as he pored over Kate's letter until he knew it by heart. By now it was late evening. He paid his bill and stumbled away from the table, making his unsteady way home to Via Bartolemeo.

Swaying on the doorstep, he tried to fit his key in the lock but couldn't focus enough to let himself in. Losing patience, he banged on the door, shouting for Sofia.

'Open the door, woman,' he roared. 'Do you have to lock up like it's Fort Knox?'

He knocked loudly again and it opened slowly. Sofia stood behind it, frowning at him. 'Stanlee? What are you doing? Why do you knock so hard to wake up the whole street? And my mother, too. She is asleep.'

Stan swayed on the doorstep and made no move to enter the house. Sofia looked at him more closely. 'You are drunk!' She laughed softly and drew him into the hallway. 'Come. We must get you to your room, or you will be sleeping in the street.'

'Sleep,' Stan said solemnly. 'Mustn't sleep. Must get on the telephone. Important.'

Sofia guided Stan up to his room. He leaned heavily on her, stumbling, pulling them both back down the stairs. Sofia dragged him to his feet again and pushed him patiently, step by step, until they made it into his room.

Stan sat heavily down on the bed, looking blankly around him. 'Thish my room?' He looked puzzled. 'Thish where I sleep? No,' he said loudly, 'sleep with ... sleep with...' he tailed off uncertainly.

Sofia giggled and put a finger to her lips. 'Sshh. Quietly now, Stanlee.' She fingered his T-shirt gently. 'You are not going to sleep in your clothes, Stanlee,' she said. 'Come, I will help you get undressed.'

Stan did not protest. He was feeling the effects of no evening meal and too much wine and did not resist as Sofia peeled off his clothes, stroking his skin and kissing his neck. She helped him into bed, slipped in beside him and began gently nibbling his ear.

'Mmm, gerroff,' Stan giggled and batted Sofia away. He struggled to sit up in the bed. 'Got to ring ... ring ... you know. Got to ring...'

Sofia eased him back down to the bed. 'In the morning Stanlee. Right now ... kiss me.'

******

The next morning was Saturday and Stan had no classes. The sun was streaming in the bedroom windows when he awoke. His head ached and his mouth was dry. He turned to look at his bedside clock and was horrified to see Sofia lying next to him. He turned away quickly and stared straight ahead, unwilling to believe what he had seen. After a few moments he turned his head slowly. Sofia was still next to him, sleeping peacefully.

Stan moved gingerly out of bed. To his horror he found he was naked; he grabbed a towel to wrap around himself and tiptoeing to the door, opened it quietly.

Sofia's soft voice stopped him in his tracks. 'Good morning, Stanlee darling.'

He turned. She was propped up on one arm in the bed, smiling invitingly at him. 'Where are you going? Come back to bed. There is no school today.' She pouted at him. 'The teacher is on holiday too. Let's take up where we left off last night.'

Stan froze in the doorway. Where had they left off last night? He had a dim memory of getting home, being on the doorstep, but after that...

'Did you, er...? Did you help me to bed, Sofia?'

She laughed, throwing back the covers to reveal her lithe, naked body. 'Mm, I think it was you who helped me to bed, Stanlee. Now I know you English men are not the cold fish you are made out to be. Quite the reverse.'

Stan had to ask. 'Did we...?'

'Don't you remember? Oh, Stanlee. How ungallant. Was it not memorable for you?' Sofia slid out of bed and wrapped herself in a robe. Then she was at Stan's side, putting her arms around him. 'Let me remind you, Stanlee.'

Stan backed off through the open doorway. 'I know I was a bit drunk last night, Sofia...'

She smiled at him. 'Not so drunk, Stanlee. Come on, come back to bed.'

'No.' Stan was fierce. 'Please tell me, we didn't...'

Sofia shrugged. 'If you don't remember...' She sashayed to the stairs and looked back at him. She began to descend, keeping her gaze fixed on him.

Stan ran to the stairhead, looking down at her. 'Sofia!'

She laughed up at him and blew him a kiss.

Stan crumpled in a heap in the bathroom doorway. All the things he had accused Kate of doing and she had been innocent, whilst he...

CHAPTER 48

'Annabel! It's a beautiful day out there. Come on, you must get out of the office and take a break.' Barney Anderson was smiling down at her. 'It's too nice for paperwork today. Why don't you take the afternoon off and join Jackie at Bishopthorpe Hall Spa, like she suggested. They have a fantastic outdoor swimming pool. You could top up your tan.'

For a moment Annabel was tempted.

'Maybe you could convince her at the same time that I'm not the womanising monster she thinks I am.' Barney looked hopeful.

'I don't think I could do that,' she smiled ruefully. 'We don't know each other well enough.'

'That's why she wanted you to go with her, so that you could get to know each other better, become friends. She needs a friend Annabel, and I don't know, but somehow you two look like you were meant to be friends.'

Annabel hesitated. She thought back to the telephone call she'd had from Jackie a week ago, suggesting a spa day together. She'd said no, making her decorating project at the flat her excuse. Maybe another time. She could hardly bear the disappointment in Jackie's voice and almost changed her mind. But how could she spend a day in her sister's company, tortured by the knowledge of what she had done to her? Jackie had accepted her excuses, but Annabel sensed the hurt behind the friendly tones.

'I'll take a lunch break, Barney,' Annabel said firmly. 'But not the afternoon, thanks all the same. You and Jake are far too popular. The clients can't get to your door fast enough and if I don't get some accounts sent out soon, there'll be nothing in the kitty to pay the bills.'

Barney looked disappointed.

'I do want to be friends with Jackie,' she said softly. 'It's just that... I just need a little space at the moment. Sort of get my bearings, you know?'

Barney didn't know. The more he saw of women, the less he understood them. Walter was right. Don't even try.

******

Annabel had been avoiding Café Paradise for a while, but when she came out of the offices of Anderson and Cranton, she took the familiar route from Little Stonegate to Castlegate. She felt drawn to it, needing to sit once more where her mother, Marilyn, had spent so much of her life and where her sister carried on that life. It was easier knowing that Jackie would not be there. She would not have been able to meet her friendly, welcoming smile.

It being a Wednesday, Kate was not at the café. Genevieve and the new girl, Louise, were waiting at the tables. After the bright sunshine outside, Annabel's eyes took a few moments to adjust to the interior of the café; it was too late to turn back when she saw Walter manning the coffee counter where Jackie usually stood. Taking a deep breath, she moved forward and said a pleasant hello, before taking a seat as far away from his counter as possible.

She picked up the menu and hid her face in it. It had been a mistake to come here. She hadn't expected to see Walter at such close quarters. He always looked at her as if he saw right into her soul. She would have a cold drink and leave.

Genevieve came to take her order. Annabel enquired how she was getting on.

'Alright, I think.' Genevieve sounded dubious. 'At least, I haven't broken anything so far this week, or mixed up any orders, or made Monsieur Henri cross. So,' she brightened, 'that's all good, isn't it?'

Annabel chuckled and ordered a fruit juice. Genevieve carefully wrote down the order and gave it to Walter at the coffee counter where the iced drinks were kept. He waved Genevieve away and summoned Louise to take charge. Annabel's heart sank as she saw Walter approach with her glass of fruit juice.

He put it down carefully on the table and took a seat opposite her. 'I'm pleased to see you in here today,' he said.

Annabel smiled cautiously and took a sip of her drink. 'It's nice to be made welcome.' She wondered what was coming.

'Oh aye, you're always welcome. Jackie's always pleased to see you.'

In the short silence that followed, Walter looked steadily at her across the table. Annabel kept her eyes on her glass. 'Believe it or not, I'm pleased to see you an' all,' Walter continued. 'And you'll never guess why.'

This remark was so unexpected, it threw Annabel off balance. Walter never looked pleased to see her, he usually scowled at her from afar. She waited.

'So,' Walter continued as she made no reply. 'Can you guess why?'

'No.' Annabel was nervous now. What was coming?

'I'm right pleased to see you because you take me back to my younger days. Back to the time when Jackie's mother, Marilyn, was your age and I was nobbut a year older. It's a right strange thing, but you're the image of her as she was then.' He saw Annabel's startled look. 'Aye. Her double. Her hair, her eyes, skin. Even her voice and some of her mannerisms.' Walter sat back in his chair. 'What do you make of that?'

Annabel was too overcome to speak. She'd had no idea she resembled Marilyn so closely. Had Jackie seen it as well as Walter? Did he suspect her secret? She made herself say something. 'I think that's very interesting, Mr Breckenridge.' She was surprised at how steady her voice sounded.

'It is that,' Walter said laconically. 'I'll tell you summat else of interest while I'm on it.' He leaned in closer across the table. 'It was a big surprise to me to see you wearing Marilyn's garnet necklace and earrings at Jake's birthday party.'

Annabel shook her head, but Walter ploughed on. 'I don't know how you come by them, but they were Marilyn's. How do I know? Because I bought them for her years ago, and they were a one-off. Original pieces by a local jeweller. He put them to one side for me and I saved long and hard to buy them. I just about knew every stone in that necklace by the time I was done. And now here you are, the spitting image of Marilyn and wearing them. Now, what am I to make of all that?'

He knew. Annabel felt like a cold vice had clamped itself around her throat and was squeezing the breath out of her. This would be the end of everything; her deceit would be discovered and Jackie would never speak to her again. She had to get away. Away from Walter's intense gaze, away from his knowledge.

'I can't...' Pale and breathless, she pushed her chair back and ran out of the café doors, running as far away from the Café Paradise as possible.

******

Annabel thought she was going mad. Her mind was in turmoil as she waited for the roof to fall in on her carefully constructed world. She had not carried out Tom Young's demands and spread the mouse droppings at the café, or contacted Environmental Health to report them. He had wanted her to do it quickly and after two weeks she had done nothing. Any day now he might reveal the truth about her and if he didn't, Walter Breckenridge might.

By Friday morning she could stand it no more. She had to talk to somebody. She found Walter's number in the phone book and rang his home. Luckily, Ellie had already left for a local market and Walter answered the telephone. 'Annabel,' he said in surprise.

She jumped straight in. 'Can I come and talk to you, Mr

Breckenridge, please? You obviously suspect something of my past and I would like to tell you about myself. Maybe you could help me. As soon as possible, if you could manage it.'

Walter's voice was neutral. 'As it happens, I'm not at the café today. Henri thinks he's about ready to stand on his own two feet. It's just me and daft Elvis here. Why don't you come round? I'm sure Barney can spare you for a morning. Sooner I hear the story, the better.'

An hour later and Annabel was driving up the lane to Claygate. Walter watched her parking neatly at the farm gate. He couldn't help thinking of the time, over a year ago now, when Jackie had parked up in the same spot, seeking him out when her world was crashing about her ears. Looks like a re-run, he sighed to himself. Marilyn had left a lot of unfinished business behind.

He went out to greet Annabel and brought her into the house. Elvis barked an effusive welcome and jumped up, wagging his tail furiously. Miserable as she was, Annabel couldn't help but smile at the little Border collie and bent down to stroke him. 'Oh, he's gorgeous,' she exclaimed.

'No, don't pick him up,' Walter warned her. 'He pees everywhere when he gets excited. Don't want to spoil your nice dress.'

Annabel spoke softly to Elvis. 'You'll grow out of it and be the best dog there ever was.'

Elvis licked her face enthusiastically in return.

'He'll never be nowt,' Walter said sadly. 'He were the runt of the litter, going to be drowned and Ellie were daft enough to take him when my back was turned. Ah well. Kettle's on, shall we have a cup of tea and you can tell me all about yourself, lass.'

Walter's tone was kind. Annabel sat down at the kitchen table, feeling a little less intimidated. Walter made the tea and set the mugs down. 'Here you are, lass. Have a drink of that. We've plenty of time to talk, after.' He looked closely at her. 'I meant what I said the other day, you're just like your mother. I take it Marilyn was your mother?'

Annabel nodded.

Walter sighed heavily. 'Luckily, I'm the only one left who knew Marilyn when she was younger. I knew your mother all her life and yet sometimes I wonder if I knew her at all. She was a law to herself.' Walter was lost in the past for a few moments. Elvis whined and brought him back to the present. 'Aye, this is a do, lad.' He smiled gently across the table at Annabel. 'Let's hear all about it, lass.'

Slowly, the tale came out. All about the failed adoption and the children's home, the boyfriend and the jeweller's shop raid and finally prison.

Walter was a good listener and made no comment as Annabel told her story. Then came her decision to trace her mother's life in York and perhaps, some family.

Her tears started to flow. Walter was ready and fetched a large box of tissues. Between sobs, Annabel told him how excited she was to find Jackie, but wasn't sure whether she would welcome news of an illegitimate half-sister and, as time went on, it seemed harder and harder to know where to begin.

'I was just working my way up to it when Tom Young stepped into the picture.'

Walter frowned. 'Tom Young? What dealings have you had with him? He's a bad 'un, through and through. Did Jackie a bad turn, but Barney made him put it right.'

'That's why ...' Annabel hiccupped through her sobs, 'that's why he was trying to get back at them, through me.'

'Was he now?' Walter looked grim. 'What did he do?'

'Oh, he was very clever. He got to know me, took me out and tried to find out all about me. I didn't tell him much because I didn't want anyone to know about my spell in prison. But he obviously has ways of finding out these things, because next time I saw him, he knew all about me and he blackmailed me. If I didn't do certain things for him, he was going to tell everyone about my past.'

'And what were these "certain things"?' Walter asked quietly.

'To send a text to Barney, supposedly from another woman.'

Annabel knew she was telling the worst of it now. Walter would take a very dim view of anything that upset his beloved daughter. She was frightened of his reaction but had to tell it all. 'Yes, I did it. I'm sorry I did, because I wouldn't hurt Jackie or Barney for the world, but I was terrified that Tom Young would do what he said. If I tried to go somewhere else, he would just ruin my life there for me. I thought if I did this one thing, he would leave me alone.'

'And did he?'

'No,' Annabel said miserably. 'He came back again. Wanted me to spill mouse droppings at the café and then ring Environmental Health anonymously and report them. I didn't,' she added hastily, seeing Walter's thunderous face. 'I couldn't. It was too cruel. And then I saw you the other day and you knew who I am. I had no one to talk to and it's all such a mess...'

She broke down, weeping bitterly. Quietly, Walter came to sit beside her and took her in his arms. Another of Marilyn's daughters, crying in his kitchen. He was getting used to this. He let her cry until there were no more tears left.

'Life's a funny old thing,' he said, stroking her hair. 'A bit over a year ago, I lived here all by myself. Nobody to care for me or about me, only old Sarah, my hen. And now? Now I have a wife and a daughter who try to keep me in order, a crazy dog I don't really want, but best of all, Marilyn's left me another daughter to care about and look after. If she'll let me.' He raised Annabel's face, level with his own. 'She meant this to be, you know. Leaving you those garnets. She knew that if you came looking for her and she'd passed on, that I'd know them straight away and get to the truth. Don't worry, lass. You're not going anywhere. Not away from York, nor me nor Jackie. We'll sort it all out. Just leave Tom Young to me. I know how to deal with him. He won't be troubling you any more.'

Walter's words were brave, but in reality he had no idea what he would do to crush the mighty Tom Young.

CHAPTER 49

George was feeling hung over and Penny was cross. According to her, he had ruined their gondola ride the previous evening.

'You were drunk, you thought you were James Bond and tried to kill our gondolier and then tip him in the canal. On the bus home you sang "We'll gather violets in the spring again" at the top of your voice and when you finally ran out of steam, snored the rest of the way. It's one embarrassment after another, George Montague. Any more of it and I'm going home.'

George stared at her. Penny had a vivid imagination sometimes. He may have had one drink too many, but he never did any of that. He would have remembered. All the same, it looked like he was in negative equity for brownie points. Something would have to be done.

'How about stopping off at Florence or Verona before Rome? You like your culture. Isn't Florence supposed to be choc-full of it?'

Penny's eyes lit up. He was instantly forgiven. Florence! She never thought she would get George to go there. Seeing the smile spread across Penny's face, George reached for his maps. Maybe after a good breakfast and strong Italian coffee, he might feel up to the journey.

He was busy with his maps when Penny's phone rang. He carried on looking at the route, hoping it wasn't going to be bad news from home, one of their boys sick or in trouble of some kind. Someone at the other end of the line was obviously very upset, judging by Penny's responses. 'Oh no, he didn't? Then what? Calm down. Yes, we'll go and see him and get it all sorted out. We'll explain, don't worry. Leave it to me.'

Unable to make head nor tail of it all, George returned to his maps. Some time later Penny put the phone down and jumped up briskly from her chair. 'Come on, George. We have to go.'

'Go? Now? Where?'

'Rome. We need to see Stan and explain that what he saw wasn't really what he saw. In fact, it was quite the opposite.' Penny opened her holdall and began packing her things into it.

'What about Florence?'

'She'll have to wait.' Penny paused. 'Another time. We can make a special trip and see everything then.'

'That'll be nice.' George had been hoping to 'do' Florence in a day, two at the most. What was so urgent with Stan?

'Hurry up and pack, George. We need to get off. Stan popped home to see Kate and found a man there, kissing her. Well, it looked like he was kissing her. I suppose he was, but Kate didn't want him kissing her and Stan got hold of the wrong end of the stick and punched the bloke, chucked him out and stormed off. He won't talk to Kate at all now.'

'She shouldn't go kissing other blokes then, should she?' George pointed out reasonably.

'She wasn't, he forced her. Some arty bloke she'd met when she did some modelling.'

'Modelling! I thought she worked for the Historical Trust.'

'She does. This was to earn extra money. I can't stop to explain it all now, we have to get to Rome and talk sense into Stan before it's too late.'

'What about breakfast and a nice pot of coffee first,' George suggested hopefully.

Penny zipped up her bag. 'Let's go.'

George gathered up his maps. Women. First it was this, then it was that, and when you offered to do what they wanted, they didn't want it. Now they were haring off to sort out an argument that wasn't even theirs, without any breakfast.

CHAPTER 50

David Hall had been lucky to get tickets for *Murder in the City*. The play was proving popular and was sold out for weeks ahead, but one of David's friends had tickets he couldn't use and passed them on. David decided to take Genevieve to see it. No cricket balls, no fishing line to get tangled up in and no water to fall into. It was going to be grand.

As usual, Genevieve looked effortlessly beautiful. She really was a stunning girl. Even so, David was wistful. A certain lady with long brown hair and brown eyes still insisted on haunting his every waking hour and some of his dreams too.

Heads turned to look at Genevieve as they made their way inside York Theatre Royal. David felt like he had a visiting celebrity on his arm but, to Genevieve's credit, she had no vanity about her looks. She was eager to get inside and find their seats.

They were lucky. Their seats were at the back of the stalls with a good view of all the stage. The play was billed as 'a mystery that will keep you guessing right to the end' and the cast was headed by well-known actors.

David enjoyed watching Genevieve's eyes light up with pleasure as she spotted people she knew in the audience. He knew quite a few people too and they spent a pleasant fifteen minutes before curtain up exchanging names and potted biographies of their acquaintances, although sometimes it was hard to follow Genevieve's descriptions. 'He was the one who dropped the milk in the office once. You know, the one with the beard who wanted his mother to have power of attorney for

237

his dog.' And she described a very stout lady in the front stalls as, 'Mrs Jackson from Gilbert's Farm. The one on the left with the pigs on the trees. Oh, and there's goats. Mr Jackson is quite funny about them, like his children too.'

David was intrigued, but there was no opportunity to follow this up, as the curtain was rising.

It was a modern play, very fast moving, with lots of scene changes. A man was found shot dead on a city street. He had a wife and extended family and operated a chain of casinos in major cities throughout England. There were a lot of suspects in the plot. First one member of the family looked highly suspicious and then the finger was pointed at another. The detective inspector was at the front of the stage, declaiming the wife's innocence, even though the evidence pointed to her, when Genevieve leaned over to David and said in quite a loud voice, 'Well, of course he'd say that. He's in love with her. Probably always has been. She's a local girl. I bet they had an affair and that's his son. He shot Paul Hitchins because he'd just found out he wasn't really his son and he was going to throw him and his mother out and disinherit them. Inspector Mitchell knows that, but nobody else does and he's not going to say, is he?'

'Ssh,' David was pink to his ears.

The audience around them tittered. Some agreed with Genevieve and, as the first half of the play rolled on, the word quietly spread all around the stalls. At the interval, everyone agreed, the son was the killer.

It was the only topic of conversation in the bar. There was much laughter and pointing in Genevieve's direction. People passing them with drinks said, 'Well done that lady.' 'Are you a detective in real life?' 'You had the plot nailed in no time.'

They had hardly got their own drinks when a lady in a smart suit came towards them. 'I'm Teresa Morecambe,' she said. 'House Manager here.' She held out an envelope to them. 'Your ticket money and dinner at Angelino's. On us. Provided,' she went on, 'you make an early exit from our theatre and don't give the next bit of the plot away to the audience in the first ten minutes.'

David shook his head. He'd have laid money on tonight going smoothly. Who would have thought a simple visit to the theatre...?

On the pavement outside, David looked at Genevieve. 'Well, shall we go to Angelino's, as the lady said?'

'No.' Genevieve heard the dejection in his voice and made a decision. 'Take me home, David. I seem to be a jinx on everything at the moment. Trouble just seems to follow me.'

David silently agreed. Genevieve had surprised him before, but never as much as her next words. 'Take Annabel to Angelino's. I know you really like her and I'm sure she likes you. Why don't you try again?'

He didn't know what to say. Was it so obvious? He hugged Genevieve. 'You've been the best, Genevieve. Thank you.' He looked anxiously at her. 'We'll still be friends?'

'If you don't mind being jinxed now and again.'

David dropped her home and drove on in a thoughtful mood. Genevieve wasn't such an airhead after all. Maybe he would try asking Annabel out again.

CHAPTER 51

The long, hot spell of weather had dried out the path along the riverbank. Walter had had an early start at Claygate, helping Ellie to load up for a farmers' market in Wetherby. He could have done without a stint at the café today. It was beginning to look like he was old faithful, called upon when needed and in this case, needed because they had an evening do to prepare for and Henri was going to be busy.

Walter cycled slowly, turning over the problem of Annabel in his mind. Not much shocked him these days, he was too long in the tooth for that – but Jackie? No, she was another kettle of fish altogether. She might not take this new carry-on in her stride. He would have to talk to Barney. Maybe between them they could sort it out.

He became aware of a group of schoolboys cycling behind him and increased his speed. He'd sooner get off the path before they caught up with him. Some lads could be downright rude, pushing past in their hurry to get to school.

The boys were young and had a turn of speed that was a distant memory for Walter. They were at his heels in a few moments. 'Move over, old man,' the first boy called. 'We're in a hurry, let us past.'

Walter moved to the edge of the path. 'Plenty of room, lads,' he said. 'Just be careful.'

Two boys appeared either side of him, weaving dangerously close. 'Come on, old man, get a move on.'

Walter was not going to be intimidated, especially by a bunch of lads. 'Get on your way if you're in such a hurry. You don't need all the path.'

The boy behind Walter laughed. 'Ah, but we do, don't we boys? Shall we show this gentleman just how much path we need?'

The two other boys took their cue from him and closed in on Walter, riding directly alongside him. There wasn't room for three on the path and one boy was forced onto the grass.

'Oh, now look at that,' called the boy from behind. 'Pushing my friend out. We can't have that.' He nudged Walter's back wheel with his own.

Walter wobbled, but kept on going. 'Leave off and get to school, or I'll be in to see your headmaster about you.'

'Oh yeah. Know which school then?'

Walter looked at the boys. They were in white shirts and black trousers. They could be going anywhere. 'Well, get off anyway,' he shouted.

'We don't like a sneak, do we boys?' said the boy behind. 'Sneaks always come to a sticky end, or in your case, mister...' He pushed Walter's bike hard.

Walter lost control and started slipping down the bank. His bike fell away and he rolled into the river. The boys stood on the path laughing. As Walter stood up, dripping with water and weed, the boys mounted their bikes, waved their goodbyes and were gone.

*****

'You fell in the river?' Jackie regarded Walter with exasperation. She sniffed the air. 'Have you been at Ellie's sloe gin?'

'Course not,' Walter protested. 'I told you. It was a bunch of lads larking about.'

'Well don't stand there dripping everywhere. The cleaner's just finished and we haven't got time to be mopping up after you. Henri needs you in the kitchen, so go and get your whites on, pronto.' She wheeled about and went into her office, slamming the door behind her.

Walter looked at the closed door. 'Oh Dad,' he said in Jackie's voice. 'Just think, you might have drowned. Get out of your wet clothes and I'll fetch a towel for you. And a hot cup of coffee. You must have had a dreadful shock.' He shuffled off towards the cloakroom. 'A man can always dream.'

Louise, the new waitress, came out from the kitchen. 'Oh, Walter. You're making an awful mess. That floor's just been cleaned.'

Walter shook his head. They were all the same. Did Jackie train 'em? He wondered what they'd say if he appeared with a dagger stuck in his chest. Probably tell him he shouldn't have been in the way of it.

Having got off to a bad start, the day at the café did not improve. Walter used to think Penny was irritating when she drifted off into one of her obscure rambles but he had to hand it to Genevieve, she could lose anyone in a paper bag.

'I wish now I hadn't known it,' she said, and picked up a tray and headed off into the café.

When she returned, Walter couldn't contain himself. 'Known what?'

'About the detective knowing that lady, years before. I don't know how I knew it. I just did. I don't know why everyone had to get so cross about it.'

Walter could feel another Genevieve incident coming on. He wasn't sure he had the energy to run with it to the bitter end, only she might witter on all day. It might be best if he had a vague idea what she was on about. 'Who got cross?' he asked cautiously.

'David, of course. Well, not just him,' she conceded. 'I forgot to whisper and said it out loud and then everyone around me heard and then people started repeating it and soon everyone knew and then it was the interval and someone from the management came up to David at the bar and gave him his money back. She said I'd managed to ruin the first half and they didn't want it to happen in the second, so perhaps we'd like to have an early dinner on them and goodnight. She was very cross too.' Genevieve looked troubled.

David Hall was a young man and no doubt able to cope with the dramas that accompanied Genevieve, but Walter didn't feel up to it today. He patted her arm. 'I'm sure it'll come right, lass, things generally do.'

'Not this time, Walter,' she said sadly. 'I won't be seeing him again. At least, not on a date. I think he only asked me out because Annabel turned him down and I know he really likes her. So I saved him the trouble and said we should call it a day. I don't think we were meant to be. I don't think anyone was meant for me.'

Henri bustled up. 'Genevieve! Ze fish kettle! I need it, ziss instant.'

Genevieve smiled at Walter and moved off in Henri's wake. 'Fish kettles are far more important, aren't they?'

As he worked, Walter mused on the mystery of relationships. What attracted one man to one woman and not to another? Look at him and Ellie. Chalk and cheese on the surface and yet they had settled down to a happy life together. He had thought Jackie and Kate were set fair to do the same and yet that old snake had crawled into their Eden.

At least he knew that Barney was innocent and had never looked at another woman. But how was he going to explain it all to Jackie? It was going to take tact and diplomacy and he knew he could be a bit short of those sometimes.

Today was not the day for explaining anything to her. He was too busy and she was too cross. When he had put his nose out of the kitchen, she'd nearly bitten it off. 'This isn't a holiday camp, Dad. Don't leave Henri to do it all on his own.' Hmph. A man wasn't even allowed to take a breather these days.

Kate was no better, but he couldn't solve her problems. He didn't know what they were, but she walked around with a face like a wet weekend and apparently Stan would never forgive her. What had she done? Blown their house deposit on the bingo? Danced naked at the Mango Tree Night Club? Kate could be racy when she chose. It must be bad because she hadn't confided in him like she used to.

Walter shrugged. He had enough on his plate, without Kate and Genevieve piled on to it. Henri came rushing through from his kitchen, clutching sacks of onions and carrots. 'Waltere, Waltere. Zere has been zee *catastroph*. *Oui, oui*. *Le catastroph*. Ze machine, ze one that skins ze carrots, the onions, it has gone pouff!'

'Pouff?'

'*Mais oui*. It goes bang, pouff. And black smoke, it comes from ze machine. It is defunct. A *catastroph*. Now I need you, queeckly. I need ze carrots and ze onions for my cassoulet. You get ready, yes?'

The day just got better and better. Walter looked up and said, 'Thank you, kind and loving God, for giving me such a wonderful bunch of people to work with. I couldn't ask for more.'

'Zis is no time for your prayers. I need onions.' Henri rushed back to his own preparations, leaving Walter to contemplate the mound of vegetables awaiting his attention. It looked like he would be crying his way through the rest of the morning.

******

It was a beautiful Saturday morning. Kate Peterson strolled slowly through the streets of York on her way to Café Paradise. Dully, she wondered what would happen when Stan returned from Rome. The term would be coming to an end soon. He would have to come home and then what? Would she ever be able to make him understand about Frederick Rawlings? She wouldn't need the job at the café if they split up. There would be no new house to save for.

Kate couldn't bear her thoughts and hurried on. Her route took her through the old cobbled streets of The Shambles. She looked into the shop windows as she walked, trying to distract herself. The old sweet shop, the coffee shop, the art shop and gallery. Kate walked on a few steps and then stopped. What had she just seen?

She retraced her steps and looked more closely into the art gallery window. Amongst the paintings on display was a portrait of a reclining nude. Kate froze. How dare he? This was Frederick Rawling's revenge. He had only seen her without her clothes very briefly and yet ... he must have worked on this canvas in secret. She could not even say it was without her consent, as she had modelled for the life class. A hot flush suffused her face and spread through her body. He had caught the essence of her so well. She looked like a woman sated by love. She couldn't leave it there for all to see, she was all too recognisable, but the gallery was asking a thousand pounds for it. She couldn't afford it. All her savings were tied up in a high-interest account, the condition being no instant access. What was she to do?

By the time she reached Café Paradise, shock had set in. Walter took one look at her white face and sat her down in the nearest chair. 'Something's happened, love. I can see that. Here, I'll get you a cup of tea and you tell me all about it.'

Walter went to the counter and made them a pot of tea. Kate sat at the table, thoughts tumbling around in her head. Her friends and family might see the painting or, worse still, Stan's family. She'd never live it down. And if Stan saw it...

This last thought was unbearable. Kate poured out the whole story to Walter. He listened quietly, shaking his head in dismay.

'I never sat for him, Walter. He only saw me naked that very first time and then, only briefly. He kept dressing me up in weird Roman stuff after that. He's done it all from his imagination. I look ... look ... voluptuous and sexy and ...' she buried her face in her hands, 'as if I'd just been to bed with him. What am I going to do? I can't magic a thousand pounds out of thin air and it's on full view, for all to see.'

As if Walter didn't have enough troubles on his plate, here was another one. Why did women have to complicate matters and get themselves into such scrapes? And he had to spend his time getting them out of them. He got up from the table.

'They'll not open until ten, at least,' he said laconically, collecting their tea cups.

'Who?' Kate snuffled through her handkerchief.

'That gallery place. They never open early, do they? Bohemian. That's the word. Don't they all stay up late, drinking and painting in garrets half the night? Not like us poor farmers, up at the crack of dawn to feed our stock. We've got no choice.'

Kate had lost the thread of Walter's diatribe. 'It's probably nearer eleven before they open and by then...' She dissolved into tears again.

Walter raised his eyes heavenwards. Women had endless reservoirs of tears always at the ready and out they sprung, like pressing the washer button for your car screen.

'It's all tourists down The Shambles, Kate. Don't worry. I'll have that painting out of there the minute they open the doors and no one will be any the wiser.'

'You'll buy it?' Kate said in wonder.

'Stan's been good to me,' Walter said. 'I can't have his wife on show, in a shop window, dressed or undressed. You leave it to me.'

Kate burst into tears again. Walter looked on in amazement. It didn't make any difference, did it? Good news, bad news, even no news, and they still cried. He was looking forward to leaving this madhouse soon and getting back to his smallholding at Claygate. Even the prospect of trying to train Elvis didn't seem so bad now.

CHAPTER 52

Jackie went home early from the café. Her head ached from staring at accounts all morning and she felt sick and dizzy. She lay on the bed she used to share with Barney, breathing in his familiar smell, which made her feel even more miserable and lonely.

Samson padded into the bedroom and stopped in surprise. He was used to having the house to himself in the daytime. Seeing Jackie curled up on the bed, he jumped up and snuggled in beside her, purring with contentment as she reached out and pulled him close.

'I guess you're one step up from my old teddy bear,' she told him. 'At least you're warm and alive and you don't deceive me.'

She stroked the cat absently. He shuddered with delight. More often than not, she turfed him out of the door. This was way off the cat-scale.

'What am I going to do, Samson?' Jackie stared up at the ceiling, following the intricate patterns in the roughcast plasterwork. 'We can't go on like this. In a few months' time... I need to talk to Dad.'

She continued stroking Samson. He didn't care who she talked to, as long as it wasn't right now. She was doing a fine job right where she was.

******

Later that afternoon, Ellie was busy in her dairy when Walter bumped up the track in the van. He unloaded the painting and took it into the house, propping it against the dresser in the kitchen.

He'd been in a tearing hurry when he brought it away from the gallery, refusing the offer of wrapping by the gallery owner, throwing an old goat's blanket over it instead. Now he had it home, he looked at it properly. By heck, the guy might be a first-class creep but he was a good artist. He had captured Kate's beauty and sensuality perfectly.

The back door opened and Ellie came in with Elvis capering at her heels. 'Now don't start,' she told him. 'You've only been in your run for half an... My God, Walter, what have you got there?'

She came across the kitchen and glanced at the painting and then at Walter. 'Well, I knew you liked women, but ... have you gone mad? What are you trying to do, give me an inferiority complex? How dare you go bringing nude women home? Look at her, she's asking for it.'

Elvis was not used to Ellie raising her voice. In his anxiety he peed on the floor.

'And now look what you've done.' Ellie was furious. 'Well, you can clear it up. And don't think I'm going to live with ...' she pointed to the painting, 'that.' She turned on her heels. 'I'm going back to the dairy for a while.'

Elvis sat down, watching Walter carefully. He hoped he wasn't going to start shouting too. Walter looked down at Elvis. 'Do I look like a man who would bring a large painting of a naked lady home to his wife? If she'd just give me a chance to get a word in... You stay here and don't move.'

Walter followed Ellie into the dairy and explained the circumstances surrounding his acquisition of the painting. 'I only bought it to get it out of the window. We couldn't have every Joe-Soap in York seeing her like that, could we?'

Ellie agreed. 'But you were having a good look at it just now.'

'Only because I hadn't even looked at it in the shop. Kate had been spouting tears all over the place. I wanted to see what all the fuss was about.'

'And?'

'Aye, it's good, but it's not the kind of picture you'd hang in your sitting room. I don't know what to do with it'

'You'd best ask Kate,' Ellie said practically.

Walter agreed and went back indoors to telephone Kate. In his absence, Elvis had explored the new acquisition, chewed part of the frame and was happily tucking in to one of Kate's feet on the canvas.

'Bloody Elvis!' Walter shouted. 'I told you not to move!' He scooped the dog up and put him out of the door. He turned back into the kitchen and surveyed the damaged picture. If she wanted to keep it, it would cost another pretty penny to have the damage put right.

No wonder I have to keep working, he grumbled to himself as he dialled Kate's number. If it's not Jackie, it's Ellie and a new dairy. Now it's Annabel and Kate. You watch lad, it'll be Genevieve next and then Penny'll come home and she'll be in some scrape and then I'll be ready for the funny farm and everyone'll be happy.

For once, Walter was spared. Kate never wanted to clap eyes on the hateful picture again and sincerely hoped Walter would put it on his next bonfire. She would pay him back soon and it would serve her right for her foolishness. Walter was about to agree with her but stopped himself in time. It never did to agree with women. For some reason, it always backfired.

CHAPTER 53

The course at the International College in Rome had finished. Stan had kept a safe distance from Sofia for the last two weeks and buried his head in his books, so much so that he came out top of the class and now possessed a Diploma in Roman Studies, with Merit.

Sofia looked on with amusement. If Stan saw her coming down a corridor at the college, he changed direction and heard her tinkling laughter follow him. In her classes, he kept his head down and furiously took notes, trying not to look up. On the occasions he did, he saw Sofia's sardonic smile and the mischievous glint in her eye and bent his head again to his books.

It was time to leave and Stan was packing his bags. He felt tired and confused. What was he going home to? Kate had written such a beautiful letter to him and he had not replied. He had not heard from her again. What would she be thinking? That he was the complete louse everyone had warned her against in the first place? Would she still be there? If she thought he couldn't forgive her, did she think it was all over between them?

His heart ached. He had been such a fool. Jealous over nothing, not even stopping to listen, and taking his bat home like a spoilt boy. Stan sat down heavily on his bed and stared out of the window. It was a beautiful day and the street below his window was already crowded with shoppers making their way to the local market. The busy chatter and laughter filled the air, along with the constant tooting of horns from the ubiquitous

Vespas as they wove their way among the cars and lorries.

He longed for his home in York, such a beautiful and gracious city with the river running through it, full of its own ancient history, in a green and pleasant land. How could he go home and try and pick things up with Kate after what he had done? He couldn't blame Sofia, although she had tried hard enough from day one. But it still took two to tango.

There was a knock on the door. Now what? Stan got up and opened it. Sofia was standing there, smiling broadly at him, holding a package in her hand.

'Stanlee, darling. You are leaving today. I bring you a leetle present and to say goodbye.'

'What is it?' He looked at it suspiciously, as if it might bite him.

Sofia laughed. 'Open it and see.'

Inside the paper was a small carved figure of a very muscular naked man. Stan looked questioningly at Sofia. 'Don't look like that, Stanlee. He is for good luck. He is Bacchus, the old Greek God. The Romans adopted him for their famous festivals. You are going home to Kate. You drink wine and, you know...'

Stan frowned. Bacchanalia had got him into enough trouble. He didn't want to take him home to York. 'I don't think Kate would...'

'Kate will love it. He is real, ancient.' Seeing Stan's blank expression, Sofia said impatiently, 'He is not reproduction. He is old Rome, from the Coliseum. An artefact.'

'Oh. Yes, I see. Thank you.' He turned away to put the little figure in his bag.

Sofia followed him into the room. She put her arms around him and kissed the back of his neck.

'Sofia,' Stan began.

'It's alright Stanlee. This is goodbye and I have another leetle present for you.'

'Listen, you don't have to...'

'Oh, but I do. I have enjoyed teasing you for these last two weeks, but, regretfully, now the time has come to end my leetle game with you.'

Teasing? Game? What was the woman on about? He turned to face her.

'You see, my dear Stanlee, when you woke up and found me in bed beside you, that's all it was. We slept side by side, like two innocent children.'

Stan stared at her. 'You mean, we never, we didn't...'

'No, Stanlee. We did not. You went to sleep like a leetle baby, talking about your lovely Kate. And when you woke up, you thought we had ... so I just let you carry on thinking that. It was fun. Your face was, how do you say in England? The picture.'

As Sofia's words sank in, Stan shook his head, a huge sense of relief flooding over him. He flung his arms around Sofia and kissed her soundly, dancing her around the room. 'Thank you, thank you, thank you,' he shouted. 'That's the best news ever.'

'You need not be so pleased about it,' Sofia said indignantly. 'You have missed the great experience.'

'I'm sure I have, Sofia,' he grinned at her. 'You are a very bad woman, but now I know the truth, I forgive you.' He held his hand out to her. 'In England we say pax.'

Sofia took his hand. 'Pax, Stanlee.'

******

Rome on a Friday afternoon was blisteringly hot and noisy. Cars and lorries whizzed in all directions. If there were laws governing the traffic flow, no one took any notice. Scooters, motorbikes, cars and pedestrians rushed around the squares, intent upon their own destinations, regardless of the other traffic in their way.

By the time George and Penny had found their way to Via Bartolemeo, they were dusty and tired. The journey had taken longer than they had expected and they needed to find lodgings for the night. George was longing for a cool shower and an even cooler beer but Penny was insistent that they see Stan first.

Sofia answered the door to their knock. She surveyed the two dusty travellers with amusement. 'How can I help you?'

Penny was taken aback. She didn't know what she had been expecting, probably a sun-dried elderly Italian in black. If this was Sofia, she was anything but sun-dried. She was gorgeous. Tall, elegant and very chic. Penny felt like a peasant beside her.

George let Penny do the talking. She knew all the ins and outs of the Stan–Kate situation.

'We're friends of Stan Peterson. His wife, Kate, gave us your address. As we were going to be in Rome, she suggested we pay him a visit. Are you Sofia, by any chance?'

Sofia smiled. 'Friends of Stanlee. You are most welcome. Yes, I am Sofia. Come in and I will call him down. Who shall I say?'

'Penny and George Montague.'

They followed Sofia into the cool hallway and waited whilst Sofia ran lightly up the stairs to find Stan. George raised his eyebrows quizzically at Penny. 'Stan's been lodging with that beauty all this time! No wonder he didn't remember to answer any of Kate's texts. I don't think I would have.'

'She may be very beautiful but I don't think Stan would forget he's a married man. Not so soon. Unlike some I could mention.'

George stared at her. She didn't mean him, surely? He knew a pretty woman when he saw one, but he took care Penny didn't see him looking. And she was a fine one to talk. What about that Enriquez Gonzalez, her dance partner? Did she always remember she was a married woman? He was about to follow up this thought in words when Stan came bounding down the stairs.

He swept Penny up in a joyous embrace and hugged George too. 'Penny. George. Where have you sprung from?'

'Venice,' George answered. 'We were going to Florence before coming on here, but Kate was anxious about you and asked us to call. As soon as. You know,' George shifted uncomfortably from one foot to another. 'See if we could fill you in on a few things you don't know about.' He pushed Penny forward. 'Penny knows. Wanted to have a little word with you.'

Stan looked down at Penny and smiled ruefully. 'Is it about Frederick?'

'Yes. But it's not what you think it is,' she added hastily. 'Nothing could be further from the truth.'

'Listen.' Stan looked at his watch. 'Come on up to my room for ten minutes and we can have a chat but then I have to go. My course has finished and I'm catching a flight home today. I'm going home to Kate.'

The three of them trooped upstairs. Even before they got into Stan's room, Penny could not contain herself. 'It wasn't Kate's fault, Stan. You must understand that. That fellow forced himself on her...'

Stan shut the door. 'I know. Kate wrote me a long letter telling me all about it. I understand now. I've been such an idiot, Penny. I didn't believe Kate, didn't give her a chance even to explain properly and yet things have happened to me here that she wouldn't approve of either.'

George looked at him hard. 'Stan, lad...'

'It's alright George. No bones broken. Let's just say Sofia, in full flight, is a hard woman to resist. It can be a very scary experience, believe me, a full-blooded Italian sex-siren coming on to you.'

'I like being scared,' George commented happily. 'She could...'

'George,' Penny growled.

'I was only saying. It's not going to happen, is it?'

'Stick around here long enough, George, and it will,' Stan said firmly. 'Anyway, I didn't contact Kate because of things that happened here. But I'm catching the evening flight home and check-in time is ...' he looked at his watch, 'about half an hour from now. So I've really got to get moving. Need to get a cab.'

'No need,' George said firmly. 'I've got the Harley outside. We can stash your bags on the back and I'll get you there in no time.'

'What about me?' Penny asked.

'Find a nice hotel and ring me,' said George.

'I'm sure Sofia would let you stay here,' Stan suggested. 'My room's free now.'

'No.' Penny was quite sure about that. With Sofia on the loose and George in reckless mode, anything could happen. 'We'll stick to Plan A.'

Stan said his goodbyes to Sofia and Maria. 'Keep in touch, Stanlee,' Sofia said. 'I'm sure there will be a research trip to Rome for you sometime.' She kissed him on both cheeks, a twinkling smile in her eyes. 'I will be here, waiting for my oh, so *rugged* Englishman.'

'No doubt *my wife* will enjoy a trip to Rome sometime too,' said Stan, smiling down at her. '*Arriverderci*, Sofia.'

He roared away on the back of the Harley. When Sofia realised Penny had been left behind, she took her into the city and ensconced her in a quiet hotel run by friends of hers. Penny was delighted with it and was soon soaking in a deep bath. Now they could have a few days of sightseeing and hotel luxury before setting off home again. They had come hundreds of miles on the Harley and Penny didn't relish the trip home.

A couple of hours went by and there was no sign of George. Penny tried not to get anxious. He was not answering his phone but she comforted herself with the thought that it would be turned off in the airport. Maybe he had stayed to see Stan safely on the plane back to England.

Another hour went by and there was still no word. Just as she was ready to go to the police station, her telephone rang. It was George asking where she was.

'The Hotel Romano. Where are you?'

'I'm at the hospital.' George sounded fed up. 'I got Stan to the airport OK and then had a bit of an accident on the way back into the city.'

Penny sat down on the bed. Her legs felt wobbly. 'How much of an accident, George? You must be hurt to be at the hospital.'

'I've bust my arm. The Harley's fine, thank God. I don't really know how it happened. I was going round this corner and the back end just went from under me. The bike went one way and I went another and crack, I went down on my elbow and that was it. But don't worry, Penny. I've been well looked after and the bike's safe at the local garage. I was lucky, it was a party of English folk I nearly ran into. I don't suppose they felt that lucky at the time, but they were alright about it and sorted everything out.' For a moment there was silence, then she heard him talking to someone else. 'Eh? What? Oh, that's very kind of you.' George came back to the phone. 'They say they know the Hotel Romano and they'll bring me along as soon as the hospital sign me out.'

'You won't be able to ride all the way back to England with a broken arm, George,' said Penny. 'What are we going to do?'

'I think I'll have to sell the bike and we'll fly home. Nothing else for it. I'll see you later and we can talk about it then.'

George rang off. Penny looked down at the phone, a slow smile spreading across her face. She was sorry for George, of course. He would be in plaster for quite a while. It wasn't the end to his holiday that he had imagined. But she wasn't sorry she would be flying home.

No, she wasn't sorry at all. Penny got up and did a little jig about the room. What fantastic news. No more dusty biking, no roaring engine ringing in her ears. Just a short flight and she would be home. With a bit of luck, George would be put off motorbikes for some time to come.

CHAPTER 54

The car wheels spun on the dry, dusty track as Barney Anderson bumped up the lane to Walter's Claygate smallholding. He got out of the car and looked around for signs of life. All was quiet in the yard.

'Ellie? Walter?' he called hopefully. When no one appeared, he reached into the car and tooted the horn. Looking over the field gate, he saw Walter walking towards the house with Elvis frisking about his heels.

'Now, lad. What brings you here on a Wednesday afternoon?'

Barney opened the gate for Walter and Elvis to pass through. 'Your daughter, Walter.'

Walter closed the gate carefully and looked out over the fields. 'I thought so. She hasn't been herself these past weeks. Snappy, finding fault. Sometimes nowt's right for her. Come in, lad, and tell me all about it.'

Walter led the way into the house, leaving Elvis in his basket in Ellie's new utility room. 'He can't do too much damage in there,' Walter commented. 'I've put stone flags down. He can't make much of them, even with his sharp teeth.'

When they were seated with mugs of tea, Walter looked across the kitchen table at Barney. 'Out with it, lad. I have a feeling I know what's coming but whatever it is, it won't seem so bad once it's out in the open.'

Barney hoped he was right. The appalling text had been going round and round in his head for long enough now and he had exhausted every avenue to find the mysterious Amy. He desperately needed to find a way back to the happy life he had with Jackie before this mischief had blown up in his face.

Walter listened carefully as Barney related the events of that awful evening and Jackie's withdrawal from him, how she spent nearly all her waking hours at the café these days. 'I see more of Samson than I do of her. He's even bringing me dead mice as thank-you presents these days,' he said sadly. 'Now, to cap it all, I think she's getting her own back on me and has a *friend* at Bishopthorpe Hall. I've seen them, Walter, kissing and hugging. She says he was at our wedding, but I think I'd have remembered a handsome chap like that.'

Walter reflected a moment. 'Bishopthorpe Hall, eh? Dark-haired bloke, tall, slim?'

Barney nodded. 'Yeah. Sounds about right.'

'Martin Woodside, for sure,' Walter said decisively. 'She's right. He was at the wedding. He's her best mate from schooldays and they've always stayed friends.'

'Looked more than friends to me,' Barney said miserably.

'Not in this case, lad,' Walter chuckled. 'He bats for the other side, if you know what I mean. He was there with his partner, right enough. Geoff they call him. Martin's the manager at Bishopthorpe. She probably had some legit business with him.'

Listening to Barney's tale, Walter realised how deeply Tom Young had divided this young couple by his mischief. He needed to be stopped in his tracks. He decided to take Barney into his confidence and together they could sort this out. He drew a deep breath. 'I hope you've taken the whole afternoon off, Barney lad. I've a tale to tell you and it has to do with this text lark. It'll take a bit of telling and before I start, I want you to promise me one thing.'

Barney looked at him. This was not what he'd been expecting. What did Walter know that needed a promise from him? 'Go on.'

'Promise me that when I've finished, you won't immediately go off and punch a certain person on the nose.'

'How can I promise that when I don't know who it is?' Walter waited for Barney to consider. 'You don't mean ... there's only one person I would love to punch on the nose. I don't need a reason.' Barney stared at Walter. 'Is he at the back of all this? How?'

'Promise me,' Walter insisted. 'Then we'll make a plan when you've calmed down.'

Barney frowned. 'If it's the only way I'm going to solve my problems, alright. I promise. Go on.'

'Annabel Lewis-Langley,' Walter began.

'Annabel!' Barney was surprised. 'What's she got to do with this?'

'She's Jackie's half-sister.'

The world had gone mad. Annabel, who ran his office so efficiently, was Jackie's half-sister? Marilyn's daughter? Or Walter's daughter? And where did Tom Young come into all this? Barney had listened to many queer tales in the course of his work but his own family could beat all of them hands down.

Slowly, Walter related Annabel's story to Barney: how she had come to York to find out about Marilyn's life and had discovered a half-sister in Jackie; his recognition of the garnets she had worn at Jake's birthday party; and Tom Young's attempts to blackmail her into causing trouble between Barney and Jackie and the possible closure of Café Paradise.

As the tale unfolded, Barney jumped up from the table and paced about the kitchen, exclaiming as he learned more of Tom's methods. 'That man will stop at nothing. I thought we had put an end to his schemes last year but it seems I was wrong. He's regrouped and is looking for revenge. Well, he's not getting it this time. I need to pay him another visit,' Barney said grimly.

'Sit yourself down, lad,' Walter said calmly. 'You promised, remember. Now listen to me. I've had a bit more time than you to think about this and we can kill two birds with one stone, if we get it right. We can sort Tom Young out, but we need to put our heads together about Annabel.'

Barney sat down at the table again. 'Jackie? I think she should know, but...'

'She needs the truth, lad,' Walter said firmly. 'Leave that one to me. I know all the ins and outs and don't forget I knew Marilyn and her ways for forty years. She knew all along that I knew Jackie was mine and then she left me a message with those garnets. If Annabel came looking, she knew I'd be mixed up somewhere in bringing those two girls together. But first, we tackle Tom Young before my daughter frets herself to skin and bone.'

******

Barney had given no thought to the aftermath of his visit to Martin Woodside. As he drove back into York, he felt a small sense of relief at having at least nailed that situation down.

Now, after his afternoon with Walter, he knew the whole situation and realised he had messed up, big time, with this Martin and, worse still, with Jackie.

He was right. She was absolutely furious at Barney's cave-man tactics and wiped the floor with him when he arrived home that evening. 'Stupid, high-handed, Neanderthal, completely wrong-headed ... this was just the last straw.' Jackie slammed out of the house and into her car and was immediately away, only the smell of car exhaust fumes lingering on the evening air.

CHAPTER 55

On the flight home, Stan wondered what Kate would make of his text. He didn't trust himself to telephone. When he thought of her and all the hurt he had caused, his throat tightened and tears threatened. He, Stan the Man, ready to cry like a big girl. Imagine that in Rome airport among the chic Italians.

Recd yr ltr. I'm sorry. Back tonite.

He hadn't told her when his flight landed. An awkward public reunion and car journey home? No. The train ride to York would give him time to acclimatise and think. He didn't know how much to say about Sofia. Kate could have no idea what a maneater she was. He had done his best to keep out of the Italian woman's clutches, but he had the feeling Kate wouldn't understand why he and Sofia had shared a bed.

How could he make it up to her for ever doubting her faithfulness? Hot-headed and murderous with rage, he had turned his back on her when he should have stayed to comfort her, not cause her more pain.

As the taxi drew up outside their home, Stan was no nearer knowing what to say. He picked up his bags and climbed the step to the front door.

Kate waited for him on the other side. She heard the taxi pull away and Stan's footsteps bringing him ever nearer. Her heart was beating fast. How would he be? She longed to see him and at the same time dreaded it. They hadn't touched or kissed or even had a proper conversation in three months. Did he really understand about Frederick Rawlings, or would he reject her? His text gave nothing away. Why, oh why, had she ever suggested he go to Rome? And to Sofia, for that matter. She'd thought their love was strong enough to survive. Maybe she was wrong. What of the future, for her and Stan and...?

The door opened and Kate was there. Stan's breath caught in his throat. His lovely Kate, standing there, looking so beautiful and so uncertain. He dropped his bags and swept her into his arms, holding her tightly, never wanting to let her go again. There would be time enough to talk of Frederick and Sofia. Stan was so happy to be home, he didn't care about either of them.

Kate eased herself in his arms, looking up at him, the tears rolling down her face. Immediately, Stan was anxious. 'What is it? Kate? It's alright, isn't it?'

Kate nodded. 'I just don't want you to squash the baby,' she said softly.

Stan drew back and looked down at her. 'Baby? Did you say baby? You're having a...?'

'A baby,' Kate repeated. 'Our baby, Stan. Just before you left, three months ago ... remember? Or has the lovely Sofia driven everything out of your head?' She smiled mistily up at him.

Stan held her gently. 'Oh no,' he said. 'She never drove you out of my head. Not that she didn't try. A personable chap like me. Stan the Man and all that.' He drew Kate back into the circle of his arms. 'A baby. I'm going to be a father.' There was wonderment in his voice.

Suddenly, he realised they were standing in the wide-open doorway, the cool evening air swirling around them. 'What are we doing, standing here?' He picked Kate up and carried her into the living room. 'You have to take better care of yourself. You're expecting a baby. We need to get you to bed, rest is what you need. You can't be too careful.'

Kate groaned. If Stan was going to go on like this for the next six months, she might wish him back in Rome. 'I'm not ill,' she protested. 'It's a natural state. I can do everything I normally would as long as I take care of myself and eat properly.'

'We'll make sure you take care of yourself and you're not to do anything. I'll do it all.'

'Don't fuss,' Kate said. She hated fuss.

'Fuss? Of course I must. I'm having a baby.'

CHAPTER 56

The Europe trip was over prematurely. Back in York, George Montague stared morosely out of the window. With no way of getting it home, he had sold the beloved Harley Davidson to a garage in Rome that Sofia had recommended. He'd got a good deal, but that was little consolation to George as he patted his beloved machine for the last time.

Penny was out shopping and visiting Café Paradise. She was hoping to go back to work early, as their holiday had been cut short. She'd said being stuck in the house with him and his broken arm was worse than all those weeks on the back of the bike. You just couldn't please some women, could you?

Admittedly, it had been extremely hot and dusty travelling at times, but he thought Penny had enjoyed some of the trip. Travelling in the more temperate climes of Britain would be a lot more to her taste. George brightened up at the thought. He could go online now and have a look. After all, the money was there in the bank...

By the time Penny got home later that afternoon, George had three models lined up for her to look at. 'One's over in Doncaster. We could go and look at it tomorrow,' he said excitedly.

'No,' Penny said firmly.

'Well, if you're busy, the day after.'

Penny began to unpack her shopping and put it away. 'No, means no, George. Not tomorrow, or the next day, or even the day after that.' She turned to face him. 'Not ever.'

'What do you mean?'

'We're not having another motorbike, George, that's what I mean. You've had your fun and had a great trip out of it, but it could have ended up a lot worse. And much as you drive me around the bend most of the time, I've no desire to be a merry widow just yet.'

'Merry widow.' George didn't like the sound of that. 'Is that what you'd be?'

'If you get another motorbike and kill yourself, yes I would. I'd be very cross with you for doing it and leaving me behind. But there it is, I'd be on my own and I'm only fifty-three.'

'Out of sight, out of mind then?' George could see her planning his headstone already.

'Of course not. But you don't have nine lives. Can't you find a less dangerous hobby and then we might live to have a future?'

George clicked off the *AutoTrader* website and closed down his laptop. When Penny really put her foot down, he knew he was beaten. There would be no Harley standing in their driveway again.

'How about scuba diving?'

'No.'

'Hot-air ballooning?'

'No.'

'I know, stock-car racing.'

Penny looked at him and sighed. 'Mountaineering? All the Scottish Munros? Why not Project Everest?'

George looked at her with admiration. 'That's my girl. I knew you had the spirit of adventure in you. Now you're talking. Wait 'til my arm's healed. There'll be no stopping us.' He opened the laptop again. 'There'll be sites about it. I can start researching right away.'

Penny returned to her shopping. Surely he knew she didn't mean it? Didn't he?

CHAPTER 57

Barney dialled Detective Sergeant Roger Beesley's number in CID. This was going to be tricky. If he couldn't persuade Roger to hold back, they were all sunk, but it might be the only way.

Roger heard him out in thoughtful silence. 'If it works out, we never had this conversation, Barney. But you do realise that if Tom Young calls your bluff, my department will be obliged to investigate fully and a lot of dirty laundry will be washed in the process. It's a very risky strategy you're proposing and Tom Young is no pushover.'

'I know that, Roger.' Barney gave the thumbs-up to Walter. 'It's a risk I have to take. If I let you in on it straight away, lives are going to be wrecked. I have to take the only chance I have to make him hand over everything he has amassed about Annabel. Blackmail's a very dirty road to go down.'

'And wouldn't I love to nail Tom Young with it?' Roger mused. 'But he's not worth wrecking other lives for. He'll make more mistakes in the future and we'll be around to nab him then.'

Barney put the phone down. 'Come on,' he said. 'Let's pay our old friend a visit.'

'What, now?' Walter looked down at his shabby farm clothes. 'I'm not dressed for it.'

'You're just right, Walter,' Barney grinned. 'Blackmail's a dirty business.'

Elvis was lying quietly in his basket as they made their way through to the back door. He jumped up when he saw Walter approaching. 'Let's take him with us,' Barney suggested.

'Elvis? What for?'

'A sort of Rottweiler in disguise.'

'Have you been in the sun, lad? Elvis couldn't scare the skin off a rice pudding. He dodges his own shadow. Pees if you raise your voice.'

'Well, he's better than nothing. We'll take him.'

Walter shook his head. His son-in-law had funny ideas. He could see now where barmy Genevieve was coming from.

******

At the offices of Young's Insurance Company Limited in Swinegate, Tom Young had cleared his desk before leaving for the evening. He was looking forward to a quiet dinner with Sally, a leggy blonde he'd recently met through the York Enterprise Trust, and then afterwards, maybe back to his flat. Sally was an absolute peach. He hummed happily as he locked his desk drawers and reached for the jacket slung over the back of his chair.

The entrance bell sounded as the front door opened. Who the hell was that at this time of day? They would have to come back tomorrow. He needed to get home and freshen up for Sally. He opened his office door and went into the hallway. 'We're clos...'

Barney Anderson and Walter Breckenridge were standing there, leading a Border collie on a piece of baler twine.

'Gentlemen,' Tom said drily. He looked at Elvis. 'And ... hound. To what do I owe this unexpected pleasure?'

'Annabel Lewis-Langley,' Barney said simply.

Tom Young frowned, his handsome features twisting in a sardonic smile. 'The lovely Annabel,' he said softly. 'I know her slightly. How can I help? I hope she's not in any trouble.'

'Perhaps we could go into your office,' Barney suggested.

Tom hesitated and then turned on his heel and led the way. Barney and Walter followed, with Elvis trotting behind.

Barney closed the door and turned to face Tom. Outwardly he was calm and composed, but his heart was racing, the blood drumming in his ears. This was it. Fight or flight. He had one chance to save his marriage, Café Paradise and Annabel's new life here in York.

In the short walk into his office, Tom had time to compose himself. He presented a neutral face to Barney as he faced him across the desk.

'I would like your file on Annabel Lewis-Langley,' Barney began.

Tom raised an eyebrow. 'I don't have one. Why should I? I hardly know the woman and she's not one of my clients.'

'You know a lot *about* her,' Barney said evenly.

'I do?'

Barney cursed inwardly. Tom was far too old a hand to give anything away voluntarily. He would have to drag it out of him. Behind him, he heard Walter take a breath, as if he were about to speak. Barney checked him. 'You hired a private detective to dig around her past and once you were in possession of certain information, you blackmailed her. I would say, on that basis, you know a great deal about her.'

Tom sat back in his chair and drummed his fingers lightly on his desk. 'Fairy stories, dear boy. You really should find more interesting bedtime reading. I had no idea Miss Lewis-Langley had such a vivid imagination.'

'She didn't imagine it,' Walter said sternly.

'Her word against mine, I think,' Tom said tranquilly. 'You've no proof.'

'You admit you approached her on two separate occasions to carry out certain deeds for you, with a view to jeopardising my marriage and causing the closure of Café Paradise.' Now he'll know we know it all, Barney thought grimly. Time to turn the screws.

'The ramblings of an over-excited mind, surely.' Tom was at his most bland. 'Now, really gentlemen and ...' he smiled thinly down at Elvis, 'that thing on the rope.'

He got up from his chair and walked towards the door. 'If that's all, I must ask you to leave. I have an appointment and even though it's always a pleasure to encounter you both, I must be on my way.'

Walter and Elvis stood between him and the door. 'You're going nowhere,' Walter said, a hint of steel colouring his voice. Elvis looked up at him and then at Tom. Tom continued to approach. A long, low growl came from Elvis and he bared his teeth. He didn't like this man's tone of voice.

Tom hesitated. 'Would you and your dog kindly step aside? He may be small, but he is a little, ah, menacing, shall we say.'

Walter covered the doorway. 'We're not going anywhere, Tom Young, until you hand over that file on Annabel.'

'How many more times? I don't have one.'

'You do and it's in this office,' Barney said. 'I know it. I know you too well, Tom Young. You wouldn't keep something like that lying around in your flat. It will be here, under lock and key.' He looked around the office and spied the wall safe. He nodded towards it. 'Of course. It's in there.'

'Another fantasy,' Tom said, although he wasn't looking so cool now.

Barney pulled out his mobile phone. 'Five minutes, Tom, or I contact York CID, and maybe you'll open the safe for them.'

'Always the bluffer, Barney Anderson.' Tom managed to keep his voice steady but Elvis caught the note of anger in it and growled more loudly.

'No bluff, Tom. Just try me.' Barney looked theatrically at his watch. 'Five minutes and counting. Give that file to me or to the police. You choose.'

There was a long silence in the room, broken only by low growls from Elvis. Barney checked his watch. 'Three minutes, Tom.'

'Alright!' Tom shouted. 'Stop bloody counting. I'll give it to you.'

Barney kept his eyes on his watch. He couldn't let his guard down yet. Tom Young might have a last twist up his sleeve.

'Two minutes.'

Tom sprinted to the safe and punched in the combination to open it. He brought out a slim manila folder. 'Here. Take it. No police. Get out of my office and my life and take your smelly friend with you – and that thing.' He gestured in disgust at Elvis.

Barney rapidly examined the file and was amazed to find the lengths Tom had gone to in documenting Annabel's life. 'This is highly confidential information,' he remarked. 'None of this has been come by legally. If I ever hear a whisper of you doing anything like this again, the police will know about it, you can be sure of that.'

'Oh, get the hell out of it,' Tom said wearily to Walter. 'And take Goody Two Shoes with you.'

'What now?' asked Walter when they were out on the street once more.

'A gathering of Clan Langley, I think,' said Barney. 'We need to get Jackie and Annabel together and tell the story, with Annabel's permission, of course.'

'Leave it to me,' Walter said confidently. 'Me and Elvis, I should say.' He looked proudly down at the little dog. 'Fancy you coming up trumps, little fella, and finding your growl. You're not such a runt after all.'

CHAPTER 58

The next day was a Saturday. Barney knew Jackie would be out at the café from early morning. He was up before her, feeding Samson, when she came down to the kitchen.

'You give him too much,' she said shortly. 'He's getting fat and lazy. We'll be overrun with mice if he's not hungry enough to do his job.'

Barney was shocked at how poorly Jackie looked. Quite ill, he thought. 'Are you alright?' he asked her

'I'm fine. Just a bit queasy, that's all. Henri uses a lot of butter in his cooking. I don't think it agrees with me.' She put the kettle on. 'Coffee? It's decaffeinated.'

Barney made a face. 'No thanks. I think I'll have tea. Since when did we have decaff?'

Jackie shrugged. 'Don't know. For a while, I think. Better for you.' She made her coffee and headed for the door.

Barney seized the moment. 'We need to go to your Dad's tonight,' he said casually.

Jackie looked back at him. 'What for? It's not his birthday. Don't tell me it's Ellie's. I haven't got her anything.'

'No, nothing like that. A bit of a family get-together. We've a lot to talk over, especially about the recent past.' He looked steadily at her. 'Explanations and some family news for you.'

'Why do we need to go to Dad's for that? Has he been getting funny texts too?'

Barney flushed. 'No. But between us we can explain what's been going on and, I hope to God, you'll understand and forgive.'

Jackie felt the tears pricking her eyes. So, it had all been true. If that wasn't a confession, she didn't know what was. Understand and forgive! He was knocking on the wrong door for that. She would never be able to trust him again. And to think they were going to... 'I'll see you tonight,' she mumbled and fled back up the stairs. If Walter thought he could talk her round, he could think again. Barney might not have taken his marriage vows very seriously, but she had.

******

That same Saturday morning saw Walter knocking on the door of Annabel's flat in Clifton Moor. Very cautiously, she opened the door a crack and peered round it.

'Oh, it's only you Walter. Thank God for that.' She opened the door wide and Walter went inside.

'What do you mean, *only* me? Who were you expecting? Her Majesty?'

'I thought it might be Barney come to flay me alive for what I did. I thought you'd have told him by now and I knew something would happen.'

'Never fear, lass,' Walter said stoutly. 'Do you think I'd let you face all that on your own? You don't know me well enough yet, I can see that.'

He looked about the small, bare room. 'Is this it?' he asked. He sounded puzzled.

'Is this what?'

'Is this your living room? Only, there's isn't much to it.' He saw the sadness flit across Annabel's face and hastened to add, 'I don't mean to be rude lass, but a deckchair and one coffee table. It's not exactly the Ritz, is it?'

'Don't forget the nice table lamp,' Annabel said defensively. 'I had nothing when I came out of prison,' she said simply. 'A bag of clothes and some money. A few books. The court took what we had in reparation, as they never recovered the jewellery taken in the raid. I'm starting again.'

She looked around the little room. 'I've loved it here. My own place.' She sighed. 'At least, if I have to move on, I won't have much stuff to worry about. There's hardly anything here. That's why I never let Jackie come here, you know.'

Walter looked at her.

'Well, one deckchair and a tiny coffee table. Not much to show for a professional woman, is it? She'd be bound to wonder. I didn't want to tell more lies, so I kept putting her off. I know she was hurt but I didn't know what else to do.'

In the normal way of things, Walter was not a demonstrative man but Annabel's story and acceptance of her situation moved him beyond words. He put his arms around her and held her close. 'It's not right, lass,' he said softly. 'Marilyn should have done better by you. She was young and daft, I know, and took the only way out of her situation that she could at the time. But afterwards...'

'Afterwards it was too late,' Annabel pointed out. 'I'd been adopted and as far as she knew, was having a happy life with my new family. She wasn't to know it didn't work out and what happened afterwards.'

'Maybe not,' Walter conceded. 'But, things being as they are now, it's not right. Marilyn had two daughters. One has her home and her business and the other has nowt. I can't have that.'

Annabel was alarmed. She drew back from Walter. 'I haven't come to make any trouble,' she said. 'I just wanted to find my family. I don't want anything from them. And I don't suppose Jackie or Barney will want anything to do with me after this, anyway. I'll be back where I started.'

'No, you won't,' Walter said firmly. 'As I said yesterday, I've got two daughters now. One's provided for, one isn't. And I can provide for you and I will. I loved Marilyn all her life. She didn't love me for much of it, right enough, but I still feel in a funny way that you're mine too.'

'I've often wondered about my father, Walter. Have you any idea who he was?'

Walter walked over to the window and looked out. 'I've been thinking about that. She went away to London when she was twenty-five,' he said slowly. 'She wanted to be a cook. She was always interested in food, ever since we were youngsters together. Probably because we didn't get much of it in those days. We used to go thieving off the market stalls, can you believe?'

Annabel shook her head.

'Aye, she went off to this college to learn cooking. That's all we knew about it. And then, six months later she was back. Said she didn't like it, didn't like London either. I never thought any more about it. I was so pleased to have her back. And then, when you appeared, it made me think back. Marilyn was going with a lad called Tommy Hargreaves at the time. He was a good bit older than her. He was a plumber, worked with his dad. A nice enough lad, tall and broad shouldered, thick brown hair and brown eyes. I reckon that's where you get your mop from.' Walter smiled at her.

'This Tommy Hargreaves,' Annabel asked eagerly. 'Is he still around?'

'I'm sorry lass, no,' Walter said gently. 'He died very young. Meningitis – he went within two days. It did for his mum and dad too. He was their only child and they idolised him. Anyway, Marilyn and me - we got back together when she came back, just for a while.'

Annabel shook her head sadly. 'I should have left well alone,' she said. 'I wasn't meant to find my family. All it's done is cause pain and heartache all round.'

Walter wasn't having that. 'It's going to be alright, Annabel, you'll see. How brave are you?' he asked.

Annabel's chin went up. 'As brave as anyone else, I think. Why?'

'It's time we all put our cards on the table, so to speak. I've invited Jackie and Barney over to our house tonight and I want you to be there too.'

'To tell her the truth?'

'Tell her about you and where you fit into this family. And yes, what happened with Tom Young.'

Annabel drew a deep breath. 'I can be brave, if she can forgive me. If she can't, it's the end of all my dreams. I might not be so brave then,' she ended shakily.

'You will be,' Walter said confidently. 'You're not Marilyn's daughter for nothing.'

CHAPTER 59

Jackie was very tired after a busy Saturday at Café Paradise and in no mood for a get-together at Claygate. Everyone around her was happy. Penny was home from her travels in Europe and grinning like a Cheshire cat because George had broken his arm, so no more motorbiking for him – or her. Kate was looking more beautiful than ever now that Stan was home and all was right between them. Not only that, but she was blooming in early pregnancy. Genevieve was going around singing like a bloody canary because Henri was teaching her to cook and, amazingly, she seemed to have a talent for it. It was a great relief to get her away from waitressing; at least the customers would get what they ordered now.

Life was so unfair, Jackie thought resentfully. She was up to her ears in paperwork that would take all weekend to sort out, she had an unfaithful husband, a father who had been mysteriously unavailable when she needed him most, and a future she didn't even want to contemplate. But her mother had managed, hadn't she? Maybe she wasn't Marilyn's daughter for nothing.

Annabel arrived first at Claygate and was warmly welcomed by Ellie. She saw how nervous Annabel was and tried to reassure her. 'It'll be alright. I know it doesn't always look like it, but Jackie sets a lot of store by Walter's opinion. He'll make her understand about everything.'

Annabel tried to smile, but her jaws had locked tight with tension.

Walter came into the sitting room, an unfamiliar sight

in slacks and a shirt. 'Aye, I know,' he grinned. 'She made me smarten up a bit. Said it would give me gravitas. I thought that was something yon Henry made at the café, salmon and stuff. I got a clip round the ear for that.'

Annabel knew he was trying to help with a little joke. 'You look very nice,' she said.

There were voices in the kitchen. She stiffened, gripping the arms of the chair.

'It's alright, lass,' Walter echoed Ellie's comments. 'We'll make 'em understand.'

Jackie and Barney came into the sitting room and paused in surprise when they saw Annabel. Jackie looked questioningly at Walter. 'I thought it was family matters...'

'It is and Annabel comes into it. That's why she's here. Come and sit down, lass. There's things that's happened in the past that have a bearing on the present and you need to know about them. When you do, I hope you'll understand why things have turned out the way they have.'

Jackie looked at Annabel. 'Does any of that make sense to you?' she asked.

Annabel nodded, too afraid to speak.

Jackie looked at Barney. 'Do you know about this?'

'I didn't, until yesterday. Listen to what Walter has to say, darling. It's important.'

Jackie settled back in her chair. 'Go on.'

Walter launched into his story. 'It starts with your mother.'

Jackie grimaced. 'Doesn't it always.'

Walter ignored her. He related the events of Marilyn going off to cookery school in London and returning six months later. 'She was lonely and she didn't like London, she said. We thought nowt of it at the time, or ever again. Until recently, that is.' He paused and looked at Annabel. She flushed and fidgeted in her chair.

Jackie regarded her silently.

'Fact was, Marilyn hadn't gone to cookery school at all. She was pregnant and went away to have the baby. I remember her going with a local lad, quite a bit older than her. We'll never know what happened there but they didn't get married and Marilyn had the baby adopted.'

Walter had Jackie's full attention. No one in the room moved or spoke. The tension was palpable.

Into the silence, Jackie said wonderingly, 'You're my sister?' Annabel nodded. 'Oh! That's amazing.'

'Hold on,' Walter said. 'I haven't finished.' He moved the story on to Annabel's unhappy adoption and subsequent return to the children's home, her growing up in ignorance of her parentage or any kind of background history.

Then he came to the part where Annabel had been innocently duped into taking part in the jeweller's raid and jailed. Jackie's violet eyes were like saucers. She leaned forward on the edge of her seat, looking closely at Annabel. 'Prison?' she whispered. 'Terrible.'

Walter exchanged a glance with Barney. So far, so good. No bodies on the floor as yet.

'This next bit is just as difficult as the rest,' Walter continued. He drew a deep breath. Would Jackie be as sympathetic when it got really personal? He related Annabel's release from prison and the quest to know more about her mother that had brought her to York, where she discovered Café Paradise and, best of all, Jackie. 'I knew there was a rabbit off somewhere when I saw her, because she's the image of Marilyn at that age. But, unfortunately, someone else suspected something was up as well. Our old friend, Tom Young.'

Jackie's face darkened. She looked at Barney. 'I thought we'd seen the last of him.'

'So did I,' Barney agreed. 'Unfortunately, he still has the capacity to make mischief.'

'He blackmailed Annabel,' Walter said baldly. Quickly he related the events that led up to the sending of the text to Barney's phone. Walter laboured the point that Annabel did not want to do it or hurt anyone. 'She knew she would lose everything if she didn't do as he wanted.'

Hearing this, Jackie glared furiously at Annabel. 'How could you? I thought we were friends. You nearly succeeded in wrecking my marriage.'

The tears were running down Annabel's face. 'I never wanted to, please believe me.'

'Oh yeah, like I'd believe anything you said now.'

Annabel, white faced, rose from her chair. 'I said it was no good.' She looked at Walter. 'I knew she wouldn't understand, let alone forgive me. This was a mistake. I made a mistake in coming here. It's all gone so wrong.' She fled from the room.

Ellie followed her but within minutes she was back. 'I couldn't persuade her to stay,' she said sadly. 'I think she'll leave York altogether now.'

'Good riddance,' Jackie said sharply. 'Who needs a sister like that?'

It was Walter's turn to be angry. 'You do, young lady, and if you don't realise it soon, you'll have lost the best sister and friend you're ever likely to have.'

'She sets out to break up my marriage and you're telling me she's a wonderful sister! I never had one before and I don't need one now, thank you. She can go to blazes, for all I care.'

'And she most likely will if you don't do something about it.' Walter sat next to Jackie and took her hands in his. 'Think about it, Jackie. You had Marilyn all your life. She loved and cared for you. She left you a successful business and a good, solid house. You've got a husband and a father who both think you're the bees' knees. What's Annabel ever had? Adoptive parents who didn't want her, an anonymous children's home and a boyfriend who set her up for prison. She's only made it because she's Marilyn's daughter through and through, just like you. She has strength of character and was trying to make a new life for herself. She cared enough about you not to spring any surprises on you that you might find unwelcome. She might never have got around to telling you who she was.'

He took a deep breath and continued. 'She just wanted to be near you. She didn't come in with all guns blazing, wanting her share, did she? It's quite possible she could have made a claim and a nice mess that would have been. She was backed into a corner by Tom Young and she only did the one thing. He came back to her for more, you know.'

Jackie was startled by this piece of information.

'Aye, you might well look,' Walter said. 'He wanted her to spread mouse droppings all over the café and then tip off Environmental Health. Now that would have caused real trouble for you. And would he have stopped there? I doubt it.'

'He really hates us, doesn't he?' Jackie said slowly.

'He lost a lot of money because of you and Barney stopping his dodgy insurance practices and now he's lost his hold over Annabel too.'

'How come?'

'Barney and I paid him a visit.'

'And Elvis,' added Barney.

'Aye. Elvis. You should have seen him, lass. He growled and bared his teeth, ready to take a chunk out of Tom Young if I'd told him to. He came up trumps did the little beggar.'

'So Elvis, all by himself, stopped Tom Young's games, did he?' asked Jackie.

'With a little help from Barney. You should have seen him, Jackie,' Walter said admiringly. 'He's a smooth operator is your husband, when he gets going. I don't think Tom Young will be troubling you or Annabel again. Whatever else, lass, just remember this: Annabel wouldn't do you or your business harm. She was prepared to leave all this lovely new life she was making for herself, rather than see you ruined.'

There was a long silence. Walter wondered if he had done enough. Barney was waiting hopefully at the door, eager to get his wife back.

'I need to see her,' Jackie said decisively, getting up from her chair.

Walter beamed. 'Your mother's daughter.'

'My father's too. I don't like injustice.' She headed for the door.

'I'll fix it up tomorrow,' Barney said, shepherding her out.

'I'll go now,' said Jackie.

'*Carpe diem*,' said Walter, grinning at Barney. 'That was Marilyn's saying and Jackie's just like her mother.'

******

Half an hour later, Jackie pulled away from Barney's embrace. 'I said I was going to see Annabel.'

'I know.' Barney grinned at her. 'But, as your very *faithful* husband, I felt I had first claim on your time.'

Jackie winced. She had put him through so much these last few weeks. However would she make it up to him?

'Happiness is making me hungry,' Barney chuckled. 'I could eat a mountain. Do you fancy an Indian later?'

Jackie could feel the bile rising in her throat. For weeks now, the slightest whiff of spices from Henri's kitchen had made her dash for the toilet. She swallowed hard. 'I don't think I could manage one tonight,' she said.

Barney was disappointed but determined not to let anything spoil these magical moments. 'Oh well, maybe a cheese sandwich then.'

Jackie had been going to wait for the right moment but was there ever a right moment? This would seem to be it. 'The smell of spices makes me feel sick,' she said carefully.

Barney looked at her closely. 'They never used to.'

'No. Well. That was then. This is now. I've been feeling sick a lot lately.'

'We'd better get you to a...' Barney sat bolt upright and looked into his wife's face. 'Did you say "feeling sick", as in "feeling sick"?'

Jackie smiled and rolled her eyes. 'Yes, feeling sick. The clues are there.' She snuggled up against him. 'I'm having a baby, stupid.'

'A baby! What? A real...'

'Yes, a real one. Two eyes, a nose and mouth. Two arms, two

legs. Maybe a boy, maybe a girl, but definitely a baby.' As she joked, she could see the tears appear in Barney's eyes. Her heart smote her. She should have trusted him and told him ages ago *and* have put him out of his misery about Martin Woodside.

'Should we leave Annabel until tomorrow?' he suggested. 'You've had enough emotion for one evening. You need to take care of yourself. I'll take you home.'

'You'll do no such thing, Barney Anderson,' Jackie said firmly. 'Annabel was in a terrible state when she left Dad's house. And when I think what I said... We're going there right now. You can drop me off and I'll get a taxi home later.'

Barney started the engine. 'I'll drop you off if I must, but there'll be no taxi home. I'll wait. My baby is not going home in a taxi.'

*****

Annabel lay on the bed in her flat and stared up at the ceiling. She needed to keep her eyes open as every time she closed them, the awful scene at Claygate replayed itself in horrible technicolour. Ellie, sitting discreetly near the door, smiling encouragingly; Barney, seated in an armchair, looking anxious, rumpling his blond hair every time Walter started to relate a new phase of her life. And Jackie. Her beautiful sister, head on one side listening carefully as the unlovely tale unfolded, her expression changing from wonder to disgust.

Unable to bear another re-run of the scene, Annabel jumped off her bed and prowled restlessly around the little flat. She would have to leave, of course. There was no point in staying on in York now. She could not bear to witness her sister's anger or be cut dead if she met her in the street.

The doorbell rang. Annabel checked her pacing. The friends she had made since coming to York usually telephoned. She did not encourage visitors. Cautiously, she opened the door.

Jackie was standing there. Annabel stared at her. 'Please,' Jackie said quietly. 'Can I come in?'

Annabel stood aside to let Jackie into the living room. She saw the deckchair and table but made no comment. Turning to face Annabel, she said, 'Forgive me, I've been a stupid fool.'

Annabel gaped at her. This was not what she had been expecting. Another spurt of Jackie's anger, a warning to stay away from them, but forgiveness?

They stared across the empty room at each other for a few moments.

'I have nothing to forgive,' Annabel said. 'You've done nothing wrong, whereas I have harmed you – and could have harmed you more, if Tom Young had had his way.'

'But you didn't,' Jackie said quickly. 'You came to Walter and told him everything. I know now that you never meant any of us harm, least of all me, your sister.'

Hearing Jackie acknowledge her as sister was too much for Annabel. The tears gathered in her eyes and rolled down her cheeks.

Jackie took a tentative step towards her and in a moment was hugging her tightly. 'I'm so sorry, Annabel. Please forgive me. I said some horrible things. Can we start again?' She looked at Annabel and smiled. 'I can't believe I have a sister. We have so much to catch up on. You're not going to go away, are you? This is your home, here in York, with us.'

Annabel dabbed at her eyes. 'I'm staying. All these years I've dreamed of a family. I'm not abandoning the dream now.'

'Good,' said Jackie. 'Because now you have all this family, including batty Genevieve, and soon a little niece or nephew will be joining the party.'

'Are you...?'

'Yes. Aunt Annabel. Bring it on!'

CHAPTER 60

David Hall had been taken aback by Genevieve's suggestion about trying again with Annabel Lewis-Langley. But she was right. He liked Annabel a lot, more than a lot. Maybe she would say yes this time.

He telephoned her on the Sunday morning and received a rather guarded response. 'Have you spoken to Barney recently?' Annabel asked.

David wondered what that was all about. Since when did he consult Barney about his love life? 'No,' he said.

'Only, there's been quite a lot going on lately and I wondered... It's just, I haven't heard from you for a while, I thought perhaps it wasn't coincidental.'

What was she talking about? 'I've no idea what's been going on. I was ringing up to see if you'd like to go out to lunch today. Maybe you could fill me in then?' David crossed his fingers and waited for her answer. He was surprised and delighted at the enthusiasm in her voice as she accepted.

'That would be lovely. It would be great to see you and I have a lot to tell you. Be prepared for surprises.'

When she'd rung off, David looked thoughtfully at his phone. He hoped they were good surprises and she wasn't about to tell him she'd just got engaged to Tom Young.

Two hours later, over lunch at The Dog and Duck, he sat back in his chair in amazement. 'Jackie's half-sister? I had all sorts of ideas going around in my head, Annabel, but I never dreamed of that one. That's fantastic.'

Annabel was relieved. This was the first time she'd told an

edited version of her story to anyone outside her new family and she had wondered what the reaction might be. It looked like it was going to be alright. David was smiling so sweetly at her. His next remark jolted her slightly.

'Have you seen much of Tom Young lately?' he asked, keeping his voice casual.

'A little,' Annabel said quietly. 'A little, which is too much. I shan't be seeing any more of him. He is not a nice man, to put it mildly.'

'No.' David wanted to jump up and punch the air. Instead, he raised his glass and proposed a toast. 'To the future,' he said and smiled.

Annabel smiled back. 'To the future, David.'

'Now,' he said. 'I have the offer of dinner for two at Angelino's. I was wondering if a certain beautiful lady would care to join me there.'

Annabel smiled again. Did she deserve all this? A new family and now this lovely man eager to take her out? She hoped so. There was such a lot to look forward to now.

CHAPTER 61

Everyone knew it was Sunday morning, except Samson. He wanted his breakfast. He padded up the stairs and jumped onto the bed, watching Jackie and Barney for a few moments. Barney was his best bet; Jackie only booted him off. She wasn't to know he'd been out hunting all night and for the first time, without success. He must be getting old. Since when was a field mouse faster than him? Now he was hungry and he wasn't going to take no for an answer.

Quietly he made his way up the bed and sat on Barney's chest. He meowed loudly and gently kneaded his paws, but got no response. After a few moments he stretched out a paw and tapped Barney's face. Barney stirred but did not wake up. Hunger spurred Samson on. He tapped Barney hard on the nose and meowed plaintively. That did the trick and Barney opened his eyes. Samson meowed again. Barney looked at the clock and groaned.

'Why can't you learn when it's the weekend, Samson? It's only six o'clock. Can't you wait a bit for your breakfast?'

Samson definitely could not. He stared at Barney and meowed again loudly.

'Alright.' Barney kept his voice low. 'Get off me and don't go near Jackie. Give her a bit of peace for once.'

He started to climb out of bed, but it was too late. Jackie stirred. 'Is that Samson?'

'Yes. Sorry. I was trying not to wake you.'

'No, don't apologise. It's great. I wanted to get up early and I knew I could rely on Samson. What a great cat. Better than any alarm clock.'

Samson looked back from the bedroom door. Had he heard right? A great cat? He arched his back with pleasure. It was nice to be appreciated sometimes.

CHAPTER 62

At Walter's suggestion, Café Paradise was hosting a party. He wasn't keen on word getting out piecemeal about Annabel, or her having to explain what her situation was over and over again to everyone she met.

'Family solidarity,' he said solemnly to Jackie. 'Let's invite all our friends and acquaintances and put on a good spread at the cafe. We can introduce Annabel properly. Then everyone will see that we're thrilled to bits with her.'

Jackie agreed and added, 'And spread the word about the new baby.'

'I think we can leave it to Kate to...'

Jackie patted her stomach and smiled. 'Grandpa Breckenridge.'

'Not you an' all,' he exclaimed. 'Well, I never. I can't take much more of this. Not so long ago I was on my own. Now I've got a wife, a daft dog, two daughters and now a grandchild.'

'Nice to see where we come in the pecking order,' Jackie said drily. 'Elvis has been promoted.'

'I should think he has been,' said Walter. 'He showed Tom Young who was boss. A grandchild, eh? All the more reason for a party.'

And now it was Sunday morning and there was a lot to prepare. Jackie, Annabel, Kate and Penny were meeting at the café at nine o'clock to prepare a buffet and arrange the tables for the party.

*****

Annabel need not have worried about her welcome at the Café Paradise. She knew Kate slightly and Penny soon had them all laughing with her stories from her European trip with George. 'I was pleased when he broke his arm,' she ended up. 'I pretended I wasn't, of course. George was so disappointed when we couldn't come home on the bike but really, I could have kissed the ground in Rome where he came off.'

By lunchtime everything was ready and the girls stood back to admire their handiwork. A cold buffet with tempting savouries and salads was laid out on the main table, cheese and fruit on another table and cold puddings on yet another. Kate and Penny went off to the ladies' cloakroom to change. The guests were due to arrive shortly, so Jackie took Annabel into her office to get changed.

It was the first time Annabel had been in this part of Café Paradise and she looked about with interest. This was the place where her mother had spent a lot of her time. It was much as it was in Marilyn's day, as Jackie had given all her energies to the public part of the café and the kitchens. Old filing cabinets were pushed against one wall and the room was dominated by a large mahogany desk with a computer and printer and a battered chair behind it. Out-of-date calendars and faded postcards dotted the walls. Marilyn must have had friends holidaying all around the world, judging by this collection.

'We'll have to get a move on,' Jackie said, taking their dresses from the hook behind the door. 'Mum did a lot of this, quick change in the office before going off to some do or another.' She looked about her. 'I bet Marilyn, in her wildest dreams, never thought this day would come.' She hugged Annabel impulsively. 'I'm so glad it has. Come on, let's hurry up, we have a lot to celebrate.'

It didn't take them long to get changed, although Annabel was starting to feel nervous and fumbled with the buttons of her dress.

'Come on,' Jackie said again. 'We're Marilyn's daughters, up for anything.'

Annabel wasn't sure she was ready for this, but it was too late now. 'Just give me a few moments,' she said.

Jackie went out into the café, ready to greet the guests. Barney was waiting for her. 'Where's Annabel?' he asked.

'She'll be out in a minute. I think she just needed a bit of time to collect herself.'

In the office, Annabel sat down gingerly on Marilyn's chair and looked out across her desk. Her mother had sat here. All those years, I wonder if she ever thought of me. I don't suppose so, she thought sadly. She had Jackie and a new life, she was probably far too busy to worry about what had happened in the past. I know Walter likes to think Marilyn laid it on so that I could come to find her if I wanted, but I'm not so sure. I wish I could have known her. Maybe I'll get to know her through Walter and Jackie...

Whilst Annabel was lost in her thoughts, part of her mind unconsciously absorbed the details of Marilyn's desk. She leaned forward and looked more closely at the drawers. They were beautifully made with intricate carvings around the edges and sides. She cleared some papers from the top of the desk and looked at it thoughtfully. Annabel's design studies in prison had included furniture and, if she wasn't mistaken, this was a very valuable desk.

CHAPTER 63

'If you don't come in now, Walter, you'll be introducing Annabel wearing your wellies and farm trousers,' Ellie called out in exasperation. 'That, or I'll go without you. This is your last call.'

Walter looked at Elvis and shook his head. 'Women. If you know what's good for you, lad, keep away from them.' He nodded towards the farmhouse. 'What they don't understand is that it only takes a man ten minutes to wash his hands and get his suit on. We don't faff around with frocks and face paint. It takes *them* hours. And now there's three of them. You wait lad.'

Elvis looked at him enquiringly.

'How long do you think it will be before Annabel starts telling me the road I know? I'll give it a week and that's being generous. They're all the same. They can't help it.'

Ever since the encounter with Tom Young, Elvis had found a new identity. The unexpected praise and attention from Walter had boosted his confidence. He felt he was a proper dog now, with responsibilities towards Ellie and Walter. He followed his master everywhere, trotting attentively at his heels. Walter found he enjoyed the little dog's company and had many a good talk with him about the pressing issues of the day.

They entered the house in harmony. 'I'll not be long,' Walter said. 'And if Ellie thinks you're wearing that big yellow bow, she can think again. I'll get you in the car before she can catch you.'

******

Café Paradise was full. Friends from all over York had been invited to the party. The wine and chatter flowed as latecomers crowded in. David Hall made a beeline for Annabel, kissed her gently on the cheek and looked down at her admiringly. 'You look beautiful,' he said simply.

'Thank you. I feel very nervous about this afternoon.'

'Don't be.' David was confident. 'Everyone will be delighted for you. Yes, a bit surprised at first, that's only natural, but now they know you they'll be pleased for you to have found your family.'

When all the guests were primed with glasses of champagne, Walter banged on the table. The chatter subsided. 'Welcome to Café Paradise everyone, and thank you for coming today. It probably seems a bit odd to be having a party here in the middle of a Sunday afternoon but we have a lot to celebrate.'

He drew Annabel and Jackie towards him. 'I didn't want the rumour mill starting up in the city and all sorts of tales doing the rounds, so I thought you could have it straight from the horse's mouth, so to speak. Me being the horse.'

The guests laughed, wondering what was coming.

'I don't want to go into the ins and outs, but you all know Jackie here and you knew her mother, Marilyn Dalrymple-Jones. Well, it turns out Marilyn, who could always surprise us, left us one final surprise. She had another daughter. She was young at the time and the baby was adopted. But babies grow up and come looking for their roots, as did our Annabel here.'

Everyone was listening attentively to Walter and at this, their collective intake of breath could be heard in the silence.

'Aye.' Walter looked proudly at Annabel and at Jackie. 'I'm not her real dad but I look upon her as my daughter. I must be a glutton for punishment. I've got two daughters now. I'm the luckiest man in the world, or the unluckiest, depends which way you look at it. Double trouble. Two daughters, plus my wife to keep me in order. What chance do I stand? Me and Elvis'll have to stick together, won't we lad?'

Elvis barked and wagged his tail.

'Anyway, I would like you all to raise your glasses and welcome my daughter Annabel and on that happy note, I now declare this party open.'

Loud applause followed Walter's speech. Annabel was relieved to see everyone smiling at her.

'Go on.' Walter gave her a little push. 'Time to meet and greet. Don't be afraid, they're on your side.'

'Yes, go on Annabel,' echoed Jackie. 'Everyone's pleased for you. I'll gather the girls and we'll refill the glasses and get the food ready. Off you go.'

Annabel looked around and saw David Hall clapping wildly and smiling. He nodded encouragingly. She took a deep breath and plunged into the crowd.

Walter and Jackie were right. Everyone was delighted with the news and keen to hear Annabel's plans for the future. She was nonplussed; she didn't really know herself what she would do next. Barney, overhearing this exchange with some friends, interrupted. 'At the moment she's working for Jake and me but I don't suppose we'll keep her forever. She's far too talented to moulder in our offices. You'll just have to watch this space.'

Penny, moving around the guests and topping up glasses, overheard George talking animatedly in a corner to Kate's Stan.

'Good job I didn't know you were an expectant father when I took that sharp corner in Rome,' George said.

'If I had known, I would have got a taxi as I'd planned to do,' laughed Stan. 'How you ever got from England to Rome in one piece, I'll never know. You ride like there's no one else on the road.'

'Is there?' George grinned. 'Ah well, I loved every minute of it.' He pointed to his arm in plaster. 'Penny won't have another bike, you know. Frightened it could be even worse next time.'

'It probably would be.'

'I thought you were a friend,' George said in an injured voice.

'I am, mate. That's why I'm telling you straight. Take up

something else.'

'How about go-karting or drag racing? I quite fancy those.'
Stan shook his head. 'Nothing involving speed, George.
Something a bit slower. How about rock climbing? It's the
great outdoors. It's sporty, it's got an element of danger in it,
but not too much to get Penny worried. Sounds ideal to me.'

Kate had been standing nearby, listening. 'Stop it, the pair
of you,' she said. 'Haven't you put Penny through enough,
George? You dragged her all the way to Rome in the heat and
dust and now you think she'll take kindly to being thrown off a
mountain. Stop encouraging him, Stan.'

'But it's very safe these days,' Stan protested. 'I wouldn't
mind a go myself.'

'If you think we're going up mountains with a new baby...'

'No, maybe not,' Stan said sadly 'We'll have to think of
something else, George. Cross-country skiing, or kayaking...'

'Oh, for heaven's sake...'

Penny took the tray away from Kate. 'He's winding you up,
Kate. Take no notice. No one will be going mountaineering or
anything else until that arm heals, and then it might be a gentle
walk by the river and that's it.'

The girls moved off.

'A gentle walk by the river?' George was appalled.

'We'll have to soup-up the baby buggy,' said Stan.

George brightened up. 'Great idea. A whole new sport.
Buggy racing!'

The party was in full swing. Ellie and Penny were busy
serving puddings. Martin Woodside stood with his partner,
Geoff, watching the proceedings. Barney sidled up to them, an
apologetic grin on his face.

'Sorry,' he said quietly. 'How wrong could I get it? I was a
crass idiot and I can't apologise enough. Thank you for coming
today. It meant a lot to Jackie and to me.'

Martin smiled back at Barney. 'I'm just glad we've had a
much different reception today. I've known Jackie most of my
life and wouldn't want to lose her friendship.'

Barney winced inwardly. 'You won't. Not on my account. In fact,' he beamed at Martin and Geoff, 'we're expecting a baby next year and wondered if you two would do us the honour of standing as godparents to the sprog. Long-standing friends of Jackie's, upright citizens and all that. Friends of mine...' Barney held out his hand tentatively.

Martin shook his hand. 'Friends.' He looked at Geoff, who nodded. 'And, yes. We'd be delighted.'

Seeing Walter sitting quietly with Elvis, watching the proceedings, Jackie joined him at the table. 'Penny for them, Dad?' she asked.

Walter looked at her. 'I was trying to imagine Marilyn amongst all this. Me, here in a suit, married to someone as good and kind as Ellie and now with two beautiful daughters to mind.'

'I'm glad you've taken Annabel under your wing, Dad. She needs us all behind her.'

Walter pointed to David Hall as he watched protectively over Annabel. 'If I know anything, that young man will be taking over my role soon enough.'

Jackie followed his gaze. 'David? Oh yes. Now that would be great.' She eyed them speculatively.

'Don't go interfering,' Walter warned her. 'I can see what's in your mind. Leave off. You're just like your mother, always wanting a finger in the pie.'

'And you never do, I suppose,' Jackie challenged.

'It's you women,' Walter protested. 'I get dragged in. Sorting out your troubles.' He looked down at Elvis curled up at his feet. 'We mind our own business, don't we, lad? When we get a chance to.'

'Hmph,' Jackie snorted. 'The day you mind your own business, I'll eat hay with all your horses. But here's one bit of business you might be interested in. Marilyn's desk.'

'What about it?'

'Annabel thinks it's very valuable. She's had a good look around it and thinks it's from the 1880s.'

******

Grace Anderson looked on anxiously as Genevieve carried trays of dishes back to the kitchen.

'Relax, Mum,' Barney said, coming to join her. 'She's doing fine.'

'I'm waiting for the crash,' Grace said dolefully.

'You're making it a self-fulfilling prophecy, Mum.'

Grace looked at her son. 'Barney Anderson, how can you say that? I've always encouraged the three of you in everything.'

Barney knew better than to lay down the law to his mother. She could be very formidable when roused. He didn't want her stalking out in high dudgeon this afternoon of all afternoons.

'Just ease up on her, Mum, that's all,' he said. 'Don't fuss her. I think it makes her worse. Jackie's made it clear to Gen that she expects her to do well, and it seems to be working. She works things out in her own way. OK, it might not be our way, but it works for Genevieve. She has her catastrophes, but then everyone expects her to do better and she does.'

Grace was silent. Genevieve had had some spectacular catastrophes in the past and had to be rescued from her own folly. Was Barney saying they were causing the problem?

'Isn't it time she moved out, Mum?' Barney asked gently.

Grace's startled expression told Barney a great deal. 'Let her make all the mistakes she needs to. She's too old for nannying.'

'Nannying!' Grace was indignant.

'You do nanny her, Mum,' Barney said quietly. 'It's time to let go, let her make her own mistakes. We're all here if she needs us, but let her ask for help first.' He stood up. 'I've got to go, Jackie's looking tired. I might take her home soon. I'm sure the girls can manage without her now.'

Grace watched him cross the room to his wife. Maybe that son of hers knew a thing or two, after all. She watched Genevieve quietly making her way through the crowds with plates and glasses. No accidents befell her and she soon returned for more. Barney was right. The time had come to let go.

CHAPTER 64

The last guest had left and Café Paradise was closed for the night. David and Annabel strolled hand in hand through the quiet Sunday streets of York, enjoying the peace after the noisy afternoon. They passed billboards advertising ghost walks around the city. 'Have you ever been on one?' David asked.

'Not yet.' Annabel sounded doubtful. She wasn't too sure about pursuing ghosts.

The bells from the Minster summoned the faithful to Sunday worship. 'That sounds better,' she said, smiling up at David. 'It's a beautiful evening. We could sit outside and listen to Evensong.'

The square outside the ancient Minster was bathed in sunshine. They sat on a bench and let the music flow over them. When it had finished, Annabel sighed with contentment. 'Just think, we can come here and listen to this whenever we want. How lucky are we?'

'We can and I hope we will,' he said, smiling. He felt a sense of rightness, sitting here with his arm around her. 'Sunday evenings stretching away, all down the years.' He turned towards her, taking her hands in his. 'Maybe as Mr and Mrs Hall?'

Annabel hadn't been expecting this. She looked up at him. 'I think so. I hope so,' she said. 'It's just a bit too soon, David. I've only just found out who I am and I have a family to get to know. Give me a little time.'

David kissed her gently. 'All the time in the world. I'll be here.'

CHAPTER 65

Samson pushed through the cat flap and walked into the kitchen. Jackie was busy preparing the breakfast. Samson sat down, curling his long black tail around him.

'Good morning, Samson,' Jackie said cheerily. 'Isn't it a wonderful morning?' She looked down at him. 'Mm, you're looking a bit thin, old boy.'

Old boy. Who was she calling old boy? He was in his prime.

Jackie picked up the packet of Kattibix and poured some into his bowl. Samson looked at them disdainfully but made no move towards them. If this was all he was going to get, he might have to consider moving house.

Barney came into the kitchen and saw Samson sitting silently by his bowl.

'Kattibix again, old lad?'

There they went again, calling him old. Samson meowed loudly.

'I think Samson deserves a treat,' said Barney. 'After all, he's soon going to have new responsibilities.' He reached into the cupboard, pulled out a tin and briskly opened it. Samson sniffed the air hopefully. Was that best salmon? What did new responsibilities mean?

Jackie smiled as Barney put the salmon down for the cat. 'I suppose we should spoil him a bit. He must be sick of the sight of Kattibix and he'll soon have a new baby to get used to.'

Samson paused over the salmon. A new baby? Oh no. That was a small human, wasn't it? His friend Fergus down the road had one of those in his house. Samson didn't like it at all. Quite a scary thing. It shrieked and wailed and smelled strange. Why did Jackie and Barney want one of those? If they did get one, he might *seriously* have to consider moving house.

He wolfed down the salmon and hung around hopefully for something else, but it seemed only the Kattibix were on offer. Jackie and Barney were busy with their own breakfast, still talking of babies. Samson decided to get along to Fergus's house and share the news. They might have to make plans.

CHAPTER 66

Mike Fernhough from Fernhough and Stackpole, Auctioneers and Valuers, straightened up from his examination of Marilyn's desk and whistled softly through his teeth. 'It's a gem,' he told Walter and Jackie. 'A very early Gillows partner desk. It's worth a lot of money. How did you come by it?'

'It came with Marilyn,' Walter said. 'She never said anything about it, just had all her stuff laid on it.'

'Well, if I might make a suggestion to you.' Mike looked consideringly at the desk. 'We take it away and,' he looked apologetically at Jackie, 'give it a bit of a dust, but that's all. Don't want to disturb the patina. Then we can advertise it in our next catalogue, circulate known collectors with the details and put it in the sale. We could be talking forty or fifty thousand pounds. As I said, it's a rare piece.'

When he'd gone, Walter and Jackie looked at each other in silence. Walter was the first to break it. 'That's serious money, lass. I wonder if Marilyn knew what she had.'

'I don't know, Dad. Maybe she did and was keeping it against a rainy day. If she was, it never came for her. But I know someone who's had a lot of rainy days and could do with a sum like that.'

Walter raised his eyebrows. 'That's my lass. I was thinking the same thing. We can put some with it and get her a decent place. Marilyn owes her that.'

******

A week later Mike Fernhough called to see Jackie at Café Paradise. He held out a yellowed envelope. 'How about that? I found a secret drawer. I'd looked for one when I examined the desk here, but couldn't find it. It took me some time back at the workshop but I found the mechanism eventually. It's a really clever device. You have to press the right panels in the right order. Marilyn must have found it, probably by accident, and she made use of it.'

Jackie took the envelope. It was Marilyn's handwriting, addressed to Walter. She thanked Mike and put the envelope in her pocket. She would deliver it to Claygate later. She didn't want to summon Walter to the café to read it. Who knew what bombshell it would contain?

She left the café early and made her way to the farm. Ellie welcomed her warmly and put the kettle on, summoning Walter from the field where he was trying to turn Elvis into a proper sheepdog.

Walter came across the yard, shaking his head. 'Bloody Elvis. I ask him to go right and he goes left, sit and he runs off. I was beginning to think he had half a brain, but now I'm not so sure.'

Elvis could tell by the tone of Walter's voice that all was not well. He got straight into his basket when they reached the house. Walter came into the kitchen, grumbling quietly to himself. 'He eats like a horse and thinks like a donkey. Whatever am I to do with him? And why I have to do it, I don't know. I thought as how he was going to be Ellie's blinking dog.'

Jackie got up to greet him. 'Hello, Daddy dear. Happy as ever, I see.'

Walter grinned and rumpled her hair. 'It's you women, you hand me nowt but trouble. But it's good to see you, lass. Have you come for tea?'

Jackie sat down and produced the old envelope from her bag. Walter took it slowly and looked down at it. It was Marilyn's writing alright. She'd never written to him in forty years. What on earth could this be doing hidden away in a drawer? He looked doubtfully at Jackie.

'Go on, open it. It might be nothing at all, but she put it away carefully and obviously kept it for a lot of years.'

'Happen she forgot about it,' Walter said. He opened it and drew out a sheet of paper. It was a letter, addressed to him. He scanned it quickly and looked up. 'Well, by gum,' he said slowly.

'What?' Jackie and Ellie leaned forward eagerly.

Walter shook his head wonderingly. Would Marilyn ever stop surprising them? She'd had a tender heart after all. What a pity she'd kept it so well hidden. He began to read the letter to them.

My dear Walter,

In nearly forty years I've never written a line to you, but I think the time's now come to set a few things down. The years are going by all too quickly and although I've kept my secrets, I don't want to take them to my grave. You and I grew up together and probably what you don't know about me isn't worth knowing. But I still have surprises for you, Walter, and if I die before you, I want you to take care of things for me. I know I can trust you completely in this. You have always been so faithful and I know I do not deserve the love and support you have always given me.

I know you guessed long ago about Jackie. You were right, of course, she is your daughter, but I could not face a life at Claygate, scratching a living from the soil. I'd had too many years of hunger and poverty. So, I opted for the easy way and all that Barry could provide. Weak, I know, but I had been stupid enough to let it happen once before. Only that first time I had to give my baby away and I was determined not to let that happen again, or be forced to bring a child up in poverty.

Surprised Walter? Something you didn't know about me? No one ever knew, only my parents. I'm telling you this now because if I die and Annabel ever comes looking for me, I want her to know the truth. I want her to know how much I loved her, absolutely adored her and desperately didn't want to give her up for adoption. But I was only young and my parents didn't want to know. In fact, they insisted I had her adopted. Do you remember that cookery course I went on in London? That was the excuse to get me away.

Can you guess who the father was? Tommy Hargreaves, the plumber's son. He wasn't interested at the time and now he's dead. My lovely Annabel couldn't even meet her father now if she wanted to.

She was so beautiful, with melting brown eyes and fluffy brown curls. I only had her with me for a few short weeks in the mother and baby home. Then the adoptive parents came to take her away. I think that was the worst day of my life. They had to wrench her from my arms.

By the time I was in a position to care for her, it was too late. She was with a family and I could not intrude on that and wreck her new life. But I have never forgotten her, Walter, never. I think of her every day and wonder what she looks like now, what she is doing, and if she is happy?

We have had the pleasure of watching Jackie grow up in our care and she is provided for after I die. If I go before you, I want you to take care of Annabel if she comes to York. Make her welcome, love her, as I know you love Jackie, and make sure she is provided for in whatever way you can.

I'm asking a lot of you, Walter. I always did. When I feel the time approaching when I can no longer do this myself, I'll post this letter to you and trust you with its contents.

With love and thanks, always,
Marilyn.

Walter stumbled over the last few sentences and put the letter down with a shaking hand. 'She knew that I knew, all the time. She was some actress, was Marilyn. Now what? It's a bit late for this. Annabel's beat her to it.'

'No, it's not,' Ellie said. 'Let Annabel see the letter. What a joy it would be for her to know how much Marilyn loved her and that she didn't abandon her willingly.'

'I agree,' Jackie added. 'If I was in Annabel's place, I would love to read this. It would make all the difference.'

'There'll be tears before bedtime,' Walter foretold gloomily.

He was right. Annabel read the letter with tears streaming down her face and then wept all over Walter and all over Ellie. It was cathartic. When there were no more tears left, a new Annabel emerged, calm and serene, confident of her place in her mother's affections.

Walter wanted her to stay the night, but she could not. David Hall was taking her to Angelino's restaurant in the city. 'What better place to celebrate?' she said. 'I can't wait to tell him.'

When she had gone, Ellie said, 'Are you thinking what I'm thinking?'

'Aye, I'm sure to be,' Walter replied and sighed. 'And if we're right in our thinking, there'll be another wedding to pay for afore long. Why didn't she have a pair of lads? It would have been so much easier.'

CHAPTER 67

Grace Anderson watched her daughter as she stared listlessly out of the window. Now that Genevieve wasn't seeing David Hall any more, she didn't seem to know what to do with herself. The house was clean and tidy, Grace's fearsome daily saw to that and woe betide anyone who left a mess for her to clear up. Grace could see now, there was nothing for Genevieve to do here and all her friends were nearer the city. Barney was right. It was time to stop clucking over her like an old mother hen.

'Do you think you would like to live in a flat, Genevieve?'

'I don't know, Mummy. I never have. Why? Are you thinking of moving?'

'No. *I'm* not, but I wondered if you might think about it.'

Genevieve looked at her blankly. 'Why would I do that?'

Grace felt the familiar irritation rising in her. 'Because it might be nice for you to live on your own now. Do what you would like to do, without having me watch over you all the time.'

Genevieve continued to stare at her. Had she understood, Grace wondered?

Surely she'd been plain enough. 'A flat, by yourself,' she repeated.

'Yes. I heard you. Mm. Does that mean I could have what I liked for breakfast? And be untidy. Spread my paints out and not worry about Mrs Dawson shouting at me?'

Dear Lord, had they regimented the poor girl that much? 'Yes, all of those things,' Grace said quietly.

'Then I think I would,' Genevieve said. 'Are we going to look for one?'

'When your father comes home at the weekend. He and Barney know all sorts of people in the city. Someone's bound to know someone who has a flat to rent. You'll be an independent girl about town before you know it.'

'Cool,' said Genevieve. 'Wait 'till I tell Barney.'

And on his head be it if we all go to hell in a handcart over it, thought Grace.

CHAPTER 68

M ike Fernhough checked the bidding on the Internet. 'I have sixty-five thousand on the Net. Sixty-five. Any advance on sixty-five?'

The room was quiet. The Gillows partner desk had been well advertised and it seemed that half of York had crowded into the auction room to watch the star item in the sale go under the hammer.

'Seventy, Sir. Seventy-two on the Net. Seventy-four in the room. Any more now? Last chance, Internet. Seventy-six. Seventy-eight. Eighty in the room. Eighty-five on the Net. Any more? No? It's eighty-five on the Net.' He glanced rapidly around the room. No more bids were showing. 'Eighty-five it is, on the Net. Selling once, selling twice.' He paused and then brought down his gavel. 'Sold, Bidder 472 on the Internet.'

A spontaneous round of applause broke out amongst the buyers. The Gillows desk had drummed up huge interest and fierce bidding, driving the price up from the expected fifty thousand pounds to eighty-five.

Barney and Walter could hardly believe what they had just seen. They went outside to telephone Jackie with the good news. She had stayed at the café, unable to stand the stress of the auction room.

'Eighty-five?' Jackie shrieked down the phone. 'That's fantastic. Good old Mum. I bet she never knew what she was working on all those years. I might be able to buy a new desk too, out of that.'

'Not for eighty-five grand, I hope,' said Barney.

'A large table from a car boot would probably do me,' laughed Jackie. 'Space for the computer and printer and that's me done. Say fifty quid tops.'

'Oh, the extravagance.' Barney rang off.

******

The sisters were on a spa day at Bishopthorpe Hall. Jackie had been intrigued at Annabel's complete lack of curiosity about the sale of Marilyn's desk.

'It's not really any of my business,' she said. 'It was part of the café and I suppose I thought you would plough the money back into the business.'

Jackie wiggled her toes, helping the nail polish to dry. 'The business is doing well. It can pay for any renewals itself.'

Annabel shrugged. 'Will you invest it?'

'Yes.' Jackie grinned at her sister. 'In you.'

'Me?' Annabel was startled and nearly fell off the treatment table.

'The money is yours, Annabel. Marilyn left me well provided for; it's your turn now. She wasn't stupid, you know. The more I think about it, the more I'm sure she knew the value of that desk and meant this to happen one day. This is Marilyn's investment in you. You must take it and use it in whatever way you wish. She would have wanted that.'

Annabel was too overcome to speak. Not caring if her nails were dry or not, she leapt off the bed and hugged Jackie tightly. 'Does Walter know? And Barney?' she asked anxiously. 'What do they think?'

'What do you think? They're all in favour of the idea. All you have to do is decide what to do with it.'

Annabel sat on the bed and regarded Jackie thoughtfully. 'I've always wanted my own gallery,' she said slowly. 'A space to showcase good interior design, furniture and decorative pieces.'

'Perfect,' Jackie enthused. 'You've a proven track record already, spotting the Gillows desk. You could set up in the centre of York, we could help you find somewhere, fit it out...'

'Hang on, I've only just thought of the idea,' Annabel said. 'You'll have me moved in tomorrow, if you have your way.'

Jackie laughed. 'We're Marilyn's daughters Annabel. We follow her motto, *Carpe diem*.'

******

Previous title by Patricia Comb

Cafe Paradise

ISBN 978-1-908098-93-1

A romantic comedy set in York, North East England.

After Jackie finds her domineering mother lying dead, face down in a bowl of porridge, she has to take over the running of Café Paradise. Her plans to modernise are not met with enthusiasm by her staff.

Zumba dancing, feckless chickens, cross-dressing and Roman re-enactments all play their part in helping the characters at the Café Paradise resolve their misunderstandings and find true love.

Both titles also available as eBooks

Lightning Source UK Ltd.
Milton Keynes UK
UKOW06f2326180515

251811UK00001B/2/P